FALLING FOR HER SECRET BILLIONAIRE

REBECCA WINTERS

CONSEQUENCE OF THEIR DUBAI NIGHT

NINA MILNE

MILLS & BOON

First published in Great Britain 2023
by Mills & Boon, an imprint of HarperCollins*Publishers* Ltd,
1 London Bridge Street, London, SE1 9GF

www.harpercollins.co.uk

HarperCollins*Publishers*
Macken House, 39/40 Mayor Street Upper,
Dublin 1, D01 C9W8, Ireland

Falling for Her Secret Billionaire © 2023 Rebecca Winters

Consequence of Their Dubai Night © 2023 Nina Milne

ISBN: 978-0-263-30636-1

01/23

FALLING FOR HER SECRET BILLIONAIRE

REBECCA WINTERS

MILLS & BOON

I adored my doctor father, who made my life heavenly.

He deserves every adulation.

It's for him I dedicate this novel.

CHAPTER ONE

THANK HEAVEN FOR a day off from the hospital!

This Friday morning, Françoise packed up some items in her apartment in Nice to ship to a storage unit in Paris. She didn't want to have to take anything with her except a suitcase. In less than three weeks she'd be flying home to take the last of her medical boards. With luck she'd receive her doctorate.

The last item to go in the box was her father's black medical bag. He'd never had another one and it was her most prized possession. Sixty-one-year-old Patrick Valmy, who had died five months ago, had been a distinguished doctor. His fatal heart attack shouldn't have happened. Her mother, an incredible nurse who'd worked with him, had died a year before from pneumonia. She missed both of them horribly.

As she looked inside the bag one more time, it slipped from her hands and fell upside down on the floor. Out came the percussion hammer and stethoscope she'd played with as a child.

Surprised, Françoise leaned over to pick up everything, including an old dark brown billfold. For some reason it had been lying in the bottom of the bag with everything on top of it. She'd never seen it before.

Curious, she looked inside and discovered a faded document of some kind. When she pulled it out and opened it, the first thing to catch her eye was the print at the top of the paper.

Groupe Français pour l'Adoption

Adoption? She frowned. What was this paper doing in the bottom of her father's bag? According to the information here, he'd delivered a baby. His patient's? Or someone he'd helped in an emergency?

Une enfant femelle. Née 10 Fevrier
Docteur attitré: Patrick Valmy.
Mere: inconnue
Pere: inconnue

Inconnue... Unknown.

Françoise looked down at the signatures of the adopters.

Patrick Valmy and Dionne Valmy

What?

Those were *her* parents' signatures!

They'd adopted *this* baby?

Françoise had been their only baby because her mother couldn't have more children. She'd gone through three miscarriages before Françoise's birth.

If they'd adopted this child and it had died, why hadn't she known about it?

Beneath their names was the year of the adoption. Twenty-eight years ago. She'd just celebrated her twenty-eighth birthday on February 10. Françoise did the math.

No, it couldn't be!

She let out a gasp and fell back on the couch.

Something was very wrong here. She read it over and over again.

If this were to be believed, *Françoise* had been their adopted baby!

She wouldn't have cared about being adopted, but she couldn't imagine them not telling her everything. They'd had her whole life to be honest with her. Why hadn't they wanted her to know? Why the secrecy? Did they think that she would love them any less, or resent them if she'd learned the truth?

The questions kept coming. Her mother had always said she wanted more children. Why hadn't they adopted another child to give her a brother or sister? How had they kept her adoption a complete secret?

Françoise's great-aunt on her mother's side lived in a rest home at Bouzy-la-Forêt southeast of Paris. Their family had driven the two hours to visit her there on many occasions. The older woman who suffered from emphysema had never breathed a word about the adoption. Had it been so secret, her mother's *own* aunt hadn't even known?

There were no details of the baby's weight, no names of the birth parents, no city or country named, no hospital, no official stamp with the name of a functionary. Nothing she could link to anything.

Who were her birth parents? Were they still alive? If so, *where* were they?

Until now, her parents had never hurt her. But this purposely withheld information caused her more pain than she'd known in the whole of her life.

Devastated, she reached for her phone to call information and discovered there was no adoption agency with that name in Paris. She asked the operator to do a global search around France. *Nothing came up!*

Shaken to her core, she looked up the number of a private investigator here in Nice and phoned for an appointment. She asked about their fee. Though she didn't have much money, she would spend every last euro to get answers.

At two that afternoon she entered the office of Lameaux & Briand. Guillaume Briand invited her in. She showed him what she'd found and told him that no adoption agency by that name existed anywhere. "Is this even an official document?"

"I've never seen one like it, but the fact that it exists and has been hidden inside your father's medical bag must be troubling for you until we can arrive at the truth. Where did your father get his medical degree?"

"In Paris at the Sorbonne. Both my parents were Parisians, lived there and did their studies there." She gave him a full history on the family of what she knew, or *thought* she knew.

"That helps. So do the dates. You say you're twenty-eight?"

She struggled not to tear up in pain. "Yes. With the same birth date as on the document."

"Why did your parents move to Nice?"

"They didn't. Three years ago, he was invited by the French government to start a health program in Rabat for the Moroccan government. I was already a resident working on my medical degree in Paris. My parents got me enrolled at Sophia Antipolis University here in Nice so I could continue my residency and be closer to them. When I could, I visited them in Rabat and they came to me."

"I see." He removed his glasses. "I'm going to do some investigating. Leave your number and address with the secretary and I'll phone you the minute I have information."

"Thank you. I'm still shocked that my parents kept this from me." She prayed that during his search he'd discover a valid reason for what her parents had done without telling her.

"I'll do my best to get answers for you."

"Thank you." She left his office so upset she didn't know how she'd be able to function until the reason behind the adoption was uncovered.

The layout of Nice came into view as the military transport plane descended. Ten years out of the country hadn't done anything to make this moment easier, but Jean-Louis Causcelle had been discharged from the army two weeks ago and forced to return to France for medical reasons. He'd been offered a medical discharge twelve months ago but had resisted until he had no strength left to refuse.

The medic who'd done what he could to help him during the last horror in Mali couldn't tell him what was wrong. It didn't matter. Jean-Louis had been suffering with certain problems that couldn't be diagnosed in a war zone. For the last two weeks he'd sensed he was dying of some hideous disease picked up in Western Africa. He could still walk, but his recent weight loss and attacks of sickness seemed to have robbed him of strength.

There were hospitals throughout France where wounded vets could go to be treated. Since he couldn't bring himself to return to his birthplace in eastern France, he opted to fly to Nice, the home of his war buddy Alain, who'd been killed in the Sahel two months ago. Once he'd paid his respects to his best friend's family, he'd report to the vet hospital here in Nice, where he would learn how much longer he had before leaving this earth.

Once the plane landed, he got in line while an official looked through everyone's paperwork. Jean-Louis still wore his uniform, but it hung on him.

"*Le prochain?* Capitaine Robert Martin?"

"*Ici.*"

Jean-Louis handed his papers to the man at the desk. Ten years ago he'd signed up for the army with a fake name. A friend had known a friend who'd helped him obtain a fake driver's license and birth certificate. He'd shaved his head and grown a moustache so he wouldn't be recognized in the photo as one of the famous billionaire Causcelle triplets.

Joining the army had made it possible for Jean-Louis to disappear. The deception had worked well enough to get him enlisted. However, regulations forbade facial hair, so he'd been forced to shave off the moustache.

The man stared at him for a long moment. "Now you have hair."

"My bald head made me a target. But it no longer matters." Nothing mattered.

"*Soyez le bienvenu.* Here is your stamped card. Show this to an official at any hospital for vets to get the treatment you need. *Bonne chance.*"

Welcome home and good luck?

Right.

"*Merci.*"

With his military career over, possibly his life, he walked out of the building on a Saturday morning in June carrying his duffel bag. He signaled for a taxi. "Darrieux Reparations Auto, 210 Rue Rossini, *s'il vous plaît.*"

After climbing in, he sat back taking in the sights of a world he'd been away from for a decade. Yet it wasn't a world familiar to him. Ages ago Jean-Louis had taught himself not to think about the place his soul hungered for. To do so tortured him beyond endurance.

The driver took him along the Promenade des Anglais clustered with tourists toward his destination. The chatty man gave him a running commentary on great spots for soldiers, but Jean-Louis lost any concentration after they passed the glistening white Causcelle

Prom Hotel. A nuclear bomb might as well have gone off inside him.

He closed his eyes tightly, trying to shield himself against the invisible radiation from so many past memories. But it was too late. They penetrated to all his senses. The only reason he'd come back to France was to die.

After a few turns, the taxi came to a stop. Jean-Louis opened his eyes in time to see the small shop front where Alain had helped his father before joining the army. Both guys had been about to turn twenty. Alain's family had little money and had never traveled anywhere. He'd wanted to see the world and enjoy a different life. He'd sent part of his monthly pay to his father over the years, and the rest he'd invested for his family's future.

Jean-Louis, on the other hand, had only wanted to get away from the evil intrusion of the press and his widower father's expectations. More than that, the military had offered him a solution to become anonymous and throw off his dreadful guilt over one family having such an insane amount of money.

He and Alain met in boot camp and had served together until recently. Early death and unexpected illness hadn't figured in their plans to become career officers. Now it was time to face Alain's father and mother. Their son had worshipped them and his younger sister. That much Jean-Louis could share with their family, plus a few photos.

He asked the driver to stay put because he'd be back out again in a few minutes. Leaving his duffel bag on the seat, he walked inside the small shop wishing like hell Alain were there with that great smile on his face.

"*Salut, soldat!* What can I do to help you? Our service building is in back where the service writer will fix you up."

Jean-Louis turned to a man probably in his thirties. His nameplate said Michel. "I'm looking for the owner, Etienne Darrieux. Is he here?"

"Yes, of course. Is he expecting you?"

"No. I'd hoped to surprise him."

The man nodded. "That's his office right there." He pointed. "Just give him a heads-up."

"*Merci bien.*"

He didn't have to walk far. Alain's light brown-haired father had just gotten off the phone and looked up when Jean-Louis tapped on the doorframe. "Monsieur Darrieux? We've never met, but I'm Robert Martin, a friend of—"

He got no further because Etienne jumped out of his chair and came around to grasp Jean-Louis in a strong hug. "I know who you are…" He spoke with deep emotion. "I can't believe you're here!"

The resemblance between father and son through coloring and facial features couldn't be denied, but it was their natural warmth that got to Jean-Louis. Meeting Etienne explained a lot. He saw framed photos of Alain on the desk.

"Please—sit down."

"I can only stay a minute. I'm due to check in at Mercy Hospital here for a full medical examination, and my taxi is waiting. But I wanted to come by first and tell you how sorry I am about Alain. He thought the world of his family. No one ever had a better friend."

Etienne's brown eyes filled with tears. Jean-Louis struggled to fight his own. "He wrote about you so much, Robert, I feel like you're part of our family."

"I know the feeling, and I have some pictures of your son I'm sure you'll enjoy." He reached in his pocket for a dozen little photos. There was much more he needed to do for Etienne if death didn't take him first.

The older man wept as he looked at them before his head lifted. "You *have* to come back for dinner this evening. The family will want to meet you and talk to you."

"Thank you, but I won't be able to. I've been discharged from the army because I'm ill. It all depends on what the doctors tell me. It could take a while." But he doubted he'd see Etienne again. "I'll phone you."

"I'm going to hold you to that promise."

Jean-Louis left the shop. He asked the taxi driver to drive him to Mercy Hospital, where he got out at the emergency entrance with his duffel bag. Once inside, the staff processed him and took him to an examination room.

Up front the doctor on his case told him he'd have to stay at the hospital for tests for at least a week. *That long?* Jean-Louis figured he'd be dead in less time. He felt so exhausted and breathless, they moved him to a private room immediately.

Incredible but true, when the seventh day arrived after endless blood tests, X-rays and cardiograms, he realized he was still alive. "What's the verdict, Dr. Marouche? How long do I have?"

"When you came in, you said you believed you were dying, but you're not! Our epidemiologist has discovered your problem and will be in shortly to discuss it with you."

His response angered Jean-Louis. The way he felt, he couldn't imagine living any longer. "I can take bad news, and I'm not here to play word games. You don't need to pretend with me."

"I never pretend," came the sober response.

Jean-Louis didn't believe him. Since Alain's death and his illness, he'd been waiting for this pointless existence to be over. His best bud's friendship had helped compensate for the loss of his brothers, Nic and Raoul, from his life. Alain's death had compounded his grief over the loss of his family when he ran away.

Ten minutes later, a different doctor entered his room. It was a brunette wearing a mask that hid her face from view. But her white lab coat didn't prevent him from noticing her long legs and lissome body as she walked toward him. She looked attractive, as far as he could tell. Given how terrible he felt inside and out, it surprised him that she'd caught his interest at all.

Over the years in the army, he and Alain had enjoyed many women, but he'd never cultivated a long-lasting relationship. Besides his trust issues about being wanted for himself and not his money, he couldn't envision himself settling down to marriage.

His own father had lost his life's companion when Jean-Louis's mother had died in childbirth. He didn't dare put himself in the position of losing a wife. Nothing could be worth that anguish. Better to stay unattached. Safer.

It had been hard enough losing his best friend. They'd been through everything together. Alain's death had been the coup de grâce, devastating him. He'd seen too many losses in war with his own troop and with the people in Africa. He was done with it all.

"Monsieur Martin?" The woman's cultured voice forced him to pay attention. "I'm Dr. Valmy. Dr. Marouche asked me to talk to you." She moved a chair over to his hospital bed with a certain grace and sat down. He watched her pull an electronic pocket notebook from her uniform.

"He says I'm not dying. But I don't believe it when my body feels like I've just done ten rounds with a heavyweight boxer, and my head is like cotton wool. I'm twenty-nine, but I might as well be sixty."

"By your morose reply, I get the impression you wish you *were* dying." She'd said it kindly. "I can recommend an excellent psychiatrist here on staff you could talk to about your feelings."

Jean-Louis shook his head. "No thanks. I'd really prefer not to waste anyone's time. I'm not worth the trouble." As he spoke, he looked up into compassionate green eyes staring at him above her mask. They were the color of the lush grass surrounding the château on his family's estate.

"I'm sorry you feel so ill, but we're here to help you. I'll say it again. You're not dying, and if you take care of yourself, you should live a long time."

He still couldn't comprehend it. After learning of his friend's death, he'd sensed he would be next. Yet for the first time in many months, those beautiful eyes were giving him hope, something he'd thought was gone.

"I see here you joined the army at nineteen and served ten years. What I'd like you to do is think back before your military experience. Tell me if you had any of these symptoms you listed for Dr. Marouche when you were a teenager."

He blinked. "A teenager?" Her question had surprised him.

"Yes. Tell you what. I'll read each one you told him in order to jog your memory. Let's start with tiredness and weakness. When did that begin?"

"To be honest, I can't remember a time when I didn't feel that way."

"Can you give me an age?"

"Around fifteen I guess."

"You never saw a doctor about it?"

"No. After school I liked to fiddle around in the garage and just figured I never got enough sleep."

"I see. What about sweating at night?"

"I guess that's what I've been doing for years. I thought it was normal."

"Hmm. Around fifteen too?"

"Probably."

"There are other symptoms here. I'm most concerned about the difficulty you have breathing when you're lying down. Did you experience that in your teens?"

"Once or twice. When that happened, I assumed I'd caught a cold in my chest."

"Your weight loss now is understandable considering how awful you feel. You did mention blurry vision. Did that happen at school years ago?"

"I think a couple of times."

"You still said nothing to your teacher?"

"No. It went away fast. I played soccer at school. The coach warned us to drink a lot and not get dehydrated. I figured that was the reason."

She flicked him a speaking glance. "You're quite the doctor for a man with no medical training." Beneath that professional exterior, the woman had a sense of humor.

"I hated going to one."

"I understand. Most children hate it almost as much as twenty-nine-year-olds do." She had him there and he actually chuckled. "Monsieur Martin, what I've found out from the latest tests is that you have an enlarged spleen. Your answers just now verify everything. You show no signs of malaria or other illnesses you assumed you'd picked up in Africa."

"That doesn't seem possible considering I feel like the walking dead. What does an enlarged spleen signify?"

"The spleen clears blood cells from the body, but it's on overload. You have a blood disorder called polycythemia vera, or PV for short."

"I've never heard of it."

"PV occurs when there are too many red blood cells. These extra red cells make your blood thicker than normal, and the thickened blood flows slower and may clot. Red blood cells carry oxygen to organs and tissues throughout the body, so if the blood moves too slowly or clots, the cells can't deliver enough oxygen. This situation can cause the kinds of complications you've been having since you were fifteen. Left untreated, they can lead to heart disease and stroke."

He sat up in the bed. "That's truly what's wrong with me?"

"I'm positive. Twenty-two out of every one hundred thousand people have PV. But it usually hits men over sixty."

"I'm not *that* old," he murmured.

"No, you're not." She chuckled back, charming him.

"Why does it happen?"

"Because of a genetic mutation. You have one in the JAK2 gene. In most cases, PV isn't usually hereditary, but it can be passed down. I found mutations in your TET2 gene too. PV is rarer in women. Are there any men in your family who have suffered from the same symptoms?"

"I don't have family, and I've been in the army for a decade."

"I see."

Did either of his brothers have the same problem? He prayed they didn't. The news about his condition astonished him. *He really wasn't dying?* Then that meant—that meant there was still time to make restitution for so many things. "What can be done about it, Docteur?"

"We treat it with a phlebotomy that removes blood

from your body. The red blood cells contain large amounts of iron. By getting rid of the iron, the production of red blood cells by the bone marrow slows down. We'll get you started today."

"The vampire method," he muttered, but she heard him and her eyes smiled.

"Since I hope you trust me a little, *I'll* do the procedure for you this first time."

"Just to make certain I don't live forever in a different sense?" he quipped.

"Exactly. You'll die as a mortal when it's your time, that is if you follow my instructions. Give me five minutes to get what I need and I'll be back to help turn you into a new man."

"*Turn* being the operative word."

She laughed. "I may have superpowers, but would I do that to a courageous vet?"

Her friendliness had caught him unaware. He watched her womanly body leave his room and he realized he'd enjoyed talking to her. Another surprise on this day he hadn't thought could happen.

In less than five minutes she returned wearing gloves. Within seconds she'd started the procedure by inserting a needle in his left arm. "I promise this won't hurt."

She did meticulous work. Finishing up, she put a plaster over it. "How was that?"

"On a chart of one to the proverbial ten for pain, it was a zero. Thank you."

Her eyes searched his above her mask. "I'm glad to detect a change of mood in your voice. Good for the army for discharging you in time to help you get on with a new life. Not everyone is so lucky."

With that last remark, Jean-Louis sensed a kind of sadness in her tone that puzzled him. He had an idea she was talking about herself, not him.

"We'll do this in another seven days. Just so you know, you won't be able to leave the hospital until after your next treatment because you'll need monitoring for one more week. After that, you'll have to come here every week and have this done until your red blood cell level gets closer to normal. Soon you'll start to feel much better."

"Is that a promise?"

"So, you really *do* want to live! Wonderful!" For a doctor, she had a refreshing personality and was easy to talk to. "In that case you'll need to come for a phlebotomy every three months to keep levels normal. You'll need treatment throughout your life because there is no cure, but it should be a whole long life and a rich one."

"Is that a promise too?" For the first time since losing his friend, his world had started to open up to him. Her bedside manner had everything to do with it.

"I wouldn't lie to you."

"Dr. Marouche told me the same thing."

"Out of the mouths of two witnesses," she reminded him. "I'm prescribing aspirin, which will be given to you every day for the next week. There's also a medication called hydroxyurea you take that slows the production of red blood cells. Little by little you're going to get back to normal. I wish all the patients here had a prognosis like yours. I'm sorry you don't have family who will rejoice at your good news."

But he *did* have family with brothers and sisters and a father he loved heart and soul. To have the chance to see them again...

"Take care of yourself."

Before he could tell her to wait, she walked out of the room, leaving him oddly bereft. Her intelligence and appealing nature spoke for themselves. He hadn't wanted their conversation to end, and it wasn't just because he'd found out he wasn't going to die.

The next week came and went with lots of sleep and good food. Dr. Marouche checked on him daily, but to his disappointment, there was no sign of Dr. Valmy. The rest of the time he spent on the phone putting Alain's plans for his family into action.

On the weekend he had a surprise visitor before dinner. He recognized her from some of Alain's latest photos. His sister was an attractive twenty-three-year-old with trendy short brown hair. She carried a sack in her hand. Etienne must have told her where he'd been hospitalized. The two men had talked several times on the phone in the last week.

"Capitaine Martin?"

"You have to be Suzanne."

She broke into a smile like Alain's. "Yes. Maman made you my brother's favorite *mille feuilles* and I decorated them." She put it on the bedside table. "My parents want you to come to dinner as soon as you're able."

"That's very kind of them, but I'm still undergoing tests and don't know when I'll be able to leave the hospital."

Her brown eyes wandered over him. "I'm sorry. It must be so boring for you lying here. Papa hopes when you're better you'll stay in Nice with us for a while if you don't have other plans. He'd like you to come work for him too. I work there. I'm a service writer."

"No doubt you brighten up the place. Alain told me you were the greatest sister in the world. He missed you a lot."

She nodded. "It was never the same after he left."

"I can see why. He was my best bud."

They both heard voices outside the door. "The nurse told me I couldn't stay long, and I don't want to tire you out so I'd better go."

"It means a lot to me that you came. I'll call your father when I know more. Give my best to your family and tell your mother I'll relish the *mille feuilles*. I happen to love them too. Thank you for your contribution."

"*A la prochaine*, Robert. Is it all right if I call you that?" Her unexpected visit and the hopeful look in her eyes convinced him not to get involved. Now that he didn't face a death sentence, he had other plans he'd only dreamed about. First and foremost, he needed to see his father again and hope to be forgiven for the impetuous actions that had separated him from his family for too many years.

"*Bien sûr.*"

She turned to go just as someone else came in. To his surprise it was Dr. Valmy, masked as usual. His pulse quickened. All week he'd been wondering why she hadn't been to see him. "I didn't realize you had a visitor, Monsieur Martin. How nice! I'll come back."

Dr. Valmy would have checked his daily history on the computer and knew he'd had no visitors until now.

"*Non, non.* Mademoiselle Darrieux was just leaving."

He saw Suzanne stare at the doctor and cast him a frustrated glance before disappearing. She hadn't been happy about this particular interruption.

The doctor walked closer to his bed. "You're looking healthier and more human than a week ago. Are you feeling a little better in yourself? I hope so because I came in to tell you that the latest test indicates you're not making more unwanted blood cells. That's a good sign."

She'd delivered her message, and he sensed her desire to escape, but he wanted to keep her talking. "I'll admit I have a new lease on life and have been formulating some hopefully worthwhile plans to make up for lost time."

"I'm happy to hear that." Her warmth enveloped him. It came as a surprise. He saw sincerity emanating from those lovely eyes, but he also noticed something else. It was that unexplained sense of loss in her gaze he'd seen before and it haunted him. "Just so you know, before dinner you'll be given a second phlebotomy. Antoine will be here in a minute to do the procedure."

Jean-Louis didn't want someone named Antoine doing anything. "You're not able to?" He trusted her. *She'd* been the doctor to find out what had been wrong with him.

"I'm off duty now, but be assured, he's strictly human," she teased. "Tomorrow you can leave the hospital and do whatever you want, but come back in one week. The staff at the front desk will arrange all your appointments from now on. If you have any problems, get in touch with Dr. Marouche, your doctor of record. *Bonne nuit, monsieur.*"

CHAPTER TWO

JEAN-LOUIS HADN'T WANTED Dr. Valmy to leave yet, but over the years he'd grown used to losses. Since he wouldn't be staying in Nice, saying good-night to her also meant saying goodbye. He'd always been able to walk away from a woman. For the first time ever, that didn't sit well with him.

A few minutes later Antoine appeared. He was a talker who told him he was a med student. He had a brother in the air force and chatted with Jean-Louis for a long time after his blood was taken. The conversation eventually turned into a discussion of Dr. Valmy, who he learned was here on a fellowship. Antoine was crazy about her and he was a fountain of knowledge.

The brilliant epidemiologist, daughter of a renowned Parisian doctor now deceased, had turned down every guy working at the hospital, including Antoine. Hospital gossip said she was involved with one of the men on the French trade commission to Morocco. The man had distinguished himself and was headed for an illustrious career that might include running for the president of France.

Apparently, this man was a Moreau whose family

lived in one of the famous Auteuil villas of the nine-teenth century in Paris. Before leaving for military service, Jean-Louis had known of their family. It would probably be the marriage of the season.

He'd thought Dr. Valmy was a Niçoise and about twenty-four years old. But with all her schooling, she had to be a few years older. She might not have a ring on her finger yet, but it sounded like it was going to happen. The news disturbed him in ways he didn't want to examine. Poor Antoine.

As for Jean-Louis, he needed to make up for lost time. Ten years' worth. The next morning, he left the hospital with his duffel bag. Before he did anything else, he hailed a taxi to drive him to the bank to withdraw some funds accrued from his army pay. From there he checked into a hotel and went out to buy some casual clothes. The rest of the day he worked on the plans Alain had shared with Jean-Louis. It was up to him to carry them out.

On the following day, he took a taxi to the Darrieux body shop. Alain had cried to him many times over abandoning his father and mother after joining the army. But he'd died before he could be with his family again. No one understood how that felt like Jean-Louis did. Now that he knew he was destined to live, he wanted to act for Alain and help out his best friend before leaving Nice.

Etienne looked up from his desk in surprise. "Robert—"

The two men hugged. Jean-Louis sat down. "I hope you have some time for me, Etienne."

"I'll make time. You look much better."

"I'm feeling better and I'm here for a specific reason. I have a present for you from your son."

"A present?"

"You'll have to come with me to see it. He said you've wanted it for at least thirty-five years. It was a dream of yours."

The older man squinted like he couldn't understand.

"Let's go and I'll show it to you." They left in the taxi and drove to a big Ferrari dealership about a mile away. It took up a lot of the block. A huge sign towered over it with the name Etienne Darrieux. He watched the older man's expression. His head jerked around.

"What is this? Some kind of joke?"

"Not at all. Your son has been paying for it since he was deployed. He planned to help you run it after he got out of the army. He felt terrible that he'd been gone so long and couldn't wait to go into business with you."

Etienne shook his head. "He never had that kind of money."

Jean-Louis had secretly mined his own wealth and connections to seal the deal, but Etienne would never know that. "He earned it month after month. Four months ago, he put it all in your name. Let's go inside and meet the manager, Jules Villon. He'll have all the banking and paperwork to show you signed by your son."

He scratched his head. "You're putting me on."

"I swear I'm not." Jean-Louis got out of the car and Etienne followed.

They no sooner walked in the front door and the

manager walked up to them. "I've been waiting to meet the new owner. I'm Jules." He shook both their hands. "I understand you have a body shop over on Rue Rossini, Monsieur Darrieux. Are you keeping that too?"

"I don't believe this is happening," he murmured to Jean-Louis, who hoped his deceased friend could see his father's happiness now. They spent the next two hours going over the books. Jules gave Etienne a tour of the whole place and he met the employees. When he returned to the office looking dazed, Jean-Louis got up. He felt a joy beyond words to have fulfilled Alain's wish.

"I have to get back to the hotel, so if you want to stay here longer, I'll call for a ride, but I promise to stay in touch."

"No, no. We'll take a taxi to my shop together." Etienne was so overcome, he wept. En route, he thanked Jean-Louis profusely. When the taxi pulled up in front, Etienne got out. "What are your plans?"

"Tomorrow I'm renting a car and taking a trip to see the country. I haven't been behind the wheel of a car since I was nineteen." He needed to put substance to ideas that had been percolating since Dr. Valmy had assured him he'd live a long life. Home was his ultimate destination. "I won't be back, but I'll keep in touch with you."

"Please keep me posted, Robert. You're like a second son."

Jean-Louis felt touched to the core. "That means more to me than you'll ever know. You're like family to me too, and one day we'll see each other again."

"Where are you going now?"

"Back to the Excelsior Hotel, where I stayed last night."

Etienne tried to hand him some money, but he refused. "I've saved my pay. No worry there, but thank you."

Jean-Louis saw the question in the older man's eyes that he'd never put to words. *What about your family, Robert?* It was a question he couldn't answer yet because it was too painful. After he'd seen his family, then he'd tell Etienne the truth.

"*Dieu vous protégé*, Etienne. You're the best man I know."

Except for my father, but I learned that truth far too late.

They hugged once more before he told the driver where to head. After he got dropped off at a café near the hotel and had dinner, he walked back. No sooner did he reach his room on the second floor when he heard a pounding on the door. Actually, he heard separate poundings, both insistent. Was the hotel on fire or something? He hadn't heard an alarm.

"Monsieur Martin? *Ouvrez la porte, vite!*"

He rushed to open it.

Two mirror images of himself stood before him. He thought he was going to pass out and stepped back in shock.

"*Grâce à Dieu* we've found you!"

Jean-Louis had no defense against his own tears as his brothers broke down with him. They all kept hugging each other and thanking God for this miracle.

To be with Raoul and Nic again... It was too much. He couldn't handle it and fell back in the sofa, burying his face in his hands while his body heaved with happy sobs. He finally lifted his tear-stained face. "How in heaven did you find me?"

Raoul smiled. "With the help of a retired secret service agent named Claude Giraud and a lot more from above. He found out a Robert Martin had been at boot camp ten years ago and became best friends with an Alain Darrieux. But out of all the enlistees, he could find no proof that a Robert Martin had ever existed before signing up. Then he discovered that both of you were master mechanics. You had already earned that reputation at home."

Nic nodded. "That gave him his second clue and from there he identified the forger who made up your documents. He also learned that Alain died two months ago and soon after, you were discharged from the army for illness. It's obvious you've lost weight and look drained. We've been desperately worried since learning the truth."

"I feel a whole lot better than I did two weeks ago. You should have seen me then."

"We're glad you're getting better, but why were you so sick?" Raoul questioned.

"I have a blood disorder called polycythemia vera that doesn't have to be fatal, but I make too many red blood cells. Some of my blood has to be drawn once a week and eventually every three months to stay healthy. I'll explain in detail later, but I'm feeling better and want to hear how Claude caught up to me."

"He traced you to Nice," Raoul explained. "All he had to do was flash your photo at Alain's sister in his father's shop and she identified you at once. Robert Martin is a big name around there."

He shook his head in wonder. "Do they know who I really am yet?"

"Nope. We told Claude why you joined up in the first place. He would never give you away."

Relief swept through him. He wanted to be the one to tell Etienne the truth.

"Is Alain's sister someone special?" Nic teased with a gleam in his eyes.

It looked like he had Suzanne to thank for a positive identification, but Jean-Louis wasn't complaining. He'd been through too much. After seeing Etienne's pain over the loss of his son, he was tired of running away from his life.

"Only special enough for your super sleuth to have figured out my deception. I'm thankful he did." He stared at the two of them. "Tomorrow I'd planned to drive home to see all of you, and here you are. I can't believe I'm not dreaming."

"We can't either." They both hunkered down in front of him. Nic looked into his eyes. "With you gone, life's never been the same for us or our sisters, and definitely not for our father. *Frérot?* It's why we hired Claude to find you."

Raoul gripped his arm. "Papa hasn't been well and yearns to see you. His pain over the way he treated you ten years ago has plagued him. He's wanted to see you again and ask for your forgiveness."

Jean-Louis moaned. *He* was the one who needed to ask, *beg* his father to forgive him for being such an ungrateful son. To his joy it *wasn't* too late. With maturity he realized his flight from home had been rooted in a teenage rebelliousness against circumstances that weren't anyone's fault.

No one could have prevented his mother's death. Their family's obscene wealth had its naissance centuries earlier. His father had only tried to preserve that legacy. Certainly Jean-Louis's responsibility for a troop of soldiers had opened his eyes to the challenges his father had to overcome to raise their large family alone.

"We flew here in the family jet and want to take you to La Racineuse tonight before more time passes. Two months ago the doctor made him retire. He has a medical helper named Luca. Corinne moved into the château with Gaston and the kids, but everyone is trying to take care of him," Raoul explained.

Jean-Louis started to tremble. "What's wrong with him?"

"Heart disease," they said at the same time.

He remembered a question Dr. Valmy had asked him about any male in his family who suffered from the same symptoms. His brothers seemed well enough. *Had his father developed PV over the years?*

"My life hasn't been the same since either. I need to see him more than you'll ever know." He got to his feet. "I'm ready to go right now. Let me throw my stuff in my duffel bag." While in La Racineuse, he'd go to the hospital there and have his blood drawn. But he wished Dr. Valmy would be there to do it.

He'd only met her twice, yet her warmth and sincerity had drawn him to her. She'd helped him with his depressive thoughts in a straightforward and compassionate manner. Putting all that together, combined with a compelling physical attraction despite the fact he'd never seen her without her mask, and he couldn't get her off his mind. After he'd paid his hotel bill, they went out to a waiting limo that drove them to the airport. Once on board they congregated in the lounge compartment and the jet took off. Jean-Louis didn't know the pilot or steward. Too much time had gone by, but the new staff recognized the missing triplet and went out of their way to welcome him home.

Maybe his eyes deceived him. "Nic? Is that a wedding ring I see?"

His brother grinned. "I married the woman of my dreams three weeks ago. She's the attorney Papa hired right before he had to retire. One look at her and that was it for me."

"Felicitations!"

"We're building a home in Roselin Woods as we speak."

"That's what we named it when we found all those finch nests that day on our bike ride."

"That was one fun day."

So much life had gone on without him. He turned to Raoul. "What about you?"

"I haven't been lucky like Nic." His brother averted his eyes and his face clouded over. Jean-Louis realized this wasn't the moment to question him.

"There's too much trouble going on at La Racineuse," Raoul explained.

"What do you mean? Don't tell me old man Dumotte is still doing his worst?"

"Worse than his worst," Nic broke in.

"How is that possible?"

His brothers looked at each other. "We have some sad news. Oncle Raimond died of ALS the night I got married," Nic informed him.

"I loved that man," Jean-Louis murmured.

"We all did. Papa asked Raoul to leave the corporation we were running together and come home to run the estate. He's doing what he was always meant to do. But the second Dumotte found out, he went into a meltdown and burned one of the barns in protest."

"I knew it!" Jean-Louis blurted. "He's always hated Papa. The man's irrationality has finally turned him into a maniac." He looked at Nic. "I take it you must be running the whole corporation in Paris now."

"No. I help when I can, but to my joy Causcelle is now in the hands of our inimitable cousin Pascal and Papa's assistant George Delong."

"There never was anyone like him!" Jean-Louis cried. "He was always my favorite cousin."

"Everyone likes Pascal. You'd think he was born to it."

"Another Papa?"

Both brothers nodded.

"Then what are *you* doing, Nic? Besides being a new euphoric husband, of course." The look in Nic's eyes confirmed his happiness. How would it be to have found the love of his life and experience that kind of joy? For the first time in years, Jean-Louis began to think marriage might be something to aspire to rather than reject. Nic's delight and contentment was real, and once again unbidden thoughts of Dr. Valmy entered Jean-Louis's mind.

For the next few hours he listened as his brothers caught him up on everything that had gone on over the years. Nic went into detail about the reconstruction of the church where their mother's brother Gregoire had died in a fire years ago.

He explained about the free hospital/hotels he wanted built around France, secretly in honor of Gregoire and the other monks who'd lost their lives. This first one would include a bovine research center, but all of it was still in the planning stage.

"You should have gone into science, Nic." He knew his brother's heart.

"That's old ground now."

Shivers raced through Jean-Louis's body. He couldn't believe what his brother had just told him. Nic's ideas coincided very much with his own future dreams that had developed while he'd been in the hospital. Maybe this was a triplet thing to be on the same wavelength. But it was something he'd talk about with them later.

The Fasten Seat Belts sign flashed, bringing their conversation to an end. The plan was to drive the fifteen miles from Chalon Champforgeuil airport to the château where his old bedroom had been waiting for him. He felt intense remorse over the childish anger that had caused him to run away from his birthright, from all that had been precious to him.

He owed everything to his father, who'd had to go it alone when their mother had died in childbirth. He'd be home soon to see the whole family and embrace his beloved parent. He wanted to make up for so much while there was still time with his father.

Jean-Louis no longer gave a damn about being recognized as one of the world-famous triplet billionaire sons. Like Nic, he planned to turn all of it to the good. Even better, Raoul had gone back to the estate he'd never wanted to leave. Happiness was possible for all of them.

What was it Dr. Valmy had said to him? *So, you do want to live!* She had no idea... His only problem was that he found himself thinking about her way too much. But right now his thoughts were on the father he hadn't seen for years.

The drive to the château didn't take long. As soon as they drove up, Jean-Louis leaped out of the car and hurried inside to look for his father. He found him on the terrace at the rear of the château sitting in a wheelchair. His caregiver smiled and nodded to him.

A boulder had lodged in his throat. "Papa?"

His father stirred, then looked over at him. "Jean-Jean, *mon fils.*" He called him by his nickname and threw out his arms to him. Jean-Louis ran into them and they hugged for a long, long time. Both men wept.

"Forgive me for leaving you, *mon père.* I love you and have missed you so much."

"There's nothing to forgive. I thank God you've

come home and that your life has been preserved. That's all I've ever wanted. I love you, Jean-Jean."

"It's heaven to be home. I'll never leave you again."

Today had been Françoise's last day at Mercy Hospital. She'd done her packing and tomorrow she would be leaving for Paris. As she got ready to walk out of the lab for the last time, she received a call and prayed it was Guillaume Briand. Her concerns over the adoption had grown more troubling while she'd been waiting for news from him.

To her consternation it was Eric who wanted to explain that he couldn't fly to Nice this weekend because of official business in Rabat. He was terribly upset and promised to make it up to her in Paris in a few weeks.

That phone call was an answer to prayer.

Their relationship should never have happened. When he contacted her in Paris, she would have to tell him goodbye. They'd met at her father's funeral in Paris and he'd started dating her after she'd flown back to Nice, but her attraction to him hadn't grown. She knew it was time to stop seeing him.

Her boards couldn't have come at a better time. She wasn't in love with him, and finding that hidden adoption record had turned her inside out so she couldn't concentrate on anything else. Her fear now was to try not to fail her exam while she waited for news from Monsieur Briand.

Suddenly Antoine rushed in to say goodbye. She could tell something was wrong. "What's on your mind?"

"Besides your leaving?"

She smiled at the younger man. "You knew it had to happen, but I'll miss you too. Now tell me what's wrong."

"I did all the lab work for today's patients, but our army vet didn't show."

That caught her off guard. "Maybe he came yesterday."

He shook his head. "Nope. No one has seen him all week. He never kept his appointment."

"That's not good."

"I talked to Dr. Marouche. He's worried our patient might have had a serious death wish and didn't want answers."

There'd been a time when she'd thought the same thing. Antoine's comment about Dr. Marouche confirmed it. "He said that?"

"More or less. I liked Robert."

Liked wasn't the right word when she thought of her patient. The first night after she'd met him, she'd had a dream about him that still shocked her. She was glad to be leaving for Paris, where she wouldn't be seeing him again. It haunted her even now.

"I'm sure he'll show up soon, Antoine. Maybe he's been too sick to come."

"Maybe."

"He had one visitor who might be looking after him and will see that he comes."

"You think?"

"Yes." Françoise had to admit it wasn't possible for a woman to ignore Robert, certainly not the one who came to his room the other day. She'd seen the hungry look in the young woman's eyes. Despite his illness, he was unusually attractive and possessed an intriguing personality. His sense of humor had made her laugh. To think he'd managed to get through twenty-nine years of life doctoring himself.

Françoise found it miraculous that he had such an amazing constitution and strength of will considering his PV. But lurking in the black recesses of his eyes, she'd seen hurt and sorrow. She couldn't be sure if war had done that to him, or something, or...someone. Both she and Dr. Marouche had gotten the idea he'd been welcoming death until he was told he was going to live and why. The change in him had fascinated her, as if the words had pulled him out of a terrible nightmare.

Remembering that illuminating moment after she'd told him he'd live a long life, she said to Antoine, "I'm sure he doesn't have a death wish now. Don't give up on him."

She kissed his cheek. "*A bientôt*, Antoine. Take care of yourself. I know for a fact dozens of girls are out there waiting for you to date them." No doubt there were thousands of them waiting for Robert when he'd recovered. "Email me when you meet *the one*, and bring her to Paris so I can meet her."

"I'll do that, and I know you'll ace your boards."

"Let's hope so."

She grabbed her purse and hurried out in front of the hospital to get a taxi.

No sooner had she given the driver the address of her apartment than her phone rang. Seeing the ID, she clicked on immediately. "Monsieur Briand? I'm so glad it's you. Please tell me you have good news for me."

"I'm afraid not. This is a case that has been specially sealed in the strictest legal sense."

Her spirits plunged. "What do you mean *specially*?"

"It means it contains information that mustn't come to light under any circumstances."

She could hardly breathe. "In other words…"

"In other words, there's nothing more I can do," he affirmed in a serious tone. "It isn't a case of needing more money. I'm so sorry."

"So am I," she said in a tortured whisper. "Thank you for all your help."

"It's been my pleasure, Dr. Valmy."

Françoise hung up in a stupor.

She knew nothing about her birth parents and the kind of people they were. She never would. Did she have other siblings? Grandparents? Aunts and uncles? So many questions haunted her. She couldn't conceive of her adoptive father and mother hiding this from her and was shattered by it.

It was a good thing she wasn't in love with Eric because she realized she wouldn't be having a relationship with any man unless she got answers.

What if her birth mother or father had some kind of inherited disease or a psychiatric disorder that could have been passed on to her? Had her adoptive parents decided not to let her know anything because she'd shown no signs yet? How could she ever marry or have children if such a thing were a possibility?

Equally horrible, what if it turned out her father—lauded by the government for his contribution to medicine—had done something to ruin his stellar reputation? If that delivery had been on the up and up, there'd have been no need to hide it from her forever.

Torn apart by too many ugly thoughts, she made up her mind that once she'd passed her boards—*if she did*—she'd leave Paris and go someplace where her adoptive father hadn't been known. All these years everyone had commented about her inheriting her father's fabulous genes. Nothing could be further from the truth.

She didn't know the identity of her birth father or mother. Finding that adoption paper had robbed her of her identity as a Valmy. All of her life she'd taken such pride in her family history and lineage. The hidden document made her feel like she'd just been born. Welcome to a world where her birth parents could be out there. Did they wonder or worry about her? Life as she'd known it had turned into a nightmare.

After two and a half weeks in Paris to convince the jury, Françoise had just received her doctorate. She could claim it officially, but the phone call from Guillaume Briand in Nice might as well have slammed her through a wall.

She hadn't been the same since he'd discovered that the adoption case had been specially sealed under the law. In his opinion it meant something did have to be concealed. Unfortunately, there was no way ever to learn the facts.

Feeling as if she'd been permanently frozen in a void, it was a miracle she'd gotten through her exams.

"Dr. Valmy?"

She looked up from the computer. "Christophe!" The married, sixty-year-old head of epidemiology known professionally as Dr. Soulis had just left his private office in the lab on the fifth floor of The Good Shepherd Hospital in Paris. He'd been in touch with her for the last year and was responsible for hiring her the moment he knew she'd received her degree.

He winked at her. "It's good to have another Valmy back at the helm. Your father was a legend around here before he left us to serve France in Morocco. Now that you're here, all is forgiven. We expect wonders from you."

She groaned inwardly. "Are you trying to terrify me after my third day on the job?"

"You're his daughter. What is there to fear?"

"You don't want to know."

He laughed and said good-night before disappearing out the door. How lucky for her to be working under someone so likeable and pleasant, but not for long. The sealed adoption had changed everything. Once she'd found another hospital position far from Paris where her father hadn't been known, she'd turn in her notice.

As she studied the latest case, Celestine, the young clerk at the fifth-floor desk, came rushing into the lab. "Dr. Valmy?"

"Yes? Right here."

"Oh, good." She ran over to her. "I saw Dr. Soulis leave and was afraid you might have gone home too."

"Is there a problem?"

"A man came in at the last minute for blood work. He didn't have an appointment. I told him he was too late, but I thought I'd check one more time."

"I'm just leaving, Celestine." Eric had flown into Paris today and would be coming over to her apartment tonight to celebrate her graduation. She dreaded it, but she had to break off with him. "Will you tell the patient to come back tomorrow at ten and one of the staff will take care of him?"

"Yes, of course. Ooh, I wish I were a phlebotomist."

"You can certainly train to become one."

"That isn't what I meant."

"I don't understand."

"He's the hunkiest man I ever saw in my life and he's a vet! I didn't know there were men like him in existence! See you on Monday." She rushed out.

"*A bientôt*, Celestine."

Back in Nice, Françoise had also met a hunky vet, one who'd infiltrated her mind in a dream she needed to get out of her head. Maybe looking for a new car to buy tomorrow would help erase him from her thoughts.

After years of commuting by bus and taxi, she looked forward to having her own transportation no matter where she ended up. Eric would have picked her up, but she didn't want to be beholden to him in any way.

She closed the file and removed her uniform. Beneath it she'd worn one of her work blouses and skirts. After grabbing her purse, she left the lab for the elevator down the hall. As she stepped in, a woman and man followed. She'd assumed they were together until the woman got off on the third floor.

After reaching the main floor, she got out first and headed for the entrance. Once outside the busy hospital, she waited at the *tête de taxi* for a ride. If one didn't come soon, she'd phone for one.

Several cars drove past coming out of the parking lot. A black Mercedes actually stopped in front of her and an incredibly handsome man at the wheel got out. He walked toward her. She felt his eyes studying her. "Excuse me. Is it possible you're Dr. Valmy?"

"Yes, but—" She'd been going to say she didn't recognize him. Then she looked into those compelling black eyes that were so familiar. "Monsieur Martin!"

"Yes, I'm Robert, your former patient in Nice. The one whose life you saved and promised would live for a long time. I thought it was you in the elevator, but I never saw you without your mask on until today."

This man *couldn't* be the same one, but he was. "It *is* you. *You're* the patient who wanted your blood drawn here a little while ago?"

"How did you know that?"

"Because I work at this hospital now. The clerk said a vet had come without an appointment, but I was on the verge of leaving. If I'd known it was you, I would have taken care of you. I'm so sorry when you took all the trouble to come here."

"No problem. It's my fault. I got so busy today, I didn't make an appointment. I'd hoped I could get it done before going to my hotel. It doesn't matter. I'll come again tomorrow morning. Why are you in Paris?"

"Paris is my home. I came to take my final boards and now I'm employed here."

He rubbed the back of his neck. "I thought you were from Nice."

"Only living there for the last three years. When my parents moved to Rabat for a government assignment, I worked at Mercy Hospital in Nice to do my residency and fellowship through Sophie Antipolis University. That way I could see my parents more often."

"Now I understand, but I have to admit I'm surprised to find you here."

"It's a surprise for me too." He was the embodiment of the man in her dream. "Before I left Nice, Antoine told me you didn't come in for your phlebotomy. What happened to you? I had no idea I'd see you here."

"I've been in the east of France and received treatments at another hospital there."

"Well, it shows. In just a month you seem healthier. It's amazing what those treatments along with nourishing food and rest have done for you."

"You promised I'd get better," he said with a smile.

She'd never seen him in anything but a hospital gown because he'd always been in bed. The tall, rock-solid man who had to be six foot three was dressed in a pullover and jeans. In a word, he looked sensational.

The two times she'd been in his room, he'd appeared down and out. Clean shaven now with vibrant black hair, she found his transformation astounding. He no longer resembled a wounded animal. She saw life in those black eyes that hadn't been there before.

Just then a taxi pulled up to the *tête de taxi*. "It looks

like I've got a ride. That's good because I have plans and need to get home. I've enjoyed seeing you again, Robert, and am so glad you're doing well." She feared she'd be dreaming about him again tonight.

"Please wait a moment, Dr. Valmy. After what you've done for me, I want to repay you for saving my life. That's not lip service," he claimed in a more serious tone of voice. "Would you consider letting me give you lunch at my hotel tomorrow? It would mean a lot to me. Circumstances in Nice prevented me from talking to you one more time. We might never see each other again. Please say yes."

Like Antoine, she liked Robert. How could she possibly say no? "Since you were turned away from getting your blood drawn, I'd enjoy lunch with you. But it will have to be a late one since I'm buying a new car tomorrow."

His eyes held a gleam. "Then let's say four o'clock. Will that give you time to negotiate the sale and try out your new purchase to your heart's content?"

She smiled at him. "So you know what that's like."

"Oh, yeah. There's nothing more fun."

"I've never owned my own car and I'm really excited."

"I'm excited for you. Do you have a make in mind?"

"None that I can afford."

He laughed. "Then it will keep me guessing until you arrive."

"I'll try to get there on time. Thank you. By the way, where is there?"

A chuckle escaped. "23 Marais Place. I'll be out in

front to meet you." He walked over to the taxi. After saying something to the driver, he opened the rear door for her. "Don't take too many chances. There are other sick people in desperate need of your particular services. You're a rarity and I for one will always be grateful. Your diagnosis brought me back to life, and this chance meeting allows me to do something for you in return."

She felt his sincerity to her bones. "You're very kind." And too appealing for her own good. "*A demain*, Robert."

The drive to the apartment that the hospital had arranged for her to live in didn't take long. Meeting him had been a surprise that shouldn't have thrilled her so much. He'd put her in a different mood as she got ready for Eric to come over. Robert's words of appreciation had been a balm to her soul even if she didn't know her true origins or destiny.

Now it was time to do the one thing she *could* do something about. Eric deserved his freedom even if he didn't know it yet. He was a terrific man, but not the one for her.

A half hour later she heard the knock on the door. When she opened it, dark-haired Eric swept her into his arms and kissed her hungrily. "I thought this day would never come. You aced your exams. Now we can get engaged and plan our wedding."

She eased herself away from him and walked in the living room. "Eric?" Françoise turned to him. "Sit down for a minute so we can talk. I've enjoyed our times together very much, but the truth is, I can't marry you. It hurts me to say it, but for the last month I've tried to be honest with you so you'd understand."

His features creased in confusion. "What do you mean you can't?" He hadn't been listening to her. "I understood your hesitation before your exams, but now—"

"Now it's truth time," she cut him off. "I'm not in love the way I need to be in order to marry you."

His brown eyes looked incredulous. "I don't believe you're saying that to me."

"I know, and I'm so sorry. I tried to tell you before."

"There's someone else."

"No. No one." Her dream had nothing to do with reality. "Something has held me back from committing. Time away from you has made me realize how I really feel."

He shook his head. "You've been alone too much since the deaths of your parents. You aren't yourself. We need more time together. I'll call you tomorrow. We'll drive out to the house I want to buy for us and we'll really talk before I have to get back to Morocco. I have big plans about my campaign, and they include you."

"It won't work, Eric." She paused. "In fact, I'm not sure I'll ever get married." She meant it.

"That's crazy."

"No, it's not, but I have my reasons. I don't want to be cruel to you. You're a marvelous man, but I can't do this anymore. Please try to understand. And right now, I'm very tired and need to get to bed."

He got up and came over to kiss her cheek. "Be warned. I'm not letting you get away from me."

She knew he was in pain, but one day he'd meet a woman who would make him happy. Françoise couldn't be that person.

CHAPTER THREE

THE NEXT MORNING Françoise took a hot shower and washed her hair. To her relief she hadn't dreamed, but that was probably because she'd be seeing Robert before the day was out.

Normally she'd wear pants and a top. But because he'd invited her for a meal, she chose to dress up a little and wear her blue-and-white-print sundress. It had the same print on the short-sleeved jacket. She brushed her hair and put on some pink frost lipstick. After slipping on white sandals, she felt ready to go.

By three o'clock Françoise had bought a metallic blue Nissan Versa she liked and felt she could afford. After driving it around overjoyed, she did a few errands and headed for Robert's hotel in the Marais district. She'd been away from Paris for three years and welcomed the familiar sights with all its older charm and glory from past kings.

In another few minutes she slowed down to turn into the courtyard of a modernized two-story palace with a fountain she'd passed many times over the years. It had never been open to the public.

Françoise knew she'd come to the right address, but this palace couldn't be a hotel. There had to be one behind it. She wound around, but saw nothing except some security guards at the entrance. Hopefully, they could tell her where to find it. After parking, she got out and heard footsteps.

When she turned around, there stood Robert. Instead of casual clothes, he wore an expensive-looking light blue suit with white shirt and tie. For a second, Françoise couldn't think as she studied the chiseled features that made him the best-looking man she'd ever seen in her life. Those black eyes gleamed beneath luxuriant jet-black hair.

"I'm crazy about the color of your car, Dr. Valmy. A Nissan is always dependable. That's important considering you're a doctor. Congratulations on your choice."

"Thank you. I love it. But tell me something. I thought you said this was a hotel."

He nodded. "It is. However, everyone who stays here calls it the *palais*. Shall we go in?"

She walked inside with him. He called to the guard at the front desk. "I don't want to be disturbed, Guy."

By whom?

He cupped her elbow and walked her down the hall and around a corner to another wide corridor. They soon came to an elevator and rose to the next floor. She experienced more surprises when the door opened into the foyer of an elegant suite.

Her host walked her into the salon with its sumptuous furnishings and floor-to-ceiling windows. She noticed the intricately paneled walls—this had been a palace after all, but it had a comfortable, inviting feeling you didn't often associate with such a magnificent building. How had he obtained permission to be here? He'd been a mystery from the first. That hadn't changed.

"The restroom is down the hall on the right. Go ahead and freshen up first."

When she came back to the salon, she found him waiting for her. He'd removed his suit jacket. "Sit down, Dr. Valmy."

"Thank you. Please call me Françoise."

"I'd like that." He sat on an upholstered chair. "After our talk, we'll have dinner in the dining room."

"A talk?" What did he mean?

"I want you to understand the depth of my appreciation for you. I wouldn't be alive if it weren't for you. Please let me get this off my chest."

"I'm glad I happened to be the doctor who discovered your problem, but let's not make more of it. Any epidemiologist would have found it."

"That isn't what Antoine told me, and I need to unburden myself to you."

Once again, she found herself concerned by that pained expression in his eyes. "What's wrong?"

"When I was your patient for that brief period in Nice, I lied to you about certain aspects of my life. Since seeing you yesterday, I know I must tell you the whole truth. The first thing I want you to know is that my name isn't Robert Martin."

Françoise had found a place on the end of the damask-covered couch and folded her arms, trying to relax.

It proved impossible when his admission had surprised her. First her parents' sin of omission. Now his.

He leaned forward with his hands on his powerful legs. "I've got a picture to show you. It may explain a lot, then again, maybe nothing."

"Where is it?"

"On the coffee table in front of you."

She hadn't noticed the framed five-by-seven photo lying facedown next to the vase of flowers.

"Go ahead and take a look at it."

She reached for it and discovered a black-and-white picture. What she saw were three young handsome guys with black hair. They all looked like Robert, who'd said he wasn't Robert Martin. All were dressed in the same pants and pullovers with the name Racine Rams imprinted from their high school. They were triplets! How incredible. She studied the picture for a minute. *Racine Rams.*

Wait a minute... *Triplets!*

All of a sudden she remembered hearing about a famous set of triplets before her parents moved to Morocco three years ago, taking her to Nice to be near them. They'd been a year older than she and were the sons of a multi-multi-billionaire who'd lost their mother. Their pictures had been all over the media and the news, and her girlfriends had been gaga over them. What was their father's name? She searched her brain. Over time she'd lost track, but seeing this photo brought it all back.

She felt dark eyes on her. "You're a brilliant doctor,

and I can see it's on the tip of your tongue." He could read her mind.

"I've almost got it. Don't tell me."

He chuckled. "Take your time. We've got all night."

"Something *scelle*. Porscelle? No. Borscelle."

"Try starting with the first letter of the alphabet."

"Aurscelle?"

"Keep going." His smile had turned into a grin.

"I've done *A* and *B*. That leaves *C* next. Corscelle," she blurted.

"Close," he quipped.

She jumped to her feet and walked around looking at the photo. "Conscelles."

He shook his head.

"Curscelles."

"Je regrette..." he teased.

"Oh, why can't I think of it?"

The man who had called himself Robert sat back in the chair putting his hands behind his head. He was so attractive, it shouldn't be allowed. "Think of the Promenade des Anglais in Nice."

She nodded. "I've walked along there hundreds of times."

"In that case, why don't we eat our meal while it's hot. I'm sure it will come to you in time."

"I can't until I've solved this."

"You're probably a whiz at crossword puzzles."

"My roommates have hated me for it. My mother was the only person who could beat me." *My adoptive mother.*

"So, you inherited your smarts from both sides of your family."

She'd inherited everything from her birth parents. Who they were? She didn't know and never would. "Maman was smart enough to marry my father. Why aren't I smart enough to come up with the name I'm looking for?"

"You're trying too hard."

"You're right." She stopped and looked at the picture again, then flicked him another glance. "The Promenade des Anglais, huh?"

"Plain as the lovely nose on your face."

She shrugged her shoulders in defeat. "I know you're hungry, so I give up."

"I can wait."

"No, you can't. I heard your stomach growl."

At that comment, rich male laughter poured out of him. "I'll give you one more hint. Think of a celebrity hotel."

Celebrity...

Suddenly the light dawned. "The Causcelle Prom Hotel!"

He stood to his full height. "You got it in six. *Bravo!*"

By now the blood had started to drain from her face and she felt light-headed. "*You're* one of the world-famous Causcelles—do you know the odds of that happening? Which one are you?"

"Jean-Louis."

"I think I'm going to faint."

He rushed over and put her on the sofa, pushing

her head down. The picture fell to the floor. When the world stopped spinning, she lifted her head and stared at him. "It's my turn to owe *you*, Monsieur Causcelle. If I'd fallen, I would probably have cracked my head open."

"At least I'm good for something." He still had his hand on the back of her neck. One of his fingers played absently with a curl, sending darts of awareness through her.

Françoise couldn't stop looking at him. "You're the missing son everyone used to wonder about." The man in my dream.

He smiled. "They still do."

"Jean-Louis. Good heavens. You have a fabulous heritage with a family tree that goes back centuries! I remember now." She couldn't believe it. "And here you thought you were dying. They must be overjoyed beyond belief that you're back." Françoise envied that he knew without a doubt who'd parented him.

"I'm still trying to take it all in. Your diagnosis turned my world around. That's because you're the genius daughter of a renowned doctor. Genes don't lie. Antoine bragged about you and I can see why."

Françoise averted her eyes. "I had no idea Antoine was a walking encyclopedia."

"The man's in love with you, that's why." She'd suspected Antoine cared for her, but it jolted her to hear this man put it into words. "He's suffering because word has it you'll be getting married soon."

Wrong again. "He didn't leave much out, did he?" She laughed to cover her distress.

"You have to forgive him. For your information, you're the only person outside my family who knows I'm back after dropping out of sight ten years ago."

"I'm still in shock that you're the missing Causcelle."

"Then you need to eat first to restore yourself." He put the picture on the coffee table and helped her up from the couch. "Now that I've confessed, I'm ready to enjoy our dinner."

A knot of guilt prevented her from moving. "I'm afraid I can't eat until I reveal *my* lie."

That caught his full attention. By the way his hand tightened on her arm, she knew she'd surprised him. His eyes searched hers for an answer.

"Since you've told me the truth about yourself, Jean-Louis, I can do no less because I've been living a lie too. Three weeks ago, I found out my famous father and mother weren't my birth parents after all. Their genes aren't mine. Now *you* have the distinction of being the only person alive who knows that fact aside from the PI I hired to get at the truth and couldn't."

Jean-Louis's heart missed a couple of beats while he absorbed that information before he helped Françoise to the dining room table. "While we enjoy the *saumon en papillotte*, I'd like to hear your story first. Then I'll tell you about mine and the PI my brothers hired to find me, if you're interested." He sat across from her and poured their wine. "What's your real name?"

"Françoise Valmy. I was never given another name." She eyed him curiously. "Why Robert Martin?"

"There are millions of Roberts and Martins in France. I needed to get lost in the shuffle, but we're talking about you." He took a sip of wine. "What happened three weeks ago that turned your life inside out?"

"That's exactly what it did." He watched her eat before she rested her fork on the plate. For the next few minutes, she told him about her father's medical bag and the discovery.

"They never told me I was adopted. That paper lay hidden in the bottom of his bag for twenty-eight years. If it hadn't fallen upside down, I would never have seen it. Maman told me she had three miscarriages before they had me. Of course, I wouldn't have cared about being adopted. What I don't understand was the secrecy. Finding it has left me with too many unsettling questions."

He sat back in the chair, studying her intently. "Considering the caliber of your doctor father, who represented France in Morocco, are you afraid he might have had an affair with a patient before or after he was married? Are you frightened his reputation would be forever tarnished if it came out?"

The man had seized on one of her fears. "Yes. What if he had delivered me, or done something unethical?"

He finished his food. "Maybe he had a lover who couldn't take care of the baby, and he felt responsible because you were his child?"

"You really do know how to ask the right questions. I've thought of that possibility too. Is my birth mother still alive out there somewhere? That's what is killing me. Maybe he was investigated for breaking the rules of the Hippocratic Oath. My father was an attractive man, and there would have been opportunities. He married my mother, who was a beautiful nurse."

"I can believe that," he said under his breath, but she heard him.

"The problem is, I know my parents loved each other. So, if that's true, then it's possible he could have delivered the baby and secretly put it up for adoption before he married. Then he could have talked Maman into going to an adoption agency and they adopted me. I'll never know if she knew or not. I've been lying awake nights wondering about that."

He poured more wine. "Then again, he might have been protecting his patient who'd had an affair with another man. Maybe the father was a government official who couldn't bear exposure at any cost. Or, the woman might have been underage, had a boyfriend and was afraid her parents might find out?"

"The possibilities are endless, Jean-Louis. But perhaps their reason for not telling me had more to do with me. Because I'm a doctor, I can't help but wonder what fatal illness I could have inherited.

"Or is there something in my future like a psychiatric disorder that my parents didn't want me to know about? Will I grow up to be unstable? What did my parents know when they adopted me?

"All this time I thought this omission had to do with some action of my father. But what if they wanted to hide something about my mental or physical condition? These questions are torturing me and make my life uncertain."

Jean-Louis sat forward. "You say this Guillaume Briand from Nice claimed the case was specially sealed under the law."

She nodded. "He said it was done that way because the highest discretion had been necessary. At that point he assured me he couldn't do any more investigating for me and wouldn't take money."

"The man was right. I'm not saying he wasn't good, but it takes someone with years of savvy and certain political connections to get a document like that unsealed. It would be wrong to assume anything yet. What you need is a different kind of expert."

Her eyes narrowed. "Like a man who can get secret and private permission through the help of the president of France himself for example?"

He sensed she wasn't joking. Neither was he. "Maybe."

"That takes more money than I could make in a lifetime. I'm going to have to live with it."

He shook his head. "Knowing you're the best epidemiologist around, you'll never rest until you have answers. But for now, everything you're worrying about is sheer speculation with no basis in truth."

"I realize that, but it has changed my life."

Françoise took another drink of wine. "You're a good listener and I've told you too much. Thank you. Now it's your turn. I want to know why you wanted to drop off the face of the earth for ten years, but I'd love to know the story about this *palais* first. Over the years I've been by this place and the Causcelle Corporation many times, yet I never understood about it since the public wasn't allowed in here."

He lowered his wineglass. "This palace was purchased when my great-great-grandfather bought the other palace to set up Causcelle headquarters a block away. He wanted all the family close by, so this became the family home in Paris complete with a fully staffed kitchen. This suite has always been mine and was still waiting for me after ten years."

"Does it feel good being here again?"

"*Good* isn't exactly the right word. My brothers also had suites while we all went to business school here. But it wasn't home, and contrary to my father's dream for us, I didn't want to go into business. My grades suffered. We had many arguments before I told him I was leaving. Before he could stop me, I joined the army, which I did for many reasons. I made certain he couldn't find me."

There was that pain in his eyes again. "You really did want to get away, didn't you?"

"You'll never know how much. Just now you asked me why I wanted to drop off the face of the earth for ten years. It's interesting you would use those exact words." A low sigh escaped his lips. "How to sum up my twenty-nine years in a few minutes. That's a real challenge. Maybe what I have to show you will help you understand some of my reasons more than anything else could."

He pulled his phone out of his pocket and opened it to his messages. After he'd scrolled to the next text he wanted, he handed his phone to her. "Take a look at that article from *Paris Now*. It came out in May of this year. When I first asked my brother Nic what was going on in his life, he told me to read this and he sent it to my phone. I believe you'll find some of the answers to your question."

Beyond curious, Françoise picked it up and started to read.

New Love for one of the Bachelor Billionaire Triplets? For the second time in two years, gorgeous, hunky billionaire Nicolas Causcelle is off the market! All female hopefuls will have to look elsewhere now.

Insider sources report that his former fiancée, Denise Fournette, is "devastated" that Causcelle has found love again so soon after brutally casting her off. Sadly. she didn't have the financial means to make the grade for a Causcelle.

His new lover is reputed to be media-shy Anelise Lavigny, only child and daughter of multimillionaire Hugo Lavigny. In this case it took money to capture money.

Mademoiselle Lavigny was said to be "inconsolable" after losing her engineer fiancé, Andre Navarre, in a car crash only nineteen months ago, but this liaison between two of France's biggest commercial dynasties seems to have soothed her pain.

Who says money doesn't talk?

The Causcelle triplets have long been the target of scheming mamas. Although, since one of them appears to have disappeared off the face of the earth, that leaves only two delicious men to snap up.

Françoise shuddered when she realized what she'd just asked Jean-Louis.

Good luck, Mademoiselle Lavigny. One has to wonder if the golden boy has staying power this time, or if he'll cast you away in the end.

After reading it twice, Françoise was so sickened she got up from the table and walked back into the living room still clutching his phone. She felt his presence behind her.

"I take it you've figured things out to a certain degree."

She turned around slowly to face him, and handed him back his phone, unable to articulate her feelings.

"What you read only explains part of the agony our family has always faced. The intrusion of the press will never stop being unbearable, but it was my own inner turmoil at nineteen that caused me to run and not look back.

"I couldn't bear the guilt of our family having so much money. Not when there were millions of people in the world who didn't know where their next meal would be coming from. I don't need to tell you what I saw in Africa."

His explanation had reached her soul and helped

her understand that wounded look she'd sensed when she'd first met him. "I'm so sorry."

"Not as sorry as I am for behaving like a selfish wretch and walking out on my father. I was the third triplet to be born and didn't have what it took to look life squarely in the eyes like my brothers did. To make my anguish worse, I'd just lost my best friend, Alain, of ten years. When I entered the hospital in Nice, I believed I was dying and I wanted to. It was the coward's way out."

"Not cowardly, Jean-Louis," she rushed to make him feel better. "Anyone wanting to die has to be in a kind of pain that surpasses human understanding."

"You have a remarkable way of putting things, Françoise. I'm afraid Dr. Marouche doesn't have the same bedside manner. To my complete and utter shock, he bluntly said in a loud voice, *You're not dying!*"

"You sounded just like him." It made her laugh.

"My first instinct was to tell him to go to hell because he didn't know what he was talking about."

"It's a good thing you didn't do that."

"I felt too ill to take him on, but I couldn't believe it. I wanted it all to be over so I'd never have to face what a miserable excuse I'd been for a human being. Then you walked in my room and verified what Dr. Marouche had told me. I wanted to hate you, but I couldn't when you were only doing your job and had shown me a lot of understanding."

She could hardly breathe from the remorse and regret pouring out of him.

More than ever, she understood when he'd told her he'd needed to get this off his chest.

"My next shock came when there was a knock on my hotel room door and I discovered my brothers standing there. They'd been looking for me and had finally found me. I felt more shame because they'd had to search the earth for me. Worse, they told me my father was dying. If I wanted to see him before it was too late, I needed to leave with them right then."

"Oh, no—" Françoise wanted to comfort him, but didn't know how and didn't feel she had the right. "How bad is he?"

"Bad."

"That explains why you didn't go in for your next phlebotomy."

"I took care of it at the hospital where my family lives. We live in eastern France outside a little town called La Racineuse."

"Thank heaven you didn't put it off. That's what is making you well. I realize you wouldn't have told me this much and asked me for dinner if you hadn't gone with them."

He nodded. "The Prodigal Son returned and I made my peace with him. With *all* of my family. To my joy, my father is still alive. It's a long story I won't bore you with now."

A soft moan escaped her lips. "I'm so happy for you about everything, Jean-Louis. More than that, I want to thank you for this evening and for listening to me. I've needed someone to talk to about my problem too. It helps to be able to share the burden with someone we trust. Now I'm afraid I have to go." She was enjoying this way, way too much.

"Are you in a hurry?"

"I want to get an early night. In the morning I'm driving to Bouzy-la-Forêt to visit my great-aunt for the day. She's suffering from emphysema. I promised I'd visit her after taking my boards and want to show her my new car. It'll be fun to try out the Nissan."

"Does she have family with her?"

"No. Her husband died four years ago and they couldn't have children."

"Then you must be a great comfort to her."

"I hope so. I also have to admit to another objective. Now that my parents and grandparents have passed, she's the only person alive who could possibly tell me about my adoption. That is *if* she ever knew about it. But they might have sworn her to secrecy. She and Maman were very close. Still, I have hope that she'll understand my pain and tell me what she knows, *if* she knows something."

His compassionate smile filled her with warmth. "I knew you'd go on digging. It's in your nature."

"You're right. So, tell me. Are you flying back home?"

"In a day or two after I've done some more research."

She rolled her eyes. "You've left out the details, but that sounds interesting."

He cocked his head. "It could be. How about I tag along with you tomorrow and I'll tell you about it? Bouzy is as good a place as any to start on a project I've been planning. While you visit your great-aunt, I'll do some searching in and around the village. For what it's worth, I'm a good mechanic. If anything should happen to your car en route, I can repair it."

"Are you serious?" The thought of spending a day with him made her dizzy with excitement. She was out of her mind.

"Ask the army. Alain and I got ourselves out of many a fix."

How terrible he'd lost his friend. "If you really want to, of course you can come with me. I'd planned to leave town by seven thirty."

"Whenever, wherever you say."

"Why don't I pick you up at the entrance."

"I'll be ready."

"You don't mind a woman driver?" she teased.

"Women make some of the best drivers. I found that out after I joined the military."

Before she knew it, Jean-Louis had walked her out to the elevator and they descended to the main floor. When they'd come here earlier, she'd had no idea what to expect. All she knew was that in the sharing of their stories, she'd felt a connection that had made them friends.

Jean-Louis walked her to her car. "Maybe the visit tomorrow will settle all your fears."

"Certainly Monsieur Briand couldn't give me any hope."

"I didn't think I had hope either until you found a cure for me. That was a miraculous moment in time. I've discovered that I like being alive and human." His comment reminded her of her dream about him. "It's long past time I started to redeem myself. Thank you for having dinner with me."

"The pleasure was all mine, believe me." Jean-Louis could never know what it meant to her.

He shut the door and she drove away while she thought about what he'd said. *Redeem himself.*

Françoise still didn't know which part of his story brought him the most pain. He'd been one of the walking wounded that had taken him on a long ten-year journey. But he seemed to be recovering. As for her pain, it had started three weeks ago and she had the terrifying thought it would never end.

CHAPTER FOUR

SUNDAY MORNING, Jean-Louis had been chatting with Guy for twenty minutes when the sight of the metallic blue car pulling up to the *palais* entrance suddenly quickened his pulse.

"That's one beautiful female, Jean-Louis."

He'd found that out the day before yesterday when he'd seen her for the first time without her mask. It had struck him then that she had to be the most gorgeous woman he'd ever met in his life.

"I agree. See you later."

When he climbed in the car outside, he couldn't help but notice her neck-length black-brown hair that framed a perfect oval face. "You've chosen a beautiful day for a drive, Françoise."

"We're lucky. It shouldn't take us more than two hours to reach Bouzy."

"It took my brothers and I a little longer on our bikes years ago."

"I'll bet." She chuckled before driving them out to the street.

Beneath those finely arched dark brows glowed the

lustrous green eyes with dark lashes he'd remembered in his hospital room. As for her mouth, its natural curvature would drive any man wild with desire to taste it. He thought of the man intending to be her future husband. Jean-Louis understood Antoine's dilemma.

"Does your great-aunt know you're coming?"

"No. I want to surprise her. Thank you for being on time. Have you eaten?"

"Not yet." He was starving.

"I haven't either. There's a café called L'Auberge I like in Bouzy. They serve the most scrumptious, creamy scrambled eggs on toasted baguette slices you've ever tasted. Their hot chocolate with *crème fleurette de Normandie* is to die for."

"I used to dream about food like that after my company had been out of rations close to a week."

She made a groaning sound and he laughed. Before long they'd joined the A-6 going south. "Where were you and your brothers headed during that bike ride?"

"We wanted to explore the Loiret area and see the bawdy wooden friezes at Bellegarde castle."

"Guys." She shook her head.

"Yup. We can be kind of awful."

"I would have loved a brother. Do you have sisters? I only remember that you were triplet brothers."

"We have three."

"How glorious! Six children."

"Four spouses and five nieces and nephews. It's been fun being with everyone again after a decade."

"I envy you your large family." She darted him a glance. "You said you'd tell me about this project of yours. What is this research you're doing? I'd love to hear about it."

Françoise showed an interest that made her fun to talk to. "First, I need to explain that from the beginning I had decided to become a career officer. When I met Alain, he thought that's what he would do too."

"You had to have undergone an incredible change the moment you entered the military, yet you adapted to it over all those years."

"We didn't have a choice. During that time, we saw soldiers being discharged because of one problem or another. Many of them had joined at a young age and didn't have the schooling or means to thrive back in society. I spent those years wondering how to help them. Some vets with all kinds of wounds and injuries were released with little hope and nothing to look forward to."

She nodded. "I've taken care of some of them."

"Of course you have. Well, it wasn't until Alain died that I decided to leave the service and put my ideas into action. But by then I began to feel so ill, I was certain I didn't have long to live and was discharged. You know the rest. When I realized I wasn't going to die, I used those two weeks in the hospital to put real substance to my ideas."

"I could never have guessed what was going on inside that brain of yours."

A half smile broke out on his mouth. "When you told me I didn't have to stay at the hospital anymore, I couldn't wait to get started. I made dozens of phone calls to the veterans' division of the army to trace returning veterans and ask them to get in touch with me. That's when my brothers found me."

"And to Antoine's alarm, you took off. Please go on. You have me riveted."

"Everything in my family has changed because my father is dying. My brothers no longer work or live in Paris like they once did. When I flew back here a few days ago, I walked around the empty *palais* and thought what a waste. It contains twelve suites like mine, a staff kitchen that makes all the meals, maids, housekeeping, security. But for what at this point?

"When I fly home in a few days, I plan to ask my father and family how they would feel if the *palais* could be used for a real purpose. It's asking a lot, but—"

"But worth a try," she interrupted, "for an amazingly worthy cause. So many returning vets need help."

"Yes! If they could have housing and go to school to learn a trade, it would make a difference in a few lives. What I'd like to do is set up a fund to aid them in going to school here in Paris. They could live free at the *palais*."

"How fantastic would that be!"

"I agree. When they've achieved enough schooling, I'd arrange for different businesses around France to hire them. Some could be nurses, armed guards, firefighters, parole officers, substance abuse counselors, computer operators." He angled his head toward her. "What do you think?"

She was quiet for a minute. "You *have* to know the answer to that question." Her voice trembled. "Your desire to do good knows no bounds. The world needs more men like you."

"You mean a guy who left his family for ten years when they needed him?"

"Stop belittling yourself," she scolded. "You know what I mean. We've arrived in Bouzy, Jean-Louis. Breakfast will be my treat."

Françoise drove into the quaint village and parked in front of the family-owned L'Auberge. They went inside to eat breakfast. Later, over a second cup of cocoa, he said, "Why don't you leave me here? I'll walk around the village and start doing my research. Let's trade phone numbers to stay in touch. When you're ready to go back to Paris, call me."

Françoise pulled the phone from her purse. With that accomplished, she got to her feet. "Stay there and enjoy yourself." She put some euros on the table. "Expect a call from me this afternoon when I'm ready to leave Silver Pines."

He nodded. "I think I'll start my quest right here with the man over at the counter. I'll feel him out about hiring a vet who's been a cook and has credentials from a cooking school."

She smiled. "Knowing you, I'm convinced anything is possible. Go for it."

"Thanks for the encouragement."

Within ten minutes she reached the rest home and spoke with Thea, a daytime nurse who took care of the residents. Françoise loved her. "How is Nadine doing? I'd like to take her outside."

Thea shook her head. "I'm sorry, but she's not well.

Almost overnight she developed bronchitis and needs oxygen. The doctor came in to check on her last night. You'll see on his notes that her dementia has grown worse. She only says a few words now. I'm sorry. If you need anything, ring the desk."

"Of course. Thank you for all you do for her."

With a heavy heart she walked to the room and leaned over her eighty-five-year-old great-aunt. There'd be no going anywhere with her, the poor darling. She lay under the covers looking exhausted each time she coughed. Tears filled Françoise's eyes.

"Mame?" She whispered her pet name for her after kissing her forehead.

The older woman made a sound. "Dionne?"

The doctor was right. Nadine's dementia had grown worse since the last visit. "No. It's Françoise."

She coughed again. "Who?"

"Dionne's daughter," Françoise answered.

"I wanted one."

"I know."

She muttered something about Albert, her deceased husband.

Françoise leaned closer. "What did Albert say, Mame?"

After another coughing spasm Françoise heard, "No adoption."

Her stomach clenched. Was that proof that Nadine knew something? Or did she mean her husband hadn't wanted to adopt a child? She sat down on a chair at the side of the bed. Her great-aunt didn't want to talk and

Françoise wouldn't dream of wearing her out. There'd be no answers here.

She stayed with her until a few minutes after three. During those hours against a background of more coughing spells, Françoise told her about her life now. She explained how she'd met one of the famous Causcelle triplets. Françoise talked about taking her boards and that she was now working in the hospital in Paris where her father had worked.

Only when she told her that she'd broken it off with Eric Moreau did the older woman make a sound. "Sad…" she murmured.

"It's for the best, Mame."

"No baby…"

The words broke Françoise's heart. Nadine had suffered because she hadn't been able to have children. Neither had Françoise's mother. Her mind was in a different place.

After giving her a final kiss, she left the room and asked the staff and Thea to keep her posted no matter the hour. Françoise was responsible for her. After phoning Jean-Louis, who would wait for her at the petrol station on the north end of the village, she left the rest home with a whole new heartache.

Bouzy was too far away from Paris for Françoise to visit every day. Maybe she could find a position at a hospital in a town closer to here, so she could make daily visits. Even though her mind was still deep in thought when she reached Jean-Louis, she couldn't help but notice him because he stood out. Not because of his tan suit and white shirt his build did wonders for. It was the man himself.

What had the newspaper said?

Gorgeous, hunky billionaire Nicolas Causcelle is off the market! All female hopefuls will have to look elsewhere now.

Those words described all three brothers. If Françoise needed proof, she only had to recall Celestine's reaction to meeting Jean-Louis at the desk at the hospital. It had reminded her of his female visitor's similar reaction at the hospital in Nice. Her face and eyes had worn the same infatuated expression.

He's the hunkiest man I ever saw in my life and he's a vet! I didn't know there were men like him in existence!

No, Françoise thought to herself as she drew closer to him. There weren't, not like the inside or the outside of that particular male.

She pulled to a stop so he could climb in. After he buckled up, she looked at him. "How was your day?"

"Successful in several ways. How about yours?"

Françoise started the car and drove toward the main street leading out of the village toward Paris. She told him about Nadine and her bronchitis. "I don't know how much longer she'll live."

"I'm sorry, Françoise."

"So am I. She didn't recognize me. She thought I was my mother."

"Poor thing. I take it she couldn't shed any light on the adoption paper you found."

She told him what her great-aunt had said. "I don't know. If she did give something away, I'm sure it was by accident. Her comment could have been taken two ways."

"You're right, and I can see you need cheering up. I'll call ahead to Chez Aline, near the Bastille. Have you ever eaten there?"

"No, but I've heard others rave about it."

"I'll order us some Prince de Paris *jambon-beurre baguettes*. It'll be a meal as delicious as our breakfast after our return to the *palais*. My treat this time." He set the address on her GPS.

"I'll be salivating all the way back."

He pulled out his phone and made the call to the restaurant before putting it in his jacket pocket. She felt his gaze on her and sensed something was on his mind.

"Françoise? I know a man who might be able to help you. He's the one my brothers called to find me. I hesitated to say anything before you spoke to your great-aunt, but now I know you could use his services."

"I could never afford them, Jean-Louis."

"It would cost you nothing."

She shook her head. "I appreciate your magnificent offer more than I can say, but I have to refuse. One of the reasons you left France for a decade was to get away from a world that wanted a piece of you. You've shared one of your dreams with me that has revealed the selfless side of your nature. I couldn't let that generosity extend to me."

"Françoise—listen to me. I—"

"I'm not a vet without a home or a career," she cut him off. "I've had the best life with the best parents anyone could ever have. Whatever went on in my father's past, he and my mother showered me with love. While I sat with my great-aunt today, I realized her one dream was to have a child, but that hope never materialized. Yet she endured her trial and led a wonderful life.

"I need to learn from her and endure something that hurts too. I have to find the strength and faith to know my parents kept the adoption a secret because they believed it was right."

"That's a laudable speech, but if you ever change your mind…"

"Thank you, but I won't. For now, I'd like to hear about your successes today."

He put on his sunglasses and turned to her. "Even though it's Sunday, some businesses were open. I talked to managers and owners throughout the day. Do you know that every one of them was willing to consider hiring a vet after I told them my plan?"

Her mouth curved upward. "Even the owner of the café where we had breakfast?"

"He told me they usually hire family because he belongs to a large one, but he'd be willing to give a vet a chance. There's goodness in most everyone. People want to help. Today has proved to me this experience will be repeated wherever I go and gives me hope for my plans."

"That doesn't surprise me."

"I have you to thank for spurring me on, Françoise. I know you think it's because I'm a Causcelle, but I introduced myself as Robert Martin and told them I had formed a company to aid returning vets."

She gripped the wheel harder. "Actually, I didn't think about that at all. But whether you had told me or not, I know it's *you*, Jean-Louis, and your sincerity after serving in the military that spoke to their minds and hearts. I'm so thrilled for you."

"I'm happy for you too."

"What do you mean?"

"Back in Nice I learned about a certain important man in your life."

Françoise gritted her teeth. "That Antoine is a menace."

"You know you don't mean it. He intimated you've been involved with one of the men on the French trade commission to Morocco. Apparently this one is a Moreau, and I know that family happens to live in one of the famous nineteenth-century Auteuil villas in Paris. Antoine said you'll probably be getting married soon and it will be the match of the season."

She took a quick breath. "Antoine got ahead of himself along with all the hospital gossip."

"Am I wrong to be congratulating you yet?"

"I'm afraid so, but it's not your fault. Eric and I were never engaged and we won't be getting married."

Out of the corner of her eye she noticed Jean-Louis's hand suddenly clench on his thigh. Why?

"I guess Antoine isn't in the loop on that piece of news."

"No. But he did notice on your chart you had a visitor after you didn't show up for your next phlebotomy."

"Who?"

"The young woman holding a sack." Was she someone special to him? Françoise got angry with herself for wanting an answer to that question.

"You mean Suzanne, my friend Alain's sister. The day I stepped off the transport plane, I visited his father, who runs a small body shop. I wanted to pay my respects and give his family some photos of their son. He knew I was headed for the hospital. Before I left Nice, I presented Alain's father with a gift from him. She brought me some dessert her mother had made. It was their family's thank-you."

That answered that. "They sound like a lovely family. What was Alain's gift? One of his possessions?"

"In a manner of speaking, yes. It's a Ferrari dealership his son eventually bought and paid for after having given ten years of his life to military service. He died before he could turn it over to his father, so I acted in Alain's place to take care of it."

She was speechless for a moment as she pondered what he'd said. "That's the most wonderful thing I ever heard. Not only his love for his family, but your love for him."

"He took the place of my brothers over those ten years. Every time he talked about his terrific father and mother, I suffered shame over the way I'd treated mine. My father pushed me into business though I'd wanted to be a mechanic on the estate. But that's all in the past. Enough about me. Françoise, I'm truly sorry about you and the man you were involved with. Forgive me for bringing up something painful."

"You didn't!" she blurted. "It was never meant to be. What I'm facing now is the question of my whole life. Think about it, Jean-Louis. When you look in a mirror, you *know* who you are. I envy you that more than you can imagine."

"I'm not inside your skin, but you're still Françoise Valmy to me, epidemiologist extraordinaire. Whether you have your adoptive parents' genes or your birth parents', it has nothing to do with the woman you've become. I, for one, owe you my life. That's all that really matters."

She shook her head. No. That wasn't all that really mattered, but Jean-Louis didn't need to hear more about the agony she'd been going through. "I'll try to maintain a positive attitude." By now they'd reached Paris and she needed to be alone before she broke down.

Within the month she'd like to find work at a hospital where her father hadn't been a fixture. It needed to be in a town near Bouzy so she could visit her great-aunt every day. Nadine was her only family now. She'd get an apartment and settle in to take care of her. It would be a new life.

"Françoise?" A deep male voice broke in on her thoughts. "Keep following the map to the Rue de la Roquette and wait out in front of the café. I'll run in to get our food."

"I can't wait."

CHAPTER FIVE

ANTOINE HAD BEEN a menace after all.

Jean-Louis had assumed he'd been safe around Françoise, a nearly married woman, but the information fed to him in Nice about Moreau hadn't been reliable. This was the exact situation he'd never wanted to happen with any woman. It had been a mistake to drive to Bouzy with her. She'd burrowed so deeply under his skin, he might not be able to get her out. He feared in his gut that he was already beyond the point of no return.

Once he'd picked up their food, Françoise drove them to the *palais* and they ate outside in the car. He couldn't help admiring the way she looked in her yellow two-piece summer suit, like a vision in the sunlight.

"Thank you for this, Jean-Louis. I didn't realize how hungry I was."

"You've just reminded me I haven't thanked you for buying us breakfast."

No woman had ever paid for him before. That was crazy when she'd been the one to save his life. It was his fault that he'd asked if he could come with her today…because…because he had to admit he craved her company. But he feared acknowledging it. To get close to a woman only to lose her terrified him.

As he sat there, Jean-Louis realized he was in serious trouble. He'd thought he was safe until she'd dropped the bomb telling him she wasn't going to marry Moreau and had never been engaged. Once he went inside the *palais*, would he have the willpower never to see her again?

She turned to him. "You were right about these sandwiches. Food for the gods."

"My brothers and I went there often between classes."

"I can see why."

Get out of the car. Make a clean break. Now!

He'd finished the last of his baguette. "Unfortunately, all good things have to end. I can't thank you enough for letting me drive with you today. It was a rare treat with you at the wheel of your new car. I accomplished more than I dreamed."

I've also learned I've been holding a live grenade in my hand.

He opened the door and got out with their empty sacks. She leaned toward him. "I'm so glad you came with me. Take care of yourself and never fail to make an appointment to get your blood drawn."

"Believe me I won't. Try not to worry too much about this mystery in your life. One day you may get answers. Let's hope your great-aunt recovers soon from her bronchitis. *Au revoir*, Françoise."

Once inside the *palais*, Jean-Louis hurried to his suite before he ran back out to stop her from leaving. After he took a shower, he could hear the phone ring and threw on a robe to get it. In his heart of hearts, he hoped it was Françoise who hadn't wanted to say good-bye either. He reached for it on the bedside table. When he saw the caller ID and realized it was coming from his sister Corinne, he grew alarmed. They all worried about their father.

He clicked on. *"Eh, bien, ma soeur. Qu'est-ce qui se passe?"*

"I'm glad you picked up. I'm calling on behalf of Papa. He hasn't stopped brooding about your blood disorder. He feels so guilty for not knowing how you suffered. Dr. Simonesse came by earlier and they got talking. Papa's wondering if the disorder grew inside of him and that's why he has heart failure."

"I've wondered too."

"The doctor is willing to consult with your doctor because Papa would rather your specialist came here to take care of his blood work. But you know Papa. He fears it might be asking too much of you, and he wouldn't blame you if you turned him down. I told him I'd find out. What do you think? Would it be possible?"

The chance of being with Françoise again shouldn't have filled him with this rush of exhilaration. His watch said eight thirty. "I'll do anything for Papa. Let me try to get hold of Dr. Valmy and maybe I'll call you back tonight."

"That would be wonderful. Thanks, *frérot*. I love it that you're home after all these years."

"I love it more." He clicked off and called Françoise without hesitation, but she'd put her phone on call forwarding. After leaving his name, he asked her to phone if she could, no matter how late. It was important. He'd never forget that moment when his loving father had held out his arms to him and forgiven him. The man didn't have his physical strength anymore, but inside him lived the soul of a saint and Jean-Louis would do anything for him.

He was still pacing the floor two hours later when his cell rang. She was calling him back. He grabbed it and sank down on the side of the bed. "Françoise?"

"Jean-Louis—I'm sorry I couldn't call back until now." She sounded a little out of breath. "Are you ill?"

Of course she would ask. She was a doctor. "*Non, non.* I'm sorry if you thought it was urgent. But it *is* important. I know you didn't expect to hear from me. Forgive me for disturbing you."

"That's nonsense. What's wrong?"

He gripped the phone tighter. "This concerns my father." He explained about Corinne's call. "I know Papa, and he's agitating over it."

"Well, we can't have that. I'd be happy to do this for you."

He heard no hesitation in her voice. She couldn't know what this meant to him. But since she was a doctor, he didn't dare read more into it beyond her need to be of help. "The whole family thanks you."

"No problem, but your father's doctor will have to contact my boss, Dr. Soulis. Let me talk to him tomorrow and I'll get back to you. If he says yes, then we'll make the arrangements and I'll plan to take some time off from the hospital. I realize your father can't travel."

"You're a saint."

"Hardly that."

Something in her tone worried him. "Françoise? Are you all right? You don't quite sound yourself."

"I'm not. You're very perceptive. Eric was waiting for me when I got back to my apartment. That's why I couldn't call you right away."

He took a quick breath. "I see."

"It's good he has to go back to Morocco in a few days."

Jean-Louis smothered a moan. The sooner the better. "Try to get some sleep if you can. We'll talk later."

The second they hung up, he phoned Corinne and told her it would probably work out fine. He'd call her tomorrow with details. When he clicked off, he fell back on the bed thinking about being with Françoise again, this time on his home turf.

His feelings for her dominated everything, including any thoughts of self-preservation. After years of avoiding entanglements, it was finally happening.

But he couldn't afford to forget.

An entanglement took two.

"Entrez!"

Françoise opened the door to Dr. Soulis's office Monday morning. "Can we talk for a few minutes when you're not busy?"

"I'm all yours. Come in and sit down." He studied her. "Are you all right?"

"I'm not sure. You were so wonderful to consider hiring me, and now I find myself in a real dilemma I couldn't have imagined before today."

"What's wrong?"

"Two things. First, I need your permission to leave work for a day to attend to a man dying of heart failure. You'll recognize the name Louis Causcelle."

His eyes widened. "Who doesn't know about the most famous entrepreneur of his generation? How are you associated with him?"

She cleared her throat. "His son was a patient of mine in Nice for two weeks." Françoise went on to explain everything to him. "His doctor will phone you to ask permission for me to fly to eastern France and draw his blood."

Christophe smiled. "In a heartbeat."

"Thank you, but that's not all. This is about my great-aunt." She told him everything, including her desire to live near her. But a move would mean giving up this coveted position with him.

"Say no more, Françoise. As you know, my widower father is very ill and depends on me and my wife for everything. You're her only relative and she needs you as much as you need her. Since you haven't even worked here a week, why don't you take a week's vacation now to look into everything and arrange for some interviews. As for Louis Causcelle, I'll tell his doctor you have my permission to draw his blood. That shouldn't take too long out of one day."

Tears fell down her cheeks. "I don't know how to

begin to thank you. I feel so honored to be working here with you, but I just need to sort things out first."

He sat back. "I'm glad this has happened now. You can't do your work if you're worried about your only loved one. If you do move from Paris to work at a different hospital near her, I won't be happy about it, but I'll totally understand. You're free to leave now. I'll see you in a week."

Françoise had been wrong. Jean-Louis wasn't the only male on the planet with exceptional goodness coursing through his veins. Christophe was right up there too.

On Tuesday morning at eight thirty Françoise walked out of her apartment building with her overnight bag to wait for Jean-Louis under a partially cloudy sky. He'd called earlier for her address and told her not to eat breakfast. They'd have a meal on the jet.

Yesterday Dr. Soulis had talked with Louis's doctor and encouraged Françoise to do whatever she could to satisfy the ailing older man's questions.

Since learning that Jean-Louis was a Causcelle, Françoise had a natural curiosity about their whole family and had to admit she was looking forward to this visit with more anticipation than was warranted. Jean-Louis had everything to do with it. Besides his background, she'd never met a more complicated, fascinating man in her life.

She found it ironic that the door to a new life had just opened for him. Yet another door had slammed shut on her, crushing her dreams for a normal, fulfilling future.

While Françoise stood watching for his black Mercedes, he came for her in a white limo. Her heart raced faster as he got out to help her in with her case. This time he'd arrived in a dark blue suit with white shirt and tie. In trying to describe his dark male beauty, she'd run out of superlatives.

He sat down next to her and the limo drove off. "I like that dress you're wearing." Their gazes met. "The color matches your eyes. You would never know you're the same masked doctor from the hospital in Nice."

"You don't resemble the sick vet lying in that hospital bed either."

They both smiled before he said, "There aren't enough ways to say thank you for doing this. It's asking a lot."

"No need for more thanks. I'm a doctor and am as curious as you to see if there's any connection between your father's condition and yours."

"Then I hope you won't mind if I ask you another favor while we're there."

She never knew what he was going to say next. That's what made him so intriguing. "Why would I mind?"

"It's about my brothers. Since we're identical triplets, I—"

"You're worried they might have your disorder too?" Françoise broke in while she studied his arresting profile. "Have they been showing symptoms too?"

"If so, they've said nothing to me, but I'll tell you more after we're in the air."

They'd reached the small airport where a sparkling

white jet with the Causcelle name and logo stood on the tarmac. Jean-Louis pulled her overnight bag from the back seat and helped her on board. They sat in the lounge compartment and strapped themselves in. Before long they taxied out to the runway and took off. Being with him made everything they did an unprecedented experience for her.

When they'd gained altitude, they undid their seat belts. The steward, on friendly terms with Jean-Louis, served them a meal of quiche Lorraine and wine, which she thoroughly enjoyed. "That tasted delicious." She wiped her mouth with a napkin. "I've never flown in a private jet. This is wonderful."

He nodded. "It beats the transport plane that brought me into Nice."

On that flight he'd believed he was returning to France to die. She wanted to change the subject. "Tell me more about the concern for your brothers."

Jean-Louis turned to her. "At the hospital, when you asked me if I had any males in my family showing symptoms, I lied to you, which I'm sorry for. But you got me thinking. When I reconciled with Papa and told him the reason for my discharge, I'm afraid it got him thinking and he's been worried about it ever since. He wants my brothers tested along with himself."

"After learning what's wrong with you, of course he's anxious. Do they know I'm coming?"

"Yes, but not to test them. The problem is, Nic and Raoul are as stoic about themselves and what goes on with them as I am. If they've ever had any of my symptoms, they never told our father. But now they're going to have to for the sake of their health."

"Will they cooperate?"

"If my brothers resist, my father will urge them to get tested in such a way they won't be able to say no."

It sounded like Louis Causcelle was the source of the irresistible force Jean-Louis had inherited. "I'll make it as painless as possible. To keep things simple, let me run a basic blood test on them and your father immediately. If I don't find any abnormalities, then there'll be no need to put them through the tests you had to undergo and your worries will be over."

"And you'll conclude I was the only abnormal child in the Causcelle household."

"Correct. There's usually one of those in every family."

His chuckle tickled her. "We'll be landing at Chalon Champforgeuil airport in a minute. From there we'll drive to the château."

"What's it like?"

"The original building was deeded to the family in the twelve hundreds by Philip II. There've been dozens of renovations since. My sister Corinne and her husband live there with her family to help take care of our father and his health caregiver, Luca. Raoul lives there now as does Nic with his wife, Anelise. They occupy another part of the château.

"They're building a home on the estate and will be moving out of the château in another month or two. My other sisters and their families live on our grounds too.

Everyone comes in and out. But don't worry. There's a guest room waiting for you at the château."

The Causcelle family lived larger than life. No doubt there were many guest rooms. "I imagine it's a big estate."

"Yes, with everything you can think of, including the fromagerie, grange, a hothouse, gardens, orchards, farms, barns, a dairy, outbuildings, storage sheds, pastures, cattle, sheep, corrals. The list goes on and on."

She angled her head toward him. "Why didn't you mention a garage? You told me you used to work in it after school and that's why you felt so tired. Does it still exist?"

He smiled. "You never forget anything, do you? Yes, it's as pathetic as ever."

"That's because you've been away ten years. Now that you're back, I presume you have plans for it."

"We'll see."

"Have you spent time in it since returning from Africa?"

His eyes searched hers. "I would have liked to. You know too many of my secrets already."

"Well, I know you were a captain in the army, but I'm positive they gave you a mechanic's job in the beginning."

"Alain and I got assigned to work on machinery."

She smiled. "A match made for two guys who liked using their hands while your genius brains figured out what was wrong."

The jet lounge resounded with Jean-Louis's laughter.

"You *are* geniuses, Jean-Louis. My father used to

say that creating a world required an engineer/mechanic to start the whole process. The engineer would figure out what was needed and the mechanic would start fixing it."

Jean-Louis grinned at her. "Your father left himself out."

"When I said that to him, he shook his head. 'My darling daughter, God was *the* great engineer/mechanic and healer. Everything else came after.' When I thought about it, I knew he was right."

"*You* are a healer, Françoise, in more ways than you know. I'm curious to see what secrets you discover after drawing our blood."

"So am I. Maybe I'll find the genius gene that set your family apart from the beginning. But I'll keep it a secret. Otherwise, it will give the world another excuse to invade your privacy."

He sent her an intense glance. "You really do understand, don't you?" Just then the Fasten Seat Belts light flashed. They were about to land in the world Jean-Louis had been born to. She'd never been so eager for anything in her life.

The conversation with Françoise had sent new thrills through him. His euphoria stayed with him as he found one of the estate cars at the small airport to drive them to La Racineuse.

When they passed the town sign, she turned to him. "I know *racine* means root—your high school logo. What does *racineuse* mean?"

"As you know, the *euse* part means doer. Put it on

the end of *racine* and around here the word has come to mean a man who is tenacious, stubborn and a doer."

The car filled with her laughter. "It goes right along with everything you told me about your father."

He sent her an answering smile. "Papa is the biggest tenacious, stubborn doer of this century. Do you think when you draw his blood, you'll be able to identify that particular stubborn gene? Will it show up in Raoul or Nic?"

"That's a question I've never even thought about. You've just suggested a whole new field of research for me."

"Your mind never stops working. As long as we're nearing the town, we'll swing by the hospital first. That way you can get what you need and be able to draw Papa's blood after we reach the château today."

"You're making this so easy for me."

"That's because you're going out of your way for our family. He's afraid he might die before he finds out if he has PV. As you know, he blames himself for not having known what was wrong with me. I told him it was my fault for never mentioning my symptoms, but he can't get over it."

"The poor darling. While at the hospital here, I'll get what I need to take your brothers' blood too. Then they won't have to make a trip unless it becomes necessary."

"Thank you for being so thoughtful and generous, Françoise. How was I lucky enough to end up with you as my doctor in Nice? I still marvel."

"You can stop thanking me. I'm still amazed that I met *you*." She cocked her head. "Jean-Louis? Do you know how rare it is for the mother's egg to split into three? And that all three of you were born identical and healthy? Your blood disorder doesn't count."

His brows lifted. "One in ten thousand?"

"That's with the help of fertility drugs. Did your mom use them?"

"No. My parents already had three girls. They decided to try one more time for a boy, but they had little hope."

She laughed again. "Without those drugs, you're looking at a case of one set of triplets in *one million*!"

"You're joking—"

"*Non.* You Causcelle triplets have defied the odds. With your permission, I'd like to write it up for the medical journal. The press won't see it, but doctors around the world will love it."

"I'll think about it." But he doubted he could ever deny her anything. On he drove until they reached the hospital, where he pulled up in the front parking area.

"Is this the place where history was made?" she cried.

He turned off the engine and smiled at her. "You mean where an emergency room doctor sewed up my hand when the air hammer jammed a chisel bit into it? *That* made history."

"I'll bet it did when you were supposed to be in bed."

"You're right. The ambulance came to the garage at midnight to cart me away. I had a biology test at school the next day and failed it miserably by mixing up paramecium and protozoa. Needless to say, my father was not a happy man."

More chuckling rippled out of her. "That sounds

pretty traumatic, but it still doesn't match your sensational birth. I liked that high school photo of the three of you, but I have to admit I'm eager to see all of you together in person. It'll be a privilege."

Being with Françoise made him thankful to be alive. He jumped out of the car and they went inside. "The lab is on the second floor, west end."

The doctor on duty had been alerted they were coming and helped her gather the items she'd need. Before long they left the building and drove to the château.

When his home came into view, Jean-Louis heard her slight cry of wonder. The unexpected sight of it in the distance always affected visitors that way. After being gone ten years, seeing it again that first day and all it represented had been so overwhelming, the guys had left him alone in the car for a little while to deal with his emotions.

"Oh—" Her gorgeous face had lit up. "You just don't expect to see a glorious château in the distance that looks like it should be in Paris."

Jean-Louis agreed about the glorious sight, but at the moment his whole attention was focused on the breathtaking woman who'd infiltrated his every thought.

He drove to the front area of the château, facing one of the rose gardens, and pulled her bag and hospital case from the car. Together they entered the foyer. "Your room is upstairs where you can freshen up. Then I'll take you to meet my father."

Dozens of framed family pictures decorated the walls as they climbed the stairs. Françoise would love to have time to look at all of them. An attractive brunette was just coming out of the bedroom on the second floor.

"Jean-Louis! I didn't know you'd arrived. I wanted to make sure there were fresh towels in here."

Françoise watched him give her a hug. "Corinne? Meet Dr. Valmy, the epidemiologist who diagnosed my problem. Françoise? This is my sister Corinne, who's taking wonderful care of Papa."

To think their mother had died before she could finish raising her daughters or hold her baby boys. How terrible that Jean-Louis and his siblings had lost their incredible *maman* that night, and so tragic for their father, who'd lost his wife.

"It's a pleasure to meet you, Corinne." They shook hands. "I don't want to cause you any inconvenience."

She shook her head. "We're all ecstatic you're here. You've not only saved our brother's life, you've brought new hope to our father, who never thought to see Jean-Louis again. I honestly believe he's looking better today."

Her words touched Françoise. "That's remarkable news."

"I'll join you downstairs and we'll visit Papa in his bedroom. He knows you were coming to draw blood so he agreed to stay in bed." She walked away.

"He doesn't sound too *racineuse* to me," Françoise whispered to Jean-Louis. His black gaze fused with hers. The shared moment remembering their conversation in the car set her vital organ fibrillating. Who had the heart problem right now?

Jean-Louis carried her things into the bedroom.

"You go ahead and freshen up, Françoise. My bedroom is two doors down the hall. I'll meet you in the salon on the right of the foyer. Take all the time you need."

"I won't be long." She closed the door and looked around. Seeing his magnificent home made her wonder how he could have left for ten years, except that she *did* understand the reasons.

After opening the lab kit, she washed her hands in the en suite bathroom and pulled out a wrapped packet of surgical gloves. Once she'd put on a surgical mask, she picked up the kit and left to go downstairs, anxious to meet the dynamo of the Causcelle Corporation.

Finding herself alone, she wandered over to the portrait above the hearth. The beautiful raven-haired woman had bequeathed parts of herself to Jean-Louis and his sister. A special spot in Françoise's soul ached for the woman who'd died before she got to know all her wonderful children. It hurt her to realize Jean-Louis had never known his mother. Francesca had never known her birth mother either. That was something they had in common.

"Papa had this hung after my brothers and I were born." Jean-Louis had just come in the room. "He said he wanted our mother to be front and center so we'd never forget."

"As if you could. What was her name?"

"Delphine Ronfleur."

How wonderful that Jean-Louis could look at that painting and know it was his mother.

Clearly, Louis Causcelle had loved his wife. That was the kind of love Françoise had always wanted.

But unexpected circumstances had altered the course of her once-dreamed-of future. As she'd told Eric, *I'm not sure I'll ever get married.*

She turned to Jean-Louis. "Your mother is so lovely."

"I think so too," but he was staring at Françoise. "I can see you're ready. It's a shame you're wearing your mask. Papa won't be able to see all of you, and he won't like it."

"That's not important."

"I couldn't disagree more." Everything he said in that deep voice made her tremble. "Let's go."

They went back out to the foyer and walked down a hall. Corinne and the health caregiver she introduced as Luca met them in front of a set of double doors. They were opened into a veritable apartment with its own sitting room.

"Papa?" she called out. "We're coming in."

The four of them entered the bedroom. By its appointments, Françoise could imagine a duke or a count living in here once upon a time. Her gaze flew to the balding man sitting against pillows, his long body under the covers.

At a glance she could see he'd given his sons their striking bone structure and height. When he'd had hair, he would have been a very handsome man. Right now, his color looked surprisingly good for a patient in this stage of heart failure.

He studied Françoise out of dark eyes. "Please pull down your mask for a few seconds, Dr. Valmy. I want to see the face of the woman who saved my son's life."

The source of the irresistible force had spoken. She did his bidding, then put it back in place. Out of the corner of her eye she could tell Jean-Louis was trying hard not to smile.

"It's a good thing you have to wear one around your male patients," he kept talking. "A woman who looks like you needs all the protection she can get. I appreciate your dropping everything to come here so quickly. I'm anxious to know if this PV has invaded the whole male side of my family."

"We'll find out very soon, Monsieur Causcelle."

"Please call me Louis."

"If you'll call me Françoise."

"Done." The older man smiled.

Jean-Louis put one of the chairs next to the bed, where she sat down and reached in the kit for the stethoscope. "Let me just check you out first. By the way, Louis, I like your blue silk pajamas."

"My grandchildren gave them to me."

"They have excellent taste. All right. Just breathe in and hold it."

She took her time listening to his chest and back. When she'd finished, she said, "I think you're a fraud. You sound much better than I thought you would. Like I told your son when he thought he was dying, there's life in you."

Jean-Louis stood next to her. She noticed his eyes suddenly glisten with the news about his father.

"Let's draw your blood and that will be it."

"Thank you for coming, Françoise," his father murmured.

She heard the same kind of sincere tone in his voice that described his son's. "I'm honored, Louis. You're a man who did all the work after your wife passed away. Few men qualify as a superhero. You're one of them." Add another name to her list of exceptional men.

The older man cleared his throat several times.

Françoise took the gloves out of the packet and put them on. "Let me push up your sleeve and we'll get this over." Another few minutes and she'd obtained the precious blood.

When she'd finished, she looked around and saw that Jean-Louis's male siblings had come in the room and were staring at her. The three gorgeous brothers together was a heady sight she could scarcely believe. "Am I dreaming, or what?"

They chuckled and nudged Jean-Louis.

Their father pointed to them. "Nic? Raoul? Françoise is here to draw your blood too. I want no argument. Find a place to sit so she can do her job."

Like obedient little boys who knew better than to argue with their father, they did his bidding and made it easy for her. Before long she had three samples of blood and put them in the case.

Smiling at them, she stood up. "Back at the hospital in Nice, when I told Jean-Louis about the procedure, he was afraid I might turn him."

"He's always had a thing about vampires," one of them quipped.

She grinned. "I found that out," she said, thinking of her dream.

At that comment they all burst into laughter. "Thank

you so much, gentlemen. I'll take these vials to the hospital now and analyze them. We'll have answers soon. As I told your brother, even if there are abnormalities, you can be assured it's still human blood."

More laughter ensued.

"Stay in bed until tomorrow, Louis. Don't be tempted to get out like your restless son wanted to do at the hospital."

Their father reached out to grasp her hand. "Bless you."

"I'll make sure he stays put," Luca answered with a smile.

Jean-Louis picked up her kit and walked her out, leaving the rest of the family behind them. "You have to be hungry. There's a good restaurant in town."

She shook her head. "Thank you, but I couldn't sit down to a meal right now. Could we pick up something at a deli maybe?"

"I know the exact one. They make tasty meat pies."

"That sounds perfect. We can eat on the way to the hospital."

Twice now they'd eaten in the car. Was that her way of letting him know she was all business so he wouldn't think she wanted something more from him?

After they left the château and got in the car, she removed her mask and gloves. He put the kit in the back seat. "How long will it take to analyze the samples?"

"Since I know what I'm looking for, we'll have some if not all the answers tonight."

He started the engine and they took off in the semi-darkness. "Did you mean what you said about my father's condition?"

"He had good color and seems to be in better shape than I would have imagined. Maybe having been reunited with you, his body is responding to moments of spiritual rejuvenation."

"You think that's possible?"

"I do because I've seen what pure happiness can do for some patients."

After stopping for meat pies and coffee, they ate during the short trip to the hospital.

"Mmm. That filled the bill, Jean-Louis. Thank you. Now I can get right to work."

More than ever, he got the idea she'd only come to La Racineuse as a medical doctor. He ought to be relieved, but instead it disturbed him so much he could hardly think.

They hurried inside to the lab. "I'm staying in here with you."

"Of course. Go ahead and sit at that desk over there. No one else is here right now. This won't take me long."

Watching Françoise at home in her world came as a revelation to Jean-Louis. This woman's knowledge and years of study humbled him. Despite his personal frustration, her delightful bedside manner with his father and brothers had elated him.

During the exam, he'd shared a glance with Corinne, who'd noticed their father's improved condition. Even a temporary reprieve was a reason to rejoice.

While Françoise worked now, he took some pictures of her with his phone camera. When he couldn't be with her, he'd be able to look at them and remember this night of nights. A month ago, he'd thought he was dying. Back then a miracle like this night wouldn't have been a possibility in his mind.

Sooner than he'd imagined, she turned her face to him, wearing a mask and gloves. "I have the best news. None of your family has PV or anything else. *You* are the only one. Chances are you won't pass it on to any boys you might have one day."

He shot out of the chair. Joy filled him that his brothers and father didn't have his problem. "So, I'm the freak."

"Yup."

"You're one in a million too, Françoise."

She averted her eyes. The woman had trouble accepting praise. "Give me five minutes to clean up everything. Then we'll go back to the château and make the big announcement."

They left the hospital without her wearing a mask or gloves, and arrived home in record time. Jean-Louis found his brothers in the bedroom talking with their father. Their heads turned to see him and Françoise walk in. They couldn't take their eyes off her. No man could.

"*I'm* the only one with PV." His voice resonated in the room. "You're all good to go."

Relief broke out on their faces. His father wept.

Françoise smiled. "Congratulations, gentlemen, and thank you for your cooperation. This has been a wonderful visit for me. It's truly a privilege to meet all of you. As I told Jean-Louis, your miraculous birth only happens one in a million times. It's textbook stuff for the medical journals."

"You're kidding—" Nic sounded shocked.

"Ask your little brother."

"Wait till I tell Anelise."

She smiled. "While you celebrate, I'll go up to bed since we'll be flying back to Paris in the morning. Unfortunately, I have patients who are waiting to undergo tests you don't want to know about. *Bonne nuit.*"

Like she did in the hospital in Nice, she ran away before Jean-Louis could stop her. Something was going on with her. Obviously, she didn't want him getting any ideas about her being interested in him other than as a friend. He refused to believe it.

"Is that true?" his father asked. "I thought it was one in ten thousand."

"What?" For a moment Jean-Louis's mind was somewhere else.

"The one-in-a-million chance?"

"Oh. *Oui.* Without the help of fertility drugs, the odds escalate. Whenever you've done anything, Papa, it has always been more spectacular."

His father shook his head, then stared at him out of watery eyes. "I'm sorry I didn't know about your suffering."

"Enough of that. I didn't know I was ill. Those symptoms came in bits and pieces. Françoise says if I take care of myself, I'll live to a goodly age like all of you."

"Thank heaven, son."

"Thank heaven you're feeling a little better this evening, *mon père*." He leaned down to kiss his forehead.

"Amen," his brothers chimed in.

Raoul looked at him, eyeing him earnestly. "Little brother? What's the story on Dr. Valmy?"

Jean-Louis knew what Raoul was asking. He'd like the answer himself, but he didn't have one yet. In the silence, Nic and their father were also waiting. "She was my doctor, but no longer."

"And?" Raoul prodded.

Deep down he knew Françoise was in search of answers and living in a world of pain. For the time being, the reason for it would have to stay privileged information he had no right to divulge. The two of them had developed a strong connection, but Jean-Louis wasn't on her mind at the moment. He couldn't live with that much longer.

"And nothing. I have to get her back in the morning. That's all. *Bonne nuit, tout le monde.*"

"Wait, Jean-Louis," his father called to him in a surprisingly strong voice.

He wheeled around. "What is it, Papa?"

Louis sat forward. "You can't leave yet. I have things to say to you. First of all, I'm giving you the garage. Other families on the estate have wanted it, but it has always had your stamp on it. Do whatever you want with it since it's empty."

Jean-Louis knew that these days the estate vehicles and machinery were repaired in town. "That's very generous, Papa, but—"

"I'm not finished, *mon fils.*" Jean-Louis hadn't seen

this coming. "Now that you're home again and needed here in every way, don't forget about the land I gave you years ago. It's still waiting for you."

Nic grasped Jean-Louis's shoulder. "Anelise and I would love it if you built your own place near Raoul's and we were all neighbors together. You could teach the Causcelle kids how to fix cars."

He nodded. "It's an exciting idea, whether they be boys or girls. The women in the military could do it all."

"Just like the women on this estate who've always been able to do everything," Raoul murmured. A lot of personal pain went into his remark.

Jean-Louis cleared his throat with difficulty. "I love the idea of it too. And marriage or no marriage, I plan to do any job you want me to do on the estate from now on. But as for building a home, you've got to have a wife in order to plan one." For the time being that wasn't the case for Jean-Louis, and maybe not for Raoul. Only time would tell about their futures.

"You don't have to have a woman to make plans," his father asserted.

"You're right, Papa, and your generosity astounds me. But before I can think about anything else, I've been working on a project. In fact, I wanted to talk to you about it, but this isn't the right time."

"Of course it is!" his father came back. "Come sit by me and tell me what's on your mind."

He did his bidding. "It's an idea I thought about nonstop while I was in the military. But it really hit me hard when my transport plane flew into Nice and dropped me off. After ten years I was back on French soil. I tried to put myself in the place of any returning vet who had nothing to return to."

"We should have been there for you," Nic muttered.

"My selfishness made that impossible, didn't it?"

"Let's not go there." This from Raoul. "Tell us your idea."

"Because I'd been discharged, I at least had a hospital to go to where they took care of me for two weeks. But what of the thousands of the walking wounded getting off transports everywhere? How would the poor devils live now without family or promised work? Where would they turn? Who would hire them?"

Raoul shook his head. "I haven't been where you've been, but I hear you."

"The only money I've used for ten years has been my army pay. But after you and Nic found me and we were all reunited, I—"

"You want to do something with your family money," Nic broke in on him. "You think we don't get it? That's what drove me to want to build free hospitals with research centers."

"Of course."

"How can I help?" his father asked.

He sucked in his breath. "It's very ambitious."

Raoul smiled. "Only successful plans are."

"I've stayed in touch with half a dozen vets. They were in my company for three years before going home and we became friends. They're destitute with no college education or family help. They've been wounded mentally and physically in war. After one job, then another, they're let go. It crushes me to compare my circumstances to theirs."

"Tell us your idea, *mon fils*."

"All right. Since none of our family stays at the *palais* anymore, I'd like permission to use it for a hotel/halfway house for these vets. Naturally I'd set two suites aside for family use when necessary. But there would be ten suites standing empty."

"Just waiting for needy vets," Raoul filled in.

"Yes. Bed and food for free."

Nic stared hard at him. "It's inspirational."

Françoise had said the same thing.

"I'd fund their schooling in Paris and help them get scholarships. When they're certified to work, I'd place them in any city in France where they'd like to be employed. They'd start to earn a decent wage so they can live a good life and raise families. This first group would be the beginning of more. But I know that's too presumptuous and I have no right to ask."

Their father sat there with his head bowed for a long moment. Then he lifted it and his eyes pierced Jean-Louis's.

"Serving in the military for ten years did more to teach you about life than all the prestigious business degrees could ever have done. I've never been more proud of anyone in my life. You've found your *raison d'être*. I want you to take over the *palais* and anything else you need with my blessing. If your mother were here…" His voice trembled.

Jean-Louis reached for his father and hugged him for a long time. "There's no one like you, Papa." When he let him go, his father's eyes were closed and he looked like he had finally fallen asleep.

The three of them said good-night to Luca and left the room. Overjoyed that his brothers were totally on board with his ideas, Jean-Louis went to the kitchen with them to enjoy a cup of coffee.

Near midnight they were all ready for bed. Jean-Louis hugged them and hurried upstairs past Françoise's suite. Much as he longed to share his news with her, it would have to wait until morning during their flight back to Paris.

He also had an idea he wanted to run by her before he took her back to her apartment. She'd probably fight him on it, but it was worth a try.

CHAPTER SIX

AFTER BREAKFAST ON board the Causcelle jet with Jean-Louis, Françoise realized that this interlude of being treated like a princess was fast coming to an end. She'd loved being in his world for a little while and regretted that it was over.

As they talked during the flight, his black eyes came alive. He told her that his dreams for helping vets were going to come true now that he'd had the important talk with his father and family. He also explained that he'd be living on the family estate and working there from now on. It meant he'd only be in Paris once in a while to check on his project.

Since she'd been given a week's freedom to plan out her life, she'd made up her mind to drive to Bourges and check out the hospital there. If she were hired, that would mean no more chance meetings with Jean-Louis.

His latest news shouldn't have bothered her, but it did in ways she was afraid to acknowledge. Much as she longed to be with him, a relationship with him was out of the question right now.

"Françoise?"

She glanced at him.

"You've been wonderful to my family, but I know there's a pain inside of you that won't be going away soon. I've given it a lot of thought and an idea came to my mind during the night. Do you live by a certain faith, or go to a certain church?"

His question astonished her coming out of the blue as it did. "Yes. Our family is Catholic."

"So's mine, although I stopped going years ago." She could understand that since she hadn't gone for a long time either. "Did your parents have you baptized at a church here in Paris?"

"Yes. My great-aunt is my godmother and witnessed it. That's why we've been so close."

"What if we stop by there on the way to your apartment and talk to the priest? Trying to get information online won't tell you anything. But if you see him in person, maybe he can show you the written document, or answer some of your questions. It's possible that he or someone else in the clergy who knew your parents could shed some light on the adoption for you."

She sucked in her breath. "You're brilliant to have thought of that, Jean-Louis. I don't know why it hadn't occurred to me to go there for answers right away."

"I'm sure you would have thought of it at some point. But remember, you just took your boards. And you've had too much on your mind with your move back here and helping my family."

"Thank you for being in my corner. The truth is, I haven't been to church for ages. No wonder it wasn't my first thought."

"That's one thing we have in common," he murmured.

"Actually, we have three," she claimed. "Neither of us knew our birth mother. And neither of us told each other the whole truth about ourselves right off."

He shook his head. "My lie was premeditated ten years ago."

"But I've been claiming to be a Valmy *all* my life."

"Unpremeditated doesn't count, Françoise. Maybe you'll find an answer you can live with before the day is out." The Fasten Seat Belts sign flashed on. "We're about ready to land. When we get in the limo, shall I tell our driver to take us to your apartment or the church?"

She buckled up. "You didn't need to ask that question since you already know the answer. It's on the Rue des Moines." Every time she was ready to say goodbye to him— wishing it wouldn't be their last—something else came up that pulled her in to him again.

Before long they'd been picked up and Jean-Louis told the driver where to take them. When they'd pulled up in the church parking area, he turned to her. "Since this is a totally private matter, would you like to go in alone? If so, I'll stay in the limo."

Françoise appreciated his consideration. In fact, there wasn't anything about him or his behavior she didn't like. Except that *like* wasn't the right word. She didn't dare say the word that fit her true feelings.

"Please come in with me. It was your idea and I can't thank you enough."

He got out to help her and they walked to the side

door that let them into the church office. A middle-aged woman seated at a rectangular table greeted them and asked them to be seated. She wore a tag that said Annette Larue. "*Bon après-midi.* How can I help you?"

Françoise sat forward. "Twenty-eight years ago, on February 10, I was born and eventually baptized in this church. Do you keep the original document here? I'd like to see it if I could."

"I'll consult the parish register. Please fill out this form and I'll take care of it." She handed Françoise a clipboard with a pen and the attached paper.

It didn't take Françoise long to write down the information. She handed it back to the other woman.

"I'll go into the archive room and be right back."
"*Merci, madame.*"

After the woman left, Françoise looked at Jean-Louis. "This seems too easy."

Those black eyes gazed steadily into hers. "That's because your baptism didn't need to be hidden."

"I know. I'm being ridiculous."

"Not at all. Once you've verified everything, we'll look at the name of the priest officiating. Then you can ask to talk to him. Maybe he'll remember something that will help you."

"That is if he's still serving at this church." Then a groan escaped. She lowered her eyes. "Forgive me, Jean-Louis. I'm behaving like a fractious child."

He reached over and gave her hand a little squeeze. "You have every reason to be anxious." His support comforted her. Without his help, she wouldn't even have thought to come to the church.

"Here we are." The woman walked back to the table carrying the cumbersome register. "I found the correct volume." She put it on the table in front of them and opened it to the right place. "Please be careful. These pages are fragile."

"Of course." Françoise examined everything. "Oh, Jean-Louis—look at that handwriting."

He sat closer to inspect it. "A lost art these days."

"I can't believe it. This is the original document." She couldn't prevent the tremor in her voice. "'Parents: Patrick and Dionne Valmy. Infant daughter: Marie Françoise Valmy. Godmother: Nadine Bonnet. Priest officiating: Father Alexis Marquette.'"

"Is the name Marie significant?"

She nodded to him. "My grandmother's first name."

He took another breath. "Do you remember hearing the name of that priest?" Jean-Louis whispered.

"No. It means nothing to me."

She looked up at the other woman. "Can I please make an appointment to speak with Father Alexis Marquette?"

"I'm sorry, but he died two years ago."

No... Her heart sank. She fought not to break down. "He was the one who baptized me." Devastated because another door had just shut in her face, she closed the register.

"Father Benoit could talk to you."

"No. He wouldn't be able to answer my questions... But thank you."

In the next breath Jean-Louis got to his feet. "Thank

you for helping us, *madame*. We won't take up any more of your time."

Françoise murmured her thanks before he took hold of her arm and walked her outside to the limo. Without his help, she doubted she could have walked out on her own.

He gave the driver the address to her apartment and they drove away. Earlier on the jet when he'd talked about them visiting the church, she'd been filled with hope. Now that it was dashed, she felt numb inside. *And ashamed.*

It was too embarrassing for her to imagine what Jean-Louis must think of her. She might be a grown woman and a doctor, but she couldn't handle what life had handed her with even a modicum of grace.

"This doesn't have to be the end of your search, Françoise. At the time you were born, did your father have a confidant or best friend? What about your mother? Think back."

"They must have had a close friend or two, but none I remember from that long ago."

"Have you kept some of their memorabilia?"

"Maman saved things in a box. It's in storage at the moving company I used."

"Here in Paris?"

"Yes."

"Why don't you pick it up and go through everything? Who knows what you might find?"

She lifted her head. "You mean now?"

"I don't see why not. I can't see you getting much sleep later tonight, and closing time won't be for another hour. When we reach the apartment, you can leave for the moving company in your car. Before you go to bed, you may have found a photo of a friend or someone who can shed light on what happened."

"Oh, if I thought that were true..." This man was a marvel. "Would you come with me?" Françoise had said it so automatically, she shocked herself.

Jean-Louis almost jumped out of his skin with excitement. The concern in those gorgeous green eyes slayed him. "What do you think?"

"You really don't mind?"

Mind? For the first time since he'd known her, Françoise had asked him to do something *with* her. It had nothing to do with her being a doctor, or her trying to help him. "I'll ask the driver to take us there right now. What's the name of the company?"

"Gilbert Demenagement. It's not too far from the hospital where I work."

He spoke through the intercom to give the driver directions. In a few minutes they arrived at the moving company. Jean-Louis asked the driver to wait and they went inside. When the box had been brought out, he carried it to the limo and they headed for her apartment.

Once there, she brought in her overnight bag while Jean-Louis took care of the box. He told the driver to leave and followed her to the second floor, where she lived.

She put down her bag. "As you can see, this furnished apartment isn't the *palais*, but it's close to my work and convenient until I can find my own place. Several of the hospital staff live here too."

Jean-Louis had been so preoccupied with thoughts of her wanting his help, he scarcely noticed the surroundings. "After the army, this apartment *is* a palace."

She turned to him. "How do I thank you? I hardly know where to begin after what you've done for me. I know you're anxious to get back to your project and the limo is still waiting for you."

"No, it isn't. I told him to leave. It's too late for me to work on anything tonight. I saw your face at the church when you heard the priest had died. I felt your pain and I'd like to help you learn the truth about the adoption. It's the least I can do after you brought me back to life."

Her velvety green eyes filled with tears. "I'm so glad you want to stay. The thought of going through that box alone—" But she couldn't finish.

"I know. When the taxi drove me along the Promenade des Anglais after I got off the transport plane, the sight of the Causcelle Prom Hotel almost destroyed me. The memories of my former life flew at me, and the only thing that saved me at that moment was knowing I'd come home to die."

"Oh, Jean-Louis. You understand better than anyone else in the world could."

Without conscious thought, only need, he drew her into his arms and she sobbed quietly against his chest. He rocked her as she clung to him. Holding her felt so right, he never wanted to let her go. The fragrance of her hair and skin, the feel of her against his body—

nothing compared to the feelings and sensations she aroused in him. But a sudden loud knocking on the door broke his trance.

Françoise pulled away from him. "Jacques?" she called out. He assumed it was the concierge. "Is there a fire or a burst pipe?"

"No," a wintry male voice answered. "It's Eric."

Jean-Louis's body tensed.

"But how did you get in the building?"

"I have my ways. Open the door. We have to talk."

She walked over to it. "Lower your voice. We've said everything there is to say."

"No, we haven't!" he countered. "You told me there wasn't anyone else, but you've been lying to me. I saw a man come in here with you a few minutes ago and he hasn't left. I'd like an explanation."

"We've said our goodbyes, Eric, and I have a guest with me."

"Are you going to make me wait out here?"

Jean-Louis walked over to her. "Eric sounds more than determined," he whispered. "If you want me to deal with this, I will." The other man was crazy in love with Françoise. That much was obvious.

He heard her sharp intake of breath. "No, I'll let him in, but stay with me."

That was music to his ears. "I'll sit on the couch while you talk." He sank down in the middle and waited for her to open the door.

Eric walked in and almost stumbled over her overnight bag. "Where have you been, Françoise? I've been calling this apartment and your phone for two days!"

"I had to go out of town overnight on a case and just got back. Why are you here?"

"You know why." His glacial gaze flew to Jean-Louis, then back at her. "What's going on?"

"I've been attending this man's father, who's ill."

"That's a good story. Where's the patient now?"

She folded her arms. "Eric—what do you want?"

"I want to talk to you. *Alone.* I have the right."

"We've said our goodbyes."

"But I *haven't*! So, this man's going to spend another night with you? How many have there been during the time I was working in Rabat?"

Jean-Louis had heard enough and got to his feet. "I don't think we've ever met." He walked over to Eric, not a bad-looking man if he weren't torn up with jealousy. "I know you're a Moreau. I'm Jean-Louis Causcelle."

His head flew back. He studied him. "That face is familiar. You *are* one of the Causcelle triplets."

"That's right. I was discharged from the army a month ago with an illness that Dr. Valmy found and diagnosed in Nice. She flew to my home in La Racineuse to attend my father, who's dying of heart failure. He wanted to know if he has my blood disorder. It turns out he doesn't. We just flew back to Paris. I offered to help her with that box over there before leaving."

"Your disappearance turned this country upside down." Clearly he hadn't heard a word of Jean-Louis's explanation.

Eric switched his gaze to Françoise and stared at her through narrowed lids. "Well, well, well. I *was* right.

You did find someone else with a lot more money than I could ever make, even when elected."

Elected? That's right. Antoine had told Jean-Francois the man would be running for president of the country.

"Who else but a Causcelle with his billions? *Bonne chance, cherie.*" Eric flew out the door.

Jean-Louis stepped forward and closed it. In his gut he knew the man was out of her life permanently, *grâce à Dieu.*

"Jean-Louis?" She sounded fragmented.

He turned to her. "Nothing needs to be said. I'm immune. The poor devil is in love and hurting, just like Antoine." There wasn't a woman on the planet like Françoise. No one knew it better than Jean-Louis. "You need to dig into that box and forget everything else."

After a long pause, "You're right. If you'd like to freshen up in the bathroom down the hall, I'll fix us some coffee and get started."

"You're reading my mind."

A few minutes later he walked into the living room where she'd put their mugs of coffee on the table in front of the couch. She'd pulled the box over to one end and knelt on the floor.

He took a seat near her and started to drink the coffee while she sorted through various old photos and keepsakes. "I don't see any recognizable people in these old group pictures. No letters. But here are my parents' framed certificates and awards. I don't think I'm going to find a clue in here after all."

Jean-Louis leaned forward to look through them.

One caught his eye. "Didn't you say your parents went to medical school in Paris?"

"Yes."

"How come this internship certificate on your father says Asclepius Hospital in Rouen?"

"What?"

"An appropriate name for a hospital, don't you think? Wasn't Asclepius the son of the god Apollo, known for healing?"

She shook her beautiful head. "How do you know so much about an obscure piece of Greek mythology?"

"One of my high school teachers was big on it. Here. Take another look."

Françoise took it back from him and studied it for a moment. "I can't believe I didn't notice this. According to the date here, Papa must have done a rotation at this hospital after they were married." Her brows furrowed. "But Maman never mentioned anything about them being separated. I guess she went with him. I'm surprised."

"Maybe that's worth investigating," he declared.

She looked up at him. Hope radiated from those divine green orbs. "What would I do without you, Jean-Louis? All these things have been in this box for years. If you hadn't suggested looking at some memorabilia, let alone catching this, I would have missed it completely. Now that you've discovered it, I need to talk to the administrator at that hospital."

He got to his feet. A surge of hope swept through him. She sounded as if she wouldn't mind spending more time with him. When he'd held her in his arms earlier, maybe she'd felt its rightness too. "If you can take one more day off from work, why don't I drive us there tomorrow? We'll give your car a rest."

"Oh, no. You've done too much for me already."

"I have a selfish reason since Rouen is one of the cities where I intend to make some contacts for my project. I'm also as anxious as you to find the answer to your adoption. Now would be the perfect time to do both."

She sprang to her feet. "Why don't I talk to Dr. Soulis first thing in the morning, and then phone you."

In that moment she failed to meet his eyes, giving him a frisson of fear. Was she putting him off?

"I have no doubts he'll say yes." Since her boss had been in touch with her for a whole year before she took her boards, he was probably in love with her too. Upset, Jean-Louis pulled out his phone and called for a taxi before walking to the door.

Françoise followed him. "Figuratively speaking, you've become my knight in shining armor. I hope you realize that."

What was she saying now? His desire to crush her in his arms and make love to her was all he wanted to do, but he would have to wait a while longer. "Since you literally saved my life, I'd say we're even. Get a good sleep, Françoise. Perhaps tomorrow will bring the end to your pain."

Françoise watched his incredible physique walk out the door to the elevator and disappear. She hadn't wanted him to leave. When he'd held her in his arms earlier to comfort her, she'd known then she never wanted him to let her go.

She was no different from Celestine or Suzanne, or all the women written about in the newspapers who clamored to be with one of the gorgeous Causcelle triplets. Even Eric, who could be tough as nails in a political fight, backed off the second he recognized him. No man could compete with Robert Martin, who'd become her modern-day Adonis.

After Jean-Louis had talked to her about the name of the hospital in Rouen, another Greek myth had flashed through her mind.

In Zeus's household, the goddess Aphrodite had protected the beautiful Adonis and had appointed Persephone to raise him. But Persephone fell in love with Adonis and refused to give him back to Aphrodite. Zeus stepped in. He ordered Adonis to spend a third of a year with each of the two goddesses, and a third with whichever one he wanted. In the end Adonis chose to spend two-thirds of each year with Aphrodite and had two children with her.

Would that Françoise could be Jean-Louis's Aphrodite and give him children one day. But right there her fantasy had to stop! She was living in a nightmare, not a myth. Once she'd found a place to work and live near her great-aunt, she'd leave Paris and never see Jean-Louis again. That's why she'd deliberately lied to him about needing permission to get off work. She needed to protect them both.

Françoise Valmy, or whatever your real name might have been, you can't be with any man until you have answers as to why your father hid that specially sealed adoption paper in his bag. Your whole life is in question. Don't inflict possible pain on Jean-Louis. The last thing he needs is to be associated with a woman whose father's illegal actions had to be hidden from the world. Once exposed, the result could be disastrous if it put a stain on the Valmy name.

Dr. Soulis had given her a week off to deal with her life. There was no time like the present to get going. But when she reached for her laptop to look at a map and plan her trip to Bourges, she realized she'd left it at the lab. The only thing to do was run by the hospital in the morning before leaving Paris.

Tonight, she would pack enough clothes for a week that might also include a trip to Rouen to do some digging. In her heart, however, she feared it would be a wasted journey with no results.

Before long she went to bed only to spend the most restless night of her life reliving her day. Françoise had been so off-balance around Jean-Louis, she'd clung to him. The memory still brought heat to her face. In fact, she'd said and done things that let him think she craved his company. Heaven knew she did, but that behavior couldn't be allowed to go on. No more Jean-Louis ever.

Awakening early the next morning, she dressed quickly and carried her suitcase out to the car. En route to the hospital for her laptop, she stopped at a café for breakfast. While she ate, she texted Jean-Louis, explaining that she couldn't get away because they were swamped at work. She couldn't ask Dr. Soulis for another favor. After thanking Jean-Louis for everything he'd done, she wished him well on his project.

As soon as she pressed the send button, she felt like she'd just cut the invisible tether that had joined them from the beginning. Now she was the one dangling out in the vast void of space. Since he'd come into her life, she'd welcomed every day because he inhabited her universe. With him gone from her life, Françoise knew she'd never be truly happy again and better get used to it.

Once at the hospital, she dashed inside and found her laptop in the drawer of her desk. So far there'd been no activity on her phone to suggest that Jean-Louis had texted her back. Good. He'd gotten the message and was leaving well enough alone. With her heart feeling like a lodestone, she started for the door just as Celestine came running into the lab.

"Oh, good—it's *you*, Dr. Valmy! Do you remember about that gorgeous vet who came without an appointment?"

More déjà vu.

Just the thought of Jean-Louis sent shivers of longing through her. "Yes?"

"He has come again without an appointment and is asking for *you*."

Her body quickened. This meant he'd seen her text and wasn't happy about it. "I'm afraid I'm far too busy, but I passed Dr. Loudat's office on my way down the hall. Ask him. He'll do the procedure."

"All right." She looked dejected. "I'd hoped he'd

come in early to see me, but no such luck. Whoever he's crazy about has to be the luckiest woman on earth."

Celestine knew what she was talking about. "Never fear. Someone wonderful will come along for you one day."

"But he'll never be this guy."

You're right.

"Have a good one, Dr. Valmy."

"You too."

Celestine walked away. The second she disappeared, Françoise ran out the exit door at the other end of the lab and raced down five flights of stairs. Halfway to her car she saw Jean-Louis stride toward her looking incredible in chinos and a blazer. Those eyes of his reminded her of black fires. "I'm glad I caught you before you left on your busy day."

She swallowed hard. "Why didn't you answer my text? I could have saved you this trip."

"Your text let me know you were running away again. It's your pattern."

His comment brought her up short and guilt took over. She looked around. "Could we talk in my car so people can't hear us?"

"I insist on it."

Françoise struggled for breath. His mood left no room for argument. This was a new side to him. She opened the door and climbed in. He walked over to the passenger door, which she unlocked with the remote. Jean-Louis got in without problem since he'd adjusted the seat the other day to accommodate his long, powerful legs. Then he turned to her.

"I see your suitcase in the back seat and want the truth

from you. Every time I think we're enjoying each other's company a little more, you manage to slip away. I know in my gut there's an attraction between us, but something is stopping you from getting any closer to me. Why?"

Her stomach muscles tightened, preventing her from answering him.

"When I believed I was dying, Françoise, you convinced me I wasn't. I'd like you to convince me now of the real reason you canceled our plans for today. I can take your truth, but I need to hear it. You're a doctor and should understand that better than anyone."

She gripped the edge of her seat, unable to look at him. "If an adoption document can be specially sealed, it can also be specially unsealed under certain circumstances. I live in fear of its secret being exposed one day, Jean-Louis, and it will! Trust me on this. Whatever my parents wanted concealed forever, let's agree that there's no such thing as forever. When I learn the painful truth, I don't want it to affect anyone else."

He slid his arm across the back of her seat and gently massaged her neck. She wished he hadn't done that. His touch sent bursts of desire through her body. "So that means you're not going to let me into your life any further while you wait for that terrifying day?"

"I can't!" she cried. "Don't you see? You've endured a lifetime of notoriety and illness up to now. I won't involve you or any man in my painful personal battle, no matter what it may be."

"Even if the truth should come out forty years from now?"

"That's right. A single life hurts no one else."

She felt his body constrict before he removed his arm, denying her the closeness that thrilled her to the very core. "Do you honestly think your parents would want that life for you?"

"I'm not sure. It's possible my adoptive father left the adoption paper in his bag on purpose. Maybe he hoped I'd find it one day and eventually learn its ugly secret. I've thought about it a lot."

"That doesn't make sense. Your parents loved you."

"Hear me out, Jean-Louis. Perhaps my birth mother and father have been trying to find me all these years, but they can't put their hands on the sealed document to learn who adopted me. What if my adoptive parents feared something bad could happen if they did find me? So, they decided to leave the document for me to discover, knowing I'd investigate."

"Why would they do that?"

"Maybe it was their way of warning me of something terrible before my birth parents caught up to me."

He let out a sound of exasperation. "Since all this has been building inside of you, why aren't you eager to go to Rouen with me right now?"

"I plan to, but I have to do it alone on my own time."

"After all you've done for me, is there no way you'll allow me to help you now?"

The hurt and frustration in his voice cut her to the very soul, but she had no choice. Françoise had to push him away for his own sake and hers. "Kind as you are because it's in your nature, I—I don't want your help," she stammered. "We should never have met."

She closed her eyes tightly. "I'd hoped the text I sent to you this morning had said it all."

In the next instant she heard his door open and her heart lurched. "You accomplished your objective, Françoise. The problem is, I didn't want to accept it because there's a bond between us, and I know you feel it too. That's why you run and keep running."

Without saying another word, he got out of the car and shut the door. She sat there in a cocoon of pain while he walked to the Mercedes.

CHAPTER SEVEN

JEAN-LOUIS DROVE STRAIGHT to the *palais*, experiencing an agony that was totally foreign to him. Since adulthood he'd avoided all serious relationships with women until Françoise had come into his life. This morning he'd reached out, and she'd cut through him with the precision of a surgical knife.

Kind as you are, because it's in your nature, I—I don't want your help. We should never have met.

Rejection for something normal, like she didn't have romantic feelings for him, was one thing. But she *did* want him the way he wanted her. He'd felt it when he'd held her in his arms at her apartment. Though sobbing, she'd clung to him like they were two halves of a whole. Only the shocking news that she'd been adopted had flung her into such a dark place, the true Françoise had been buried alive and was unreachable.

He knew in every atom of his body she'd never let him get close to her again until she had answers. He could imagine her living a lifetime alone waiting for them. But it wouldn't take that long if he had anything to say about it. There was only one thing to do.

After arriving at the *palais*, he raced inside his suite and looked on his phone list for the number of Claude Giraud, the retired secret service agent who'd tracked him down. If that man couldn't produce the needed miracle, then Jean-Louis would have to admit defeat and stay unattached because there could be no other woman for him. The one thing he'd been desperate to avoid for years had finally happened. Though he hadn't even kissed Françoise yet, he sensed they were soul mates.

Claude was his only hope, but to his frustration he had to leave his number. It wasn't until early Wednesday morning the other man called him back. Jean-Louis had paced the bedroom floor most of the night. When he heard the ring, he flung himself across the bed to reach his cell on the bedside table. "Claude?"

"*Eh, bien*, Jean-Louis. How is the lost Causcelle who has returned to the fold?"

Jean-Louis liked Claude. "All is well, except for my heart."

"I'm sorry to hear that," he came back in a sincere tone. "Don't tell me you have your father's condition."

His hand tightened on the phone. "*Non.* I'm afraid it's of a different kind, and I need your help. Name any price."

"I'll be very happy to assist. You know that."

"It won't be easy."

"Tell me your problem."

For the next ten minutes he unloaded on Claude all the information he could think of. "I believe the visit to Rouen might be a good place for you to start. Her father did an internship there around the time of the adoption."

"This is good. You've given me a lot to go on."

"Claude—I'm depending on you. She's my life's blood." His throat thickened. "Without her, I don't know if I'll be—"

"Don't say it, Jean-Louis," he cut him off. "Don't even think it. Give me a month and I'll get back to you."

He groaned. "A month?"

"Probably no longer. This time I won't be hunting for a soldier who wants to remain lost. In the meantime, stay busy, *mon ami. A toute à l'heure.*"

Jean-Louis hung up and forced himself off the bed. Thirty days sounded like an eternity. The only thing to do was get busy right now and fill the *palais* with vets. He would use this time to get them started on their training in any *metier* they wanted. Until Claude got back to him, he needed to put thoughts of Françoise out of his mind. *As if that were possible.*

Françoise spent the next few days in Bouzy at Nadine's bedside, sleeping nights at a nearby hotel. During that time the doctor got her bronchitis under control. However, he told Françoise her great-aunt's emphysema wasn't getting better. He estimated she could live maybe three, four more months, no longer. His news changed everything for her.

Two days later she felt she could leave for part of the day. Getting in her car, she drove the hour-and-quarter distance to Bourges for an arranged interview with the hospital director.

She enjoyed meeting the congenial administrator, who thankfully didn't link her with her father. He took her on a tour of the lab and facilities. Françoise imagined she could be happy enough working there if she had to. Before she left, he offered her the epidemiology position. She said she'd have to think about it and get back to him.

The return trip to Bouzy took longer. By the time she reached the hotel, she realized she didn't want to have to drive close to three hours a day to come and go. She needed to stay in Bouzy with her aunt and find a furnished apartment online.

Once she drove to the address of one to take a look, she ended up paying first and last months' rent on a short-term lease. In the morning she called the hospital administrator in Bourges to tell him she decided she couldn't take the position, but she thanked him profusely for his time.

With that accomplished, she left for Paris to resign her position. She had enough savings to live for six months, if necessary, without working.

First, she moved her few things out of her apartment and cleaned it. Later she canceled her phone number and got a new one. At the end of that day, she met with Christophe and told him the sad news about her great-aunt. He commiserated with her situation and accepted her resignation. She could always apply again one day when circumstances had changed.

Françoise asked him to tell no one why she'd left or what her plans were. She wanted complete privacy. Not that Jean-Louis would ever venture near after what she'd said to him. Christophe assured her of his silence. After a tearful goodbye, she left the City of Lights for Bouzy.

The old season of life had passed away. A new one had begun. She and Nadine would face it together.

Don't be tempted to look back, Françoise.

What a joke. During the drive, she relived every moment with Jean-Louis. Tears trickled down her face to think she'd never know that kind of joy again.

"Hey—Jean-Louis. We're almost filled up."

He flicked his gaze to Guy. They'd been talking at the front desk. Guy had agreed to be in charge of the new vet hostel, and over the last week the man had become his right arm.

"You're right. I'm waiting for Remy, the last one who'll be coming in the van from the airport within the hour. You'll like him. He served under me for a time."

"I like all of them. It's a grand thing you're doing, Jean-Louis. My wife cried over your generosity when I first told her about your plan for the *palais*."

"Thanks, Guy. We'll see if this experiment works out. I couldn't do it without you."

"It's going perfectly, and you're paying me too much."

He shook his head. "Guy? There isn't enough money to compensate you for all you're doing. When I'm back in La Racineuse, I'll be able to do my work on the estate knowing you and the staff have this place running better than the finest Swiss watch."

"It's a pleasure."

"The guys think the world of you too." He patted Guy's shoulder. "Tell you what. I'm going upstairs to make some phone calls. Let me know when he arrives."

"Will do."

He walked down the hall to the elevator that took him to his suite. He no longer felt guilt that he was the only one living here. None of the men were in the army now, but they had a camaraderie no one else could understand. Guy was getting a taste of it.

He grabbed a cola from the fridge and sat down on the couch to deal with the phone calls that had come in while he'd been setting up a new computer in Remy's room.

With each call, he'd prayed to see Françoise's name to no avail. This evening there were three calls from La Racineuse he needed to return. Halfway through his conversation with Raoul, another call came in. *Claude Giraud!*

Jean-Louis sprang to his feet, coming close to cardiac arrest. He clicked on.

"Claude? *Grâce à Dieu.*"

"Sorry it has taken me this long to get back to you, Jean-Louis. To make a long story short, you'll have noticed on the news that the president of our country has been on a tour and just got back yesterday."

He blinked. "I don't understand."

"The problem you gave me led me from one obstacle to another. It was very unusual. In fact, I would say impossible. I finally realized I needed the highest authority in the land in order to look inside that particular adoption."

Hadn't Françoise said something about that long ago? Jean-Louis could hardly breathe. He started walking around. "What are you saying?"

"I met with the president today and explained your particular situation. The name Dr. Patrick Valmy, plus the name Louis Causcelle, worked magic on my former boss. He holds both men in the very highest regard. In an unprecedented move, he allowed me to look into the adoption brief long enough to understand why it had been specially sealed."

That meant Claude knew everything! Jean-Louis's gut clenched.

"I've been instructed to tell no one but Françoise Valmy what I learned. I can't tell you. Not even the president knows. He trusts me not to violate what he is allowing, or I could be imprisoned. This isn't about politics. It's beyond top secret."

What?

"No one must ever know what I've done. It will be up to Dr. Valmy if she ever tells you. Do you understand what I'm telling you?"

Imprisonment? He leaned against the wall for support. "I hear you."

"If you'll give me her number, I'll get in touch with her tonight."

"Claude?" he said after doing his bidding. "I don't know what to say, or how to thank you for this. You're saving my life."

"I hope that's true for your sake."

The man's choice of words troubled Jean-Louis, but he couldn't worry about that right now. He was too grateful for what Claude had done. "Whatever you should want or need, name it and it's yours."

"I appreciate that. Just remember, not a word to anyone ever, or my life isn't worth a *sou*, let alone the president's."

He heard the click. This time Claude's wording sent a strange tremor through his body. While he tried to absorb the implication in the man's warning, his phone rang. It was Guy. That meant Remy had arrived.

Jean-Louis left the suite to meet the vet and help him get oriented. Before the end of the night, he knew he'd be hearing from Françoise. Whether the news from Claude brought her happiness or dreaded pain, her wait would be over. Though she'd declined his help earlier, she would feel obligated to call Jean-Louis. Just the thought of hearing her voice again sent a lightning bolt through him, bringing him to life once more.

An hour later he said good-night to Remy and headed for his suite. Unable to settle down, he returned the calls from La Racineuse while he waited for his phone to ring. Five minutes after he and Raoul had finished talking, he saw Claude Giraud's name on the incoming call.

He grabbed his cell. "Claude?"

"I'm glad you answered. Will you give me Dr. Valmy's phone number again? I must have written it down wrong."

Jean-Louis groaned inwardly. The former agent hadn't even talked to her yet? "Here it is." He repeated it slowly. Claude thanked him and they hung up. Two minutes later he rang him again and he picked up. "Claude?"

"Sorry, Jean-Louis, but it's no longer her number. I checked with the phone company. As soon as you get the new one from her, let me know and I'll call her immediately."

She was still running from him. "Thank you, Claude. You'll be hearing from me soon."

The only thing to do was drive over to her apartment. Even if it was after ten, he would have to disturb the landlord because this constituted an emergency. Five minutes later he reached the complex, but saw no sign of her car. A visit with the man named Jacques and he learned she'd moved out two weeks ago with no forwarding address.

His frustration off the charts, Jean-Louis returned to the *palais*. After a shower, he went to bed and spent a sleepless night. At six he got up and dressed before taking off for her place of work. Though he didn't see her car in the hospital parking, it didn't matter since she probably wouldn't arrive until eight. He went inside and waited for her in the fifth-floor lounge. Two cups of coffee later, he approached an older nurse at the desk who'd just arrived. He'd seen her before.

"How soon do you expect Dr. Valmy?"

"I'm sorry, *monsieur*. Dr. Valmy doesn't work here anymore."

The news ripped his insides apart. "Since when?"

"I believe she left two weeks ago."

This couldn't be happening. "Do you know where she's working now?"

"I don't. I believe you're the vet who came in to get your blood drawn a while back. What can I do to help you this morning?"

He needed to get a grip. "Is Dr. Soulis here? I must talk to him. It's an emergency."

"I'll see if he's available." She made a call and a short conversation ensued before she hung up. "Dr. Soulis will be right out."

"Thank you." He paced in front of the desk until Françoise's sixtyish-looking former boss appeared.

"I understand you wanted to talk to me. The nurse mentioned an emergency."

"It is. Dr. Valmy was my doctor in Nice before she moved here. I have to talk to her."

"Unfortunately, she's no longer available. I'll be happy to recommend another doctor in her field to help you."

Anger kindled inside him. "You don't understand. I need *her*. Where is she working now?"

His hands opened. "I have no idea."

Jean-Louis got the feeling the other man could be speaking the truth. No doubt Françoise had told her boss to say nothing. "Do you at least have a phone number for her? It's vital."

"I have no information on Dr. Valmy since she left our employ." Of course not. "I'm sorry."

So am I.

"Thank you for your time, Dr. Soulis." Jean-Louis wheeled around and left the hospital.

Once in his car, he phoned Claude and told him of

Françoise's disappearance. "Can you do me one more favor and find out her new phone number?"

"I wish I could, but I made a vow to the president. No more investigation on this case that could leave tracks, if you know what I mean."

His eyes closed tightly. "Forgive me. I'm desperate."

"I know you won't give up trying to find her. I'll be waiting for your call."

He clicked off, leaving Jean-Louis frantic.

The only tie Françoise valued in her dark place lived at the rest home in Bouzy-la-Forêt. In another two hours he could be there. First, he would go back to the *palais* to throw some things together in a duffel bag. He might have to stay in the village for a few nights.

Thirty minutes later he took off on the A-6 headed south. En route, he talked with Guy and answered several calls from the registrar enrolling Remy in a beginning EMT program. Everything in Paris seemed to be going well by the time he drove into Bouzy and found the Silver Pines rest home.

Searching all around, he couldn't see Françoise's car, but for once he wasn't alarmed. She would never leave her godmother. He'd stop at the L'Auberge for a meal, then drive over to the rest home to wait for her.

Today was Nadine's eighty-sixth birthday. Françoise left the store with another jigsaw puzzle to help with dementia. It would fit on the overbed table. This one featured eight famous French châteaux for her great-aunt to identify. One of them turned out to be the Causcelle family home and gardens in La Racineuse.

Françoise melted at the sight of it and she couldn't resist buying it. That visit had changed her life, leaving her with an aching sense of loss that would never go away.

She'd also purchased Nadine's favorite snacks at the grocery store so they could celebrate. Françoise would have loved to bring her red roses, her godmother's favorite flower, but she'd developed a serious allergy to pollen. Françoise had also chosen foods that were good for her while she battled emphysema.

The day wore on as they munched on grapes and nuts. Nadine only nodded over three of the châteaux on the box though she'd visited all of them but one.

Françoise pointed to it. "This château located in Eastern France was deeded to the Causcelle family in 1200. I went there to see a patient with a heart condition."

"Sad," her godmother murmured.

"Yes. Louis Causcelle is a remarkable man."

Suddenly Nadine looked up at Françoise, struggling to say something. The word finally came out. "Triplets?"

Françoise almost fell out of the chair. "Yes. You remembered his name! Three triplet sons."

Just then Thea poked her head inside the door. "You have a visitor on your special day, Nadine. Is it all right?"

"She'd love it, Thea." Françoise glanced at her great-aunt. "I bet it's your friend Fria from down the hall."

"No." Thea shook her head. "It's a man I've never seen before, but he says he knows you."

"What's his name?"

"He wants it to be a surprise."

"Oh. I bet it's my landlady's son, Fabien. She said she would send him over with some *pains au chocolat* for Nadine's birthday. Tell him to come in."

When Jean-Louis walked in the room looking jaw-droppingly gorgeous in a heather-blue suit, she thought she was hallucinating.

Those black eyes blazed as they took in every inch of her, making her feel faint. "It's good to see you, Françoise." His deep voice permeated the room. He walked over to the end of the hospital bed. "I've wanted to meet your great-aunt. Nadine Bonnet, isn't it? The nurse said she's recovering from her bronchitis. I'm glad to hear it. I'm Jean-Louis Causcelle, Nadine. It's a real pleasure to meet you."

Her godmother lifted her hand and pointed at him. "Triplet."

His low chuckle invaded Françoise's body. "Yes. I'm the youngest one. Happy birthday. It looks like I've interrupted you putting a puzzle together."

Françoise's cheeks turned to flame when he leaned over to look at the lid of the puzzle.

"May I help? I haven't done a puzzle in years." He reached for a chair and pulled it up to the other side of the bed.

Nothing could have shocked Françoise more when her great-aunt smiled at him and nodded. He knew all about her condition. While he fit puzzle pieces together, he just kept talking as if it were the most natural thing in the world that she didn't answer.

"I've been busy helping returned veterans from war

get settled into schools to train them for work. Ten of them now live where I live in the Marais district of Paris. You know when Françoise came out to La Racineuse to take care of my father and draw his blood, I took some photos of her working in the hospital lab there." She gasped in more surprise. "I'd like to give them to you for a birthday present."

In the next instant he produced six small photos showing Françoise checking out the blood samples. Her great-aunt studied them before staring at Françoise. She put a hand to her own face. "Mask."

He laughed. "I don't like it when she wears one either. It hides her beauty."

Most amazing to Françoise was the touching way she put her hand on his to thank him for the gift. Françoise knew she was going to cry. "Excuse me for a moment." She jumped up and hurried out to the hall. After giving way to tears, she wiped her eyes and went back to the room.

Jean-Louis just kept on talking about life at La Racineuse and the rose garden in the back of the château. For the last two weeks she'd been dying to know how he was doing. Today she'd learned more during these few hours than she would have dreamed. He was so wonderful with Nadine, she could never thank him enough. There wasn't a man alive like him.

That's what made this so hard. He shouldn't have come. More memories had been made that would live with her forever. More pain to endure after they said goodbye.

Dinner arrived. They ate together, but Nadine fell

asleep before she could finish. The day had worn her out, and Françoise helped her get ready for bed. Jean-Louis waited for her out in the hall.

"Do you sleep here now?" he asked when she joined him. "I discovered you gave up your job and your apartment in Paris."

She took a quick breath to combat her guilt. "I rent a nearby apartment. She needs constant care now."

"How wonderful she has you. I'll follow you to your place. We have to talk."

"I wish you hadn't come, but since you're here, let's go out to my car. We can talk there."

He didn't argue with her, they left the building and got in her car. He'd parked next to her.

She trembled from his nearness. "You were so sweet to Nadine. It's obvious she enjoyed your visit very much."

"But you weren't happy to see me."

Françoise had never been more conflicted in her life. How could she answer his question honestly? She was desperately happy to see him. His kindness to Nadine only made that worse. She was in agony to be so near him. But she had to remain strong and resist, do everything she could to deter him. It had to be this way for his sake as well as for her own sanity.

"No. I told you I have to do my own thing from now on. Why on earth are you here?"

He turned to her. "It's called desperation. I called Claude Giraud. You wouldn't let me do it before, but I couldn't bear the separation from you. I ended up contacting him. He was able to obtain the information you need so badly so we can be together."

"What?" she cried in sheer disbelief.

"He tried to phone you, but couldn't reach you with the phone number I gave him. That's when I found out you were nowhere to be found. I went to your apartment, your work. No one could or would tell me anything. My one link to you was your great-aunt, so I came here today. For all I knew, you might have moved the two of you to some other town."

She pressed her hands to her face. "I don't believe what I'm hearing. How dare you go against my wishes! That wasn't your right, and I could never have afforded it. You've betrayed me! This means *you* know every painful, maybe even criminal thing my father might have done. Do you have any idea how much that hurts me?"

He groaned. "How could I hurt you? I was trying to erase your pain. Claude has told me nothing because it's not my business. But if you'll give me your new phone number, I'll pass it on to him. He'll call and tell you all that you want to know about your adoption. It'll be between the two of you and no one else. Ever."

Her head reared. "Don't you understand what you've done? How could you go behind my back? I thought I could trust you."

"Don't you get it, Françoise? I did everything I could to bring us together because *I'm in love with you*!"

His declaration filled the interior of the car, shaking her to the foundations.

"I want to be your husband. I want to make love to

you for the rest of our lives. I want to have children with you. The love I have for you will never go away. There's no other woman in the world for me. I came here fighting for a life with you. Only you. Nothing will make sense if you're not my other half."

He reached in his jacket pocket and drew out a card. "Since you can't bring yourself to give me your phone number, then you call Claude. It's up to you. He's ready to give you the answer you've been waiting for. Despise me if you want, but he put his life on the line to get this information for you." He put the card on the dashboard.

She'd started to shiver.

"I thought you felt the same way about me, but I was wrong. You have my solemn promise that I'll never come near you again."

He climbed out of her car and turned to her. "I've already thanked you for saving my life, but at this moment I have to ask myself if it was worth it when it means I've lost you. I wish you and your great-aunt well in the future, Françoise." The door closed.

She hugged her arms to her chest, filled with soul-destroying shame over her reaction to his revelations. Only Jean-Louis could have given her such a priceless gift motivated by pure love. To her horror, she'd trampled all over it out of an irrational fear of the unknown.

And your own despicable pride, Françoise. A man as truly magnificent as Jean-Louis doesn't deserve a pitiful woman like you.

Long after she heard him drive away, she stumbled out of the car and hurried back to Nadine, dying inside.

Her godmother looked up and lifted a hand, as if

to ask why Jean-Louis hadn't come in with her. He'd made a friend while they'd put that puzzle together.

"He's gone, Mame."

The older woman's hand holding one of the little photos fell to the sheet and tears dripped down her pale cheeks.

Françoise sank down in the chair. *What have I done?*

CHAPTER EIGHT

JEAN-LOUIS HAD JUST come downstairs in jeans and a T-shirt when he saw his sister in the château foyer. "Corinne? If anyone needs me, I'll be at the garage."

She turned to him. "You don't want breakfast first?"

"Not now, thanks. I'm meeting the kids in a few minutes. We'll grab some food later."

"Everyone's excited you've had it rebuilt. Did you know that Honoré and Theo are dying to work with their Oncle Jean-Louis now that it's ready?"

"Old news, *ma soeur*. See you later."

A week ago he'd flown home after the disastrous confrontation with Françoise. His world had disintegrated before his very eyes. During the time he'd been home, he'd supervised the birth of the new garage. Jean-Louis had needed to keep so busy he wouldn't have time to think.

The building contractor who worked on the restored church/hospital for Nic had sent out more crew to help Jean-Louis. Now that school was out, his fifteen-year-old nephews had been pestering him to start working there. Maybe it was a genetic thing with some of the family that made them want to repair cars, trucks and tractors. He wondered what Françoise would make of—nope! That era was behind him.

He climbed in the new truck he'd bought in town to get around the estate. This morning he headed for the garage. While growing up, his old refuge had been a place of peace and pleasure for him. When Jean-Louis had first opened the creaky door after being gone a decade, he'd experienced an overpowering sense of nostalgia.

Beneath a dim light he'd looked around the big, empty relic. His old toolbox had been sitting there lifeless and untouched since he'd left for Paris with his brothers at eighteen. Where had the years gone?

Today he used the new remote to open the garage door. In seven days, the whole place had been transformed into a mechanic's state-of-the-art facility. He parked the truck and walked inside. Last evening he'd put one of the unreliable estate cars up on the lift for the boys to work on.

In a minute they appeared on their bikes. They hopped off and walked inside with huge smiles.

"Good morning, gentlemen. Right on time." They looked excited. Nothing like the soldiers Jean-Louis had been assigned to train in the army. No doubt at his nephews' ages, he'd worn the same goofy expression.

Honoré eyed the car. "Are we going to work on that old clunker?"

"How did you guess?"

"It hasn't run for a long time," Theo piped up.

"Then imagine how surprised everyone will be after

you grease monkeys get it cranking again. Once you guys turn sixteen, it'll be your car to drive around in on the estate." Both of them had birthdays coming up.

They high-fived each other on a burst of pure happiness.

Jean-Louis walked over to the lift. He'd forgotten what that kind of emotion felt like. In one week he'd turned into a hundred-year-old man.

At four thirty in the afternoon, Françoise finally found the deli she'd been looking for in La Racineuse. Needing sustenance after the flight from Bourges to Chalon Champforgeuil, she parked her rental car in front and hurried inside for coffee and a meat pie to take with her.

A few minutes later she ate on the way to the Causcelle château. Memories of the night she'd done the same thing with Jean-Louis en route to the hospital assailed her. She'd never known such happiness.

Her whole life had changed the first time she'd met Robert Martin. Yet a month and a half later, she'd done the unthinkable by wounding him and destroying what could have been divine happiness.

Françoise didn't expect forgiveness, let alone anything else. But she had to find him and bare her soul or she couldn't go on living. It would serve her right if he refused to see or talk to her. Still, she'd do whatever it took to convince him she never meant to hurt him. She wanted the chance to tell him he was the literal answer for her having been created.

The sight of the château hurt, because of all the wonderful memories Françoise had tried to put out of her mind. She pulled up in front, desperate to see and talk to Jean-Louis. After changing her mind half a dozen times, she'd chosen to wear a new periwinkle-colored silk blouse with pleated white pants.

She checked herself in the mirror. The little periwinkle earrings had been the right touch. When Jean-Louis told her she'd wasted her effort to come here, she wanted to have made a favorable impression before leaving.

Girding up her courage, she slid out of the car and hurried to the entrance. Two bikes stood outside. Before she could ring the buzzer, two teenage boys came bursting out the door. They stopped immediately when they saw her.

"Bonsoir," she greeted them. "I'm looking for Jean-Louis Causcelle. It's very important. Do you know if he's here?"

"He's over at the garage," the dark-haired boy answered her.

The famous garage. Jean-Louis was there.

She almost melted on the spot.

"Yeah," said the one with the blond hair. He carried a sack of something in his hand. "We're going there right now to take him dinner. Follow us."

They took off like speed demons. Overjoyed by this accidental meeting, she hurried back to the car and drove behind them a mile to the place on the estate he'd cherished. She saw a new truck parked outside, but the garage door was closed.

The blond boy got off his bike and knocked on the

door. "Oncle Jean-Louis? Open up. Tante Corinne sent your dinner."

"Thanks, guys," came his deep voice. "Just leave it and I'll get it in a minute. Right now, I'm draining the oil pan."

"Okay."

"See you tomorrow, same time."

"Ciao!" they both called out.

"I'll see that he gets it," Françoise whispered to them.

They nodded and rode away, but kept looking back at her. She picked up the sack, wondering how long she'd have to wait. Her heart lodged in her throat. After a minute she grew so nervous she couldn't take it any longer. Praying for help, she walked over to the door and knocked.

"I thought you guys had left."

In a moment the door lifted and she found herself three feet away from the most gorgeous male on earth. Oil covered parts of his face, T-shirt and arms. He'd been wiping his hands with a paper towel, but he stopped when he saw her.

"Jean-Louis—" she cried. "Please don't close the door on me yet. You would have every right, but I need to talk to you and beg your forgiveness. Then I promise I'll go away."

He didn't move. "How long have you been out here?"

"Just a minute. I drove to the château and your nephews were just leaving on their bikes. I asked if you were there and they said to follow them. This is your dinner." She started to hand the sack to him.

"I can't do anything until I get this oil washed off."
His face had such an impassive look, her heart plum-
meted to her feet. This wasn't her Jean-Louis. "I'll
meet you at home."

Still, one prayer had been answered. He hadn't yet
told her to get out of his life and stay out.

"Thank you."

On trembling legs, she got in the car and put down
the sack before driving to the château. Before long
Jean-Louis trailed behind her in his truck. He parked
next to her near the entrance and they both got out.

The moment seemed surreal when he opened the
front door for her. "Come upstairs with me where we
can be private."

Another prayer had been answered because they
didn't run into any of his family as they climbed to
the second floor. She'd done this before, but he didn't
stop at the suite she'd used on her first visit. He kept
walking down the hall to his room and opened the
door for them.

"Come in while I shower and change." After shutting the door, he turned on the TV in the sitting room
and handed her the remote. "I won't be long."

Françoise sat down on the couch to wait. It was in-
conceivable that he'd let her into his suite when she'd
been so cruel to him. She couldn't believe he would
be this decent after what she'd said and done. His polite formality was killing her, yet decency was one of
his many exceptional traits. She turned off the TV, unable to concentrate on anything and too anxious for the
final confrontation,

"Do you want something to drink?"

She jumped up in surprise and turned around. Jean-Louis had come from the shower wearing a casual tan sport shirt and white cargo pants. The wonderful scent of the soap he'd used clung to his powerful body.

"I don't want anything, thank you, but you need to eat." She looked down at the couch. "Oh, no—your dinner is still in my car! I forgot."

"Don't worry. I'm not hungry."

She clasped her hands in front of her. "Jean-Louis? All I want to do is apologize until you believe that I never meant to hurt you." Her eyes swam with tears she couldn't prevent.

He rubbed the back of his neck. "I know it's not in you to hurt anyone deliberately."

A little moan escaped. "You don't have to pretend with me. What I did can never be forgiven. There's no excuse for the way I reacted when you told me about talking to Monsieur Giraud."

"You had every right to be furious, Françoise. I went against your wishes."

"But I know why you did it, and I've been out of my mind ever since for the unconscionable way I treated you."

"That's because you were traumatized the day you found that adoption paper."

A groan came out of her. "A mature woman doesn't act like that. In the beginning, my fears escalated out of control. When I met you, part of me was terrified that in learning something terrible about my father, you'd hear about it and I'd *lose* you!"

He moved closer. "Lose me? What are you talking about? I meant nothing to you."

"You're so wrong about that." His eyes narrowed, as if he hadn't heard her correctly. "When you asked me to lunch to repay me for saving your life, I was already so crazy about you, I couldn't think."

She heard his sharp intake of breath. "Say that again."

"I *want* to say it again. The truth is, I fell in love with you at the hospital in Nice."

After a long silence, "You're serious."

By now the tears had started running down her cheeks. "Unfortunately, up until a week ago I was too blind with fear to tell you I love you more than life itself. If my father had done something unpardonable, then it would taint me too and you would never want anything to do with me." Her voice broke.

"*That's* been at the root of your fear? That I'd reject you?" He sounded incredulous.

She clung to the end of the couch. "I've known losses in my life, but the thought of losing you meant my life would be over. I shrank from facing it."

"Françoise—"

She looked up. "That first night after drawing your blood, I went home and had dreams of the most gorgeous vampire in existence entering my room. It was *you*, Jean-Louis. You devoured me with those eyes of black fire and willed me into your powerful arms."

"You're making this up."

This man she adored didn't believe her. Maybe she'd done too much damage and he couldn't. "I swear I'm not. I ran to you and we started to make love. It wasn't enough. I begged you to bite me with your beautiful white teeth so we would live together forever."

He shook his head. "Do you hear what you're saying?"

She'd never seen him in shock before. It made her smile in spite of her tears. "I *know* what I'm saying. When I first awakened, I was giddy with joy to have been turned by you and I needed you desperately. But you weren't there! I was frantic to find you until I realized it had only been a dream. I'd never been so desolate in my life."

More fire flickered in his eyes. "I wish I'd been there," he teased. Her old Jean-Louis was finally coming out of shock.

"From that moment on, my palpable hunger for you frightened the daylights out of me so much, I purposely stayed away from you for that whole first week."

An enticing smile broke the corner of his compelling mouth. "I wondered why I hadn't seen hide nor hair of you. Now I understand the reason why you've always been running from me."

"You don't know the half of it. It only took one more time to lay my eyes on you, and I knew you were part of my heart, mind, blood and soul. I told myself that if I got away from you immediately, my fantasy would dissipate with time."

That deep chuckle of his escaped. "Did it work?"

Heat crept into her face. "You know it didn't. I never stopped willing you to come to me, not even when I was six hundred miles away from you."

"That was a great disappearance trick you pulled on me, Dr. Valmy."

"Disappearance nothing. Lo and behold, a few weeks later there was my vampire. I'd willed him to Paris and he'd found me, appearing out in front of the hospital. He drove a Mercedes, no less. You'd taken on a new identity in breathtaking human form, not even wearing hospital pajamas."

A dashing smile appeared. "Which version do you like better?"

"You're an amalgam of both I adore. As the clerk on the fifth floor had described, you were the hunkiest vet she'd ever seen in her life. I already knew that and wanted to scratch her eyes out along with Suzanne's because you were *mine*. I'd already drunk of your essence in my dream."

"Don't I wish. We're going to have to reenact that particular dream right away." The throb in his voice resonated to her insides.

"I'll never forget it. We'd said our vows to each other during that night of impossible rapture no human could imagine. But again, I had to face the stark fact that being a human, I couldn't be with you. My earthly existence had been marred by an event of my parents' choosing, an event beyond my control."

Jean-Louis put his hands on her upper arms. "Which brings us to the matter of your adoption."

"But I'm not worried about that anymore."

Her words brought him up short. "You're not making sense."

"Listen to me, darling. On the evening after you left

Silver Pines, I drove to my apartment and wrestled with my thoughts and emotions all night. By morning, I'd come to my senses with only one thought. Because of your sacrifice, you had risked everything so we could be together. The quote about greater love hath no man had been indelibly impressed on my soul. I realized nothing else mattered. As soon as I could, I flew here."

His hands squeezed her shoulders. "Then you mean—"

"I never called Monsieur Giraud," she broke in on him.

"But—"

"No *buts*. You did everything humanly possible to help me get my life back, yet I trampled all over yours. I'll spend the rest of my life showing you how sorry I am and how much I love you. The only important thing is to tell you I want to be your wife. I don't want to live without you." She slid her hands up his chest. "But only if you think you can forgive me."

"Forgiveness doesn't come into this." The tears in his voice told her everything.

"Oh, yes, it does. Don't you know I want to marry you as soon as possible? Do you still—?"

The rest of her words were smothered as his mouth closed over hers with a fierce hunger that had been building from the first moment they'd met. He wrapped his strong arms around her, enclosing her against his heart. They drank deeply, trying to show each other what they'd had to hold back for so long. She felt the imprint of his body run the length of hers. Desire exploded more potently than what she'd experienced in her dream.

"Darling," he cried, covering her face and hair with kisses. They were both out of breath.

"I love you, Jean-Louis. I love you. You couldn't possibly know how much." No kiss lasted long enough.

A new dream started as he picked her up like a bride and carried her to his bedroom. Once he lowered her to the bed, she got lost in the ecstasy of being able to show him her love. She had no cognizance of time while they were finally giving in to their passion. Then suddenly he groaned and pulled away from her, getting to his feet.

She gazed up at him. "What is it, Jean-Louis?"

"I'm so in love with you, I'm ready for this to be our wedding night, but it isn't. Not until we've said our vows and I've put my ring on your finger. And that can't happen until you've spoken with Claude."

She sat up and moved to the edge of the bed. "No, darling. I told you it doesn't matter."

"Yes, it does, deep down. While Claude is still alive and able to tell you everything, you need to hear it before the information is gone forever. Whatever you learn, I know you'll handle it and I'll be with you all the way. Be honest with yourself. Then we can plan our wedding with no shadow marring our happiness."

Jean-Louis had spoken from his heart, and those words reached her soul.

"You're right. You're always right." She checked her watch. "It's ten to ten. Do you think—?"

"He'll still be up."

"Will you stay in here with me? I want to do everything with you. We'll listen together."

He took a fortifying breath. "Do you still have that card?"

"No. I'm sorry, but I tore it up. You'll have to give me the number again. My phone is in my purse in the sitting room."

"Stay right there. I'll get it." He rushed out and came back in another minute with her purse. She pulled the phone out and handed it to him to program Claude's number from his phone.

After he gave it back to her, he sat on a chair near the bed and waited for her to call the agent. The loving smile Jean-Louis flashed gave her the confidence to go through with this. She pressed the digits and heard the voice mail say to leave a number. Françoise followed through.

"He'll call back, *mon amour*."

Seconds after he'd spoken, her phone rang. She clicked on. "Monsieur Giraud?"

"Dr. Valmy. I wondered when I'd hear from you."

"There are no words to thank you enough for what you've done."

"The Causcelle family has been a good friend to me. I'm only happy to help. Are you ready?"

With the man she loved seated right in front of her, holding her hand, she was ready for anything. "Yes. Please tell me what you know."

"Your mother's birth name is Vivienne Fortin. She never knew her parents and was left inside a church in a blanket on a pew. She was taken to an orphanage in the village where she grew up. All the children attended church when old enough. In her teens she struck up a friendship with an altar boy from the village.

"They fell in love at seventeen, but fate stepped in and his family moved from the village. He never came back. She learned he'd been headed for the priesthood. Vivienne decided to become a nun. Before taking her final vows, she became ill and was sent to a regional hospital. Your father, Dr. Patrick Valmy, happened to be the intern on duty late that night.

"The initial examination proved she was near seven months along and in labor. He delivered a live baby. Her habit had hidden her pregnancy, so no one knew.

"She told your father she'd repented of her sin and could still be a bride of Christ. It was what she wanted with her whole heart and soul. Would he arrange for her daughter to be adopted? Since she'd never known her parents, she begged him to find her the best home possible with a loving mother and father. Then she confided her secret.

"The boy she'd loved was the grandson of a cardinal close to the pope in Rome. If word got out that his grandson was the baby's father, it would be disastrous for him, his family and the Church. Since he didn't know about the pregnancy, Vivienne wanted to spare the man she'd loved as much pain as possible.

"Your father sent her back to the nunnery, indicating she'd had a bleeding problem, but it had been corrected. He honored her wish by having her sick three-pound baby transported to a hospital in another city for expert care. Six weeks later that hospital sent the well baby to another orphanage.

"Your father and mother talked it over. Since she'd gone through three miscarriages, they would adopt this baby, which would be a blessing to everyone. Your parents applied for the adoption and brought you home. Your father slowly gathered all this information and wrote it down. At that point it was sealed by special order.

"To this day your birth mother and birth father are alive, serving God as a nun and as a priest in different areas on this planet. I'll say this, Dr. Valmy. Not every adopted child has such a lineage of earthly and spiritual parentage in their DNA. You're a blest woman to claim these four dedicated, saintly people as your parents. Your father wrote that he and your mother considered raising you as their sacred trust.

"Jean-Louis confided to me that you've been his savior. After what I've learned about your heritage, it doesn't surprise me. It's been my privilege to assist you both. My lips are sealed. I'll say good night." He clicked off.

Françoise broke down sobbing.

Jean-Louis stood up and pulled her into his arms. He brushed his lips over her wet face, only able to imagine her joy and wonderment. They clung for a long time. This answer meant their lives could begin, starting with a marriage ceremony he wished were happening this very second.

"You're my heaven-sent miracle, Jean-Louis. I wish

we were man and wife right this minute. I need you closer," she cried, flinging her arms around his neck. He crushed her against him and she lifted her mouth to his. Their long-suppressed hunger for each other began to set off sparks until they reached flash point.

"That's one miracle we need to arrange for tomorrow," he murmured against her lips. "Since I can't take my hands off you, let's go back to the sitting room where I can try to think. I don't trust myself in the same space with you, least of all this one." After another scorching kiss, he let her go and walked into the sitting room.

She hurried after him. "Jean-Louis—"

He turned to her, but was afraid of giving in to the passion she'd aroused in him. "You heard what your father said, Françoise. Your parents considered you their sacred trust. I do too, and I want to do this right. You're going to have to help me."

After eyeing him for a soulful moment, she stood on tiptoe to kiss his cheek, then she sat down on the couch.

He drew a chair close to her. "I've dreamed of this day since I first looked into your lush green eyes that reminded me of the grass surrounding the château. Where do you want to be married, *mon coeur*?"

She smoothed a dark curl off her forehead. "With my parents gone, you're going to be my family and you belong to a big, loving one. If you could have your heart's desire, where would it take place?"

"Besides claiming you for my bride and selfishly wanting to live on the estate with you all our lives?" He drew in a deep breath. "I wish we could be married in the church here. Father Didier, a younger, modern-thinking priest, married Nic in a short ceremony the way my brother wanted it. My sisters told me about it. I envied him."

She laughed gently. "A short ceremony sounds perfect to me. So does living here with you. Please tell me we don't have to wait three weeks to allow for the banns."

"That won't be a problem." He couldn't stay away from her, and slid onto the couch, kissing her long and hard. "Your love has transformed me," he spoke at last. "I want a church wedding especially for you, but it isn't possible. Because of a long-standing hatred that a certain man on the estate has for our father, Nic had to arrange for his marriage to Anelise to be performed in the living room here. He would have married her in the church otherwise."

"How awful that one man could create that kind of enmity. I'm so sorry."

"We're all sorry about it. This man has sown seeds of discontent among some of the estate workers for years. While my father has been alive, not even my sisters' marriages could be performed in the church. Every wedding has taken place in the living room to avoid serious repercussions that the Causcelle family has already paid for in the past. I'll tell you about that later. Not tonight. I'm too happy."

She looked into his eyes. "I hope you realize I'd love to be married downstairs in front of your mother's painting. It would be an honor."

Emotion took over. "You're an angel, Françoise."

He kissed her again, needing to pour out his love for her. "But I'm thinking of another place. The weather is still perfect. It came to my mind while I was visiting you and your great-aunt. Let's go downstairs and I'll show you."

They left his suite and walked down the hall to the stairs, kissing several times before they reached the foyer. He drew her down another hallway that led to the rear entrance of the château. He flipped a light switch before they walked out on a large patio with wrought iron furniture. The outside lights illuminated a rose garden in full bloom.

"Oh, darling—" she gasped quietly. "This is like a dream. You can smell the heavenly scent of the roses."

"How would you like to be married out here with the family looking on? My mother started the original garden years ago. Papa kept it going after she died. You mentioned that your great-aunt loved roses. Do you think she'd like this setting for her precious Françoise? I know my father would."

He heard a cry before she hugged him until it hurt. "How did it happen that you came into my life? What did I ever do to be loved by you?"

"I'm still asking that same question about you. Since your great-aunt is your entire family now, I want her blessing. Her needs have to come first."

Françoise kissed his jaw. "Do you know she wept when I walked in her room and told her you'd gone? You won her over that day putting the puzzle together."

"I enjoyed it too. In fact, I've thought of nothing but you two ever since. There's an empty suite on the main floor across the hall from Papa's. We could fly her here, where she can convalesce in comfort indefinitely. Between you and Luca, she'd have all the medical help needed, plus the château staff."

Sobs shook her body while she clung to him. "You're so wonderful, you're unreal."

Emotion gripped him. "Don't get me started on you."

She lifted her head and covered his mouth with her own. "I wish there were another word I could say to let you know what you mean to me. I love you too much."

"I don't think there is such a thing as too much, not where my feelings for you are concerned. Let's go in the kitchen and grab a bite to eat while we plan. I'd like us to be married within a few days."

"Is that possible?"

"I don't see why not," he said as they went back inside the château. "We will be married in the eyes of God, which is most important to us, I think? The civil ceremony can follow later." He turned off the outside lights and led her to the kitchen. "The whole family except for your great-aunt lives on the estate, but we'll take care of her tomorrow."

He fixed them sandwiches and coffee. Her arrival had brought back his appetite. He was starving for food, for her, for the life they were going to have together.

They sat at the kitchen table. "Forgive me that we haven't even talked about your career yet."

She eyed him over the coffee cup. "I've been thinking about that too. When I drove into La Racineuse earlier today and stopped to eat, I passed the hospital where I tested the blood samples. Maybe they need an epidemiologist?"

He leaned toward her and kissed her cheek. "I'm way ahead of you. After we visit the priest in the morning, we'll fly in the family jet to Bourges to pick up your car. Once back at Bouzy, we'll get you moved out of your apartment. Nadine's going to be surprised when we take her from Silver Pines and drive her to Bourges. During the flight here, we'll make her as comfortable as possible."

"You think we can do all of that in one day?"

"Why not? Tomorrow night the three of us will sleep on the flight back here because I don't want to be separated from you ever again. Until the wedding you'll stay in your old suite."

She chuckled. "I was only here for one night."

"The room is yours until the wedding."

"Jean-Louis? No one in your family knows about us yet. This is going to come as a huge shock."

"My nephews would have spread the news of your arrival to everyone hours ago."

"I forgot about that. They were so cute."

"My gorgeous Vampira—I'll let you in on a little secret. The male members of our coven were expecting an announcement the night you came to take their blood."

"You can say that again," sounded another deep male voice. Both of them looked around to see Raoul, who'd come in the kitchen. Jean-Louis got up, recognizing a certain glint in his brother's eyes.

"You have the same goofy look on your face that Nic still wears around here." Raoul stared at Françoise. "Thank heaven you came when you did. None of us has known what to do with him. Papa was overjoyed after Theo and Honoré spread the news that you'd arrived."

Her gentle laugh filled the kitchen. "It's a good thing no one was around me before *I* flew here."

He grinned. "Welcome to the family, Dr. Valmy."

"Please call me Françoise!"

"*Entendu.* How soon is the wedding?" He poured himself a cup of coffee.

Jean-Louis put his hands on her shoulders. "As soon as Father Didier can do the honors. Hopefully in a few days. We'll be meeting with him in the morning."

Raoul nodded. "Another Causcelle non-church wedding." He eyed Françoise. "I presume he's told you why."

"Only some of it, *frérot*," Jean-Louis responded for her. She didn't need to hear about Dumotte. Not yet. He leaned down to kiss the side of her neck. "It's late and you must be exhausted. If you've finished eating, why don't you go up to your room? I'll run out to the car for your suitcase and bring it to you. Did you lock it?"

"No. I only had one thing on my mind when I drove up to the château. I couldn't believe you hadn't told me to go away and never come back."

"I can promise you one thing. That will never happen, not in all eternity," he whispered. "I'm still in a daze. It's a miracle I'm even functioning. That's all because of you, my love." After another kiss on the back of her neck, he walked over to Raoul. "Come with me. I need to tell you our plans."

Raoul smiled at her. "Good night, Françoise, and congratulations. My brother is a lucky man."

"Thank you, Raoul. He's my life! As for marrying into your marvelous family, I'm the lucky one. I never had brothers or sisters. Now I'll have both. Nothing could thrill me more. *Bonne nuit.*"

After they left the kitchen, Françoise cleared the table and did the few dishes. Eighteen hours ago, she couldn't have imagined standing here in the château kitchen planning her marriage to the most wonderful man on earth.

No sooner had she gone upstairs and entered the suite she'd slept in before when she heard a knock on the door. Her heart leaped. "Come in."

"I don't dare. I'm leaving the suitcase outside the door with your purse and phone. Call me in the morning when you're awake and we'll drive to the church. I can't get married soon enough."

"I love you, Jean-Louis. I hope I don't wake up to find this has all been a dream like my first one where you vanished."

"That couldn't happen, *mon tresor.* We took vows in your dream, remember?"

She ran to open the door, wanting one more kiss from him, but he'd already disappeared down the hall. Françoise brought the case and her purse inside and quickly got ready for bed.

By some miracle she did fall asleep, but she woke

up at seven the next morning so excited, she rushed to shower and wash her hair. Today she wanted to look perfect and chose to wear a light blue two-piece summer suit. The periwinkle earrings matched. After putting on lipstick, she slipped on high heels and felt ready.

As she reached for her phone, it rang. Jean-Louis! She clicked on. "Darling?"

"My prayer has been answered. You didn't run away from me."

She clutched her phone tighter. "I'm all ready to run away with you right this minute. Where are you?"

"In the foyer."

"I'm coming down."

Françoise grabbed her purse. She flew out the door and down the stairs. Jean-Louis caught her in his arms. "You're a dazzling sight." He kissed her so thoroughly, she lost her breath. "We'd better go or I'm going to take you back upstairs, *mon amour.*"

They left the château in one of the estate cars. He reached for her hand. "I'm taking you to my favorite café for a celebration breakfast first. They serve the specialty of this local region, *saucisse de Montbéliard* with sensational Montbéliard *crème* and eggs."

"With one exception at the *palais*, breakfast has been the only meal we've ever sat down to," she teased.

"It's my favorite meal of the day." He squeezed her hand.

"I'll have to remember that. Since meeting you, it has come to be mine too."

The charming, family-owned café owner treated Jean-Louis like the prince she believed him to be. They were shown to his regular table. While they waited for his favorite food, he pulled something from the breast pocket of the immaculate dove gray suit he wore. He was so incredibly handsome she couldn't help staring at him.

Françoise didn't realize what he'd done until he'd reached for her left hand. She looked down and let out a small cry as he put a diamond ring on her finger. Not just any diamond. It was pear-shaped and probably three carats in the most glorious plush green color she'd ever seen.

He rubbed her palm with his thumb. "Now you know how I felt when I first looked into your eyes above the mask."

She'd never seen anything like it except in museums. He'd paid a king's ransom for it. "Oh, Jean-Louis. How did you get it in such a short amount of time? Did you have it with you when you came to the rest home before I ruined everything?"

He winked at her. Something he'd never done before. "There have to be some perks to being a billionaire."

At that moment the waitress brought their order while she sat there dazed. After the woman walked away, Françoise reached for his hand across the small table. "I love it." Her voice trembled. "I love you beyond comprehension." Tears filled her eyes. "I'll cherish this forever."

"I plan to cherish you forever. Now we're ready to meet the priest."

He began eating his food with relish. She ate, but she kept watching the way the diamond sparkled with every movement her hand made. The beauty of it fascinated her all the way to the church, where they were shown into the priest's office. Jean-Louis introduced her to Father Didier.

"We're anxious to be married as soon as possible. Like Nic, whom you married recently, our ceremony will have to take place at the château. We've planned to say our vows on the patio. How soon could you perform the wedding? It would be at your convenience, whether morning, noon or evening."

Françoise adored her husband-to-be. He was so eager he hadn't given the priest time to talk or even ask questions.

A smile broke out on the priest's face. "You not only look like your brother, you're as excited as he was. I've never seen two men more anxious to become husbands." His gaze flicked to Françoise. "But after meeting you and Mademoiselle Lavigny, I have a perfect understanding. Here's my dilemma."

Jean-Louis gripped her hand tighter.

"I'm leaving for church business today and tomorrow. On the following day when I return, which could be late, the ceremony would have to take place in the evening. Shall we say seven?"

"We can't ask for more than that, Father."

He lifted a hand. "I know you want it short. Would you like to say your own vows? I'll just officiate."

Françoise had never seen her fiancé beam before. "The Church needs more priests like you, Father. We'd love it."

"How do you feel about that, Dr. Valmy?"

"Jean-Louis and I are in total accord on everything. You're so kind to arrange your schedule for us."

"It'll be my pleasure. I'm glad you came when you did. I'll be leaving in a few minutes."

"Then we won't take up any more of your time. We'll see you on Wednesday evening, Father." Jean-Louis reached for Françoise and they left the office. Before he helped her in the car, he pulled her in his arms and buried his face in her hair. "I don't know about you, but I'm considering going back to church again."

Her laughter got smothered when he covered her mouth with his own. There was a little boy inside this remarkable man she loved with unleashed intensity. The thought of giving birth to a son like him one day thrilled the very daylights out of her.

CHAPTER NINE

THE FLIGHT TO Bourges from Chalon Champforgeuil on the private jet only took an hour. The drive in Françoise's car to Bouzy took fifteen minutes longer, but pure, unadulterated joy filled Jean-Louis's being. While Françoise drove, he talked on the phone with the rest of his family to make final arrangements. His father sounded elated and spoke to her, welcoming her officially to the family.

She stopped at the apartment. While she talked with the landlady and took care of the rent and lease money owing, he carried the few belongings out to her car.

Now to go to the rest home. He could only hope that in time her great-aunt would be happy with this move. When they walked in her room a little while later, she looked up at both of them from the bed.

"Triplet." She pointed to him.

"Yes, Mame. Jean-Louis is now my soon-to-be husband." She walked over to kiss her and show her the ring.

"Ah." The older woman's breath caught.

Françoise reached for the puzzle on the overbed

table and tapped on the picture of the Causcelle Château. "We're going to live here, and we want you to live with us. Will you come?"

Jean-Louis could tell it took time for everything to register. He moved closer. "I love Françoise and want her to be happy. You're Françoise's family, and I love you too. We won't be happy if you don't come to live with us. Please say you will, Nadine, and you'll make me the happiest man on the planet." He tapped the château on the lid again. "We'll be getting married out by the rose garden, where you can see everything."

His heart thundered in his chest. This was the moment he'd been worried about. What if she didn't want to leave Silver Pines?

While he waited for a response, Nadine smiled and put her hand on his. Françoise stared at him in utter bliss. Nothing could prevent a happy marriage now. A new degree of joy seeped inside him. At that moment he remembered what she'd said to him in Mercy Hospital.

"So, you really do want to live! Wonderful! In that case you'll have to come for a phlebotomy every three months to keep levels normal. You'll need treatment throughout your life because there is no cure, but it should be a whole long life and a rich one."

By seven that evening, they'd eaten and boarded the jet for the flight to Chalon Champforgeuil. Earlier Jean-Louis had called ahead for a local ambu-car service that drove them to Bourges. Françoise left her car in the rest home parking area to be collected later.

They made her great-aunt comfortable for the flight.

Once in the air, he turned to Françoise. "Raoul will meet us at the airport and drive us to the château. He told me our sisters are getting the suite ready for Nadine. When we arrive, she can go straight to bed."

Françoise turned to him with her heart in her eyes. "You and your family are heaven-sent. I'll spend the rest of my life trying to repay you for everything."

"Just keep loving me. It's all I'll ever want."

"That's my wish too. Darling? Tonight I think I'd better spend the night with Nadine in her room."

"I was going to suggest it so she won't be nervous. Though she doesn't know it, she makes the perfect chaperone to keep me away from you."

A chuckle escaped. "That works both ways. Do you know what amazes me? She's managing so well despite her illness."

"She reminds me of Papa, who has rallied somewhat. You're the one who said happiness could bring on rejuvenation."

"I know one thing," Françoise commented. "Happiness radiated from her when she saw you walk in her room earlier. That means more to me than you'll ever know. She saw me baptized, and now she's going to see me married to the man in my dream. You're my one and only," her voice trembled. "If we do have a son one day, I want to name him Robert Martin Valmy Causcelle."

Jean-Louis loved the sound of that. "Maybe we'll have twins. I'd like the second one to be named Alain."

"And if another miracle happens and we have triplet sons, what do you want to name our third one?" she prodded him.

"Don't you know already?" he asked with a smile.

"I know what I'd like, but I want to hear *your* choice."

"I'll tell you on our wedding night."

She groaned. "That's two nights away—I love you so much it sounds like a lifetime."

"Don't I know it."

After the long wait, Wednesday evening arrived. Everyone had assembled out on the patio, where candles flickered in the perfumed night air.

Françoise had bought a knee-length wedding dress in town the day before. Nic's wonderful wife, Anelise, had gone with her. They'd both loved the vintage lace she'd found with a high neck secured at the back. The dress had long lacy sleeves and an A-line skirt that flared from the waist with a lace border at the hem. She'd felt it was a dress her mother and her birth mother would love too. After looking at several veils, she'd decided not to wear one.

Jean-Louis had sent her white roses to carry. He'd also sent a white rose corsage for Nadine to wear.

Feverish with excitement after doing her makeup, she slipped on new white satin high heels and left the room carrying her sheaf of flowers. Corinne's husband, Gaston, stood in the foyer filming her as she descended the staircase.

To her surprise, she found Louis waiting for her in his wheelchair. Though he had heart disease, he looked dapper in a navy dress suit with a white rose in his lapel. He smiled up at her. "I'm sorry your father isn't here. If you'll allow me, I'd consider it a privilege to escort you down the aisle."

Tears smarted her eyes. "I'd be honored."

With Luca pushing him, they started down the other hall to the rear of the château. "I never thought I'd live to see the day my Jean-Jean came home, let alone watch him marry a woman as angelic as my Delphine."

His words touched her to her soul. So did the revelation that he'd called his son *Jean-Jean.* "I love you, Louis." She squeezed his shoulder gently before they moved out to the patio. Among his sisters and their families, her great-aunt sat in her own wheelchair. Louis joined Corinne and her family. Father Didier stood waiting in his traditional wedding vestments.

Next to him stood her gorgeous Jean-Louis wearing a navy dress suit and white shirt like his father. He too wore a white rose in the lapel. She walked up to join her fiancé, whose eyes were like flame as they played over her. Brigitte, Corinne's daughter, took the roses from her.

Father Didier opened his arms wide. "Once again, we've all come together for a very sacred occasion. This time to join Jean-Louis Ronfleur Causcelle and Marie Françoise Valmy in holy matrimony. God intended for us to live in families and cherish each other. This evening I see a perfect example in front of me.

"The bride and groom have asked to say their own vows and exchange rings now. I'm honored to be here to officiate.

"Françoise? If you'll turn to Jean-Louis and tell him what's in your heart."

By now hers was so full, she could hardly breathe, let alone get the words out. She gazed at him. "Less than two months ago, I met you, Jean-Louis. You were a vet at the hospital where I was finishing my fellowship in Nice. You thought you were dying of an illness you'd contracted in Africa.

"Unbeknownst to you, I was going through the greatest trauma of my life. I'm convinced now we were supposed to meet by some divine plan because you were the answer to my every prayer. Not to mention that you're such an unbelievable specimen of the perfect man, you're the answer to every maiden's prayer."

Chuckles erupted from his family.

"Your kindness and love for others, your selfless generosity is so inspiring that I want you to know it's a privilege to be loved by you. Few women on this earth will ever know the joy I feel. I can't wait to have a family with you. As your wife, I vow to love and cherish you today and throughout all eternity. I want to give you this ring as a token of my love and fidelity."

Françoise reached for his hand and slipped the gold wedding band she'd bought yesterday on his ring finger. She knew it had surprised him when she heard his quick intake of breath.

Father Didier spoke next. "Jean-Louis, if you'll turn to Françoise and tell her what's in your heart."

She saw her beloved swallow hard.

"Less than two months ago I entered Mercy Hospital in Nice believing I was dying, and I wanted to die. I knew I'd been a failure as a human being to my family and feared it was too late for me to find redemption. I decided it was good I'd reached the end of my life.

"Then you came into my room, Françoise, and told me I wasn't going to die. You said I had a blood disorder, and you promised me I'd live a long rich life if I followed your instructions.

"Your mask hid your face, but not your eyes, which were green like the fields of paradise. I looked into those eyes and thought I'd been transported to heaven. After you helped put me on the path to health, you left for Paris. That's where we met again, but there was no mask this time. Believe me, the goddess Aphrodite has nothing on you."

More happy sounds came from the family.

"I vow to love and cherish you forever. I long to be your husband, to take care of you in sickness and in health. I want to have children with you. I thank God for you, Françoise." He reached for her left hand and slid a gold wedding band next to her engagement ring. Then he leaned over unexpectedly and kissed her hand. It was a gesture only he would think to do. She almost melted on the spot.

Father Didier smiled as he looked at the two of them. "May the Lord in his kindness strengthen the consent you have declared before the Church. May He graciously bring to fulfillment his blessings within you.

"By the authority vested in me, I now pronounce you husband and wife. What God has clearly joined together, let no man put asunder. In the name of the Father, the Son and the Holy Spirit. Amen."

In the next breath Jean-Louis swept her in his arms and gave her a husband's kiss. This was where she'd longed to be. It sent electricity through her body as she clung to him and forgot everything else.

While deep in Jean-Louis's embrace, she heard Father Didier say, "I don't think this groom needs to be told what to do next, do you?" More chuckles ensued from their audience. "If you'll notice, the first Causcelle son to be married got carried away just like Jean-Louis. I know they're both part of a set of triplets, but they're even more alike than I thought."

Laughter exploded, causing her husband to lift his head while she blushed. Father Didier cleared his throat. "Members of the Causcelle family, I have the honor to present Monsieur *et* Madame Causcelle."

Everyone clapped and gathered round to wish them happiness. Nic and Raoul gave them special hugs. Her new husband belonged to an exclusive triumvirate. Next came his father, who hugged him, followed by the rest of the family.

Luca wheeled her great-aunt over so Françoise could kiss her. Then Honoré and Theo walked up to their uncle. "You'll be working in the garage with us tomorrow, right?"

Jean-Louis grinned. "Afraid not. I'll see you two characters on Monday."

Brigitte stood behind them. "You guys—they'll be on their *honeymoon*!"

"Zut!" they both said at the same time and walked over to the buffet table to eat.

Françoise tried hard not to laugh, but she couldn't

help it. Jean-Louis grabbed her around the waist from behind. "Welcome to *our* family," he whispered against her ear. They *were* her family now. She loved them. "It's time we went upstairs, where our own private feast is waiting, Madame Causcelle. One day we'll take a honeymoon to some exotic place," Jean-Louis promised.

"I'm glad we're not going anywhere. The château feels like home to me already. It's a blessing that Nadine seems so happy. Did you see her and your father putting a puzzle together yesterday?"

"Luca knows what he's doing. Now it's our turn, *ma belle*."

When they reached the foyer, he caught her up in his arms and carried her effortlessly up the stairs and down the hall to his suite. "We'll have this wing to ourselves until we build our own home." He opened the door and closed it with his foot before carrying her through to the bedroom. She kicked off her high heels on the way.

"Since meeting you I've dreamed of keeping you prisoner in this room that became my childhood haven once I could sleep in a bed. But until I came back from Africa without hope, I had no idea the best part of my life was yet to happen," he cried, lowering her to the floor. "I can't believe you're my wife! I love you so much I'm in pain with it. Help me, darling."

"My dress fastens at the back of my neck."

She felt him reach around. "Whoever designed this piece of temptation made sure the groom went through agony first."

How she adored him! "I'm in my own agony waiting for my groom to figure it out." His impatience delighted her. She kissed his jaw. "I thought you were a mechanic."

"Maybe I'll just rip it off you."

"Ooh. I can see you haven't had practice on this sort of problem. Let the doctor do it." She reached behind her and undid the four hooks and eyes in an instant. Her dress slid down.

"Françoise—"

Sunlight filtered through the windows when Jean-Louis woke up. His beautiful dark-haired wife was draped across his chest, sound asleep. After the indescribable night of loving each other into oblivion, he wanted to know that rapture over and over again.

He raised up on one elbow to study the exquisite, giving woman he'd married. How was it possible he'd met his soul mate at the very darkest moment of his existence? When she'd spoken her vows to him last evening, she'd talked about a divine plan that had brought them together. That's what it had to be.

Unable to resist, he slid his fingers into her hair, needing to touch her. The thought of ever being apart from her killed him. He didn't even want to think about the pain his father must have gone through when he lost his wife. But he needed to stop dwelling on his fear of losing Françoise. He'd been given the most precious gift imaginable and would always relish this living, breathing miracle who was his wife.

All of a sudden, he felt her stir. She made a strangled sound.

He cradled the back of her neck. "Darling?"

She thrashed around, obviously still in a deep sleep. "I can't find you," she cried out. "Jean-Louis—where are you? Don't vanish on me. I'll die if you don't come back to me. Where have you gone?" By now she was virtually sobbing tears.

That dream she'd had before...

"Sweetheart! Wake up!" He pulled her into his arms and covered her wet face with kisses. "I'm here, my love."

Those heavenly green eyes slowly opened. She stared at him in disbelief. "You're here! Thank heaven, thank heaven." She threw her arms around his neck and clung to him for dear life.

Eventually the tears subsided and she looked at him. "We were in paradise, and then you disappeared like you did before."

"That was a dream, Françoise. When you told me about the first one you experienced in Nice, I had trouble believing you, but not anymore. Just know that before you go to sleep in my arms every night from now on, I'll be here when you wake up. I may not be a vampire, but we're bonded forever. You'll never be able to escape me."

"I don't want to escape. Not ever. Love me again." She kissed him as only she knew how, thrilling him to his very core. To think he had this to look forward to whether waking or sleeping all the days of their lives was beyond his comprehension.

Another hour of bringing immeasurable pleasure to each other, and she brushed her fingers across his jaw.

"You need a shave, my love, and I know we both need to eat. But before we budge from this bed where I've known rapture, I want to confide something to you."

His black eyes danced. "Are we pregnant?"

She chuckled. "Don't I wish."

He kissed the corner of her mouth. "Is it a secret?"

"No. It's something your father said on the way out to the patio last evening. The tender sweetness in his tone caught at my heart."

"Now I'm really intrigued."

"He said, 'I never thought I'd live to see the day my Jean-Jean came home, let alone watch him marry a woman as angelic as my Delphine.'" She sat up. "He called you Jean-Jean. For one moment I caught a glimpse of the father he'd been when you were his little boy. I'm so thankful you made it home in time for the two of you to pour out your love to each other again."

His eyes glistened with unshed tears. "I only wish he had enough time to see our children born."

"Well, that settles it. If we have triplets, one must be called Louis."

He crushed her in his arms. "Have I told you how much I love you? I've been thinking about the names if we have triplet girls. Our first will be Dionne in honor of the mother who raised the perfect daughter."

She kissed his chin. "We'll call the second one Delphine for the beautiful mother in that portrait downstairs."

His arms tightened. "And the third one we'll name Vivienne for the angel mother who gave you birth and made my world complete. A divine plan if there ever was one. Before we do anything else, I need to love you again, Françoise."

"If I had my way, we'd never leave this bed. Come here, my darling Jean-Louis."

* * * * *

CONSEQUENCE OF THEIR DUBAI NIGHT

NINA MILNE

MILLS & BOON

To Rosalind,
my wonderful, all-singing, all-dancing mother-in-law.

With love. xx

CHAPTER ONE

MAX SAT ON the rooftop bar of the five-star hotel and looked out at the extravagant vastness of the Dubai skyline. The sheer size and scope of the architecture, the buildings that loomed and spiked and curved towards the night sky in an opulent dazzle of light caught his breath and for a moment at least distracted him from his thoughts.

Thoughts that he had held at bay all day as he focused on his packed schedule of business meetings, his intent to open an office here significantly advanced. His streaming platform already had a growing audience in Dubai and after today he had a much better understanding of what to offer. Satisfaction rippled through him—today marked another step forward for his company, another step that was taking it inexorably to global success. A quote from a recent article ran through his mind.

InScreen, the entertainment business founded by the charismatic Max Durante, is one of the hottest companies in the world, smashing analysts' growth predictions this year.

But not even the knowledge that his ambitions were being realised could edge out the emotions brought about by the letter he'd received three days ago, the words etched in his mind, running on a background repeat loop.

Dear Max,
I am delighted to inform you that we believe we have made progress in the search for your mother and we believe she may well be living in Mumbai.
    As you appreciate, Mumbai is a large city but we will endeavour to continue in our search.

Not for the first time he wondered what he would actually do if the detective agency did find his mother, the woman who had left him in a cardboard box as a newborn baby. Sometimes he brooded at the cliché of it, wondered where she got the box from, what had been in it before she packaged him into it and left him outside a London fast food restaurant.

Had she ordered something specially so that the box would fit a newborn baby? Or perhaps irony of irony it had been a parcel containing gifts? Or maybe she'd simply scoured the rubbish or recycling bins. It was one of the many questions that he'd considered time and again through his childhood.

Along with the perennial question of why. Why had

she done it? Though deep down he knew why—his mother had been terrified he would be a chip off the old block. Bring her heartache and misery as his father had done before him.

Not that he had ever met his father either. But he knew about him. His uncle and aunt had turned up, un-expectedly, when Max was four, on the cusp of being adopted by the couple who had been fostering him. Even now he could recall the haze of confusion, punc-tured by the sharp, cold stab of understanding as his young self had realised what was happening. He could still remember the agonising sense of loss when he'd been taken from his foster parents, people who he had seen as parents, had been bonded to, had loved.

But love had counted for nothing—the long, cold arm of the law dictated that it was better for Max to go to 'real' family—blood had won out.

Which was ironic really.

Because his uncle, his father's older brother, be-lieved in blood all right. Believed that Max was tainted with bad blood, that his veins ran with the same con-tamination as his father's before him. Max's father, Tommy, had been a charming bastard of the first order. A womaniser, a gambler, a cheat and a criminal who had died in a prison brawl. Max was shown photo-graphs, the evidence all there that he looked uncannily like his father—perhaps his mother had seen that in those few hours she'd spent with him. Perhaps that's why nothing could change the mind of his uncle and aunt, their utter conviction of his inherent 'badness'.

He shook the thoughts away. There was nothing he

could do to change his genetic programming—he was stuck with the face that looked back at him in the mirror every morning, the constant reminder of his origins.

But just because he looked like his father didn't mean he had to be like him. He had to believe that. Had to believe that his uncle and aunt had been wrong—that he was worth something. Hell in cold, hard cash terms he had a net worth of billions, but everyone knows money doesn't equate to goodness. His aunt had told him that in their final letter to him, when he'd been on the cusp of success, still hoping to win their approval. But it wasn't to be. Soon after they had died in a car accident and any small chance of redemption in their eyes was gone.

But Max was still proud of what he had achieved.

Hopefully one day his mother would be too.

Perhaps she already knew. In the numerous interviews he did, he'd made no secret of his start in life, made it clear he was open to contact…but so far nada; his mother had chosen to remain unknown.

A movement caught his eye, a flash of colour and he turned his head. A woman had entered the rooftop bar, a woman who looked vaguely familiar though he had no idea why. He'd certainly never met her because he knew he'd remember that. It wasn't just her looks, though it was impossible not to notice the ripple of corn-blonde hair, that shone in a waterfall of waves past her shoulders; to not clock the dress, black with a sweetheart neckline and a pretty print pattern of leaves, cinched at the waist with a patent leather belt. The outfit completed with white high heels that added height to a woman already tall, the effect designed to showcase a figure that combined curves and slenderness.

But she—whoever she was—had more than looks combined with a designer dress—this woman had presence and he'd swear she knew damn well that every eye in the room, male and female, was on her. It was an entrance and one he applauded, though he had no intention of doing anything about it. For a fleeting instant her eyes rested on him and he looked away, hoped that the grand arrival hadn't been staged for his benefit. It wouldn't be the first time he'd been accosted by a wannabe actress or producer, director...

He returned his gaze to the skyline and yet it was harder than it should be to not look round to watch her. A moment later he heard the sound of a raised voice behind him, and now he did turn and saw a man approach his...no not his...*the* mystery woman as she walked towards a table. He saw her halt, saw that she'd been shocked, a jerky awkwardness invaded the exquisite grace of her movements. Then an attempt at a smile that couldn't belie the tension in her body, one that increased as a petite dark-haired woman rose from the table and came to join them.

Was it his imagination or did the woman swivel almost as though she was contemplating making a run for it? Again her gaze rested on his and this time it was too late for him to turn away. The dark-haired woman spoke and although he couldn't hear her actual words he could hear the shrill tone, saw how tightly she now gripped the man's arm. For a mad instant he considered rising and going to the rescue, stopped himself.

Mystery woman looked perfectly capable of rescuing herself and anyway who was to say she deserved saving? Resolutely he turned away once again.

But then a few seconds later he heard a voice, clear, melodious, well modulated. 'Would you mind if I join you? It would be most helpful to me and I promise it's only temporary.'

Stella Morrison put on her best smile as she asked the question, studied the man's expression as he raised his eyebrows, clearly considering his answer. Great! In truth she hadn't expected anything other than an instant agreement; in fact she'd anticipated enthusiasm.

In her experience most men were usually more than happy to be accosted by an attractive woman. Though she supposed a man like Max Durante might not be quite such a pushover as all that and yet…she'd seen his eyes rest on her for just a fraction too long as she'd walked in. Plus she'd known he'd watched her encounter with Lawrence and Juno, an unexpected meeting that still had her gut churning in sheer shock, as the past had waylaid her. But she could take pride in the fact none of that turmoil had shown on her face a few minutes before or now.

One of her many talents, along with an ability to read the room, to instinctively know who was who and what to say. But it seemed as though her usual instincts were skewed because she'd been sure she'd seen Max Durante make the smallest of movements earlier, as though he wanted to rise and come to her aid. But right now it looked as though she'd read this man wrong.

So she shrugged. 'Don't worry. Sorry to have bothered you.'

He emitted the smallest of sighs and then rose to his feet, moved round the table and pulled out a chair, with a somewhat theatrical flourish. 'I'd be delighted,' he said.

'Thank you.' She sat down, careful not to turn to look at her audience of two. 'I appreciate this and I'll keep it brief.' Summoning her best smile she added. 'Can I buy you a drink to say thank you?'

'Sure.'

A waiter materialised beside them and he looked up. 'I'll have a Macallan. On the rocks.'

'I'll have a Dance-off please.' Somehow the name suited the occasion; this was a dance-off situation, waltzing round Lawrence and Juno, about to embark on some sort of elaborate routine with the man sitting opposite her, studying her with a hint of wariness in his brown eyes. Though what he had to be wary of God only knew.

She returned the look, took her time as she assimilated his features, saw that in person Max Durante was even more compelling than he was on screen or in photographs. Dark, dark hair, tamed into a businesslike cut; eyes the colour of expensive chocolate surveyed her with a coolness she wasn't used to; chiselled features and a jaw that spoke of determination. His whole stance relaxed and yet she had the feeling his reactions were honed, that he was ready to face whatever the world threw at him. A body that must be partly due to time spent in the gym, the musculature defined without being overtly obvious, his body emanated a sense of power and entirely against her will she felt a frisson of pure desire run through her.

'So what is it you want from me?' he asked, his voice even, the words infused with an elaborate politeness.

Your body. She bit the words back, appalled at how nearly they had fallen from her lips.

Whoa, Stella. Get a grip.

This was not the time or the place—not when she was about to embark on a relationship. More than a relationship. A marriage. *If* all went to plan. And it would, because she was good at planning. And flirting with this man, any man, was not part of that plan. So 'your body' was not an option as an answer.

Instead, 'I want exactly what you've given me,' she replied. 'The chance to sit here long enough to make it look as though we agreed to meet for a drink.'

As if on cue their drinks arrived and she took a sip of her cocktail, welcomed the tang of tequila and lemon juice, diluted by tonic water and sweetened by the hibiscus foam. Saw the scepticism in his eyes and frowned. 'What do you think I want?'

A shrug, and her gaze watched the movement of his broad shoulders and tried not to be distracted. 'An opportunity to act? A promise of a meeting with a director? An invitation to some star-studded award.'

Huh. The frisson of awareness took a welcome morph into anger. 'So you think I'm stalking you? That I planned this.'

'Possibly. Or you may have seen an opportunity and

you're taking it. Nothing wrong with that. I admire opportunism, but as a rule I don't reward it.'

'Then why did you agree to let me sit down and buy you a drink?' she flashed back. 'For the pleasure of saying no?'

'I agreed on the off chance you're telling the truth. You looked genuinely shocked to see the man who accosted you. Though of course you could be an excellent actress.'

So he had been watching her, and was observant enough to have spotted something she thought she'd successfully hidden. 'I wasn't acting. Or if I was I was trying to look as though I *wasn't* shocked. And for the record I am not interested in acting, or meeting a director and I am quite capable of scoring an invitation to a glamorous event without your help, thank you very much.'

There was a pause and then to her surprise he smiled. A real smile. Which warmed up his brown eyes and caused her gaze to linger on the firm line of his mouth. 'Glad to hear it,' he said. 'So all you need from me is table space and to look as though this is a what? A date?'

A date. The idea sent a strange tremor running through her even as she told herself that he wasn't suggesting a real date. And if he did she would refuse. Because she was strictly unavailable. On the verge of negotiating a marriage of convenience with Rob, Viscount Rochester, heir to the Earldom of Darrow. A marriage that would secure the future of her home; because once she had a son her ancestral home would be safe. Her son would be able to inherit the title and one day be Lord Salvington. Failing that Salvington would be lost, inherited instead by some distant male relative who had no interest in it.

And she wouldn't let that happen. Neither for herself or for her sister. At the thought of Adriana guilt twanged inside her, strengthened her determination. Their father had never forgiven his younger daughter for not being the son he craved, the son he needed to be heir to Salvington. And so he treated her like dirt, put her down at any opportunity whilst he treated Stella like a princess. Stella had hated it, but she'd done nothing about it. Because any attempt to be kind to Adriana simply triggered her father's anger, an anger he took out on Adriana and their mother.

So Stella had allowed herself to be favoured, hell she'd reaped all the rewards with a vengeance, the generous allowance, the place in society, the parties, the balls. But through it all she lived with the constant drip feed of guilt, only alleviated by her determination to make it up to Adriana.

So the least she could do for her sister was save the home she loved. Plus it was hardly a sacrifice—Stella was fully on board with the idea of a marriage of convenience, had honed her persona to ensure she was perfect countess material.

But that was the future. At this point she and Rob hadn't even started discussions; had only agreed in principle that the idea was one they wanted to pursue when he returned from the States in two weeks' time.

So technically she owed him nothing; but a real date was not an option, would be a pointless exercise.

But the idea of a fake date held a definite appeal. Because it was exactly what Lawrence and Juno needed to see. And...prompted an inner voice...this was her last chance to sit and maybe share some banter, flirt a little, enjoy the company of a gorgeous man.

'If you don't mind, that would be perfect.'

He raised his eyebrows. 'I'll think about it, but only if you explain why you need a fake date.'

Stella focused on keeping her expression neutral 'It's complicated.' Though in truth it was a lot worse than complicated and guilt surged through her very veins, all ideas of flirting legged it over the horizon as her mind reverted to years before, led her down a shadowed memory lane. 'Lawrence, the man I was speaking with, is an ex-boyfriend of mine.'

Lawrence Tenant had been part of a wild crowd, exactly the sort of boyfriend eighteen-year-old Stella had been looking for. All she'd wanted back then was to rebel, show her father how deeply angry she was with him. Because he had betrayed her, betrayed them all, by embarking on an affair in a deliberate effort to get another woman pregnant, in a bid to get a son. If successful her father would have abandoned them without hesitation.

So she'd rebelled, decided to hit the headlines in her own right. And Lawrence had been the perfect accessory—she'd reeled him in as she knew, oh, so well, how to do. A disastrous decision that kick-started a series of even worse choices until a denouement that had ended in near tragedy. All her fault.

But she hadn't seen Lawrence for years until tonight. And when Lawrence had risen and greeted her, she, supercool Stella Morrison, had panicked. Spooked by the wave of guilt and shame, spooked too by the shock in Lawrence's eyes. And so she'd come up with her plan, said she had to rush as she was meeting Max Durante for a drink.

Now to convince Max Durante of the same. 'It was a complicated break-up,' she said. 'And Lawrence is now happily married to the woman he is here with and...'

'His wife still sees you as a threat.'

'Yes.' Stella had heard a few years ago that Lawrence had married Juno, another girl in their group, and she'd been pleased, hoped it drew a line under the horror of the past. But today she'd seen fear, had instinctively understood that Juno was scared that seeing Stella would trigger Lawrence in some way. 'Which I'm not. But I wanted to show them that, wanted to avoid a scene.' Most of all she didn't want anyone to get hurt. 'So I said that I was here to meet you for a drink.' The words had fallen from her lips without a thought.

And she'd been sure it would work. Because she'd sensed Max's interest, and let's face it, whilst he'd been checking her out she'd been returning the favour. She'd seen him the moment she'd stepped onto the rooftop bar, sitting silhouetted in the expert lighting and something had caught at her.

'So what do you think?'

CHAPTER TWO

STELLA TRIED NOT to hold her breath as she waited for his answer; he gave a quick glance behind her, managing to make it look as though he were looking for the waiter. 'Can you see them?' she asked.

'Yes. The woman is holding the man's hand and is talking. He looks a bit agitated.' He drummed his fingers on the table and then nodded. 'OK. Let's do it.' He sipped his drink. 'If we're on a date I'd better know your name,' he said.

'Stella. Stella Morrison.'

His brown eyes narrowed slightly and she could see him search his memory banks. 'Got you. High society. Aristocrat. Daughter of Lord Salvington. Few years ago you were in the papers a bit.'

'I didn't have you down as someone who follows the gossip columns.'

'Then you'd be wrong. I follow all news and trends as much as I can—it helps me work out the next best thing for InScreen. Plus I have an excellent memory. So I also know you haven't been snapped much recently apart from the usual, X attended the X ball blah blah.'

'I went through a bit of a phase a few years ago.'

A phase that had come to an end after the Lawrence fiasco. That particular scandal hadn't hit the papers, had been relegated to a few short paragraphs with her name kept out of it. In part, she knew, because her father had pulled some strings, but also because a far more newsworthy royal scandal had fortuitously struck. And Stella had been so guilt-stricken, so horrified by the consequences of her actions that she'd pulled back, returned to the 'perfect Stella persona'.

'Anyway,' she said. 'That's my name and obviously I already know yours.'

'So how did we meet to arrange this date?' he asked.

'Hmm. Let's see. Are you in Dubai on business or pleasure?'

'Business. What about you?'

'Pleasure.'

He looked around. 'On your own?' he asked and now his voice drew out the words.

'Nope.'

'You've come with your invisible friends?' he asked, deadpan and surprised a laugh out of her.

'No. They are real friends, but due to a flight cancellation they won't get here till tomorrow. So today I'm flying solo. Or I was anyway.'

'Well perhaps we bumped into each other at the airport and got a taxi here together and agreed to meet for a drink.'

'I think that's a bit dull,' she declared. 'If we're going to have a fake date I think we should give it some pizzazz.'

'OK. Go for it. How did we meet?'

'How about I saw you at your business lunch, waiting for whoever you were meeting.' She narrowed her eyes, pictured the scene. 'I'm sitting at the bar, sipping a...champagne cocktail and our eyes meet across the room and I decide to do something I'd never done before. I get a glass of champagne sent across to you...no not champagne a Hey Sugar cocktail or a passion fruit martini and a note with my phone number on it. You lift your glass in a toast and text me immediately and we end up arranging to meet for a drink here. What do you think?'

For a moment she could almost believe that was how it had played out and then he shook his head. 'Definitely wins in the pizzazz department, but it doesn't hold up.'

'Why not?'

'For a start it's stretching coincidence that we are both staying in the same hotel and ended up in the same restaurant for lunch.'

She waved a hand. 'Fate—it was fate not coincidence.'

'Plus I wouldn't have texted you.'

Stella blinked; this was a novelty she conceded. She was so used to men falling in with what she wanted, so used to being sure that rejection was not an option. 'Ouch.'

'Don't take it personally,' he said cheerfully. 'I wouldn't have texted any woman. I would have assumed you had an ulterior motive.'

'Fine. I was after a bit of pizzazz not realism. This

is an imaginary scenario remember? So let's *imagine* that I sent across a Between the Sheets cocktail with a signed affidavit saying all I was after was your body and nothing else.' *Huh?* That was not what she had meant to say at all, and from the amused glint in his eye he knew it.

'OK. I like it. Impressive knowledge of cocktails and direct and to the point. Strong on pizzazz, but perhaps slightly lacking in the romance department.'

'I felt your somewhat pedantic approach meant romance isn't your thing.' Stella suppressed an inward sigh—so much for sophisticated banter. Calling an uber-successful, gorgeous man like Max Durante pedantic? Really?

'Romance may not be my forte, but let's say I have other strengths and talents I can bring to the…table. Or—' and now he wiggled his eyebrows '—any other item of furniture you care to imagine.'

His words surprised another laugh from her, but also caused heat to touch her cheeks as a sudden vivid image of what those talents might be rushed into her mind. And when she met his gaze she saw that amusement had faded from his expression, instead his gaze had darkened and awareness suddenly shimmered in the air. Forcing herself to blink and look away she picked her drink up, saw that her fingers were trembling as she took another sip. Realised too that her brain had fuzzed and for once she was struggling to find the right thing to say.

'A table works for me.' She replayed her own words and bit back a groan. That was not what she meant to say at all. 'For another drink,' she added desperately, knew she was making little sense.

'Or...perhaps we should have dinner?' he suggested. 'Use the table that way.' He raised a hand. 'And I promise not to mention the word *table* again.'

The glint of amusement was back in his brown eyes now, accompanied by a slight upturn of his lips. Once again her gaze settled on the firm line of his mouth, once again her thought processes scrambled. 'Dinner?' she said.

'Yup. The meal you eat in the evening?' The teasing note shivered over her skin. Time to pull herself together.

'I know what dinner is,' she said tartly. 'I'm just not sure it's a good idea.'

'Why not?' he asked bluntly. 'We're both here alone, we both need to eat, and this is meant to be a date.'

Oh, Lord. Guilt jabbed at her; she'd been so distracted by Max that she'd actually forgotten about Lawrence and Juno. What sort of person did that make her? But dinner? 'I...' *I'm very attracted to you and am worried I may succumb to temptation and proposition you*, whilst being true didn't feel like the right thing to say. 'I'm very nearly in a serious relationship,' she said instead. And she didn't want to send the wrong message—wasn't sure what message she wanted to send at all.

An odd expression crossed his face. 'I'm intrigued. Because coincidentally so am I.'

Now she raised her eyebrows. 'I thought you didn't believe in coincidence.'

He tipped his palms up in acknowledgement of defeat. 'Then perhaps it's fate.' He leant back in his chair. 'A sign. So how about we have dinner, no hidden agenda. Then we go our separate ways to our nearly serious relationships. That way your ex and his wife will also think our supposed date is going well. And I'm hungry.'

The prosaic words decided her. 'In that case dinner sounds good. Apparently the menu is to die for.'

Max studied the menu, made a decision and glanced across at Stella who was still looking down at the choices. What the hell was he playing at? OK he believed Stella's story about the ex-boyfriend, though he suspected there was more to it than she was admitting. But that was none of his business.

There had been no need to prolong this fake date—yet he had.

Why? Because…because he was enjoying himself—Stella intrigued him and then of course there was the attraction—no point in denial, the attraction so strong he was surprised their table wasn't surrounded by sparks.

But it was an attraction he had no intention of acting on; if she was with someone else then she was off-limits. No way would he try and persuade a woman to be unfaithful and no way would he step on someone else's turf. He would not follow in even one of his father's footsteps and apparently Tommy Durante had been a womaniser extraordinaire. But Stella hadn't said she was in a relationship, she'd said she was 'nearly' in one. A mirror of his own situation? In which case the moral high ground took on a different hue.

His thoughts went to Dora. Dora Fitzgerald, prospective heiress, a woman who had proposed marriage to him—a marriage on paper only...a marriage made purely for business reasons. A simple deal. She needed to be married to inherit the family business. He wanted to buy the family business. She wanted to sell the family business. The answer was obvious. A no-brainer surely. Dora's words. Yet he wasn't sure and so they were both thinking about it, in pre-negotiation stages. At this stage in proceedings he and Dora were free agents.

The waiter arrived with place settings, cutlery and a complimentary platter of food.

'Are you ready to order?' he enquired.

Stella smiled up at him. 'Could we have a few more minutes please?'

Max raised his eyebrows. 'You've read it at least three times,' he observed.

'Yup.' Stella smiled at him. 'This is an amazing menu. I love Japanese food and this isn't a real date.'

'Why does that matter?'

'Well, if it was a real date I might worry that you would get bored whilst I took ages to choose. Or I might think it's better not to order something messy. Or anything that might get stuck in my teeth. Especially if someone might catch it on camera.'

Max blinked. 'For real? You would think about all those things.'

'Of course. I'd be mortified if I got caught on camera with spinach in my teeth. Or got snapped with my date looking bored. So this is my last chance to take my time and order whatever I want.'

He opened his mouth and closed it again as she returned her attention to the menu, her head tipped to one side, a small frown on her face as she muttered under her breath.

The waiter returned and Stella smiled up at him. 'Thank you. I think I'm ready now. Please can I have the *nasu dengaku*, the *kitsune udon*, *the maguro* avocado *namaharumaki* salad, the *hirame* sushi and the spider roll and the *ika* butter *yaki*. Oh, and a glass of the sauvignon blanc, please.'

'I'll have the chef's selection of sushi and a glass of sauvignon blanc as well.'

Once the waiter was gone Stella stared at him. 'Did you even read the menu?'

'I skim read it, but I know I like sushi and I am sure the chef knows what he or she is doing.' He smiled at her. 'Oh, and I didn't want you to be bored whilst I chose.'

'Ha Ha!'

'But seriously if this was a real date you would have ordered differently?'

'Sure. I'd have been worried about the noodles falling off my fork, or the sauce dripping on my dress or... there are a lot of things to think about. Especially if I have journalists set up watching me.'

'So you want to be snapped?' he asked.

'Not normally, but if I am going to be I'd rather be

in control of it and my next dates, well yes I plan for them to be in the public domain.'

'So this is your "nearly a relationship"?'

'Yes.'

'But it's not a relationship yet?'

'No.'

'But you don't want to tell me any more about it?'

'Would you tell me about yours?'

'I don't know,' he said honestly. 'It's confidential.'

She shrugged. 'So is mine. So we'd have to work on an "I'll show you mine if you show me yours" basis.' There was an infinitesimal pause and as their gazes met he saw her pupils darken, knew she was regretting the choice of words. 'That way we'd both have a hold over each other,' she finished smoothly.

'So much for trust,' he said.

'We'd be fools to trust each other. We've only just met.'

'Yet we're considering confiding in each other.'

'At minimal risk.' They paused as the waiter returned.

The risk would be minimal, but why take the risk at all? This business deal was massively important to him. Why take any chance of jeopardising it? Because dammit sometimes life was worth a little risk and he *wanted* to know Stella's story. Part curiosity, part welcome distraction from his own thoughts, and the knowledge that soon his mother might be found. Part—if Stella was a free agent then it changed the dynamics of their 'date' opened up a possibility of allowing the haze of attraction to gain a foothold.

And so, 'Deal,' he said and made to hold a hand out to shake on the deal, realised that that was hardly a 'date-like' thing to do and turned the gesture into something else. Covered her hand in his own. And felt it jump under his at the touch; her eyes shot to his face and he saw shock and surprise in the blue depths. Knew the same emotions were mirrored in his own eyes— because the touch had triggered something, a desire, a need to explore the attraction further, and had created a shimmer of awareness.

Whoa. The sheer intensity of his...their reaction shocked him and perhaps she thought the same as she gently pulled her hand away and then looked down at it, her blue eyes wide and now full of sheer desire. Before they both heralded the arrival of the waiter with relief.

Five minutes later Stella surveyed her side of the table. 'Hmm, perhaps I overordered a bit. You may need to help me out a little.'

'OK. I'll admit I was intrigued by the spider roll.'

'Crab and avocado rolled in seaweed. Then this—' she pointed, as she explained '—is the *nasu dengaku*, which is deep-fried aubergine with miso and sesame seeds, and the salad is rice paper roll with raw tuna and avocado and then there are the noodles—*kitsune udon* in a hot soup with deep-fried bean curd.' Her smile was broad with delight. 'We can slurp together.' She raised her glass. 'To fake dates,' she said softly.

He clinked his glass against hers. 'To this fake date.'

For a while they focused on eating and then, 'Right. Who goes first?' he asked.

'How about we toss for it?'

'The old-fashioned way? I'm in. Provided you have a coin.'

'I do.' She reached down into her bag and took out a small purse and tugged out a coin. 'Heads or tails.'

'Tails.'

She spun the coin up into the air and they both watched its descent into the palm of her hand. She flipped it onto the back of her hand. 'Tails it is. You win.'

'Then you go first,' he said.

She thought and then, 'I'll try to keep the background brief. My family live on the Salvington Estate. It has been in the Morrison family for generations, passed from son to son. However, my parents had two daughters, myself and my younger sister, Adriana. So no son. Which means the current heir is a distant relative who has no interest in the estate and would sell it off to the highest bidder. Unless I have a son, whilst my father is still alive. So the idea has always been that I would make a "grand alliance" and save the estate and that in a nutshell is exactly what I am planning to do. Marry a fellow aristocrat. Have an heir. I'll mix in high society, I'll have money, status; and provided I have a son I'll save Salvington.'

'Is this aristocrat someone you know?'

'Yes. Well, I mean I don't really know him, but when we were younger we went to the same parties and he is a decent sort of bloke.' Max eyed her for a moment.

'I may not be the most romantic of men but I'm not sure "decent sort of bloke" is how I'd want my bride to describe me.'

Stella frowned. 'I don't think he'd mind. We both know this is a marriage of convenience. He is marrying because he needs an heir, and he wants the right sort of wife, who will be a good countess. I will be.'

He could hear the determination in her voice. 'You must love your family estate very much.' For a moment he tried to imagine what it would feel like to know your parents and all the generations before them, to be so rooted in your family history, to have a family tree, a place that was truly home. Rather than a cardboard box.

As he studied her face he saw a shadow cross her eyes and her voice seemed strangely flat as she said, 'Yes I do.' She nodded as if to emphasise the point. For herself or him he wondered. 'I love my home very much. But it is hardly a sacrifice on my part. I'll have money, status, position, an amazing home...and life-long security.'

'But what about love?'

'Not interested.' Her voice was absolute and he wondered at the certainty. Decided not to question it; after all he didn't believe in love either. Or at least not for himself.

But... Max hesitated; knew this was nothing to do with him, yet... 'Well, what about attraction? I mean it's great that you think you'll like this guy, but you need attraction, a spark.'

Her blue eyes met his straight on and then she shrugged. 'He's a good-looking man, and I've been told that I'm a beautiful woman—I'm sure we'll manage.'

Max stared at her. 'It's not about being generically attractive. It doesn't work like that.'

'Of course it does.' She cast him a quizzical look. 'Are you saying you think he'll have difficulties managing?'

Max closed his eyes. 'No. I am quite sure he will understand the procedure and "manage" but surely you want more than just "managing".'

'Of course I do. But I am confident we'll work it out.'

An irrational surge of...what...jealousy, anger, frustration rippled through him. Along with sheer disbelief. How could she sit here with all the sparks leaping about between them and think it was OK to settle for managing.

'Really?' he rasped.

'Really. Plus attraction isn't the be all and end all is it?'

'No, but it's pretty important when you are proposing to spend your life with someone. When you last saw this guy was there even a flicker of attraction?'

'Well, no...but it was at least four years ago.'

'What happens if there still isn't a flicker.'

'We'll ignite one. How hard can it be?'

'I don't know. I've never tried to force an attraction that doesn't exist.'

'We'll work it out.'

'How? By rubbing two damp sticks together and hoping?'

'If need be.' Her eyes narrowed. 'I said we will work it out. Anyway I may set eyes on him and it will be instant lust. That can happen.'

His eyes lingered on her lips, dropped down to her

hand, the one he'd covered scant minutes before. 'I know,' he said and she flushed.

'*Anyway*.' And there was a hint of gritted teeth about the word. 'That's my story. Your turn. I presume there are sparks galore in your nearly relationship?'

'No.'

She raised her eyebrows. 'So how does that work? I thought you said attraction was an important factor in relationships.'

'Usually it is critical to my relationships, but this is different. This time I'm contemplating marriage.' The very word caused unease to ripple through him, even as he hurried to explain. 'A temporary marriage, for business reasons only. My prospective bride needs a husband in order to gain her inheritance. Her inheritance includes ownership of a business I want to buy. So the marriage is strictly one of convenience, but we need to look the part and we need to remain married for two years. So it is not a lifetime commitment.'

She studied him. 'Yet you're clearly not convinced it's a good idea.' She gave a sudden small gurgle of laughter. 'You look like a man condemned. So why do it? Your business is already massively successful.'

'This deal would make it even more so.' Which was why doubts were redundant. Yet the idea of entanglement made him edgy, worried that even a marriage in name only would remove some of his precious autonomy.

'Then what's the problem? Two years isn't that long. And if the marriage is a paper one you won't be committed to anything.'

'Thank God.' Because he didn't want to be responsible for someone else's happiness. Because he wouldn't risk failure, a failure he knew would come. He wasn't relationship material, wouldn't risk being rejected, or worse rejecting someone; he knew how rejection felt; his mother had rejected him on sight, his foster carers had been forced to reject him, his uncle and aunt had rejected him with unassailable consistency. He'd had enough rejection to last a lifetime and he certainly wouldn't court any more.

'Then if commitment isn't your thing, which it clearly isn't, you have to work out if the business advantage is worth fake commitment.'

Max considered that. 'I suppose the problem is that even a fake commitment involves some real commitment, spending time together, making it look real, fidelity in the sense we wouldn't publicly humiliate the other. That is doable for two years, but you're planning to do that for your whole life.'

'No, I'm not,' she said. 'My commitment is real. I am planning on making a real commitment to a real marriage. And I plan on being happy.'

He couldn't hold back the snort of derision. Perhaps he was out of line, but somehow this conversation had got personal and the idea that Stella was about to give up on passion, the idea of Stella with a man who sounded duller than dishwater whatever his title and position, felt wrong.

'I take it you disagree.' And now her voice held icicles.

'Yup. A lifetime without a spark sounds...flat, dull,

boring. However decent this man of yours is it can't compensate for passion, desire, the way a look can spark a shiver to run through your whole body.'

He couldn't help it now, wanted her to acknowledge that at least he had a point and so he looked at her, allowed how he felt to show in his eyes, let the desire, the passion show and saw the answer in her expression, the flush that heated her cheeks, the parting of her lips—and how he wanted to kiss her. The temptation nigh on overwhelming. 'Like that,' he said.

She blinked, shook her head and turned to look out at the Dubai skyline. 'But where does "that" get me?'

'Where do you want it to get you?' he asked.

The question was so loaded Stella could almost feel the weight of it. Loaded with promise, and possibilities. Her brain fuzzed with a sense of awareness, her whole body still shivering from 'that' look. Her brain told her she should go, before she did something foolish and yet her body relaxed back onto the seat and she saw his eyes follow the movement, dark eyes holding a seriousness and a real question.

One she didn't have an answer to. When she'd sat at his table she'd thought she was in control; had sensed his interest in her and used that interest to get her what she needed. But two hours later and she no longer felt in charge; worse she didn't even care.

Because somehow their conversation had taken her to places she hadn't expected and when he'd spoken of a life without passion, a near bleak sense of regret had touched her. The regret not strong enough to turn

her from her path but strong enough to urge her to…
to what?

'What are the choices?' she asked softly.

'We drink our drinks, say goodbye and go our separate ways or we take this further. Provided I'm reading this right, provided you are feeling what I'm feeling.'

'Depends what you're feeling,' she said, in an attempt at lightness.

'Desire. Attraction. Need. An overwhelming temptation to lean over and kiss you.' He smiled and desire rippled through her at the molten heat in his voice. 'To play another version of "I'll show you yours if you show me mine".'

Now desire interlaced with warmth as she gave a small chuckle, then met his gaze full on. 'If we play that game this time you can go first.'

'It's your choice whether we play or whether we don't.'

She eyed him. 'I'm not changing my mind about my marriage plans.'

'That's your choice. I'm offering one magical night before we both go down our chosen paths. Whatever they may be.'

Magical—it felt exactly that, as if a spell had been cast, had preordained everything that had led to this moment. This choice. Her choice.

'Would it be magical?' she asked.

'Yes.' There was no doubt in his voice. 'I promise and I'm a man of my word.'

Stella looked out at the vast illuminations, the jut and curve of a landscape that had been built at such speed, from a desert to an urban spread, a monument to wealth and glamour, a hub of power and tourism, a place where she had chosen to come to mark one last weekend before she embarked on a journey that would last a lifetime.

There was that insidious sense of bleakness again and she shook it away. She wanted to marry Rob, she did. It was the right thing to do and the right life path, the right road for her to take. But here and now she wasn't yet on that road and it seemed to her that fate was giving her a chance to experience passion and she'd be a fool to turn it down. She would carry regret with her on the road and she didn't want that. Because right here and now she wanted the man sitting opposite her, wanted him with a yearn that almost scared her.

Met his gaze and saw his pupils darken to molten brown, knew on some visceral level that he wanted her as much as she wanted him and a shiver trembled through her tummy, a twist of desire so raw and pure and elemental that she gasped. Knew she couldn't walk away from 'that'.

She gave a small, shaky laugh. 'Your room or mine?'

CHAPTER THREE

'*YOUR ROOM OR MINE.*' The words echoed in her ears. Words that confirmed a decision she knew to be right. Yet she hesitated as it occurred to her that she didn't know this man, that desire could be leading her to danger. 'And I'm going to text a friend…telling her I'm on a date and I'll check in.'

He gestured with one hand. 'I have no problem with that and if there's anything else you want to do or want me to do to feel safe that's good with me.'

Her fingers trembled as she texted, sent the text, waited for Leila's quick reply.

Intrigued. Take care. Don't do anything I wouldn't do. Leaves you lot of leeway. LOL. Check in. I'll wait up.

Then, 'Let's go.'

In one lithe movement he rose to his feet, moved round and pulled her chair out, the old-fashioned courtesy caught her off guard even as she caught her breath. The sheer proximity of him dizzied her and she forced herself to look casual, to look as though they were parting to go to their separate rooms. Forced herself to keep her walk slow and poised, even turned to see if Lawrence and Juno were still there, but they had already left and she hadn't even noticed.

They turned their backs on the skyline and headed to the door that led inside the plush hotel. The walk seemed interminable. Now that the decision was made every second where she wasn't exploring this attraction, this simmer of awareness seemed a waste. One night suddenly seemed infinitely short as anticipation swelled inside her, heightened with each decorous step. Then finally they were outside her room, in the thankfully otherwise deserted corridor.

Fingers trembling, she negotiated the lock and pushed the door open, somehow amazed that her room looked the same as when she left it, when she felt so changed. The king-sized bed, covered with the cool white duvet, the furnishings sleek and modern, a mixture of sand colours with lavender overtones. The massive glass windows that showcased the Dubai skyline, the twinkle of hundreds of thousands of lights that illuminated the nightlife of so many different people. Her open suitcase in the corner, her make-up on the dressing table.

It seemed surreal that when she'd dressed just hours earlier, applied lip gloss, brushed her hair she had had no idea the evening would end like this. With this gorgeous, infinitely desirable man who had exerted such a power over her so quickly.

'Stella?' There was a hint of a question in his voice and she knew he was giving her a chance to back out.

Or perhaps he was having doubts. 'Max?' she replied, in the exact same tone.

This pulled a smile from him, a smile that seemed to warm her this time with a sense of reassurance that somehow intensified the desire, made her feel a sense of joy.

'Any doubts?' he asked, 'We can just sit on the balcony and have a cup of tea if you prefer.'

Now she smiled, a smile that turned into a gurgle of laughter. 'I thought you promised me magic?' she said.

'You've never tasted my tea,' he dead-panned back without missing a beat and now her laughter turned full-blown and somehow with that any awkwardness, any vestige of doubt disappeared and as the laughter subsided they closed the gap between them and she looked up at him.

'Maybe later,' she said. And then in what seemed like one fluid movement, where she couldn't tell who moved first she was in his arms and he was kissing her and she was kissing him. His lips evoked an intensity of pleasure so deep the need for more was almost painful. She could taste coffee and the sweetness of wine, felt his fingers tangle in her hair and he gasped as she pressed against him, wanting, needing more. He deepened the kiss and she slid her hand under his shirt, felt his reaction, the shudder of pleasure as she ran her fingers over the glorious muscular sculpting of his back.

As the kiss continued, and desire flared and sparked they were manoeuvring their bodies towards the bed. Once there, barely breaking apart, they tumbled backwards, hands greedily exploring, touching, feeling... every sensation pulsed and roared, every bit of her lost in this glorious whirl of passion. And so second after magical second, minutes, hours passed until finally satisfied they fell asleep in the early hours of the morning.

Eventually Stella awoke, opened her eyes and knew she was alone in the bed, felt an instant sense of bereft. Opened her eyes and saw that light infiltrated the room, highlighted the scattered trail of her clothes. And then she realised she wasn't alone, Max stood by the window, fully dressed and somehow that made her clothes look tawdry.

Now what? It seemed hypocritical to be embarrassed by her nakedness—after all she had slept naked in his arms, they had explored every millimetre of the other's body for hours. Her whole body still tingled from his touch, her fingers tingled with the sense of him, the scent of him. So she'd be damned if she would start trying to do contortions with sheets.

Instead she swung her legs out of bed, her back to him, rose and walked over to where the fluffy, luxurious complimentary bath-robe hung and pulled it on, tied it at the waist and moved towards him.

'Sorry to halt the great escape by waking up.' Even as she said the words she regretted them. 'Sorry. That was snide.'

'I wasn't escaping. I was waiting for you to wake up so I could say goodbye. But it seemed wrong to stay in bed once I'd woken up and it seemed wrong to watch you sleep so…this was my solution. Coffee and the view.'

Goodbye. She knew there was no choice, knew too that she had no regrets. It was impossible to regret the previous hours, the joy, laughter, and sheer…passion, her body still felt alive, thrummed with remembered pleasure and for a mad moment she wanted to grab him by the shirttails and pull him back to the rumpled bed.

Knew in that instant that that was why he'd got up and dressed, because he knew temptation would be too much. The only way forward now was to say, 'Well I'm awake now. Thank you for staying to say goodbye. And thank you for last night—it was…'

'Incredible,' he said softly. 'I'm glad you chose my table and I wish you all the best with your future.'

'Ditto and likewise.' She stepped forward, wanted to be near him one last time. 'Goodbye Max.' As she stood on tiptoe she brushed her lips against his and moved hurriedly backwards, not wanting to make a fool of herself.

'Goodbye.' For a fraction of a second he hesitated and then turned and walked to the door. She watched, waited until it clicked shut and then ran a hand over her lips and turned to the window.

She would not cry because that would be foolish—she wouldn't even be sure what she was crying for. Coffee and the view—that was the answer. Then her friends would arrive later in the day, then she would return to England and her real life and the future she had planned.

And she'd look back on Max as a pleasant interlude. No more, no less.

Two months later, Salvington Estate, England

Stella stared down at the test result, closed her eyes and looked again. This could not be happening. This *could not* be happening. Only it was. The test had ninety-nine percent accuracy and more to the point she'd done it twice.

Fact: She was pregnant.

Fact: Max Durante was the father.

Fact: In an hour she was supposed to be meeting Rob, Viscount Rochester, for their first date, kick-starting a carefully planned, choreographed, all-singing, all-dancing schedule of dates, leading to an engagement announcement in a glossy celebrity magazine and culminating in a no holds barred high society wedding.

What was she going to do?

The question pummelled her brain as she paced the floor of her bedroom, one hand across her midriff. The sheer enormity of the knowledge so overwhelming she couldn't think beyond the one fact of her pregnancy. Having a baby. A baby, a tiny little piece of humanity with tiny fingers and toes.

But she couldn't... How could she have this baby? Baby. Baby. Baby. She and Max had created a baby. For a moment she was transported back to that magical night, a night she had tried not to dwell on, to keep in perspective, but now... They had used protection, so what had happened. Was it possible that one of those times, when he'd woken her in the early morning hours, half-asleep—could they have quite simply forgotten? Or perhaps there had been a faulty product or... What did it matter? She was pregnant.

Of course it was early days and she knew she had options, knew she didn't have to keep the baby. But...a fierce protective instinct unfurled inside her...she wanted to. Even though she could see how illogical it was, how it would mess up—no, wipe out—her entire life plan, she wanted to keep the baby.

So now what? She needed to talk to someone and who better than her sister, the one person who would grasp the magnitude of the issues at stake here. Because this baby would not be legitimate and therefore even if he were to be a boy he couldn't be the heir.

Stella left her room and headed towards the stairs, knew Adriana would be up in her study, located in the warren-like depths of the upper floor of Salvington Manor. Calling her sister's name she approached the door as Adriana pulled it open.

Stella frowned, saw a slight wariness in her sister's eyes and wondered why. Because although Adriana had every right to loathe Stella she didn't. Understood that it wasn't Stella's fault that she was the adored one, the apple of their father's eye. Understood, too, how much Stella hated that role.

'What's wrong?' Adriana glanced at her watch. 'And what are you doing here?' Her sister all too aware that she was supposed to be on her first date with Rob. A romantic lunch in one of Oxford's most expensive restaurants. Champagne and a discreetly alerted journalist in attendance.

'I can't go through with it.'

'Sorry?'

'You heard me.' Stella followed her sister into the study, resumed pacing, now in front of the battered mahogany desk.

'What do you mean? It's all arranged—you're the one who planned the whole thing.'

'I know. And I meant to do it, Ria, I really did. I wanted to do it.'

'I don't understand. What's happened? What's changed?'

Stella twisted her hands together. 'I'm pregnant.'

'What?' Shock conflated with confusion. 'But if you and Rob are...'

'It's not Rob's. He and I haven't even kissed.' Stella gave a strangled laugh. 'I had that planned for date number three in full view of the press. We were going to hold hands at date two. A peck on the cheek was scheduled for today—date one.'

'But...' Adriana's eyes widened. 'Then who is the father?'

'It doesn't matter.'

'Yes, it does. It matters a lot, given our situation. Are you going to marry him?'

Stella's strides increased. 'No. That is not an option.' Because Max was about to marry someone else, was a self-avowed commitment-phobe and they had a one-night deal. 'But neither is marrying Rob. I can't pretend the baby is his.'

Adriana studied her. 'But you thought about it? Is that why you've left it this late to pull out of this date?'

'I only did the test today. I know I should have done it before, but I thought... I hoped I would be wrong. I even thought if I were to be pregnant it wouldn't matter. I'd have an abortion. But now...' She rested her hand on her tummy. 'Now...now I know it's a disaster but I want to keep the baby.' She stopped. 'Please don't give me a hard time. I know I've messed up, messed up our whole plan, but I'll make it right somehow in the future...'

'Whoa. Slow down. I'm not going to give you a hard time—I would never do that. You're my sister and you've always been the best sister I could wish for. As for the plan, you don't need to worry about that right now. Because we have far bigger worries. If you don't go through with marrying Rob, Father is going to go ballistic.'

She could see the fear on her sister's face and guilt panged inside her again. Adriana had lived her whole life in the shadow of that terror, had to listen to their father denigrate her and put her down all her life. And Stella—she should have stuck up for her sister more, but she hadn't. Had gone along with the idea that it was 'easier' to deflect her father's anger by trying to keep him happy whilst Adriana rendered herself as invisible as possible.

The coward's way out, but she'd salved her conscience with the idea that she would save Salvington and give her sister what she wanted most—a chance to run the estate, and now…now she wasn't even going to do that. That was far worse than any fear of her father.

'What are we going to do?' Adriana asked.

'I'll have to tell Father,' Stella said. 'And there's another problem. Rob will be in the restaurant by now.'

'You need to tell him. We can't leave him stranded.'

'I know.' Stella frowned, resumed pacing. 'The problem is, I've got press all lined up to catch us. I've dropped all the right hints and I'm pretty sure there will be at least one celebrity journalist in that restaurant to scoop us. So they will see him take my call, or get my text.' Her stride increased. 'I can't think straight. But if the press get even a glimmer of suspicion about my condition, then…'

'We are up the creek without a paddle or a stick.'

'More than you know. I can't risk the paternity of this baby coming out. I can't.' Stella's voice broke. 'But there is one thing we could do…'

'What?'

'You can go in my place.'

'No way. That is the most ridiculous idea I've heard.'

'I don't mean marry him, just go and fake this date. Explain the situation to Rob. I'm sure he'd prefer that then being publicly stood up.'

'But…'

Fifteen minutes later, Adriana was primed and ready to go. At least the restaurant was only a short journey away. Once she'd waved her sister off, Stella knew what she had to do next. Face her father; her nerves fluttered at the thought, but she comforted herself with the knowledge that Lord Salvington had never been truly angry with her, even when she'd wanted him to be. Even when she'd partied and caused scandal after scandal.

Bracing herself she headed towards the east wing of the manor where her parents' rooms were, knocked on her father's door and pushed it open.

He turned from his desk and rose to his feet, a frown gathered on his forehead.

'Shouldn't you be with Rob?'

'Yes, but… I'm not going. There's something I need to tell you. I'm pregnant.'

'With Rob's baby?'

'No. Someone else's. So I can't go through with marrying Rob. I'm going to keep the baby.'

'And marry his father?'

Deep breath and, 'No. That isn't an option. So…'

She didn't see it coming, so sure that he couldn't find fault with her that it took her brain a few vital seconds to absorb the change in his expression, to see the sheer rage that mottled his features.

'Isn't an option? Are you telling me that you are going to produce a bastard, instead of an heir to Salvington, that you have sullied our name, betrayed me and everything you stand for. How dare you?'

She stepped backwards as he advanced, thought that he was going to hit her. Instinctively she pulled her phone out of her pocket, flinched as he snatched it from her hand and threw it at the wall. Saw him gather himself together and as fear grabbed her he shouted, 'Get out—out of this room and out of this house and out of my sight.'

Stella turned and fled, ran downstairs and to her car, knew she could find sanctuary in a hotel room. And sanctuary was what she needed right now, somewhere where she could somehow try and get her head round the fact that her life was now irrevocably changed, the whole carefully planned and constructed house of cards had collapsed in a fluttering heap around her. She placed a hand on her tummy. 'Don't worry,' she whispered. 'I'll look after you.'

CHAPTER FOUR

A few weeks later

MAX DRUMMED HIS fingers on his desk as he studied his itinerary for his upcoming Mumbai trip.

He had an extremely lucrative business deal in the pipeline, and a number of meetings lined up with some key players including Bollywood producers and stars. But he also wanted to soak up the culture, wander round and…and what? Bump into his mother who would of course instantly recognise him and—and run a mile in the opposite direction no doubt.

The buzz of his phone was a welcome relief from his thoughts.

'Hey,' he said to his PA.

'Um… I've got a woman here, wanting to see you. Says you met her in Dubai and you agreed to a meeting next time she was in London to discuss a reality show about first dates, but she isn't after an opportunity to act, a promise of a meeting with a director or an invitation to some star-studded award.' His PA sounded puzzled. 'Normally I'd tell her no one sees you without an appointment but oddly she sounds legit. She also looks familiar though it's hard to tell with the sunglasses, scarf routine. So I thought I'd check with you.'

Max stifled the sudden sense of shock, moved to shut down the stream of memories—memories he had held at bay for the past few months, refusing to access them, despite the ridiculous number of times Stella had popped into his head, only to be ruthlessly squashed down. He'd found himself scouring the papers for news of her impending nuptials, to see the first date hit the headlines. But nothing…and he'd wondered if perhaps she'd baulked at the idea of a passionless marriage after all. He'd hoped so, even found his hand hovering over the phone. But of course he hadn't called. There would be no point.

Especially when he had decided to go ahead with his own business marriage.

Perhaps he should refuse to see her, but that would be rude. Stella must have some reason for being here. Only one way to find out. 'Send her in,' he said.

To his own irritation he could feel the thump of his heart against his ribs, as anticipation churned inside him. Then after a perfunctory knock, Mariella pushed the door open and ushered Stella in, nodded at Max and retreated.

He rose to his feet, actually glad that his desk separated them, gave him a barrier to absorb the impact of seeing her.

She tugged the scarf off her head and pushed the sunglasses atop her blonde hair in an impatient gesture and for a long moment they stood staring at each other. Stella looked different, every bit as beautiful, but there was something he couldn't put his finger on, a subtle change. Her blue eyes held a certain something he couldn't decipher, the gloss of her hair held an extra lustre. But what hadn't changed was the instant charge, the magnetic pull of attraction, the urge to take up where they left off.

Her blonde hair was pulled back and then caught in a clip, tendrils escaping to frame her face. Blue eyes studied his face, as if she too was drinking him in, eyes that were shadowed with a trepidation that had been absent in Dubai.

'Stella. This is unexpected.'

'Yes.' Her lips twisted up into a smile that held wryness. 'I saw the article about your first date.' The article had come out two days ago, started with 'Spotted in the Wild—CEO Max Durante and heiress Dora Fitzgerald. Is it a date? The notoriously single CEO of InScreen certainly looked smitten as the possible couple…blah-blah'. 'And I'm not here to make trouble.'

'Then why are you here?' He saw her hands curl into fists as though she were digging her nails into her palms, saw her shoulders pull back as she took a step backwards as if in preparation to turn and run, and a sense of foreboding trickled through him.

'I'm pregnant.' There was a moment where the penny failed to drop where he could only look at her in bewilderment and she continued. 'With your baby.'

He rocked backwards and tried to steady himself, failed and reached out to grasp the edge of his desk. Every instinct scrambled, but it was terror that won out, topped the mix with a murky grey swirl. He couldn't be a father; couldn't…wouldn't. Shouldn't. He was not dad material, it was a path he would never choose to take, would never take the risk that he would let a child down—the idea enough to make him go clammy. He could feel all colour drain from his face, as he stared at her; his gaze dropped to her midriff and a sense of awe touched him, tried to thread through the panic. A baby, his baby was growing inside Stella.

'I get it's a shock,' she said. 'And as I said I'm not here because I expect anything. I know that you have marriage plans, but I thought you should know. Had a right to know that you are going to be a dad, but I understand that you may not want to acknowledge the baby, but one day the baby will ask me who his or her dad is and…'

Her words cut through the electric chaos that was blindsiding his brain. He had spent his whole life wondering about the identity of a parent who had abandoned him, spent years piecing together information about a father who he wished wasn't his father. There was no way he would, could or should put any child through even a fraction of that.

'Look, I know it takes a bit of time to process.' She twisted her hands together. 'Perhaps if you can call me or something in a few days, or a week or well… however long it takes. I'll write my number down and wait to hear from you.' She moved over to the desk in search of pen and paper. Clearly in a rush to leave, as if she'd done her duty and now she was going to run.

The movement, her proximity, the ridiculously familiar floral scent jolted his vocal chords into action. 'No. Don't go.' There was too much he needed to know and an instinctive part of him did not want her to walk out with his baby. What if she didn't come back? A reversal abandonment. The idea acted like the equivalent of a bucket of ice to the head, cleaved through the pandemonium of his thoughts and allowed him to focus. 'We need to talk.'

'I know, but if you want a bit of time first, or need to talk to Dora, that's fine.'

'I'm about to fly to Mumbai on a two-week business trip.' A trip he did not want to cancel; there were too many meetings lined up, too many opportunities he might lose. But the thought of being that far away from Stella, of not knowing what she was doing was not possible. 'Come with me.'

'Excuse me?'

'Come with me,' he repeated.

Trepidation vanished from her eyes, replaced by ire. 'Has it occurred to you that I might have commitments?'

The question sent a volt of unease through him. Just because there had been no publicity didn't mean she wasn't still considering marriage. Scenarios chased through his mind, a small private wedding, an engagement kept under wraps until she'd spoken with him. The very idea of his baby being brought up under another man's roof, by some boring, upper-class aristocrat, caused his hands to clench.

'Do you?' he asked, the syllables grinding past his teeth. 'Because if you do I will postpone mine.'

She hesitated, blue eyes narrowed and then shook her head. 'Why not wait until you come back?'

'Because I have just found out I am having a baby—months after the event. Why didn't you tell me straight away?'

'Because I wasn't sure what to do, whether to tell you at all. Then I saw the article and knew it was now or never, whether your marriage is a business deal or you are smitten I thought you both had a right to know.'

Whether to tell you at all. Now or *never*. Anger roiled through him. 'So you really considered *never* telling me? Letting our child grow up without knowing who his father is?'

'Yes, I did.' Her chin tilted out defiantly. 'And if I had believed that was the best thing for my baby then I would have done it. But in the end I didn't. So I *am* here and I have told you.'

And she looked as though she was regretting it and fear threw an insidious dart that pierced him. Because if she decided to turn and walk away from him there was little he could do to stop her. The realisation set his whole being on edge with both fear and powerlessness. Which meant he needed to calm down and stay calm. Do what he did best—negotiate.

'Then let's move forward from here and decide what to do next. We need to talk and I don't want to wait. So either you come to Mumbai or I'll stay here.'

She bit her lip and despite everything his gaze snagged on her mouth, lingered there as memories cascaded back of kissing her, the sheer gloriousness of those lips.

'If I come to Mumbai with you it would generate publicity and I don't want that and I'm assuming you and Dora don't either. Also surely you need time to discuss this with Dora?' She hesitated and then twisted slightly away, her voice studiedly even, though he saw her hands clench. 'Are you smitten? Did you lie to me in Dubai?'

'Excuse me?' Max blinked. 'No, I didn't lie. At all. I told you in Dubai that we needed to make the marriage look real so it wouldn't be challenged by the trustees. So that date was fake.' There was a silence and he remembered their fake date, the banter, the laughter, the simmering shimmer of mutual attraction, heightened and spun as the golden moments had gone by lit by the sprinkle of stars and the dazzling illumination of Dubai's night sky. 'Really fake,' he added. 'Orchestrated for the cameras.'

'OK.' Her gaze remained steady, but something flashed across her eyes, akin to relief. 'I'm glad you didn't lie. But Dora still needs to know.'

'I know that and I will talk with Dora.' He had no idea how Dora would react to this, but he knew that no matter what he would be there for his baby. That was the only thought that shone neon bright through the sheer panic generated by the thought of being a father. He had to be there. Whatever the cost, whatever the price. 'I'll speak with her before we leave for Mumbai.' He saw the raised eyebrow at his use of the pronoun and hurried on. 'I understand you don't want any speculation or publicity if you come to Mumbai, but there doesn't need to be. We can stick to what you told my PA. We met in Dubai, I said to look me up in London to discuss a business idea, here you are. I like the idea, I say come to Mumbai so we can discuss it further. I think it will cause more speculation if I cancel my trip and stay here and then we are spotted together.'

'Fair point. I'll come to Mumbai. The sooner I decide what to do next the better.'

Relief trumped all other emotions at her words. He had two weeks now, two weeks to cut an agreement. To make a deal that meant he would be part of this baby's life.

Stella pulled her suitcase behind her and wondered whether this was a complete and utter mistake. But... it beat what she'd been doing over the past weeks— sitting in friend's houses and then in a soulless hotel room staring at the walls, engulfed in guilt and doubts and worry and fear. Reliving the circumstances that had followed her disastrous encounter with her father. Reliving the phone call from Adriana that evening.

'Dad's in hospital. He's had a heart attack. I found him at the bottom of the stairs when I got back from the date.'

She'd stood there clutching the phone in her hand as the ramifications exploded in her brain. This was her responsibility, her bad... However complicated her relationship with her father, he was still her father. And now he was in a hospital bed because of her. She'd messed up...again.

Unbelievable.

And now, now she'd told Max about the baby—

What if that was another bad decision? After all, what did she even know about him? Perhaps she should swivel round and make a run for it.

Too late; Max had seen her. And there it was—the rush of hormones. He looked gorgeous in dark blue jeans and a black top and the knowledge that she knew exactly what he looked like, felt like under the clothes gave her a shocking thrill, which she knew she had to suppress. Because that part of their relationship was over. That magic had created a baby, their baby and her priority now was that baby. She needed to assess how good a father Max would be and she couldn't let attraction cloud her judgement or fuzz her brain. Not now, not ever. Not with her history of disastrous decisions.

So after a quick check to make sure she wasn't drooling she stepped forward, tried to access her poised Stella persona, the one she seemed to have misplaced somewhere along the way.

'Hey,' she said, glad her sunglasses hid her expression from him.

'Hey. We need to check you in then let's fly.'

A seamless fifteen minutes later she boarded the private jet, looked round its luxurious trappings that made it feel as though she was aboard a flying hotel suite rather than a plane. 'Do you usually fly privately?'

'No, not always, more when circumstances dictate. I find it's a good place to conduct private meetings and today I figured utter privacy is better. We have a lot to talk about and here seems a good place to start.'

'Agreed. Where would you like to start?'

Not even a heartbeat of hesitation. 'With your aristocrat. I assume the marriage plans are off.' Stella opened her mouth to concur as he continued. 'Obviously you cannot marry him now.'

The phrase held arrogance and she bristled. If Max Durante thought he could call the shots he had another think coming. The very idea triggered memories of her own upbringing, where her father had held all the power and the rest of the family had danced to his tune. 'I can do whatever I want,' she said. 'If I decide to marry Rob, or anyone else for that matter, that is up to me. My choice and absolutely nothing to do with you.'

'It would be everything to do with me,' he growled and the deep rumble of his voice held further autocracy. Her eyes narrowed, but his glower didn't back down.

'And would you allow me to dictate your marriage choices. I haven't asked you not to marry Dora.'

'You don't have to ask me. I've made that decision myself.'

Oh. The statement wrong-footed her. 'Why?'

'Because it wouldn't be fair. To Dora. Or the baby. There will be publicity and it wouldn't be much fun for her to go through that. But it is more than that. In order to maintain our fictional marriage, Dora would need to spend time with the baby and then what happens after the divorce? If she has bonded to the baby and vice versa.'

Stella blinked. *She* should have thought of that, instead of trying to score cheap points. Yet she also knew she couldn't show weakness, couldn't let Max think he could dictate her actions. 'I'm sorry you've lost the business deal,' she said. 'But I agree it is the right decision for the baby's sake. But me marrying Rob is a different scenario. It would be a lifelong commitment. It would be good for the baby to bond with him as soon as possible.'

'So you are seriously considering it?' Each word said perfectly calmly, but each word could have cut steel.

'That isn't the point. The point is I have every right to consider it. And it has nothing to do with you.'

'Nothing?' His tone was low, full of incredulity. 'You think I should stand back and do nothing? Watch you marry someone else, see my baby be brought up by another man, with me in the background. A man who you don't even love and I don't even know. I don't know how he would behave towards another man's child. Do you still think this has nothing to do with me?'

She could hear the pain in his voice, under the anger, and she paused, as her own anger diluted; how would she feel if biology had dictated a reversal? If Max was keeping the baby and bringing her up with Dora and she, Stella, was relegated to seeing her own child less than Dora did. How would she feel even now if he married someone she didn't know, someone who would spend extensive time with her child? The idea sheened her with panic and the anger died as suddenly as it had flared, and instinctively she raised her hand and tentatively reached out to touch his arm. 'Sorry. I'm sorry. I didn't think.' Her besetting sin really; she didn't think and people got hurt. 'I am not marrying my aristocrat. I didn't go ahead with the plans. I shouldn't have let you think I was. I'm sorry.'

There was a silence and then he exhaled and the tension in his shoulders that she hadn't even noticed was there relaxed. 'I'm glad,' he said simply and she knew the pain he'd felt had been real, not a simple desire to dictate her actions. Then he covered her hand with his own and there it was, a sudden sense of warmth, like a switch turning on, the feel of his fingers around hers exerted a pull, a sense of togetherness, a reminder they had created this baby together. And that warmth morphed into something else akin to the first spark when a fire was lit. Her gaze fixed on his hand, the shape, the strength, the memory of his fingers on her body, the magic they had wrought and as that hand brushed against hers she bit back a mewling sound of need. She knew that despite everything she still craved his touch, her skin seemed to shiver in remembered response.

As awareness threatened to escalate further, he lifted his hand just as she moved to do the same.

'OK. Good. But right now I am not planning on marrying anyone.'

'OK. Good. And neither am I.'

She essayed a small tentative smile. 'Then we can cross an item off the agenda.' She resisted the urge to rub her hand where he'd touched it, that warmth still there. Whoa. Now she was completely overreacting to a simple gesture and it was time to change the dynamic before she ended up doing something foolish. Her current speciality it would seem.

But she could at least make an attempt to be normal, poised, *together* Stella. 'Speaking of agendas, I meant to give you this as soon as we took off. In case anyone does check up on our cover story, I prepared this.' She reached into her bag. 'It's a proposal for an aristocratic reality dating show.'

She handed him a folder and he reached across to take it. Careful, they couldn't afford even an accidental brush of the fingers and she snatched her hand back and watched as the papers fluttered to the ground.

'Sorry.'

For heaven's sake—what was wrong with her? where was her famed poise and cool now?

'Sorry,' she said again and leaned forward to pick the papers up as he did the same. 'Ouch.' A shot of pain jolted through her as their heads collided and she heard his sharp intake of breath.

She sat back up. 'Shit, I'm sorry. Again.' And to her horror she felt a tear trickle down her cheek.

Instantly he was on his feet and then squatting down in front of her. 'Are you Ok? Let me see.' Before she could stop him he had pushed her hair away from her face, and was running his hand over the hurt area. 'Is it there?'

She caught her breath at the gentle touch of his fingers, swept back to that magical night. 'I—I'm fine. Really.' Wide-eyed she met his gaze, saw the concern in his dark eyes morph into something else and knew his thoughts had synced with hers. She gave a half laugh—then closed her eyes as to her horror another tear seeped out.

'You don't sound fine,' he said softly and there was genuine sympathy in his voice. But then he moved away only to return a couple of minutes later. 'Here you go. Tea and tissues.' And then with a small laugh in his voice, 'I told you my tea was magic, didn't I?'

She gave a half chuckle and picked up the steaming cup. 'Thank you and sorry. I'm not usually like this. Maybe it's hormones.'

'So what's wrong? Apart from a bumped head.'

'I… I feel…lost.' She tried to sound flippant. 'I seem to have misplaced the usual normal Stella. I mean I never cry, I certainly don't drop things and I don't then bump heads with people. And I…always know what I am doing. And now, since the pregnancy, since my father's heart attack… I have no idea about anything.'

'Whoa.' He leant forward now. 'I didn't know about the heart attack.'

She nodded, started to shred the tissue paper. 'I told him I was pregnant, told him I was backing out of the marriage and he lost it. I left and then a few hours later he had a heart attack.'

'And you blame yourself?'

'Of course I do.' However much both Adriana and her mother told her it wasn't her fault Stella couldn't help but believe it was. 'If only I'd broken the news better, if only I'd never met you, if only I hadn't agreed to one magical night. But then I wouldn't have the baby and I do want the baby and it's not the baby's fault and…my father won't even see me. And if he dies Salvington will be lost and we'll all be homeless and…' Oh, God, she was such a mess. Unable to access the cool, sophisticated persona she had spent so long cultivating.

'How is he?' Max asked.

She took a deep breath. 'He's stable, but it turns out he'd had a couple of minor heart attacks in the past so the prognosis is a bit rocky. But right now the doctors say he is unlikely to have another attack as long as he takes care.' Yet the guilt wouldn't recede, compounded by Adriana's decision to take her place and marry Rob. To save Salvington. So instead of making things up to Adriana, she'd pitchforked her into an arranged marriage.

'I'm sorry about your father and I am sorry that the news about our baby triggered his heart attack. But it is not your fault and it certainly isn't the baby's. He or she didn't ask to come into being.'

Stella sighed. 'But we didn't ask either did we? I mean I'm not even sure how it happened.'

Her gaze met his and the atmosphere changed as Stella recognised the fallacy of her words. She knew exactly how it had happened and for a moment she was transported back, to the tangle of sheets, the feel of his hands glissading over her skin, the sculpt of his back under her fingers, the slow languorous burgeoning escalation of pleasure, yielding to an urgency and desperation.

She lifted her hands to cover her cheeks, felt the heat and flush of remembered passion and stared at him wide-eyed. 'I—I mean…technically I know how it happened but…'

'But we were using protection. Or at least I thought we were. Perhaps one of the times, we didn't.'

The time they'd both woken up to find themselves half asleep in each other's arms? She closed down the memory, knew it served no purpose to relive that night.

'Whatever happened, happened,' she said. 'And here we are.' She touched her tummy. 'I want this baby, I love this baby, but… I'm terrified.'

'That's normal. Your whole life has been upended, all

your plans gone, your father is ill and you're about to become a parent for the first time and you've been carrying that alone. But now you don't have to anymore. You can share the terror with me. And we can make a new plan.'

'That sounds good.'

He held a hand out. 'Hand it over then.'

'Hand what over?' She looked at him in confusion and saw that he was studying her with a small smile of his lips.

'Half the terror.'

'Huh? How does that work?'

'Imagine it.' Now his face was serious, though his eyes also held a glint of humour at her expression. 'Imagine it. You told me in Dubai you had imagination so picture the terror. Maybe it is a big grey blob, maybe it's bright pink and wobbly with hundreds of legs. Picture it, halve it, hand it over.'

'You're serious.' She shrugged. 'I feel ridiculous but... OK.' Stella closed her eyes and pictured the terror, all the horrible feelings of confusion, guilt and panic that had assailed her over the past months, a misogynous blob, brown and sludgy interlaced with purple and red veins. Carefully she pictured halving it and handed over the imaginary mass to Max.

'I can't believe I'm saying this but that actually helped.' She looked at him, a small frown on her face. 'I also can't believe I am asking this but what are you going to do with it?'

'I'll get rid of it.'

'How?'

He shook his head with mock solemnity. 'Trade secret.'

'What trade? You're CEO of a global streaming platform.'

'Not that trade.'

'Which one?'

'Magician,' he said, and she laughed.

'So you offer tea and therapy.'

'Amongst other things.'

She gave a small intake of breath, knowing exactly what other things he was referring to.

'But it's probably best if we don't go there,' he added. 'Especially in the context of what I am going to suggest as the next part of my therapy.'

'What's that?'

'Bed. Another perk of this jet is that over there is a seat that converts into a very comfortable bed.' A funny little tremor ran through her and she saw desire darken his eyes even as a rueful smile tipped his lips. Lips that had wreaked such glorious pleasure. 'So you can sleep. You look exhausted and that's hardly surprising. So sleep. We can come up with a plan once we're in Mumbai.'

Sleep. She tried to remember the last time she'd slept properly, without vague edgy dreams or waking up in the early hours of the morning to a jumble of thoughts that wouldn't be blocked out. 'Sleep actually sounds pretty good.' And as she lay down and rested her head on the silken plump softness of the pillow she realised that this was the first time in weeks she'd felt safe.

CHAPTER FIVE

MAX FOCUSED ON his computer screen, kept his gaze resolutely turned away from the corner of the jet where Stella still slept. Knew it would be intrinsically wrong to watch her whilst she slept, however much he wanted to watch over, to guard the woman who carried his baby.

Baby. The word seemed to scroll across the screen, erasing the rows of figures and projections on the spreadsheet. Each letter undulated with a panic he knew he had to suppress—how he wished he could soothe his own terrors with tea and sleep. But he had no idea how to extract the dark thoughts and fears. Because the baby existed and the baby was stuck with him, Max Durante, for a father. Nothing could change that. In the first throes of panic he'd actually wondered if it would be better if he simply bowed out, but he couldn't do it. Couldn't abandon his baby, repeat history; that would be unforgiveable, unjustifiable. The idea of facing that child one day, trying to make him or her see that he'd done it for the best made his skin go clammy.

Because he knew if he found his mother and that was the line she spun he would try to understand, but on a visceral bone-deep level he wouldn't get it, wouldn't understand why she hadn't tried, given him a chance. Given herself a chance.

But maybe she'd been the same as his uncle and aunt, so convinced badness was baked in, bred in the bone that she hadn't seen the point in giving him a chance. That was what his aunt had told him. *'Your mother, she must have seen it in your eyes.'*

The words in their simple cruelty had rung with truth. Enough. That was then, his mother had judged him, abandoned him, but that would not happen to his child.

His child would have a mother and a father.

He turned now to look at Stella, filled with a sense of gratitude that at least Stella wanted this baby. He might not know much about her, but he did know that. She opened her eyes, clouded with sleep and a hint of confusion that morphed into a memory of where she was and she sat up, a small frown on her face.

'Sorry,' he muttered. 'I promise I wasn't watching you. I was about to wake you up. We'll be landing soon.'

She sat up, swinging her long legs over, rising and moving with natural grace across to her seat where she strapped her seat belt on. 'I really needed that sleep. Thank you.' She looked out of the window. 'I've never been to Mumbai before.'

'The hotel isn't far from the airport. I called before we left—they said an extra room shouldn't be a problem.'

'Thank you and of course I'll reimburse you.'

'No need,' he said. 'If you were really a consultant I would pay your expenses.'

'But I'm not really a consultant.'

'I know, but as I am the one who insisted you come to Mumbai I think it is fair for me to pay.'

Was it his imagination or was there a soupçon of relief on her face as she considered his statement, then nodded. 'Thank you. I appreciate that.' Surely she couldn't be in money difficulties. Though why not; it occurred to him that in actual fact he knew absolutely nothing about the woman sitting opposite him. What was her job, what was her favourite colour? He had no idea. All he knew was that she was beautiful, that there was a magnetic pull of attraction between them and she was the mother of his baby.

Fear suddenly trickled in, cancelled out the warmth he'd felt earlier. Because if he didn't measure up, just as he hadn't for his mother, just as he hadn't for his aunt and uncle then Stella had the power to take his baby from him. Or force a custody battle, or refuse to put him on the birth certificate, or move to the Outer Hebrides, or poison his child against him. And God knew he knew how easy that was to do, his aunt and uncle had dripped negativity into his very soul.

Whoa. There was no need to believe she would do any of that, but he shouldn't forget that she could.

'Max?'

He blinked and turned to Stella. 'Are you OK?'

'I'm fine,' he said as the wheels hit the runway. It would be fine; he'd do whatever it took to make it fine.

Half an hour later Max watched as streets flashed past as the driver expertly navigated the traffic-clogged roads of Mumbai, looked out at the crowds of humanity that jostled each other, looked at the streets lined with stalls and shop fronts, people and livestock. Was his mother one of those people, passed by in a flash, in the overwhelm of people, the plethora of scents and smells that assaulted his senses, the cacophony of noise.

The car pulled up outside the imposing exterior of the hotel and after thanking the driver they climbed out, blinked in the sunshine and felt the warm humidity engulf them, the air conditioning a welcome relief as they walked through the revolving glass door into the lobby.

A smiling staff member welcomed them as they approached the sleek reception area and identified themselves. 'Mr Durante, Ms Morrison. I will have someone take you up to your suite.'

Stella paused, as he frowned. 'A suite?' he queried. 'I requested an additional room for Ms Morrison.'

'Yes, unfortunately the staff member you spoke with made an error. You were emailed back straight after to explain that as we have a delegation here it was impossible to accommodate your request so we simply swapped you to a larger suite at no extra cost. It has two double bedrooms completely separated by a large living area. I know you have business meetings starting from today so I hope this will be acceptable. If not, of course I can try and find you alternate accommodations.'

Max turned to Stella. 'What would you like to do?'

Common sense told him a suite was no different than having adjoining rooms on the same floor. It just *felt* different. More intimate, more personal. But this was personal and they were here to talk in private—a suite might make that easier.

'The suite is fine,' she said, though he saw the small clench of her hands and suspected she shared his reservations.

They followed a bellboy to the suite where Stella couldn't hold back a small gasp. The living area was massive, the polished teak floor dotted with lush sofas and chairs. A state-of-the-art entertainment system and screen adorned one wall, the others were bedecked with a montage of pictures that showed Mumbai through the ages. There was a designated workspace with a sleek slate-grey ergonomic desk and the two open doors showed immense bedrooms.

'They weren't kidding when they said they'd upgraded us.'

'And it's massive, so it *really* doesn't matter that it's a suite,' she said, and instantly bit her lip in clear vexation, and he couldn't help the small rueful smile that tipped his lips.

'So you're saying it *would* be a problem if it was smaller?' he asked.

'Of course not. I just meant…well I wouldn't want to invade your space.' There was a silence that she hurried to fill. 'If you're working or you want to have a meeting up here or…you know what I mean.'

'I know exactly what you mean. Space invasion won't be a problem. But right now you can have the whole suite to yourself. I've got a couple of meetings downstairs. Once I'm back I'll grab some sleep and a shower, then we can head for dinner if you like? Maybe book at the restaurant?'

'Sounds perfect.'

Perfect. Only everything wasn't perfect Max reflected as he rode the elevator down to the ground floor, glanced at his watch to be sure he was on time. Yesterday his life had been if not perfect at least on track, a business marriage in the offing, a trip to India that would combine business and a personal quest for his mother and an exploration of his possible roots. Today he was about to become a father with a woman he hardly knew and yet was attracted to with an intensity he'd never experienced before, one that he could neither fathom or countenance. An attraction that had somehow distracted him from the focus here. That Stella was carrying his baby and she had the potential to take his baby away from him.

But right now he needed to focus on the meeting ahead—with the private detective set with the somewhat daunting task of finding the woman who might be his mother. He entered the meeting lounge, saw the man waiting for him, approached the table, shook hands and sat.

'As you are here we thought we should meet to give you a progress report. And we are progressing, but it is not easy. The woman we seek, Rupali Patel—there are many with the same name as her—we are tracking via social media and other means. We have eliminated many who we know are not your mother. You must understand too that it is possible the woman we seek is not in actual fact your mother, or if she is she will not be willing to admit it.'

'I understand—keep going and keep me posted. Send across the report showing me exactly who is left on the short list.'

'We will. Is there anything else we can help with?'

'N—' He bit the denial off as an idea slipped into his head. A way to find out more about Stella. His instinct told him that Stella was on the level, but legal facts also dictated that she was the one with the power. She had said it herself that she may have decided not to tell him about the baby at all, could marry her aristocrat, could do whatever she thought was best for the baby. So maybe it made sense to find out more about her, set his own mind at rest, make it easier for them to find a path to a good way to co-parent.

Parent... He was going to become a parent. Emotion threatened to flood him, a hapless sense of being out of control and the need to do something, anything projected the idea into a decision.

'I'd like you to do a background check for me on the Honourable Stella Morrison. Utterly confidential. Just an overview to see what she's like.' A qualm struck him and he shrugged it off before his next meeting.

CHAPTER SIX

STELLA HEARD THE click of the bedroom door and turned from the window of the lounge. She gulped, wished that the mere sight of Max didn't turn her into a hormonal mess. But as he stood there, dark hair spiked and shower damp, his shirt top button undone showing a tantalising triangle of flesh, sleeves rolled up to expose forearms that clenched her tummy with desire, her hormones went into overdrive, waved pompoms and set up a chant. Gritting her teeth, she forced herself to smile a calm, poised, civil smile, but then she saw the awareness in his brown eyes, the glint of appreciation and she couldn't help it. Her own smile changed into one of appreciation too, her gaze lingering a fraction too long on his lips.

'How were the meetings?' she managed.

'Good. One was with a Bollywood producer who has asked us on a tour of a film set if you're interested? Followed by a visit to some botanical gardens, where one of their new films is going to stage a lot of scenes.'

'I'd love that.' She really would and now at least she could change the conversation to something practical, could fend off the threatening shimmer of attraction. 'So you're planning on streaming Bollywood movies?'

'Initially, but with the view to a potential buyout or at least a stakeholding in the production company. I prefer that—it gives me more control but it also means I am more involved and invested so the relationship is more likely to thrive. But that does also mean we all have to genuinely get on, or at least all have the same general business outlook. So it's early days. This company was set up five years ago by a superstar couple, Bollywood royalty. Pria and Rahesh Khatri. It gave them control over the films they star in so they want to be very sure I am a viable partner. I hope I am.'

'So this deal is really important to you?'

'All deals are important to me, but yes this one is special and I've got a lot on the line. It's a good fit and it will take InScreen another step forward. And the films themselves—they are like nothing I've seen before... I'd like to be part of this world and I'd like it to become part of my business.'

She could hear the passion in his voice, that love for his business, that commitment and also the excitement. 'So despite how successful you already are you still have that ambition...that drive to achieve more.'

'Of course.' The words simple, and she realised that his drive was an intrinsic part of his being. 'I want InScreen to be the best everywhere—I want people to have access to entertainment, to documentaries, to news to whatever it is they want access to and I want my platform to offer it all. And I'll keep working until I achieve exactly that.'

A sudden pang of envy struck her, that he had found his vocation, that he clearly loved what he did. She could hear it in the deep rumble of his voice, the way his dark eyes shone with determination, the movements of his hands. And that enthusiasm gave him an aura of success, of power, of determination...and hell, the shimmer of attraction had somehow slipped through without her noticing.

He shrugged. 'Anyway sorry to bore on. We should head to dinner. Did you book a table?'

'Actually no. I did some research and if you don't mind I thought it might be fun to go and explore, apparently if we go to Marine Drive there are loads of street vendors that sell the most amazing food and we can watch the sunset which is also apparently a must do. If that's OK?' Everything she said was true but the real reason she'd made the decision was she had no wish to replay their last night together. The drinks, the expensive restaurant in the swish hotel, and then... Nope. This way was safer. Outside, plenty of tourists, fresh air and they could walk with a gap between them.

Perhaps he'd figured the same thing because he nodded with a shade too much vehemence. 'Good idea.'

'Then let's go,' she said. 'I think they'll call us a car downstairs.'

Twenty minutes later they alighted on the wide sweeping promenade that curved in a smooth C shape to border the lapping waves of the Arabian Sea. Stella stood and gloried in the cool evening breeze that ruffled her hair and the folds of her long floral sundress.

'I can't quite believe I am in Mumbai—it's definitely not how I saw my day panning out.'

'It does seem a bit surreal.'

She glanced up at him. 'Even more so for you. I'm guessing you're still in shock. I mean when you woke up this morning you had no idea any of this was happening. That I'd turn up, that I'm pregnant, let alone that I'd be here in Mumbai with you.' Her gaze flew to his, as an unwelcome idea entered her head. 'Were you planning on bringing Dora? For the next stage of your marriage plans?' She shook her head. 'I am sorry that you lost that deal.'

'It is as it is. And to answer your question I wasn't bringing Dora with me. We didn't think that we'd be able to pull off the whole lovey-dovey act for two weeks.'

Stella looked at him. 'Surely Mumbai is the perfect place for a lovely-dovey act. I mean look at it. Look at this.' She spread her hand out to encompass the view. 'You've got the beach, the sunset, the sheer sweeping beauty. And soon all the lights will come on and it will be magical.' She broke off, the adjective conjuring up memories she didn't want to dwell on. 'I mean *beautiful*. The perfect romantic setting.'

'Which would have made it even more obvious that we were faking. I already told you I'm not really a romantic lovey-dovey kind of guy.'

'Yes, but it wouldn't be that difficult to pretend for a few photo shoots. All you'd have to do was hold hands and…'

'I'm not really a hand-holding kind of guy either.'

Now she turned to look at him. 'You've never held hands with a date?'

A small frown creased his forehead as he thought and then he shook his hand. 'Nope. I don't think I have. I mean it's never been a thing.' As they spoke they headed towards the wall that bordered the promenade and sat down, facing the blue of the waves.

'Hmm. 'So, out of interest what is the longest relationship you've ever had?'

'About six months.' He hesitated and then shrugged. 'Well technically. But I was working abroad for a lot of that time so we probably only spent a few nights together.'

'Just nights?' Not that she could exactly judge, their entire relationship had consisted of one night.

'And days,' he said. 'But only a few over the six months. Perhaps *relationship* is the wrong word. I guess they are more like…interludes. Because right now that's all I have time for. My business, my work takes precedence over relationships, so it wouldn't be fair to embark on a serious commitment.'

Her gaze met his. 'A baby is a serious commitment.'

'I know. But a baby is a completely different type of relationship. It is forever. That relationship would take precedence over business, romance doesn't.'

She studied his face, remembered his drive, his ambition, his passion for InScreen. Would he actually be able to prioritise a child, fit them into his schedule? 'So if I were to call you up to say our child needed picking up early from school because she was sick and you were in a business meeting you'd leave to pick her up?'

'Yes.' He frowned. 'Sorry, that was too glib. If she was seriously ill of course I would drop everything and go. If not then it might depend on my schedule. I wouldn't lose a multimillion-dollar deal, and I wouldn't walk out of a meeting if people's jobs or livelihoods were at risk. But I would send someone she knew to get her. I would not let her down.'

'But you would let a date down.'

He shook his head. 'No. I am always upfront with dates that any interlude is exactly that, a temporary period of time devoted to pleasure.' And there it was again; she was sure he hadn't intended it but the words triggered memories of their time together and the sheer intensity of the pleasure.

'I remember,' she said, aware that the words had way too much wistfulness in them. 'I mean you were completely upfront, completely clear what was on offer and that business came first.'

'Until now,' he said.

'Until now. Because now everything has changed.'

They looked out over the sea and she caught her breath as the sun began its descent towards the horizon, the colours tinging the sky with a flood of orange-gold rays and the sky morphed to a purple-indigo backdrop. The whole spectacle filled her with awe and she continued to watch as the colours slowly faded to a deep pink that tiptoed across the dusk. 'It's so beautiful and right now it feels ridiculously symbolic. At the risk of being dramatic it feels like the sun is setting on one phase of my life.'

'In some ways it is. But it's the future that matters.'

A future that they were going to share and instinctively as they stood and watched the final fingers of sunshine tiptoe over the darkening blue of the sea, she moved closer to him.

'A future with no regrets?' she asked softly. 'For business deals, for life plans gone awry.'

'There are other deals. There always are.' And she knew he'd go after every one. 'Right now the most important thing to consider is the baby and how to move forward. Without regret.'

'So you have no regrets?' she asked softly. 'About the baby.'

'No, I don't. He or she didn't ask to come into this world. We made this baby—he or she is part of us and I can't regret that.'

'Thank you.' And she meant it; his words were sincere and now she felt sure that he did want the baby. Turning to face him she brushed her lips against his cheek. The sensation so sweet, and yet so sensual and she heard him catch his breath, felt something shift in her chest as she moved backwards, looked at him wide-eyed. God—how she wanted to kiss him again, kiss him properly, tangle her fingers in his hair, press her body against his.

Not happening.

She jumped off the wall, sacrificed grace for speed. 'Why don't we walk for a bit? Look for food.' The words tumbled from her mouth. 'I am really looking forward to this—in fact it's the first time I've felt properly hungry since I've been pregnant. I'm trying to eat right for the baby, but it's difficult when all you want to do is throw up. But right now I am starving.' Excellent, she'd now mentioned throwing up—well at least that should kill the mood.

'Good idea,' he said. 'Let's find food.'

Max took a moment before he slipped off the wall to make sure he had himself in hand; he didn't want to show what effect her proximity, the gentle brush of her lips, had had on him.

He glanced at Stella, silhouetted in the pink rays. She looked stunning, her blonde hair was caught up in a clip and few corn-coloured tendrils framed her exquisite face. The simple flowing dress highlighted her slender silhouette with the faintest hint of a baby bump, and that outline caught his breath with a sense of awe. Her blue eyes met his and he saw her gulp and now his gaze fixed on the slender column of her throat. Dammit—he jumped off the wall to land by her side.

'Let's go.'

Yet as they walked towards the stalls he was suddenly aware of an urge to take her hand, just to see what it felt like. Ridiculous. Unobtrusively he moved a little further away to avoid the chance of their fingers so much as brushing against each other.

'And let's make the most of you being hungry. Anything you feel like eating we'll find it.'

'What if I wanted something home-cooked? Would you be able to do that?'

'Ah. That might be a bit more difficult. If by that you mean cooked by me. No promises there. I mean some days I eat a bowl of cereal for my dinner.' He broke off as she gave a peal of laughter. What?'

'Somehow the idea of Max Durante, millionaire CEO eating a bowl of muesli for his dinner seems... well it's not what most people would imagine.'

'Muesli is when I'm eating in style,' he admitted. 'Mostly it's cornflakes.'

'So what else do you eat if you're home alone?'

'Cheese on toast is a speciality and I do have a signature pasta dish, spaghetti *al olio*. But I'm afraid that is my repertoire. Quick and easy food—I mean food is just food.'

She shook her head vigorously, genuine horror on her face. 'How can you say that. Food is...food is one of the most important things in the world.' He recalled the way she'd selected from the menu in Dubai and knew she meant every word.

'Well yes—obviously it's important to eat but...'

Another shake of her head. 'No no no! Food is something joyous. I love trying new food, new recipes, and most of all I love eating it. I mean you eat three meals a day every day—surely it's a chance to make sure you're definitely happy three times a day. It doesn't need to be gourmet food, but you can make sure your cheese on toast is special—you can add chilies, or coriander or marmite.'

'Or I'll stick to trusty cornflakes.'

She sighed theatrically. 'Well at least come and give some street food a try.'

They headed towards the line of street vendors who had congregated and he watched as she studied each menu—couldn't help but smile at the look of focus on her face, the intensity of her frown, the way she tipped her head to one side as she studied the choices.

'You do take this seriously.'

'Absolutely. It's important to make the right choice. There is *nothing* worse than choosing the wrong thing and then regretting it.'

'*Nothing* worse?'

'Right now, yes. So I think I'm going to have the *vada pav* and then come back for the *bhel puri*.'

'Why don't you choose for me and then if you don't like what you've chosen we can swap. Because I'll be fine with anything and if I don't love it I'm not fussed.'

'I've got a better idea. Let's both have the same things.'

'Why is that a better idea?'

'Humour me,' she said and as she should stood there, a speculative look in her blue eyes and a smile on her lips, his breath caught in his chest. Again.

And he tried a theatrical sigh of his own and felt an out of proportion happiness when she chuckled. 'I have the feeling I'm going to regret it but OK.'

Once they'd bought the food they wandered back to the wall and perched on it facing each other, the sea breeze ruffling her hair. 'Right,' she said. 'You go first. I want you to close your eyes when you have your first bite. And really, really savour it. Don't think about it as just food, think about it as texture and flavours and spices and then I want you to tell me about it. What it tastes like. See if you can identify the spices.'

'Do I have to close my eyes?'

'Yes. You said you'd humour me and now you have to. It'll make you think about what you eat and make you enjoy it more.' She looked at him. 'Surely intensifying a sensory experience can only make it more pleasurable? A wise man said to me once a long time ago that a lifetime without a spark, sounds…flat, dull, boring.'

'I wasn't talking about food.'

'I know. But to me a lifetime without really tasting and savouring and appreciating food sounds flat, dull and boring.'

'OK… OK. I'll give it a go, but I'm not sure I even know any spices.' He closed his eyes and took a bite of the potato patty encased in a white roll and to his surprise it did feel different to be eating and concentrating solely on the experience of eating.

Focused, chewed, swallowed and opened his eyes to see her watching him expectantly. 'OK. Go ahead.'

'The potatoes are the perfect texture, soft and fluffy but not soggy, and the coating they are cooked in is perfect, so there is still a bit of texture to each bite and that contrasts well with the fluffiness of the roll. As for the spices as I said I don't know what they all are but I am pretty sure one is fresh coriander and I can taste a hint of heat and there is definitely some garlic and that's as much as I can say.'

'See, that wasn't so hard?' Her smile was wide and as he smiled back the whole promenade lit up as the massive crescent-shaped sweep of coastline illuminated with miles of sparkling lights. 'Look. They call it the Queen's Necklace because it looks like a pearl necklace,' she said.

'It's beautiful.' But really he meant that she was beautiful. 'Now it's your turn.'

'I…' She tucked a tendril of hair behind her ear and looked down at the *food in her hand*, then back at him and now her gaze rested fleetingly on his lips, before she closed her eyes and bit into the *vada pav*. Once she'd eaten she opened her eyes and considered. 'I can taste coriander but also a hint of cumin and maybe the sweetness of cardamom and a tang of saltiness.' Now her gaze rested on his mouth and her voice was low, almost husky and whilst he told himself she was talking about the patty it didn't feel like that. It felt like she was talking about a kiss, about how it had felt to kiss him, how it would feel if they kissed now.

He took another bite and now their gazes were locked. 'I am savouring the heat of the spice and the warmth of the filling and that feeling of newness and unfamiliarity of taste. And that makes me want more, want another bite and another taste, to immerse myself in the experience. The heat, the taste, the spice, the crave for more.'

Her eyes darkened and now he knew that it was impossible to change the momentum—impossible for his brain to override the inevitability and that realisation was as close as he came to even trying. Instead he leant forward and she was close, so tantalisingly close when the swoop and dive of a seagull broke the moment, flew so near he could see the detail of its beak, felt the tip of its wings nearly brush his cheek.

Stella gave a small cry as she moved backwards and he instinctively turned to shoo off the bird and make sure she was protected.

Once the bird was gone he turned, saw that she had retrieved the food. 'Are you OK?'

'Yes.' She rose to her feet and he could see from her closed expression, the look that he'd come to think of as her stage presence, that she had no intention of discussing the near kiss. And that was fine with him. 'And I've got an idea what we should do now. Let's go back to the hotel and I'd like to watch a Bollywood film. Before our tour tomorrow. We can take the rest of the food back.' Her voice was a tad brittle, a little too high-pitched and he hesitated, wondered if they should talk about it. But what was the point? They both knew the attraction existed and they clearly both knew it was a bad idea. Perhaps the distraction of a film was exactly what they needed.

He nodded. 'We could watch one produced by the company I'm in talks with starring the celebrity couple. I've watched a few but not all.' He glanced at her. 'We could order popcorn as well?'

'Sure.' And put the bowl between them as a barrier. This would be fine.

CHAPTER SEVEN

HALF AN HOUR later they were back at the hotel, TV set up and the popcorn in place as planned. Max wondered if he should even sit on the same sofa but in the end it would be even more awkward if he didn't. So the popcorn plan would have to do. He closed his eyes—how had he come to this? Relying on some popped kernels covered in salt to save him from attraction. Self-control much Durante?

He sat down, saw that she too was sitting in a way that indicated a high level of tension, back ramrod straight, knees pressed together, legs turned at an angle away from him. A mirror image of his own body language.

'Right. Let's press Play,' he said in a voice that boomed false joviality.

And then the movie started and slowly, imperceptibly he was drawn in, the magnificent grandeur of the sets, the sheer colour, vibrancy and over-the-top extravagance of the costumes, the authenticity and detail of the props and above all the emotion, the twists and turns of the love story, the betrayals and the passion and the sheer drama so beautifully portrayed.

And somehow as all this had unfolded, and he truly had no idea how, the bowl of popcorn had been moved to the floor still half-full, Stella was curled up with her legs tucked in beneath her, right up next to him, her head on his shoulder one hand tightly gripped in his.

He blinked, remaining still, not wanting to break the moment, the tickle of her hair against his cheek, the sound of the music as the credits rolled, half of him still immersed in the world portrayed by the film.

Stella sat up, wiped her eyes. 'That was amazing.'

He could smell her shampoo, a clean floral-tinged smell that brought memories cascading back, triggered by her proximity, the way she fit in next to him, waking up next to that same scent, the tickle of hair across his chest, her head resting there, her body encased in his arms.

As he looked at her he saw a fresh teardrop sparkle at the end of her lashes and he couldn't help himself. Oh, so, gently he reached out and caught the drop on the tip of his finger.

Heard her shuddered intake of breath and now pure instinct took over, and he leant forward; and there was Stella, her blue eyes wide and full of wonder and want and then they were kissing and it was everything he'd expected and more. The taste of spices, the tang of salt from the popcorn, it was all so right, so welcome, so glorious and as he deepened the kiss her gasp of pleasure, the feel of her fingers in his hair, surged desire through him. Time suspended into a moment of pure pleasure, every sense heightened to perfect pitch until inevitably reality intruded, as the film credits ended and an ad blared from the screen.

Stella pulled away with a small gasp that he recognised as one of distress and he saw dismay transcend desire on her face. Dismay and self-recrimination.

'Dammit!' Her fists clenched, nails digging into the palm of her hand. 'What is wrong with me?'

'Nothing,' he said. 'Or if there is, the same thing is wrong with me.'

'We shouldn't have done that.' Now she twisted her hands together on her lap.

'No,' he agreed. 'But we did.' He reached out and took her hands, gently disentangled them and smoothed away the marks from her nails and even now there was still the jolt of desire, but he ignored it, refused to so much as acknowledge it. 'Stella. It's OK. We shouldn't have done it, but there is no harm done. It was one kiss. We have a massive amount of chemistry and we're spending a lot of time together and…it happened.' He frowned at her expression, could see that his words were having no impact. 'But you are clearly upset— so you do think harm has been done.'

She looked down at their clasped hands. 'Not exactly, but I do know we need to sort this out. Figure out how to not have chemistry, or at least get it under control. The most important thing now is the baby. I need to be focused on working out the best way forward for him or her and I don't want my judgement to be affected by this.'

Fear inserted an insidious tendril at her repeated

emphasis on the fact that she was the one making the decisions. Fear and affront that she believed she needed to figure it out on her own, and that meant she still didn't see them as a parenting unit.

Dropping her hands he tried to keep anger and hurt from his voice. 'So you're worried that I may be a bad bet as a father but you won't notice because of our chemistry.'

'No. Or not exactly. I mean *we* are here to try to work out what to do next and I can't work out a strategy when attraction is in the mix. It's messing with my head and I am worried it is making us both see each other through rose-coloured spectacles.' She tried a smile. 'Or if not rose-coloured, whatever the colour of desire is.'

Dammit. Stella was right. Distracted by desire, by this burning need to reach out, to touch, to kiss, to run his fingers through her hair he'd taken his eyes off why they were really here. His agenda. To make sure he was part of the baby's life.

'You're right. We're here to work out a parenting plan and we need to be focused on that. On getting to know each other as future co-parents.'

'Yes.' But he saw sadness touch her eyes. 'That's it. And that is how it will always be so we have to knock the attraction on the head now. Because if we don't, what happens?'

It was the wrong question. Because it was all too easy to imagine exactly what would happen if they succumbed—to picture her in his arms, in his bed. But then what?

'Where would it end?' she continued softly. 'We can't be an interlude…together for a few nights and then go our separate ways. We're in this together forever and I don't want our child to grow up feeling embarrassed because he or she can sense something between us, or even worse that he or she grows up hoping we'll get together. It would all be too messy and complicated.'

'I get it.' And he did. He hesitated, saw that anxiety still etched on her features. He moved closer. 'But please don't feel like we've done anything wrong. We haven't. This…whatever it is between us…this chemistry…it's what created our baby. No regrets, remember?'

She placed a hand over her midriff and now she smiled, a slow, serene smile. 'No regrets,' she said.

'And no harm done. It's good we've had this talk and we can move forward. I know the attraction won't just disappear, but as long as we don't act on it, it will fade away in time.' Though for some reason the idea felt bleak, that something so vibrant, so vital, would slowly dissipate, crumble from rose to ash. But then his gaze fell to her hand and he knew that it didn't matter. Nothing mattered except the baby.

From now on in he wouldn't forget that; this past day had been hazed by attraction. No more. From now on it would be all about the baby, all about making sure he was there for her.

CHAPTER EIGHT

THE FOLLOWING MORNING Stella studied her reflection in the mirror and gave a small nod of approval. A linen jump suit, hair pulled back in a ponytail, flat black sandals, light layer of make-up. Today heralded the return of poised, cool, together Stella ready to assess Max without the rose-coloured spectacles of desire. Because that was what she was in Mumbai for. To figure out whether Max would be a good dad and how much involvement he wanted. No, she corrected herself, not how much he wanted, how much he should have. After all her own father had *wanted* to run her life, *wanted* to make Adriana's a misery, had wanted control.

Determination bolstered her as she entered the living room, a civil, aloof smile firmly in place. And if it faltered slightly, if desire twisted through her at the sight of his sculpted, sun-kissed, muscular arm highlighted by the bright white T-shirt, the clean lines of his face, the strength of his jaw, the firm line of his mouth—well that was between her and her hormones.

Her own thoughts seemed mirrored in his brown eyes and she could see that he too was different today, sensed that he too had decided to adopt a different approach; it was in the stark white of his shirt, the sharp crease in his trousers, the way he held his body, as though he were ready for anything.

'Good morning.'

'Good morning. I've ordered room service. I've got a meeting at eleven but until then we can talk.'

'It sounds like you have an agenda.'

'Nothing so formal,' he said. 'But I would like to know more about you, seeing as you are the mother of my child and I'm sure you have questions too.'

She knew that this was the right way forward, knew that it was what they had agreed to, but dammit she missed the ease, the banter…she missed the rose-coloured spectacles. Missed the laid-back Max too. This was the Max Durante who had built a business up from nothing.

A knock on the door heralded breakfast and she smiled as the hotel staff pushed the trolley forward, covered in dishes topped by silver domes. 'We have masala *dosas* filled with spiced potatoes and a Maharashtrian speciality, *sabudana vaad*, which are sago fritters served with our chef's special yoghurt sauce.' The waiter nodded towards Max. 'As you requested all the ingredients are listed out and no unpasteurised milk has been used.' He indicated the other covered dishes. 'Under these are fruit and yoghurts and pastries.'

'Thank you. We can take it from here.'

'It all looks amazing,' Stella added, waited for the waiter to leave and then smiled at Max. 'Thank you for this and for checking the ingredients.'

'I know unpasteurised milk isn't OK, but I wasn't sure if there was anything else.'

'This all looks fine. Better than fine.' Warmth touched her that he had found time to research and had then done something about it.

'Help yourself.'

She heaped her plate and then tasted the *dosa* closed her eyes to savour the crisp lightness of the rice pancake and the contrasting spicy tang of the potato. 'This is to die for. What do you think?'

'It's good,' he agreed. 'Really good. I was reading up on it and the baby is probably able to taste some of the flavour of what you are eating—which is fascinating. Nerves from taste buds begin connecting to the brain at about thirteen to fifteen weeks.'

'I think I am going to try to introduce as many flavours as I can and then maybe the baby won't be a fussy eater.'

'Or maybe he or she will grow up to be a world-famous chef.'

'Perhaps we should just refer to the baby as 'she' from now on.' That felt better to her, a reminder that she really didn't mind the baby's gender, that she was nothing like her father, didn't crave a son and heir.

'That's fine with me.'

'And maybe she could just be a good cook, or someone who loves food,' Stella said softly. 'I don't ever want her to feel pressured to do anything,' she added fiercely. 'I want her to choose a career and I will support that choice and if she doesn't want a career but wants to go travel the world or…volunteer or…well whatever she wants to do I'll help her do it.' Would never steer her child towards a destiny that she had mapped out for her.

Max nodded. 'Of course, but it will be important to encourage our child too, introduce them to lots of options and whatever she chooses, she should be the best they can.'

Stella frowned... 'As long as she gets to choose.' What if Max wanted his child to inherit InScreen, brought them up to believe that was their path?

'Which brings me to something I'd like to know. What did you choose to do? Your job?' He poured more coffee as Stella looked at him, suddenly loath to answer the question as she remembered the extent of his success, the grit and determination and drive he possessed. He waited a polite second and continued. 'Also what are you planning to do about work? When the baby is born.'

A sense of panic was beginning to unfold, a fear that he would ask all these questions and find her wanting. Because she didn't have any answers. She fought the instinct to put her cutlery down and fold her arms. She was the Honourable Stella Morrison, beautiful, sought after, social goddess and countess material, the woman who had been going to save her family home. True her entire raison d'être had been summarily removed, she was pretty much homeless and jobless, she'd pre-cipitated her father's heart attack and let her sister and mother down *again*, but she was damned if she'd show any vulnerability to Max. Because she couldn't afford to. Because somehow now that the rose-coloured spectacles were off, she was feeling judged.

'Is that the most important thing to you? My job?' The question a prevarication, to buy time.

'No, it isn't. But I am interested and I do want to know how you are planning to juggle work and a baby and how I can help with that. I wasn't aware your work was a state secret. Perhaps you are a spy?' He sipped his coffee and raised his eyebrows. 'But either way I get the feeling you're avoiding the question?'

'I'm not.' She found herself touching the tip of her nose, almost as if to see if it had grown Pinocchio-style. 'I just don't think it will tell you anything deep and meaningful. My job history is more a question of doing 'this and that.'

'Define *this and that*.'

'I've worked as an interior designer and an events manager and I worked in retail for a while as well. But in the last couple of years I was…well practising to be a countess.' She picked up a fritter, took a bite, focused on the crunch of peanuts and chillies and the cooling sensation of the yoghurt. Told herself not to sound defensive. 'As you know I intended to marry into high society to save Salvington and I wanted to be sure I was good at what I was doing. That I could deliver. So I accepted an allowance from my parents and I organised events, I hosted dinners, I learnt how to run a big house as economically as possible, I sat on charitable committees.' The last had in fact been what she had enjoyed most; and what she'd enjoyed most hadn't been the glitz and glam of the events themselves but the behind-the-scenes involvement, the personal anonymous work she undertook that not even her sister knew about.

'So if you had to do your duty and be countess then you were going to make sure that you were the best countess possible?' he asked.

'Well yes. That made sense to me. I was essentially brokering a marriage deal and I needed to make sure I could deliver what I said I would deliver.'

'Understood.' He hesitated. 'But is that what you wanted to do? I mean I respect your decision to do it. For your family home. But did you *want* to be a countess? Do you think you would have been happy?'

She considered the question, couldn't see any harm in answering honestly. 'I don't know. I wouldn't have been unhappy. I'd have had a family. I'd have saved my ancestral home.' She'd have finally made things up to her sister and as mother of the heir to Salvington she would have had power over her father. Perhaps finally her mother could have left her marriage without fear. All of that would have made her happy and she realised she hadn't really thought much beyond that. 'But hearing you describe how you feel about your job, how it drives you, how passionate you are about it… I didn't feel like that about being a countess.'

'Is there a job you do feel passionate about? What did you want to be when you were a little girl?'

Stella hesitated. This was something she hadn't spoken about for years, had buried away as something that quite simply wasn't possible. But somehow here and now she wanted Max to know, to understand that she wasn't some entitled frippery, shallow person. Or at least that if she was it was a choice she'd decided to make.

'When I was younger I wanted to be a lawyer.' It had seemed clear to Stella from a young age that life wasn't fair. It wasn't fair that her father treated her with so much love and treated her sister like dirt. It wasn't fair that he blamed his wife for all their misfortunes and so their love had shrivelled into a bitter parody of a happy ever after. It wasn't fair, come to that, that the law said she couldn't inherit Salvington simply because she was a girl. So she'd wanted to become a lawyer, understand the law, help people fight unfairness.

She saw the surprise on his face and her eyes narrowed. 'I'm guessing you thought I'd say fairy princess or something along those lines.' And she could hardly blame him really.

'Perhaps,' he conceded. 'But I accept I was wrong. What happened to that ambition?'

'I realised I had to make a choice.' She'd told her father what she wanted to do and to put it simply he'd vetoed it. Told her it would take too long, that her priority had to be Salvington. And when she'd shown signs of digging her heels in he'd done what he'd always done. Taken out his anger with her on Adriana and his wife. And soon after that he'd embarked on his affair in an attempt to father an heir.

All Stella's fault, another consequence of her actions. And everything had spiralled from there, the scandal, her father's return to the marital fold, her own pathetic rebellion that had nearly triggered another tragedy and after that Stella had accepted her lot, had no intention of precipitating any more misery.

But she could hardly tell Max any of that, wouldn't expose her own folly. She'd worked so hard to try to put it behind her, to shut it away and move on. She'd built a new Stella Morrison, poised, cool, the perfect Lady and that was the person she needed to be and so she shrugged, regretted even mentioning the whole lawyer dream. A pointless dream that had caused misery.

'It fizzled out really. I made the choice to embrace the life that I was destined for. And what wasn't there to like about it? I had money, an amazing social life, I enjoyed the jobs I did and it was the right thing to do. For me. Being a lawyer wasn't.' She could hear the hint of defiance tinged with defensiveness in her voice, saw a small frown crease his forehead as he studied her expression. 'I guess I am more the princess type. Easier. More fun and it meant I could save Salvington.'

He looked as though he were going to pursue the subject, but to her relief instead he shrugged. 'Fair enough. But where does that leave you now? Jobwise.' The frown deepened. 'And where will you be living? At Salvington?'

'No. We have a flat in London.' Though the 'we' was perhaps ambiguous. Technically the flat like everything else belonged to her father, but Stella had always used it whilst staying in London. But now? It wouldn't feel right to stay there even assuming her father didn't have the locks changed. That's why she was currently living in... Please don't let him ask.

'So you're currently living in the flat?'

Great. 'Not at the moment. Because it doesn't feel right to do that when my father is still ill.'

'So where are you living?'

'I… Why does it matter?'

'Are you saying you don't want me to have your address?'

'No. I just don't really have an address right now. I've been staying with friends and in hotels.' She could see him process the words, and come up with the conclusion that she was technically homeless.

'Then I can help. I'd like to help. You're pregnant with my child—you need a proper roof over your head. I'll rent you somewhere. In London would work and if you aren't working right now that's OK too—we can sort something out.'

'No!' The syllable rang out, lacking any cool or poise and she took a deep breath.

She wouldn't let herself become reliant on Max. In any way. Would not give him any power in her life. Been there, done that. Her whole life she'd danced to her father's tune—now she'd dance to her own. There was that panic again because she didn't know the steps, but she'd figure it out and wouldn't reveal even a hint of vulnerability to Max, couldn't cede any power at all.

She'd watched her mother bow to her husband's wishes because she had no choice; Lord Salvington had money, power and position and he'd used them all as leverage, ensured her mother couldn't leave, was reliant on him. That would not happen to Stella and yet… suddenly as she looked at Max all she could see was a man with money, power and position.

Recalled that once her parents had been in love, her mother had trusted her father, and that trust had led to reliance and misery for them all when their relationship had turned bitter, as her father had changed from a loving husband and father into a man turned sour and miserable by the lack of an heir.

'No?' Max's voice held confusion.

'No,' she repeated, more calmly. 'That really won't be necessary. But thank you. I have it all under control.' And there it was—her nose itched again. But this was only a stretch of the truth because she would have it under control. 'I've already got it sorted. I am going back to work at the interior design place.' Talk about winging it and she was more than aware that she was skirting the edge of the truth. But when she'd left they had really wanted her to stay and had told her she could come back whenever she wanted So… 'On a six-month contract and then I'll return when the baby is older. So you don't need to worry—I can pay my bills. And rent somewhere. If you want to help support the baby then I will put aside any money for his or her future. But that's all I will accept.'

He pushed his plate away and she could see the tension now in his shoulders, the set of his jaw. 'So any money I give you now, you won't use to support our child, to pay the bills. You would prefer to live as a single parent where the father refuses to face up to his responsibilities.'

'No. I told you I will save that money for the child.'

'I can provide for my child's future as well as support them in the present. What if she would like ballet lessons or to join a football club?'

'Then I'll pay for that.'

'How? After London rents and bills and childcare how will you do that? I want my child to have the things that I can afford to give, and I don't understand why you would want to deprive her of those opportunities and chances.'

'My child will not be deprived of anything. At all. This isn't about money—there are hundreds of thousands of children who are perfectly happy without expensive classes and material possessions because they have love and care and nurturing and that is a hundred times more important. Ballet lessons do not lead to happiness.' This she knew. 'So if that's all you're planning to bring to the parenting table then…'

'Then what?' he asked and now his voice was low and she could sense his anger, knew that it was justified. It wasn't Max's fault that she was riding a wave of panic, wasn't his fault that he embodied everything she was most fearful of. But right now she couldn't stop herself, braced herself for his anger to escalate and started to utter the words, 'Then maybe there…' is no place for you at the table.

But before she could finish he took a deep breath. 'Stop. Look. I'm not sure what is going on here but maybe we should take a step back. It seems silly to argue about ballet lessons when the baby isn't even born yet, let alone pirouetting. So before you say what you were about to say maybe we both need some space. I'll go down for my meeting and we'll regroup later.'

Surprise held her still for a moment and then she nodded. 'Agreed.'

'But for the record I am not planning to only bring money to the table. I want to be there for my child. 'I want to be part of my child's life, properly, not just a token presence.'

Fear began to circulate—Max would provide pots of money, their child would be caught up in his wealth and fame and glamourous lifestyle, studded with awards and red carpets and celebrities. What if their child preferred Max. Stop. Love was what mattered, not possessions. Really? Possessions had been a balm to her soul in her childhood.

He rose to his feet and she managed a smile of sorts, knew she needed time. To process what he'd said. But also time to call Leila and turn her half lie into a truth—she had to secure a job, had to have her own money, provide her own stability.

Stella waited until he had gone and picked her phone up.

'Leila. It's Stella. Sorry I know it's early.'

'No problem. I'm up and getting ready for work. How are you?'

'It's complicated. But I was wondering if there is any chance I could have my job back. But there is something completely confidential I need to tell you first.'

Quickly she filled her friend in on events without revealing Max's identity. Leila listened and then Stella could visualise her nodding briskly as she spoke. 'Of course you can—in fact by luck my assistant is about to go on maternity leave so I need cover. But it's good you called because I've been meaning to call you. Something odd happened. But this explains it. Someone called me asking for a reference for you? I assumed you must be applying for jobs.'

Stella frowned. 'Nope. I wasn't.'

'Then it's extrastrange because I bumped into Matteo at an exhibition and he said someone had been asking about you. Kind of casually, but he still thought it was a bit off. I put it down to Matteo being Matteo but…'

'But maybe it was a reporter sniffing around.' Stella bit back a groan—the last thing she wanted was for the pregnancy story to break right now, before she and Max had figured out how to handle it. Didn't want her father to be upset, for it to affect Adriana and Rob.

'Thanks, Leila, and thank you for the contract as well.' It would at least tide her over whilst she figured out what to do next. But now maybe she'd do a quick call around and see if she could work out if there was a reporter on her case, though surely they would have tried to contact her direct?

CHAPTER NINE

MAX HEADED BACK to the suite, his mind still buzzing with the results of his meetings, satisfied that they'd gone well, alongside a knowledge that there were still significant steps to be taken to build the right rapport and trust. Just like with Stella.

He sensed he'd somehow overstepped the mark, spooked her, but he'd panicked. Needed her to see, perhaps needed himself to see that he had more to offer than money.

He opened the door to the suite to see Stella pacing the floor. 'What's wrong? What's happened? Is the baby OK?' He strode forward.

'The baby is fine. But I think we have a problem. I've spoken with some friends including my ex—well my current boss—and there has been someone snooping round. I assume it's a reporter, but oddly whoever it is hasn't approached me or my family? But someone is asking questions—and I really don't want anyone to approach my parents for a reaction or for them to see a headline hit or...'

Ah. The penny dropped around about the word

snooped and Max hurriedly scrolled through his emails, scanned the latest from the detective agency. Yup... 'A detective has undertaken discreet enquiries...'

Max was aware of a craven desire to say nothing, one he dismissed instantly. 'It's not a reporter.'

She came to a stop. 'It's not? How do you know?'

'Because I asked a private investigator to check you out, do a background check on you.'

There was a moment of silence and he watched her expression morph from worry to confusion to understanding and to outrage. 'I— You...*what?* You set a detective on me?'

'Yes. You're carrying my baby and I know nothing about you.'

'I thought that was the point of this time in Mumbai—to find out about more about each other whilst we planned a future for our child and instead you did this. Well, you can forget it, because you are going to have nothing to do with this baby at all.' He could hear anger in her voice, fury, but he could also hear hurt. 'I cannot believe you did something so low.' She shook her head. 'I'm done. I'm out of here.' Grabbing her handbag, she headed for the door.

For an instant Max stood stock still, and then two swift strides took him to the door to look out over an empty corridor. Dammit. He ran to the stairs as he heard the ping of the lift and raced down the stairs, dodged the convention of business delegates with a muttered apology even as he cursed the delay.

Reached the cool marble environs of the lobby in

time to see a glimpse of her blonde head as she headed out of the door, raced after her even as his skin went clammy at the instant hit of humid heat.

'Stella.'

She didn't so much as pause as she stormed onto the thronged street, her walk brisk though he was pretty sure she had no destination in mind. Now he didn't even bother with apologies as he thrust his way through the crowds after her, overtook her and turned so they were facing each other, didn't give her a chance to protest before he spoke.

'Because I was scared,' he said. 'That's the answer to the question, why did I do it, why did I have a check done on you?'

'Scared of what? That I'll be a lousy mum.' Hands on hips, eyes ablaze with anger, equally oblivious to the people around them.

'No.' Her words poleaxed him as he saw that her anger masked fear and also disbelief.

She shook her head. 'Why else would you do it, Max? I thought this trip to Mumbai was about us working out what was best for the baby together, a way to make this work. Time to get to know each other better. Not for you to set a detective to questioning my colleagues and my friends behind my back. Whilst plotting to take my child away.'

'I was not plotting to take your child away. At all.' How had he lost track of this conversation so dramatically? 'I was…trying to get to know you better.' Even he could hear the utter inadequacy of the defence.

'I do not need to listen to this. I thought… Oh, it doesn't matter.'

With that she'd dodged past him in a blur of grace and rage and he spun round and strode after her, all too aware how easy it would be for her to be swallowed up by the crowds.

He kept his gaze focused on the bob of her blonde head as she headed towards a massive building, one that rose in a splendour that caught the eye due to it's clearly European architectural style. Stella's stride didn't falter as she plunged into the interior and he hurried after her, instantly aware that the building housed a sprawling market, the interior lit by a stunning fifteen-metre skylight.

Noise, colour and smells all assailed him and for a moment he lost Stella. His gaze scanned the mass of people, roved over the incredible range of goods on display. Brightly coloured exotic fruit, watermelons the size of bowling balls, reds, oranges, yellows dazzled his eyes. Spices pervaded the air, stored in massive sacks—coriander mixed with cumin and the heat of chillies seemed embodied in the bright red cascades that hung in bunches. He recalled Stella's voice describing the taste of the patties just as he spotted her.

'Stella!' his voice was swallowed up in the cries of the vendors, the shouted haggling of the buyers and as he plunged towards her the caw of birds added to the cacophony of noise and he realised he was walking past a pet area. Brightly plumed birds chattered and shrieked amidst the bark of dogs and again his voice was drowned.

On past stall after stall, unsure now if they had circled round, all sense of direction lost and then finally he had nearly caught up with her.

'Stop. Stella. Please.' Perhaps she heard the plea in his voice because she slowed down and then turned, stood in front of a stall selling a vast array of vegetables, and he wished, how he wished that they were here to visit the market, to wander round, could imagine Stella looking at the knobbly kohlrabi, the vivid green garlic stalks, the light yellow lemongrass, inhaling the smell of fresh coriander and enjoying herself. Instead he knew he somehow had to get her to listen, needed to explain, to make it crystal-clear he had no intent to take the baby from her. 'Please give me a chance to explain.'

Her blue eyes narrowed, but then she nodded. 'OK. You've got three minutes.'

He'd take it. But, 'Fair enough. But not here. It's too busy, too noisy.'

Stella glanced quickly across at Max, as they exited the market; rage still churned inside along with a healthy dollop of hurt and she wondered why she was even giving him three minutes when he didn't even deserve three seconds. All that time, pretending to be kind, offering help, kissing her for Pete's sake. And all that time he'd been having her investigated, checking if she would be a good mum.

She increased her stride as he checked his phone looking for a destination. 'There's a park about ten minutes away.'

'Fine.'

Once they reached the wide-open green space, he led the way to a bench under the shade of a massive dark-leafed tree and she sank down with an inner sigh of relief, set a timer and placed her phone on the bench beside her.

Turned to face him, arms folded. But to give him his due, he met her gaze dead on. 'I would never try to take the baby away from you.'

'And why should I believe that?'

He opened his mouth, closed it again, looked down at her phone and then stared straight ahead. 'I grew up without a mother—I'd never wish that on anyone.' The words hit her as she realised she hadn't even thought about his background. 'You can choose to believe that or not. But it's the truth.'

It was, and on a gut level she knew that, but she couldn't leave it at that, not with so much at stake. 'Then why did you do it? What were you scared of?'

'Everything. But most of all I was scared you'd decide to keep the baby from me. That you wouldn't put me on the birth certificate, that you'd move to the Outer Hebrides, that you'd decide I can only have visiting rights once a year.'

'But I wouldn't do that.'

'I don't *know* that you wouldn't. We barely know each other and you were very clear that you could "do whatever you decide is best for the baby". Finding out more about you seemed a good place to start. I wanted to make negotiations easier so I told myself the more I knew about you the better. In truth I felt helpless and I wanted to do something. Because I also grew up without a father and I don't want my child to do the same.'

'I...' Stella opened and closed her mouth; had no idea what to say. She did believe the final call was hers to make but...from his viewpoint, the stance of an abandoned baby...even the smallest chance that his baby would suffer the same way he had must have been terrifying. 'I should have been more sensitive. Because I do want to do what's best for the baby, and I do want you to be part of the baby's life. You are the father.'

'Providing I measure up.'

'Yes. But I should have considered how you were feeling, should have made it clearer that I was starting from the premise that I *want* you in the baby's life. And of course I should have taken your background into account.'

'I don't want your pity.'

'I'm not offering you pity.' She could sense the tension in his body, hear it in the rasp of his voice. 'I'm offering you a qualified apology. And an explanation. I have read so many of your interviews and in all of them you sound so together about your start in life, so understanding of your mother. And because family took you in I suppose I have always read it as a feel-good story, but it's not a story. It's your truth, your life.' And she of all people should know that what you read in the press was seldom the truth. How many interviews had she given where she'd said the right thing, not what she felt? 'And I should have been more careful about what I said.' The timer bleeped and she switched it off, knew this conversation had only started.

He shook his head. 'I don't want you to be careful about what you say. I want you to be truthful. Because I need to know where I stand.' His voice was hard now. 'Because I won't fight to take the child away from you, but I will fight for my rights to be in her life. I have to.'

She could see the shadows in his eyes, the grim rigidity of his mouth set in an uncompromising line and she couldn't help herself, all thoughts of distance gone. Because this wasn't about attraction, this was about the importance of this moment, for them as parents. And so she moved forward, reached out and took his hands in hers. 'I understand and… I don't want to fight.'

She felt some of the tension leave his body, felt a sudden sense of a tenuous connection, a warmth, though there was still a wariness in his eyes.

'And it's not that I have doubts about *you* exactly. But I've been scared too.'

He blinked. 'Scared of what?'

'Scared that you would use your wealth, your position, *your* power to try and take control, to make me do things your way.' Exactly as her father had done. To her, to her mother, to her sister. He had dominated and manipulated, made them dance to his tune and yet he'd claimed to love Stella. And once he'd loved his wife. 'Because that's what happened with my dad. My parents married for love. Once they were happy and if I stretch way back into my memory banks I can remember that happiness. I have a recollection of my father throwing me up in the air, my mother laughing, family hugs. Sometimes I'm not sure if they are real memories or culled from photographs and what my mother has told me. But I do believe once they were happy.'

'And then?' His focus was complete, and she knew he was truly listening.

'Then they weren't. I mean I am sure it's not that simple—their marriage deteriorated, spiralled downwards and somehow that downwards trend wasn't reversible. My father couldn't get over not having an heir. So every month that went past, every year he became more and more bitter over her "failure" and he became more and more cruel.'

Max frowned. 'Then why didn't she leave?'

'My sister and I begged her to, but she wouldn't. Because she was terrified she'd lose custody. My father had everything, the money, the position, the power. He held all the cards and she held none.' She gave a sudden mirthless smile. 'Even when he had an affair and we were hit by scandal, through it all my mother was forced to be the wife who "stood by her man".' She wrapped her arms round her stomach. 'So I don't want history to repeat. I don't want to be reliant on you in any way. Especially as you have so much wealth and power.'

'I understand that.' He hesitated and she looked at him.

'It's OK. I sense a "but". Ask whatever you need to ask.'

'I don't understand why you were willing to marry your aristocrat. Weren't you worried about him using his power or position or wealth?'

Stella blinked, realised the question had completely wrong-footed her with its utter validity.

'It's a good question.'

He gave a small smile. 'I know.'

'For one thing I would have had a prenup with Rob.' Though they had never had a chance to get down to the real nitty-gritty of the details, which in hindsight had been foolish. 'But it was more than that. I knew Rob. I don't know you.' But in truth it had been more even than that. With Rob she had been confident that there would be no blips in their marriage, no emotions, no rollercoaster; she'd been sure of her power over him. That she, Stella Morrison, beautiful, poised, sophisticated, was so well-qualified to be Rob's wife, Countess of Darrow, that it hadn't occurred to her that he had any power. She'd felt safe because there was no spark, no overwhelm of attraction, no…no anything really. 'I liked him, respected him and… I felt in control. Around you I don't feel in control.'

'What about liking and respect?' he asked, but his voice held a soupçon of humour and she welcomed that, relieved that he seemed on board with her explanation, that he believed her.

'I'm working on it.' Her riposte was said lightly and he smiled, a proper smile.

'I have an idea. It's hard to work on liking and respect when we both feel so powerless, so scared that the other one is trying to score points. So why don't we sign a basic initial legal agreement, which acknowledges paternity, that I will be on the birth certificate, but also sets out that neither of us will fight for sole custody with no visitation rights. Then we can build on that as we do get to know each other better.'

'That sounds fair.' It really did and she gave an exhalation of sheer relief.

'Good. I'll get my lawyer to draw something up to send to your lawyer.'

She nodded. 'That works.'

'Good. So now how about we have an ice cream to celebrate? And wander round and look at some of the markets.'

'I'd like that.'

'OK. Well, there's a choice between a spice market or a jewellery bazaar.'

'How am I supposed to choose between those?'

He grinned at her. 'Toss a coin?'

The words took her straight back to their night together, she could almost see the glint of the coin against the Dubai skyline.

'Works for me. She reached into her bag and took the coin out, saw him glance at it.

'Is it the same coin?'

'Actually, yes, it is…' She wasn't sure why she'd kept it. A souvenir of a magical night, a feeling that somehow the whole evening had been precipitated by their decision to talk, to share, to confide. A superstitious belief it was a lucky coin. Who knew? 'Heads for spices, tails for jewellery.'

She tossed the coin, waited for it to land and then checked. 'Tails.'

'Gold it is, then.'

'But ice cream first.'

CHAPTER TEN

MAX FELT A disproportionate sense of satisfaction as Stella tasted the double scoop of cardamom ice cream, her face illuminated by a beaming smile. He could sense her relief and knew it mirrored his own. The idea that they had solved something and taken a step towards co-parenting felt…good.

'Good?' he asked.

'Really good. Truly scrumptious.' Realising what she'd said, she repeated the last words in song. 'I love that film.'

'Me too.' And to prove the point he started to sing the first verse. And after a second she joined in, until she broke off with a sudden gurgle of laughter as a couple of people turned to look at them.

'My mum and sister and I watch it every year—I think they do it to humour me, but I don't care—it's a tradition.'

Envy panged at the idea of a family tradition. 'That sounds nice,' he said.

'It is.' She hesitated. 'Maybe when our child is old

enough, we can all watch it together? Let my mum and Adriana off the hook. If you'd like.'

'I would like that.' Appreciated too that she was showing him that she was open to real co-parenting, planned to grant him more than minimal visitation rights.

'Good. It's a date.' And there it was again, that smile that lit up her face and brought the lyrics of the song right back.

'When you're smiling,
It's so delicious
So beguiling,
You're the answer to my wishes.'

'Were films a big deal in your family?' she asked.

'No.' His aunt and uncle had no interest in films, though they had religiously watched the various soaps together every evening, but they had told Max they wanted their 'adult time' and so he had spent time in his room, reading books instead.

He stiffened slightly, aware that he'd tensed and that she'd noticed. *Careful.* He'd never opened up about his childhood, gone along with the implication that it had been a happy one, partly because it was nobody's business, but also because if his mother was reading any interview he didn't want her to know that it hadn't worked out.

'But then one day I went on a school trip to the cinema and it changed my world,' he said, keeping his voice light and forcing his body to relax. Putting himself in interview mode. Spiel at the ready. 'I loved the visuality of them, the way the actors could make me believe in their characters, so that I actually felt I was in their world and I was fascinated by how books could be made into films and how what was in my head could then be portrayed on a screen and how sometimes a film could actually be better or other times make me rage because they'd changed something fundamental. And it wasn't just films—it was the power of documentaries, the way you can learn and the utter fascination of following the life of a particular animal or species. Or learn history from so many different perspectives—' He broke off. 'Anyway, yes I was always fascinated by film though I never thought I'd make a career from it. Until I discovered you could study film, get a degree. After that everything took on a life of its own.'

The words picked up pace, the well-rehearsed story flowed easily now, well-used during the multitude of interviews he did. Nice and easy, making the segue from childhood to college sound seamless.

'It's great that your family supported you even though they weren't interested in film,' she said, and he caught the wistful note in her voice and suddenly the lie by implication felt wrong, stuck in his craw. Because he knew she must be thinking of her own complicated childhood and the father who had dominated it with his vision for her future and for a moment he was almost tempted to tell her the truth. An urge he shut down instantly, continuing relentlessly on with his story.

'I then went to Harvard to study business and then

I combined all my knowledge. I worked hard, I saved and I started a production company with a couple of others. Figured that the way to have best control of what we produced was to stream it myself, set up a streaming company and InScreen was born and now it's here to stay.'

Stella tipped her head to one side, took another bite of ice cream and he sensed she was going to ask something else about family. Braced himself. 'I know your family died tragically young and I just wanted to say I'm sorry, but I hope they at least got a chance to see you on the road to success.'

'Thank you.' The words sounded muted, and discomfort was a bitter taste in his mouth. But his past was buried. In truth his aunt and uncle had refused to acknowledge him even after his success. He had tried, once he was established, had a job; had contacted them, had offered money to reimburse them for the cost of bringing him up: They had refused, said he 'was dead to them'. Oddly despite everything that rejection, that intractable refusal to acknowledge that they may have been wrong, had stung, 'Money and success don't grant goodness,' his aunt had written. 'Please do not contact us again.'

Soon after he had heard they had been in a fatal car accident. And to his own surprise he had felt grief, because whatever they had done they had tried by their own standards and had at least given him a chance, been physically present unlike his parents. But there was sadness too because their deaths also killed any hope they would change their minds about him.

Stella's blue eyes rested on him and he knew it was time to change the subject, knew he didn't want to directly lie to her, but what was the point of rehashing the past; it wouldn't achieve anything except make her pity him and he didn't want that. But he did now want to know more about Stella and what she really wanted from life.

'So that's enough about my career. I've been thinking and now that you aren't going to become a countess would you reconsider the lawyer idea?'

She hesitated as though she was going to call him out on the abrupt change of subject, but instead she looked away as they left the environs of the park, joined the crowds.

'I'm not sure,' she said. 'It was just a childhood dream really.'

'There is nothing wrong with childhood dreams. What made that your particular dream though?'

'I think I always knew life wasn't fair. It never seemed right to me that I couldn't inherit Salvington, because I am a girl. And that still doesn't seem right to me now. So that isn't fair. But unfairness goes a lot deeper than that.' He saw the shadow that crossed her face and wondered if she was thinking of something specific. 'I mean it's not really fair that my father's wealth and position tethered my mother to him. I got it in my head that if she had someone to turn to who understood the law it could help her, help all of us.

'Then as I grew older I realised how much unfairness there is. I told you that I helped my mother with charity events, well I persuaded her to arrange a fundraiser for women who are victims of domestic abuse and...' He saw tears sparkle in her eyes, saw her jaw set in a determined clench of anger. 'Then I realised my own problems were tiny in comparison to theirs, that even my mother's issues paled in comparison to what some women endure. And these women often have children as well and the law...it doesn't do as much as it should. Everything is so underfunded and so many of these women have no help and don't know where to turn. And yet they are so brave and dignified and so grateful. And their children, what they have seen is heartbreaking.'

Max glanced at her. 'It sounds personal, as though you have met some of these women, as well as raised money.'

She bit her lip in obvious vexation. 'The money we raised is incredibly important. So far it helped expand a refuge, helped pay for an extra staff member and most importantly meant there was another room available.' She pointed. 'Oh, look. Let's head there. It's another market. Anyway I'm sure you don't really want to know this?'

'Yes, I do.' It was like seeing a whole new Stella, a glimpse behind the woman she presented to the world, the polished, sophisticated society girl. 'And I get that the money is important but if you are involved on a more personal level that is admirable too.'

'No. It's not admirable.' Indignation flushed her cheeks and she looked so real, so vital, so involved he caught his breath. 'What I do is *nothing* and I am certainly not doing it for kudos or to make myself feel good.'

'Why do you do it?'

'Because what has happened to those women is wrong and it's tragic and if I can do anything at all to make their lives even a little better, if it's listening to them, or taking them out somewhere where they can feel safe, or take them out to do something frivolous like have their nails done or look after their children for half an hour so they can rest then I will. One woman is so terrified her partner will find her and take her child away she can't sleep, she feels as though she has to watch over Billy every second. Their life is far away from mine—so no, what I do isn't admirable.'

'Do they know who you are at the refuge?'

'Some of them, but I don't tell them—occasionally they recognise me, but I don't publicise my visits. Partly because I think that would be dangerous, could attract the attention of their partners, give them a clue where they are. But also because this is...'

'Personal. Something you truly believe in.' He could hear the passion in her voice, saw it light up the blue of her eyes, understood too that it was, something she kept to herself because it didn't vibe with the persona she had put together to present to the world. That Stella cared, but not with this raw visceral passion.

'Yes, I do.'

'I can see that, hear that. So why on earth did you give up on the dream to be a lawyer. You said it fizzled out, but I just can't see that happening.'

She caught her lip in her teeth in what he recognised now as a sign of vexation with herself, when she'd dropped her guard.

'I get you wanted to make a grand alliance but surely you could have done both. Studied law and been a countess.'

'It's more complicated than that.' She turned away. 'In the end the countess lifestyle won out. I figured I could still help people without all the hard work…'

'Stop.' He suited the action to the words, pulled her over to one side. 'You don't have to explain, but please don't lie.'

'I'm not…' She faltered under his gaze.

'I don't buy it—that you gave up a dream you are clearly passionate about for a lifestyle of glitz and glam. I don't and won't believe it.'

Her blue eyes met his and to his surprise she gave a small smile. 'Thank you.'

'What for?'

'For not believing it. And you're right.' She hesitated and then took a deep breath. 'I told my father about my dream to be a lawyer; he took that to mean that I would put off marriage, he was worried a career would take over. So he vetoed it. But I wouldn't back down, I told him I could do both. Save Salvington and be a lawyer.

'He disagreed. That's why he had the affair—he wanted to get another woman pregnant. He called it his try-before-I-buy scheme.' Her voice shuddered with distaste, a feeling he shared. 'Then once she was pregnant he waited for the gender scan. When it turned out the baby was another girl he left the woman high and dry. She went public and then tragically soon after

she lost the baby. The whole scandal, the whole tragedy of it all would never have happened if it weren't
for me and my desire to be a lawyer. I wish I'd never
come up with it, never gone to my father with it. All I
did was achieve misery for so many people. So I gave
up the idea.'

'No.' He reached out and took her hand. 'No,' he
repeated. 'None of that misery is on you. Your father
made the choices he made. That is on him. His responsibility not yours.'

'My head knows that, but it doesn't work like that.
Because if I had judged him correctly I could have
avoided inflicting pain on so many people. On my
mother, my sister and that poor woman who he lied to
and then abandoned. And who knows if she lost the
baby because of the stress of the scandal?'

'You can't take all that onto your shoulders.'

'That's easy to say.'

'I know. I do understand.' He did, recognised the
weight she carried.

She shook her head, let out a small puff of disbelief
and he couldn't blame her. But perhaps he could help,
show her he did get it.

He closed his eyes, wondered if he could do it, share
his own burden, realised he wanted to. 'My head knows
that it was my mother who made the decision to leave
me. That decision to abandon me is on her. But it feels
like it's on me. My fault. Because for whatever reason my mother took one look at me and she knew she
didn't want me.'

'No.' The word torn from her. 'You don't know that.

You can't. There could have been a reason, so many reasons.'

'I have tried to tell myself the same. But if that were the case why didn't she leave something? A letter, a note. Even just to say sorry, or that she lo—cared about me.' Even if she couldn't keep him, couldn't she have left him something, anything, even if it had been a lie.

Her blue eyes had tears in them now, tears that she blinked away as if she knew he would interpret them as pity, and a small part of him wished the words undone, hated to show weakness, hated to show he cared, as though it somehow diminished him. Because he knew there was no point in caring—his mother hadn't cared for him; caring for his foster parents had made the pain of losing them worse. And how he'd wished his aunt and uncle had cared for him even a little bit; in the face of all their loathing he'd always hoped they'd change. Pathetic. And it was time to close this out.

'But I have to try and believe that it's not on me. Not my fault. That whatever her reasons, good or bad, they are hers, her responsibility not mine. But that's hard, so I do understand why you're carrying that load, but you mustn't. Because your father is responsible for his own actions. And that's the truth. You need to try and believe that.'

'And if I promise to try will you try to believe the same about your mother?' She reached out and took his hand in hers, clasped her fingers around the palm and held on and to his own surprise warmth touched him, and some of the tension seeped from his shoulders.

'I'll try. And… I'm truly sorry about the whole private investigator—I should never have done it.'

'It's OK. I wish you hadn't but… I understand. But from now on let's also try and be honest with each other.' She smiled at him, and her fingers tightened round his. 'Deal?'

'Deal.'

'Now why don't we go and explore the market.'

'Good plan.'

CHAPTER ELEVEN

As THEY WANDERED into the narrow alleyway Stella glanced down and realised they were still holding hands, their fingers firmly entwined. She considered letting go, after all hand-holding was emphatically, surely not a good idea. But it seemed like one right now, after all they had shared. They had made a connection—she sensed intuitively that Max never spoke of his real feelings about his mother, that what he had just done was a road untravelled. Yet he had done it. For her. To make her feel better. After she had shared something—no, some *things*, plural—that she too had never shared before. And she wasn't sure what that meant but she knew something had shifted inside her, broken through a barrier, a guard, and dammit right now she wanted to hold his hand. And the very fact he clearly wanted to hold hers sent a further surge of fuzziness through her.

So for now she was going to hold on and enjoy her surroundings.

And hell, what was there not to enjoy?

The market held her spellbound as they wandered

along the multitude of stalls, some of them as tiny as one hundred and fifty feet, others large and imposing, that lined the weave and curve of narrow lanes. All of them doing a roaring trade—the glisten and shine of gold, silver and precious stones dazzled her. People everywhere, some haggling customers, other trying to transport goods through congested pathways, herding bullocks along the side, carrying items on their heads to quicken their progress. Every available space taken up.

'It's like walking through a magical Aladdin's cave; but how on earth would you ever be able to buy anything here? How would you choose?'

'It is a bit daunting, but clearly it works. There are over seven thousand shops in the market, and about sixty-five percent of Mumbai's jewellery trade is conducted here. Literally millions all sprawled out. I have no idea how you would locate a specific shop but some of these businesses have been here for hundreds of years.' She blinked, stopped outside a display—chains, bangles, anklets; the gold so bright and shiny it almost hurt her eyes even behind her sunglasses. 'They're beautiful and they define bling. But do you know what I need now?' she said.

'Food and drink,' he replied promptly.

'How did you know?'

'Lucky guess and you're in luck. Apparently this market is also known for its food. We just need to find the bit where the food stalls are.'

His fingers tightened round hers. He took one last look at his phone and tugged her back into the crowds and ten minutes later they arrived at their destination and she gave a small sniff of appreciation as she inhaled the scent of spice, of frying oil.

'OK. You stay here and I will go and get us food,' he said.

As she eyed the throngs of people she nodded her thanks and settled to wait, watched as he disappeared into the crowd. Just when she'd given him up for lost he returned, balancing a selection of containers and cups on a makeshift tray.

'Here you go. I got *bhel puri* because you missed out last night and this is apparently unique to the bazaar. I talked to the vendor and checked on line and… among other ingredients we have dry puffed rice, onions and tomatoes, chickpeas, coriander, salt, a squeeze of lemon juice and most important something called *chappan* masala, which is made from fifty-six spices ground into a fine powder. He paused for breath as they wedged themselves in position at the roadside. 'I also have something called *kachori*—which is a kind of flat savoury doughnut filled with spiced lentils. And I have mango and apple juice because I thought that was the best thing to hydrate us.'

Stella looked at him and the sheer thoughtfulness, the fact he'd remembered the *bhel puri*, the fact a man who had no real interest in food had checked and memorised the ingredients all combined to conjure up a warmth of happiness.

'Thank you.' She blinked back a sudden tear and he looked at her quizzically.

'If I'd known it would make you cry I'd have chosen the omelette option.'

'I'm not crying. Or if I am it's hormonal—I just need food.'

'Then I'm your man. Let's share it out.'

'*I'm your man*...' And as Stella looked at him, as she tasted the food, she warned herself not to take those words too literally. Max wasn't anyone's man. But... but he would be in her life forever, because they were bound together by the tiny being growing inside her.

'So what now?' she asked once the last fragrant morsel, the final crumb had been consumed.

'Back to the hotel. I for one could do with a shower and then we can make a plan for the evening. I think we should have some fun; celebrate that we're moving forward together. I'm thinking why not let our hair down a bit, enjoy Mumbai's nightlife—maybe find somewhere that does great food and plays some Bollywood music. Get us in the mood for our tour tomorrow?'

'That sounds...' Dreamy, wonderful, amazing, like a date. 'Fun,' she settled for. This was not a date, and it was not dreamy. But dammit it felt like both.

Later that evening Stella glanced through her wardrobe, wondered what to wear. Knew that she should wear something flattering but conservative, something that was not designed to attract or lure or stage an entrance. Her fingers touched the folds of a grey dress, long, flowing, cinched at the waist with a slim light grey belt, with long flowing sleeves and which would be the correct 'co-parent outfit'.

Or she could wear this...now she pulled out her red dress. Also long, but it left her neck and arms bare and the red material was shot through with a shimmer and a shine and the skirt had a strategic slit down the side, the whole thing designed to attract, lure and scream 'Look at me'.

So what to do?

There was a knock at the door and she turned, called, 'Come in' and gulped as Max entered. Dark chinos, dark collarless button-down shirt and a light jacket—smart but not too formal and he looked gorgeous.

'Sorry. I can't quite decide what to wear.'

'Then you know what to do. Toss the coin.'

'Yup. You're right.' Stella suited the action to the word and looked down. The coin had spoken. The red dress it was.

'Give me half an hour and I'm all yours.'

'*I'm all yours...*' The words danced and shimmered across the room and for some reason she didn't care. Somehow the throw of the coin, the outcome made her want to throw caution to the wind.

'I'll be waiting,' he said.

True to her word half an hour later Stella checked her reflection and a doubt, a qualm flickered. She looked...pretty good, exactly how she'd look if this were a date. Her blonde hair fell in waves past her shoulders, her lipstick matched the dress in shimmer, shine and vibrant colour; her pale pink heels added height and...and maybe she should change?

Nope. There was no harm in looking good—after

all she was headed out to Mumbai's nightlife. And soon enough she wouldn't even fit into this dress and...and she wanted to see Max's face.

Swivelling she headed to the lounge and had the satisfaction of seeing him literally gobsmacked.

'You like?'

'I like...a lot.' There was a silence. 'So much that my usual eloquence has forsaken me. You look incredible... Mumbai won't know what's hit them.'

'So the coin chose well.'

'The coin definitely knows what it's talking about. It's a keeper.' He plunged his hand into his pocket. 'And speaking of coins I got something for you.'

'For me?'

'Yes. Here.' He handed her a long flat jewellery box and she opened it, her fingers trembling as she lifted out a necklace. With a pendant hanging from it, a golden coin in a circle of gold—bright, shiny, shimmering gold.

'It's beautiful.'

'I got it at the bazaar, before I got the food. I thought...well I thought you'd like it.'

'I do like it. A lot.' She paused. 'And all my poise has deserted me too.' She handed it to him. 'Would you put it on. Because believe it or not it is perfect for this dress. Which proves that coin has magical powers.'

'Just like me,' he said, and his voice was a deep rumble over her skin and as he took the necklace and their fingers touched a shiver of desire rippled through her. One that intensified as she turned and dropped her head, presented the nape of her neck, heard his slight intake of breath. Then the cool of the gold rested on her skin and now his fingers brushed her nape and she nearly mewled as sensations rocketed in her.

'Thank you,' she said, and she didn't even recognise her voice, breathless, husky and so full of yearning. Somehow she pulled herself together, walked over to the mirror and looked at her reflection; the necklace glinted at her, shone bright against the red of her dress and the blonde of her hair. She met his gaze in the mirror. 'I love it.'

'I'm glad. I... It looks beautiful.'

Every instinct told her to swivel round on her pink stilettos, march over to him and kiss him.

But somehow, somehow instead she held her voice steady and said, 'Right let's go.'

And so half an hour later they headed towards the venue side by side. As they stood outside she craned her neck, looking up at the multi-storied building.

'One of the highest hotels in India,' he said. 'If not the highest, I think. But it also houses this place which is apparently the place to be seen.'

'Is that why we're here? To be seen?'

'No. Well maybe a little—it won't harm to say we visited here, especially as Pria recommended it.'

'Pria Khatri who owns the studio you want to buy a stake in?'

'That's the one. She said she'd speak to the management so we could turn up whenever we want.' He grinned. 'Let's hope she remembered or we'll be bounced out.'

Not something she could envisage happening to

Max Durante but she liked that he saw it as an option. 'I'm pretty sure between us we'd sweet-talk our way in.'

In any event they were ushered inside and Stella soaked in the ambiance. Huge leather sofas were strewn over the floor, illuminated by the magnificent brilliance of eclectic chandeliers. But what caught the eye and caused her to stop in her tracks was the view, made all the more stunning by the full floor-to-ceiling windows which made the panoramic Mumbai skyline look so close you could step out into the inky blue sky.

And she couldn't help but recall the Dubai night sky, that magical evening that had started with an equally breathtaking view of a different city. Back then they had one night together, but now…now they were a partnership. And in the here and now that felt…good.

He nodded to the dance floor. 'The Bollywood music is later. Do you want to dance now? Or grab a drink first. Or food.'

'Let's dance and then I'll have an appetite for the food.'

He held out a hand and they headed to join the other people on the wooden dance floor. As the DJ wandered down the decades, providing a medley that somehow morphed the years she decided that she needed to, wanted to lose herself in the moment, and perhaps Max did too as they both immersed themselves in the beat of the music, until she knew she needed to call it and she gestured to the tables.

'I needed that,' she said as she sat down, knew she was flushed and breathless. 'It was exhilarating and it was fun and it kind of regulated my emotions a bit.' A shame it hadn't regulated her hormones. But it hadn't and her hormones weren't helped by the way he looked in the dim lights, his six o'clock shadow gave him an added edge, his hair less tamed, his sleeves rolled up to show off his muscular forearms. Her eyes roved the breadth of his chest and shoulders, and she forced herself to focus on the menu instead.

'You can definitely dance,' he said.

'So can you.'

He shook his head. 'Not really. I took lessons. On how to not make a fool of myself on a dance floor.'

'No way...'

'Yup. First time I went dancing at some corporate do the DJ nearly died laughing. I figured that wasn't going to look good for my image so I took lessons. It took a long time to get me to this level.' He leant forward. 'But if you tell anyone I'll deny it.'

'Your secret is safe with me.' She mimed zipping her lips and locking away the key.

She smiled up at the waiter. 'I'll have a lavender lemonade please.'

'A Glenlivet,' Max said.

The drinks arrived within minutes, mixed behind the massive square bar, which was surrounded by spotlighted bar stools and overhung with a shelving unit that held the most varied assortment of spirits imaginable. They clinked glasses. 'To the future,' Stella said.

'The future.' He paused as the music changed and now it was Bollywood songs that surrounded them, mingled with the chatter of people and the sound of laughter. 'I've been thinking about that.'

'Go ahead.'

'I know this is too soon and I know you probably won't say yes.'

To her horror Stella realised her heart was beating a little too fast. 'Yes.'

'I've been thinking about the future. Your future. And I want you to consider the idea of becoming a lawyer and letting me help.'

She gave a mental eye-roll—what on earth had she been expecting him to say? Whatever it was it wasn't this and she realised she was already shaking her head. 'I haven't given up the idea, but if I go ahead I'll stand on my own two feet.'

They both looked down at her feet and she smiled, 'Though I may change my shoes first.' Hoped the words would take the sting out of her refusal.

'I'm not offering a handout.'

'What would you call it?'

'Part loan, part investment.' He leant forward, pushed his half-empty glass to one side. 'I get you won't just let me fund you and I admire that. But I can't see why you won't let me loan you some money—we can agree on a repayment plan and it will all be drawn up by lawyers. If we fall out on a personal level it will not affect the loan—neither of us will have the power to do that.'

'So that's the loan. I don't get the investment part.'

'What you said, about the difference between giving

money to charity and being more actively involved, on a personal level. I liked that.

'OK. So InScreen does donate to charity. I get employees to vote on which charities they want to support and I know the money goes to worthy causes. But… I'd like to do more.'

'I'm still not seeing how this connects to me.'

'I'd like InScreen to hire a lawyer who isn't corporate, who can actually go out there and help people. I'm pretty sure there is plenty of unfairness in the entertainment world and maybe we need someone to help with that. Someone too who can get involved with our charities. So I part fund you and in return you are on call for InScreen for four years. Again we draw it up legally.' He shrugged. 'Look, I'm thinking out loud here but what do you think? I promise we'll tie it up so I cannot wield any personal power.'

'I…' Stella tried to think; she knew he was wrapping this up to make the help acceptable to her, but knew too that it was a fair offer. Win-win. But had her mother once felt like this about her father? But it didn't matter—Max was factoring in the possibility trust would corrode, was protecting her from the possibility. 'I'll think about it but whatever I decide, thank you.'

'I believe you would make a great lawyer and you'd be an asset, not just to InScreen but to all the people you'd help. So give it some serious thought.' He picked up his drink. 'But enough seriousness.'

Stella nodded, but her brain still whirled, part happiness at how seriously he was taking her aspirations, touched by her belief in him and she gave the small-est of sniffs.

'Hey no crying.' He snapped his fingers. 'I know what to do. I'll tell you jokes.'

'Jokes.'

He nodded. 'I've got a whole list of dad jokes. Guar-anteed to make you laugh. Here we go. What's brown and sticky?'

'Um…'

'A stick. How do celebrities stay cool?' he paused and held his hands out in a ta-da gesture. 'They have many fans.'

She couldn't help it, she gave a gurgle of laughter. 'They are so bad.'

'Yup and there are plenty more where they came from. So if you want me to stop, no more tears.'

'No more tears,' she agreed.

Then let's order food. I saw masala fries and tan-doori lollipops and wasabi cashews on the menu.'

'Hand it over.' But not even the menu could distract her from the ever-growing fuzzy warmth and she knew she needed to be careful. But surely there couldn't be anything dangerous about being happy, getting on with the man who was the father of her baby?

CHAPTER TWELVE

'You OK?'

The following morning as the car sent by the studio pulled away from the hotel, Max turned to look at Stella, amazed at how fresh and pretty she looked, dressed in simple leggings and a tunic top. A far cry from the glamour of the evening before but every bit as beautiful.

'I'm good. Though some muscles I didn't know I had are aching.' Not surprising after the evening of dancing and laughter they had enjoyed. He grinned. 'As for all the jokes...' Now her laughter pealed out.

'Just make sure you don't bring any of those out at this meeting.'

'No, I won't. Not included in my meeting prep.' Preparation that encompassed amassing knowledge on the company and the two people they were about to meet, along with as much information on Bollywood as he could assimilate.

The limo arrived at the studio and they alighted, entered the reception area where they waited a few minutes before Pria and Rahesh Khatri appeared.

Max reminded himself that first impressions were important, felt as always the churn of nerves, the sense of anticipation, the knowledge that the next hour could make or break the deal. A quick sideways glance at Stella showed a woman who knew exactly how to act, how to work a room, and he was reminded of her entrance onto the rooftop bar in Dubai.

'Max. Good to meet you at last.'

'You too and thank you for agreeing to show us round yourselves. This is Stella Morrison, a colleague of mine.'

'It is good to meet you both and we want to show you round personally, want to make sure you have an immersive experience.'

Stella smiled. 'Can I also tell you how blown away I am with Bollywood films? Max introduced me to your films. Well he said that he started by trying to look at them analytically, but bam... Every single one sucked him in. Then we watched one together, *The Final Ending*, and I still find bits of it coming into my head. And what I really cannot get my head round is the dress you wore for the love scene. I am in awe that it weighs thirty kilograms and you danced in it looking as though it were as light as silk.' She paused for breath and laughed. 'OK I'll stop now. I promised I wouldn't gush.'

The beauty of it was that Stella was genuine—and that was clear.

Pria smiled. 'Gush away darling,' she said. 'An actor is like a porous sponge—we have massive egos combined with no self-confidence. So all compliments are manna.' She turned to Max. 'And I hope you also noted that every one of those films turned a healthy profit.'

'I wouldn't be here otherwise. Though as I discussed with your finance director there are some things that we need to go over. If we get to the latter stages of negotiation. But that is for another time. Today is about this, and for me to get an understanding of everything that goes into your movies.'

'Well seeing as you are here,' Rahesh said, 'Perhaps you would like to see one of the sets from *The Final Ending.*'

'One hundred percent yes,' Stella said.

'Rahesh, I read that you have a lot of involvement with the sets,' Max said. 'I was stunned at the amount of time that goes in.'

'Yes. For this one I commissioned and helped make an exact model replica to make sure we got as much historic detail as possible correct and—actually, hold on. I'll get one of the set managers down to meet you. She did a lot of work on this.'

A few minutes later a woman headed towards them and Max turned to be introduced.

'Max, Stella, this is Rupali. Rupali Patel. She…'

Max froze, the words slammed into him and he could feel the colour ebb from his face, even as he desperately tried to click his brain into gear. The detective had told him it was a common name, that there were scores of people called Rupali Patel.

Yet he couldn't seem to help himself, the words of introduction Rahesh were saying blurred into meaningless syllables and his vocal chords acted of their own accord, broke straight in unceremoniously.

'Rupali. That is an interesting name. I wonder have you ever been to England?' It was gauche, it was un-called for and he sensed rather than saw the two ac-tors exchange glances, sensed Stella's look of concern.

'I am not sure that is relevant,' Rahesh's voice held a note of irritation, caution even. 'We have many good colleges here and as I was saying…'

Again the words vanished, because she hadn't de-nied it, surely evidence of a sort and he stepped for-ward, his eyes devouring the woman in front of him. His eyes scoured her face, trying to assess her age.

Another step forward and now his brain was des-perately trying to get his attention, tell him to shut up, to register the confusion on the woman's face but an-other step as more words fell from his lips. 'And do you have fa—? Agh!'

Pain stabbed his foot, and he was aware of Stella standing right next to him, one hand lightly on his arm, as he bit back a gasp of pain, realised she'd jabbed her high-heeled sandal into him as she broke into speech.

'Max told me there were literally thousands of mir-rors used. Is that right? And it was here wasn't it that one of the most moving scenes took place when La-keesha thought she would never see her lover again and… I wept buckets and I'm pretty sure Max had tears in his eyes too.'

Rupali turned to Stella in clear relief and finally Max's brain engaged, focused first on the pain in his foot, a welcome pain, a distraction that had brought the world back into focus. Now he could see that the woman standing in front of him couldn't be his mother; she was way too young, midthirties perhaps. Knew too that there was every chance he'd blown it—despite Stella's sterling efforts he sensed the actors' wariness, knew they had a reputation for being stellar employers who saw their employees as family. At worst he'd come across as wildly, creepily inappropriate, at best as utterly unprofessional.

But for the next hour he did his best, as Rakesh and Pria showed them the numerous costumes, as they watched a scene being filmed, hoped he managed to get across the enormous amount of research he'd put in, tried too to show that he felt a genuine love for the genre, for the sheer extravagance of it all. Through it all he was silently thankful for Stella, who asked proper questions, made their hosts laugh and shimmered with a serenity he could only envy. And in the end before they left he decided some sort of acknowledgement was in order. 'Thank you for this opportunity and I apologise for my lapse of focus earlier.'

'You wouldn't be human if you didn't lose focus occasionally. You have made it more than clear that your interest in our business is genuine and your track record speaks for itself.'

Husband and wife exchanged glances. 'Why don't you and Stella come to a party we are throwing tonight? Nothing massive, about forty staff and a few friends to celebrate winding up a production.'

'We'd love that.'

'Good. We will see you later and enjoy the botanical gardens.' Pria smiled. 'Imagine me dancing across them.'

As they exited the studio Max wondered if it were possible to pretend the whole humiliating incident hadn't happened. Wished he could close down the aftermath of the shock, his nerves still frayed by the intensity of his reaction. As they climbed into the car he considered cancelling the trip, vetoed the idea as no doubt Pria and Rahesh would ask about them later at the party.

To his relief Stella held her peace for the duration of the car journey, fielded most of driver's conversation as Nihal navigated the stream of traffic, seemingly oblivious to the blare of horns as drivers changed lanes without warning.

She remained silent as they entered the gardens, through a pair of wrought iron gates and they both instinctively inhaled deeply and paused to allow the welcome breeze to cool them down and he took some comfort from the rolling hills and the sound of birds.

'These gardens are by the Arabian Sea,' he said. 'Twelve acres of huge green trees, butterflies, cacti and hundreds of different plants.'

'It's beautiful,' she said. 'The perfect place to come after a shock, or to calm anxiety.' She paused. 'What happened back there? I know how important this deal is to you and how much work you've put in. I also know you don't lose your cool or your nerve easily. So what happened?'

All he knew was that he didn't want to explain,

wanted to bury the humiliation, buryhis loss of cool, loss of nerve.

'And are you OK?'

That was easier.

'I'm fine.' But the words sounded forced, ragged round the edges. 'Thank you for stepping in back there. I really appreciate it.' OK better, he was back in stride. 'Or should I say stepping on it. My foot is still feeling that move. But it worked.'

'Good.' Her voice even. 'But I think that was a temporary fix. It snapped you out of it.'

'And that's all I needed.'

'What happens if you snap back in? Tonight. At the party.'

He wanted to dismiss the idea as utterly preposterous, but he could still feel the sense of helplessness, the clammy sheen on the back of his neck, the sudden conviction that the woman in front of him was his mother. The freeze of his vocal chords, only for them to utter unscripted nonsense. Throwing his business deal into jeopardy.

What if it happened again? If something or someone else triggered a response. Another Rupali, a mention of a plot involving an abandoned child, a woman who he imagined had a look of himself... the possibilities seemed suddenly endless. Each one engendered a sense of panic, a claustrophobia, a wrench of anxiety to his nerves.

OK. Breathe. He would not let this feeling win— would not lose a business deal he had worked so hard for, wanted so much. In which case he'd have to admit

the unpalatable, that he might need some help. Need
Stella to step in, as she had before. Do something to
pull him out of it before he was gripped by the paraly-
sis, the delusion or illusion.

They continued to walk the wide, sweeping path-
way, shaded by a dense canopy of trees that loomed
up above them towards the blue of the sky, providing
a welcome shade from the sun. Trees that had seen
decades—centuries even—go by, had looked over so
many people strolling or scurrying past, witnessed so
many confidences and declarations and everyday chatter.

A breeze reached them, with a tang of salt and they
could see benches overlooking the blue of the sea. Instinctively they both headed that way and sat, facing
the water, saw the bob of colourful fishing boats un-
dulate on the indigo roll of the waves.

'You're right,' he said. 'I can't risk that happening
again.'

'Then let me help. What can I do?'

He pressed his lips together, told himself not to be a
fool. He didn't need to share much, but… 'I guess I'll
need you to "babysit" me.' The very idea ridiculous.
'Make sure I don't fugue into incoherence again. And
to do that I get you'll need to know what happened.'
Stella couldn't help without some background so he'd
have to suck it up.

'I've always hoped my mother would come forward.'
Each word felt an admission of weakness, of need.
'That she would contact social services in London, or
contact me direct if she figured out who I am. I have

a pretty high profile and in any interview I've always made it clear that if she came forward I would welcome it. But she never did.

'About a year ago we did a documentary on people who traced their birth parents and it hit a chord in me. There was a woman who found her birth mother and not only that she discovered she had siblings and I thought…that I just wanted to know. Not necessarily do anything about it but to know. So I hired a private detective. Anyway, to cut a long story short they think they may have tracked her down, or at least discovered her name. They believe she that she is half Indian, that she moved to Mumbai some years ago and she is called Rupali Patel.'

He realised he was still staring out to sea, focused on the horizon as though his life depended on it.

'No wonder you reacted like that when you met Rupali earlier.' Her voice soft, no judgement. 'Your mind went into freefall.'

'I have no idea where my mind went. All I know is that my reaction nearly cost me a business deal.'

'I think you should give yourself a break—it was a massive shock.'

'It shouldn't have been. It was one hundred percent clear that she couldn't be my mother—she was way too young for a start.'

'Yes. But you couldn't have known that in that moment. It is such a huge deal deciding to try to find her and to be here in Mumbai where she may be—of course it will mess with your mind. And maybe it is a bigger deal now than it was when you made the decision,' she said gently. 'Because of the baby.'

He glanced at her, a question in his eyes.

'Technically she will be the baby's grandmother,' she said.

The words hit him with a blast, a knowledge he didn't want. What if the baby was a girl and looked like his mother? What if every time he looked at his daughter he was searching for features of the woman who had given birth to him and then abandoned him? In some sort of horrible echo of history, the way his mother had looked at him and seen his father, seen him in his eyes. What if he saw his mother in his daughter, what if he couldn't deal with that?

'Max?'

'My mother has nothing to do with this baby. When she walked away from that cardboard box and left me inside it she walked away from any rights to be a grandmother. So I am going to call the private investigator off. You're right in that she is technically the baby's grandmother, but it's going no further than a technicality.'

Stella's eyes widened. 'That's not what I meant.'

'I know. But it's what I mean. Thank you.' He rose to his feet. 'Shall we keep walking? There are some beautiful viewing points and I promised Pria we'd look at the butterflies.'

As they walked, surrounded by the beauty of the trees and plants Stella glanced at him, her mind racing, as she tried to think what to say, what to do. In truth she was still reeling herself from his reaction to Rupali, tried to imagine how he must have felt in that split second when he believed he was face-to-face with his mother.

His face had drained of colour and the anguish, the pain, the hope in his eyes had torn at her heart even when she hadn't known the origin of his emotions. But now she realised just how deep his abandonment had gone, what wound it had inflicted.

Yet now... now he was going to abandon his search when he was so tantalisingly close, ostensibly for the baby, but she suspected it went deeper than that. That exposing his emotions like that had made him feel vulnerable, weak and that meant he was closing it all down.

'Max?'

'Yes.' His voice even, guarded, remote even, but she gritted her teeth, wanted him to open up to her.

'I know it's not my decision but I don't think you should call off the detectives.'

'I don't want to complicate things.'

She took a deep breath. 'Things are already complicated and this is your opportunity to find answers that you've wanted all your life. You said you made this decision because you wanted to know.'

He shook his head. 'Now I've realised I don't. She did what she did. It doesn't matter why.'

'Doesn't it? If there are extenuating circumstances or at least an explanation for why she did what she did. Perhaps she regrets her decision. Believes it was a mistake.'

Just as she regretted so many decisions in her own life. Deeply regretted the way she'd treated Lawrence.

'Then why not contact me?'

'Because she knows you've had a good, happy life without her so she wants to leave well enough alone.' Again exactly as she had done with Lawrence. 'But that doesn't mean she doesn't have regrets. And it doesn't mean that you don't deserve answers.'

'I'm fine without them, fine without her. I've survived—dammit I've thrived without her.' They kept walking, headed now towards a large wooden viewing structure, a vantage point to watch the butterflies from and her brain swirled with thoughts.

Max *had* made a success of his life, and yet when he'd seen Rupali, believed she was his mother, that mask of success had slipped, showing the rawness of emotion, the vulnerability underneath. And something struck Stella, a deep sense of compassion, of caring for this man. One she refused to question or analyse, but she wanted to help him, wanted him to open up to her, to drop his guard. So perhaps she needed to drop hers.

'You have thrived without her, but that doesn't mean what she did doesn't hurt and maybe you should find her. Get the explanation you deserve, because that might give you closure.' Just like she should have spoken to Lawrence, told him the truth, instead of running scared after the tragic horror of their breakup, a tragedy brought about by Stella's mistakes. And now a different type of guilt touched her, that she had made bad decisions and not had the courage to face up to the consequences.

But she hadn't convinced Max, she knew that, knew that he'd hated the earlier rush of emotion he couldn't control, wouldn't risk a repeat. But if he buried it, walked away, that was wrong too.

They reached the viewing structure and started to climb the winding stairs. With each step Stella tried to decide what to do and once they reached the top they looked down over the massive trees, palm trees and magnificent weeping willows and she could see the colourful flotillas of butterflies circling, delicate flutters of orange and red and purple. And she knew what to do.

She turned to face him. 'You deserve to know what made your mother do what she did—whatever her reasons. I know you do, just like I know she may regret her decision even if she hasn't contacted you.'

His mouth set in a line of scepticism and she couldn't blame him.

'I know because I've made some decisions I regret with all my heart.' She could hear the question in the silence, carried on the beat of the butterflies' wings and she continued to talk.

'After my father had that affair I was consumed with anger. I couldn't believe that he would have abandoned me, shipped me, my sister, my mother out of Salvington, replaced us all. It was a betrayal and I wanted revenge of sorts. So I decided to go off the rails and to find myself a truly unsavoury boyfriend, to help me do that, the sort of person my father would hate. And so I targeted Lawrence. He was perfect, not because I was attracted to him or anything, but because I knew if I hooked up with him my dad would go ballistic. He was everything my father hated—rich, yes, but nouveau riche, and in addition he had piercings, tattoos, tatty torn clothes—as far away from an aristocrat as you can imagine. So I decided to lure him in—I didn't even think about how it might affect Lawrence, all I thought about was me, me, me. That was bad decision number one.'

He didn't say anything but she sensed how intently he was listening.

'Lawrence fell for me, big time. And I couldn't cope—he said he loved me, needed me, wanted me and all I really wanted was to use him, be seen with him, play the role of rebel aristocrat taking the wild path. I wanted to be pictured wine bottle in hand outside the latest cool nightclub and irony of ironies he wanted to stay in and talk about our future. I knew I was in over my head but I kept telling myself it was OK, he couldn't really love me—not when I didn't love him. I mean I tried to reciprocate I really did but I couldn't and he started to know it. He'd ask me what was wrong with me, how could I not care for him when he cared so much? I tried to split up with him but he wouldn't listen. And that's when I came up with my master plan.' Sarcasm and bitterness roiled in her voice and he reached out and took her hand in his, clasped it firmly even when she tried to pull away and that gave her the courage to continue.

'I decided to go to a party and kiss someone else in front of him. In my head that would make the scales fall from his eyes and he'd fall out of love with me and the whole problem would be solved. Ta-da! What actually happened is I did my thing, saw his face and the pain, thought it was working, so I left the party with the man I'd kissed. Then I went home, sure that all would be well. Instead… I found out the next day that Lawrence had overdosed and he would have died if it wasn't for Juno, one of the girls in our group. She'd been worried about him, found him and got him to the hospital in time. I rushed to the hospital and she told me to leave, to get out, I'd done enough damage. I left, and thank God he survived. But he might not have and that would have been my fault, a result of my bad decisions and I regret that with all my heart. But now, now I've heard your story, I truly regret that I've never contacted Lawrence, never said sorry, never explained, because I thought it would make things worse, because he and Juno got together and I hoped they were happy. And I wish that Lawrence had contacted me, demanded an explanation because he deserves one. And so do you.'

He was silent for a while, though his hand still encircled hers and when he did speak it wasn't the whole-hearted agreement she'd hoped for.

'You can't compare what you did to Lawrence to what my mother did to me.'

'I'm not. And I am not trying to excuse what either of us did. But we both made decisions that had profound effects. I could have caused a tragedy, been responsible for a death.'

'You couldn't have known what he would do.'

'But I should have guessed. I knew how much he loved me.'

Max shook his head. 'He was obsessed with you, Stella. That's not love.' He looked at her. 'Is that why you are so adamant you don't want love?'

The question caused her to pause as she looked down at their clasped hands, and then she gave her head a small shake. This was a timely reminder of her stance on love. 'Partly. I don't like what it does to people. Love resulted in my mother being trapped in a marriage of misery, and love sent Lawrence to the abyss. It causes misery not happiness. I don't think anyone's happy ever after should hinge on meeting the "one" and falling in love. In fact it seems…easier to me to find a happy ever after without love. I don't see the point of it. Sure it may work out sometimes but a lot of the time it doesn't. It causes heartbreak and hurt and pain. And… I don't understand it.' That was the truth; love was a mystery to her. Her father professed to love her but that love had been priced, by love he'd meant control. With Lawrence love had become obsession. 'So love is to be avoided.' Again she looked down at their hands, wondered whether she was telling him, or reminding herself. Then realised she'd been distracted from the point.

'But this isn't about love…this is about answers and how you feel about finding your mother.' She waited, hoped he would tell her, share how he felt, but he didn't.

Instead, 'Thank you for telling me about Lawrence. And for what it's worth I get you made some decisions you regret but in the end you didn't intend for what happened to happen—you got in over your head and you tried to get out. But he made the decisions he made and he has to take responsibility too.'

'Thank you. And I promise not to bring it up again. But please don't call off the detectives yet. Sleep on it?'

'OK.'

At least he'd agreed to that, though as she studied his expression, unreadable in the bright light, she wondered if he was humouring her. Knew though that he would keep his word.

He glanced at his watch. 'Right, we need to get going or we'll be late for the party.'

'OK and I'll be right there, by your side. If you feel any sense of panic or anxiety, take my hand.'

He smiled. 'And then what, you'll stamp on my foot with your stilettos.'

'Only in an emergency,' she said as she smiled up at him. 'But I'll wear sandals just in case. *We've* got this. And *we're* going to get this deal.'

He stilled as he looked down at her and then he smiled, a real smile which conveyed warmth and made her feel…ridiculously happy. 'Thank you.' And then he leaned down and, oh, so gently brushed his lips against hers, sending a flutter of sensation though her, a sense of anticipation and hope. 'For everything you've done today.'

He tugged her towards the steps. 'Now let's go party.'

CHAPTER THIRTEEN

'Wow.' STELLA'S VOICE held awe and Max understood why as they stood outside Pria and Rahesh Khatris's Bollywood mansion, a massive sprawling edifice, with Grecian pillars and gleaming whitewashed walls. 'It's… It's hard to believe it's real.' She counted under her breath. 'It's got six stories.'

'Yup, apparently it houses a boxing ring, a gymnasium, a cinema and multiple kitchens and living areas. Oh, and seven bedrooms and a whole room for shoes.'

'Be still my beating heart. Let's go in and check out the inside. And clinch your deal.'

'Remember I am by your side with my trusty sandals.' She hitched up the skirt of her grey dress and lifted a foot, to reveal red-and-gold mirrored sandals, the gold thread picking up the glint of the necklace he'd given her.

And as they entered now a tremor of anxiety did threaten, a sudden nightmare entered his brain of hundreds of faceless women walking towards him against a backdrop of party cacophony, all chanting, 'I am your mother', and for a moment his feet dragged. But then

Stella's hand slipped into his. 'You've got this,' she whispered and he kept walking.

Knew that next to him Stella was thinking 'double wow' as they both took in the interior. Opulent didn't cover it, though it was opulence with plenty of style. Fluffy rugs were scattered over the highly polished wooden floor, chandeliers hung from the ceilings, there were mirrors and glass, low marble tables, leather sofas, the theme black-and-white, all blending into an aura that screamed no expense spared.

Guests mingled, and tuxedoed waiters worked the crowds seamlessly moving with silver trays laden with champagne and mango juice and carefully crafted canapés. Rahesh and Pria swept up to greet them, and he let himself be caught up in the swing of the party, the atmosphere, the exquisite taste of the canapés. Though that was trumped by watching Stella eat them and her running commentary.

'Amazing... Max you have to try this. They are called *aloo tikki* and they are spiced mashed potato coins. And this...it's called a *puri* shot—and the *puri* are stuffed with black chickpeas in a fresh mint sauce...'

But Stella didn't just eat, she circulated, and he couldn't help but admire the deft touch she had with people, her ability to converse and truly listen. The episode of earlier in the day seemed far behind him until Pria approached him, a smile on her face, 'Max, there you are. Rupali wanted a quick word.'

Rupali, Rupali, Rupali... He was aware of Pria's watchful gaze as the set designer approached and he exhaled in relief as nothing happened—he could see that she was a woman in her midthirties, approaching him with a slightly wary smile on her face.

'Hi, Rupali. I am so glad you are here. I wanted to apologise—I am sorry if I made you uncomfortable—it was unintentional.'

The woman raised her hand. 'It is OK. You don't need to explain.' She smiled, a sweet smile that seemed to encompass understanding. 'And you didn't make me uncomfortable—not once I realised that you weren't really seeing me. And not when I saw Stella stamp your foot. You looked like my grandmother does when she is sleepwalking. So we're good.'

Relief trickled through him.

'And also I have found another Rupali Patel who did study in England. She also works for Rahesh and Pria as well but in the costume department.'

He could picture Stella's eyes widen as she tensed next to him, hear her well-modulated voice say *Really* in his head, with a rising of incredulity as her hand twined firmly round his.

The woman he was now keeping in his head as Rupali One stepped to one side to reveal another smiling woman. Rupali Two and now the nightmare image from earlier resurfaced and he forced himself not to look round for the faceless horde of his imagination.

Next to him Stella held a hand out. 'It's good to meet you, Rupali. When were you in England and where?'

'In Manchester about twenty years ago now.' It couldn't be her and this time Max was able to process that, able now to engage both Rupalis in hopefully intelligent conversation. Thanks in part he knew to Stella's swift intervention, the way she'd got him the information he needed, allowed him to contain the burgeon of panic before it took hold.

Appreciation touched him that she had his back, that she'd persisted earlier, and now she'd done as she promised and been by his side. They made a good partnership. Max frowned, aware that an idea was beginning to seed in his mind; he recognised the foreshadow of a plan, the ping of a possible light bulb above his head. But before he could pursue the trail Rahesh approached, his brown eyes studying Max closely. 'There is going to be an impromptu Bollywood dance, we thought you may both like to watch or better yet join in?'

'I'm in.' Stella's acquiescence was instant and as Max eyed the other man, he realised this was a test of sorts, to assess whether he would fit as a business partner, truly be part of the company that Rahesh had founded and loved and believed in.

'As long as you aren't expecting talent I'm in,' he said. 'But seeing as I am about to make a fool of myself I'd like something in return.' Time to show he really did mean business.

Rahesh nodded. 'That seems fair. What would you like?'

'Agreement that you will discuss the idea of producing some films that also include Western actors and films that don't exclusively star you.'

It was audacious, but it was the one point he hadn't been able to get across or persuade directors to put across to Rahesh and Pria—the directors telling Max that they'd never buy it. 'I know it's not your studio policy but with InScreen we could expand production, it's still your name on every movie and if you want to direct or produce you would still have creative control.'

'All this in return for a dance?'

'It's more than that. This dance is a symbol—I want to mesh our two cultures and businesses. You would still have autonomy and final choice. I wouldn't be able to produce a film you don't like, but I'd like to be able to produce more.'

'I'll talk to Pria—we decide together and I can't say fairer than that.'

'Done.'

Rahesh grinned at him. 'Now let's dance.' The actor headed off towards the dance floor that was set up in one part of the massive space and Max sighed.

Stella glanced at him. 'You don't want to do this do you?'

He shrugged. 'My lessons didn't cover Bollywood so I am about to make a massive fool of myself in front of people I'd quite like to take me seriously. But there are worse things in life. And if he and Pria agree to my terms it will be worth it.'

'We danced really well together last night. Follow my lead and it'll all be good.'

'I like the optimistic approach.'

They headed to the dance floor where Pria and Rahesh stood.

Pria started to speak, 'OK, people, for the benefit of Max and Stella I'm going to say a little bit about the dance and give some tips. You'll know from watching our movies that Bollywood dancing is highly synchronised and the movements are both graceful and energetic.

'The dance also crucially tells a story. So the fluidity of the hand, neck and head movements, the facial expressions are vital. The hand movements are in fact a type of sign language. And of course there are your feet—the moves are pretty complicated so be careful not to trip up! We'll start with a dance called a bhangra, not too hard.'

'So,' Rahesh said, 'Are you ready?'

Stella nodded, her expression serious. 'Can we watch for a few minutes and join in when we're ready.'

'Of course.'

So for the next ten minutes they watched as Pria and Rahesh and about ten of the other guests started a dance, and then Stella said softly, 'I'm going to join them. Watch for a bit longer. Don't worry too much about your feet, focus on arms and keeping to the beat.'

He nodded, watched as she moved into line, saw how easily she fitted in, her body sinuous, energy and grace personified and for a while he was mesmerised as she joined the fluid line of dancers. And as he watched her, saw her give him a quick glance and a sudden wink of encouragement, the idea from earlier put down roots and his brain raced, ran with it, and to the beat of the drums, the repeat pattern of four beats, the idea became a plan, a certainty, a path.

And he knew it was now or never and somehow the enormity of his plan made it almost easy to move in behind Stella, to focus on her, on how she moved so he could emulate it, the sway of her body, the grace with which she extended her arms, the exquisite column of her neck and the ripple of corn-blonde hair. And then following the moves he placed his hand around her waist, felt her falter for the first time before regaining her rhythm and now the tempo increased and Max just did his best to keep up. But all the time as the drums pounded and the movement of the dancers became faster and faster his plan took shape, took life as if given vitality from the exhilaration of the dance.

Then Stella moved gracefully out of line, and he followed suit and they turned and clapped to the beat as the remaining dancers incredibly upped the pace, yet maintained the fluidity of the dance until in synchronised pairs they dropped backwards until it was only Pria and Rahesh to do a grand finale. And at the end the whole room applauded and Max felt the genuine sense of family, understood truly that for Rahesh and Pria their employees mattered.

The couple walked over to them, only barely out of breath.

'Stella you were outstanding…a natural.'

'Thank you, Pria. I loved it… I'll be looking for lessons as soon as I get to London.'

Rahesh shook Max's hand. 'And Max you get points for effort.'

'I'll take that.' With a nod the celebrity couple moved away and Max turned to Stella and they simply looked at each other for a long moment and she was so damned beautiful, her face flushed, her eyes sparkling, her blonde hair ruffled.

'You were incredible,' he said in all sincerity, still blown away by the grace of her movements, the way she'd absorbed the aura, the controlled extravagance of the dance.

'I'd have kept going, but I thought it had probably been enough for the baby.' She grinned. 'Maybe she'll have picked up some moves and will be the next Pria Khatri.'

'Or maybe you will—you definitely impressed everyone here.'

'More important I think you sealed your deal.'

But by now the words were simply a show, said for the sake of saying something. But the real conversation was happening elsewhere, as awareness shimmered and rippled in the air, carried on the notes of the music that still played. And now Max didn't care, had no intention of shutting it down.

'We should leave,' he said, tried to keep his voice businesslike. 'Pria and Rahesh need to decide whether they want to go ahead and they can do that better without me here.'

'Then let's go and say our goodbyes.'

Ten minutes later they exited the mansion and headed to the car where Rahil waited.

'Why don't we go for a walk,' he suggested.

'I'd like that. I'm still pumped full of energy from that dance and...

'How about we ask Nihal to take us to the Gateway of India? It's meant to be beautiful by night.'

'Sure. Sounds good.'

Max's heart beat hard against his ribcage as the car glided smoothly towards its destination.

'Wow again,' Stella said as they walked towards the illuminated Gateway—the loom of the structure glowed golden against the indigo blue of the night sky, and the purple waves of the Arabian Sea. The fifteen-metre dome flanked by four turrets, the whole an architectural fusion of East and West.

'Amazing that it was designed by a Scottish architect, in honour of British royalty.'

'I suppose back then they couldn't have imagined how history would play out.'

'It makes you think though, doesn't it?' he said. 'How much life can change, how things we take for granted, think will last for ever may not. Perhaps it means we should seize the moment.'

She heard an edge to his voice, one she couldn't quite decipher, as they made their way through the still-populated square in front of the Gateway. Late-night street vendors sold their wares to a steady stream of custom and the smell of the sea mixed with the smell of masala chai. Nearby, the magnificence of the Taj hotel also lit up the skyline.

They found a secluded spot by the seawall, near the Gateway itself, close enough that she could see the detail of the inscriptions on the basalt walls, hear the lap of the waves. Leaning against the wall, she turned to him, her eyes open in question.

'Seize the moment how?'

'I think we should get married.'

Say what now? Stella lifted her hand to her jaw to make sure it hadn't dropped to ground level. 'Married?' The word swam around her head, images starting to form. Being with Max, a swirl of confetti in the air, having the baby together. More of the warm fuzzy feelings from today... She blinked fiercely dissipating the pictures before they could take hold, touched her tummy in a reminder of who she needed to think of first and foremost.

'Yes. Married.' His voice carried conviction. 'Co-parenting will be so much easier if we are under the same roof. Otherwise let's say the baby stays with me three nights a week or whatever we decide and the remainder with you. It means invariably one or other of us is going to miss milestones, it means our child will effectively have two homes. Getting married means she can have one stable home, it means as well there won't be the added complications of stepfamilies in the mix.'

Stella tried to think; but it was hard because every word he said seemed to make complete sense. The thought of missing her child's first steps, the thought of packing a suitcase every week, for every month, for every year as the child shuttled between homes, conversations over video calls instead of in the flesh seemed bleak. But... 'We can't get married just for the sake of the baby, because there is nothing worse for a child than growing up with miserable, warring parents.'

'Agreed and I would never wish what you went through on any child. But we won't be miserable, or warring.' His voice deep and reassuring and full of promise. 'Why would we? You said you wanted a marriage where you were partners, where both parties bring something to the table, would be good parents and have liking and respect. We tick all those boxes and we have the extra ingredient as well. Attraction.'

For a fraction of a second unease touched her and then it was gone, as anticipation thrilled through her, as the prospect dizzied her—the magic of that night in Dubai could be hers on repeat. Forever. On tap, whenever she wanted. She reached out, touched his arm, shivered at the feel of solid lithe muscle. Tried to stem the course of desire. 'We can't get married just so we can have sex.'

He smiled, a genuine smile that crinkled his eyes and turned her tummy to mush. 'I thought about that, long and, excuse the pun, hard. And we wouldn't be. I know what it feels like to just want sex and this isn't it. I want the whole package. The respect, the liking, the living under one roof with our child. *And* the sex.'

There was that smile again, and he sounded so sure, but... 'You've never had a relationship, only interludes.'

'I don't want interludes anymore, not once we have a baby. I don't want my child to see me splashed across the papers with an interlude and sure, so far I have mostly managed discretion but that's not a guarantee for the future.' He shrugged and her gaze caught on the breadth and strength of his shoulders, the ripple of his shirt against his chest and she gulped. 'The way I see it what's better, an occasional interlude or us?'

Us. That was the crux of it. They would be an us. A couple. Perhaps they could have a couple name. Stellax or Mella or… Or perhaps she should get a grip. 'But it's such a big commitment. How can you be sure? I know how resistant you were to marrying Dora even for two years.'

'That was different. There was no baby. And Dora wasn't you.' He took both her hands in his, and now his voice was serious, his brown eyes dark and intent. 'This is not a sacrifice on my part, Stella, and I don't want it to be one on yours. I believe this is right for the baby. This would give me the chance to give my child what I craved most as a child myself. A parent who is present, is there all the time and a stable happy supportive upbringing. *But* I accept we can still be good parents, bring up a child successfully without marriage. But I think marriage is right for us as well. We would be happy too—I wouldn't suggest this if I thought we couldn't make a go of it.'

Instincts warred within her. Part of her told her this was a no-brainer—every point he'd made, oh, so valid, and he seemed so very sure. Stood there silhouetted in the golden glow from the Gateway, lamplight glinted on the black of his hair shadowing the decisive planes and angles, the strength of his features.

And another part of her was terrified, petrified she'd make the wrong decision, scared, 'What if I can't make a go of it?' she asked now. 'My relationship history is hardly stellar. I was brought up by parents whose marriage was miserable. What if I say yes and then I mess the whole thing up.'

'The past doesn't matter as long as we don't ignore it—as long as we learn from it, acknowledge it. You will bring yourself into our marriage and *you* are a good person, who cares about others. I get how much your relationship with Lawrence has coloured the rest of your life. I think you've lived with the aftermath ever since.' Now he took a step closer to her and she saw the sincerity in the dark pools of his eyes. 'I think after Lawrence you decided that you couldn't be you anymore, that you had to give up your dream to become a lawyer, to have your own life. And so you built a persona, cool, poised, perfect, the Stella Morrison who would become a countess, a Stella who always made the right decisions.' Her eyes widened as his understanding blew her away. 'You don't have to be that persona any more. Whatever you decide you can make that decision as the real you. And whatever you decide I promise I will always try to be the best co-parent I can be.' His grasp tightened round her hands. 'And you don't have to give me an answer now. I get it's a lot to think about and you need to know you're making the right decision.'

And again warmth suffused her at his knowledge that she couldn't, wouldn't rush a decision, not with her track record of disastrous choices.

Words didn't seem adequate at this point and so she did what seemed natural, she closed the gap between them and brushed a kiss against his cheek, inhaled the scent of him, the woodsy cedar soap that mingled with the smell of the sea breeze. But it wasn't enough and they both shifted balance and now she slid her lips from his cheek to his lips, in a gentle imprint, that lingered for a timeless moment as he cupped her cheek in his hand and, oh, so gently deepened the pressure of their lips.

Stella gave a small gasp at the sheer intensity as sensations deepened into a lush sweetness that felt so right, so full of promise. Knowledge pooled and co-alesced inside her, a knowledge gleaned from the past hours and days and she knew she'd fallen for him. That she loved this man, and now…now she had the chance to spend her life with him. The realisation sent both joy and fear through her and she knew that now more than ever she did need time, time to make a decision. And so she pulled away, scared that he'd be able to tell somehow and she knew this love had to be kept secret for now.

She studied his face in the starlight, seemed to see him afresh; saw a good man, a man who knew what he wanted and would fight for it. But a man who she knew had his own demons and vulnerabilities. Could he grow to love her? Optimism surged through her. Surely it was possible…

'Penny for them?' he said, and she shook her head.

'No—they aren't worth it. But you've given me a lot to think about.' She summoned a smile, a poised, friendly Stella Morrison–persona smile, aware of the irony but she knew it was vital to keep her revelation private, until she worked out what to do. 'But I promise not to take long. Give me a couple of days.'

CHAPTER FOURTEEN

Two days later

STELLA CLOSED HER eyes in the welcome cool of the evening breeze, tucked a stray tendril of hair behind her ear, looked up at Max who was walking next to her and then down at their entwined hands and happiness clenched inside her.

The past two days had been…full of wonder. They'd talked about anything and everything, nothing deep or meaningful but important things nonetheless. Movies, films, music, antenatal classes, schools, private versus public education, politics, flowers, holiday destinations… They'd eaten, fed each other snacks, and every moment had felt precious, the fact that each one could be a prelude to the rest of her life seemed almost impossible. Max had made some pretext to go back to the jewellery bazaar and Stella couldn't be certain, but she suspected that a ring nestled in his pocket right now. After all where would be a better place to propose than at sunset looking out to sea.

And she'd thought about it, long and hard whilst

she'd lain alone in the massive king-sized bed, on silken sheets. Decided that marrying Max was the right choice…because she was happy and she wanted the happiness to continue, because together they could give their child a stable, secure, happy childhood. And as for her love…what did it matter? Yes, she loved him; she'd changed her mind, her attitude to love. Who was to say that Max wouldn't too?

His voice broke into her thoughts.

'Penny for them?'

Now she looked up at him and smiled, saw that he had been guiding their steps towards the seawall, saw too that the sun was just beginning its descent towards the horizon, the sky beginning to move across the spectrum of colour.

'I think they're worth more than that today,' she said softly, knew he would take his cue from those words, saw his hand descend to the pocket of his chinos.

He took a deep breath and his gaze met hers, direct and unswerving. 'Then here goes. I won't go down on one knee because that would be hypocritical, but I promise I mean every word I am about to say. Stella, will you do me the honour of marrying me? I promise to give you respect and liking and do my very best to make sure our family is a happy one and to give our child, or children a secure, happy, loving childhood.'

He opened the ring box and she looked down at the glint of diamond and gold, opened her mouth to say yes, started the lift of her left hand to accept the ring.

And stopped, as the words of his proposal rang round her head and she realised that she wanted him to go down on one knee. But he couldn't because it would be hypocritical, and Max would never be that. He didn't love her. But that was OK…because one day maybe he would.

Or maybe he wouldn't and then what would happen? Would their marriage go the same way as her parents'? They had started out assuming that they would have a son, that assumption had turned to hope and in the end that hope had withered and died, turned their marriage into a bitter morass of misery. Would that happen to Stella if Max didn't learn to love her back?

How could it end well; dammit she knew first hand how one-sided love worked out, how it could turn into obsession—would she become like that…as desperate as Lawrence had been?

His voice echoed across the years. *'How can you feel nothing when I love you so much?'*

Max didn't love her. His proposal said it all—he wanted to get married to achieve a happy family unit for the baby. Wanted an agreement founded on a bedrock of liking, respect with a no-love clause baked into that foundation. She'd fallen in love with a man who had no interest in love.

Been foolish enough to put rose-coloured spectacles back on and she had, oh, so nearly walked into a rose-coloured trap that she'd set for herself. Because she couldn't marry Max; couldn't spend a lifetime living a lie, would have to live her life with another persona, couldn't be her real self.

So there would be no romantic acceptance in the sun's setting pink rays; though her heart felt like it might burst, if only she could rip the love out, trample it, accept the proposal in the spirit in which it was given.

The jumble of thoughts whirred through her mind.

'Stella?'

What to say—the truth impossible... Her brain clicked and whirred and she knew she had to resurrect her Stella persona, the poised, cool, aloof model. That Stella would have to take over, spin a refusal he would believe and accept.

'I can't marry you.'

He stepped backwards as though the words had rocked him off balance, his expression one of confusion and the dawn of hurt.

'Why not?'

Max tried to process what the hell was going on. It made no sense and yet there was something in her stance, in her voice that told him she meant it.

'I don't understand,' he said flatly. 'I know you hadn't said yes, but over the past two days every sign pointed that way.'

'I know.' She took a deep breath. 'And I'm sorry. Truly sorry. But...this...' She gestured around them, but he didn't even turn his head, not even the beauty of the sunset could distract him. 'It's not real.'

'Still not getting it. I'm pretty sure I'm real, you're real and the baby is real too.'

'I'm not explaining well. I mean Mumbai—this isn't our reality, where we live, work. How can we decide to spend the rest of our lives together based on a few days here?'

'Fine. I don't think the setting matters, but if you prefer, we'll do this a different way. Go home, spend some more time together, move in together if you want.'

She shook her head, and he saw a hint of panic in her blue eyes, tried to get his head around what was going on. 'It's more than that. I know you aren't like my father. I do. But I don't feel comfortable marrying someone with so much wealth and fame and power.'

He studied her face 'You've known all along who I am and we've discussed this.'

'I know but I still have reservations, questions I haven't answered. If we get married our child will get used to a certain lifestyle, one that you can provide, and if something did happen, if we did decide to split up, where would that leave us?'

'Very well off. I will sign a prenup that protects you so you are never in the position your mother was in.'

'But that doesn't feel right either. I'd still be living off your money and I don't want that. And there are other things to think about. What would we tell our child about our relationship?'

'The truth.'

'That we got married for them, that's not fair either.'

'But we wouldn't be getting married for the baby's sake—we'd be getting married for all of us, to be a family.'

'It's not enough.' It was as though the words were torn from her, said with a deep pain and truth and now finally the penny dropped as he understood exactly what she was trying to say. He wasn't enough, not for her or for the baby.

Shades of his mother—he hadn't been enough for her. Shades of his foster parents—couldn't they have fought harder; shades of his uncle and aunt—they'd wanted their own child not the 'bad option'. A wave of anger, an echo of how he had felt as a child threatened to tsunami, crashed into the even bigger wave of bleakness because this was different. This was a judgement on him, as he was now. The finished version so to speak and he still wasn't enough.

And that meant losing what he'd achieved with Stella, the warmth, the laughter, the comradeship. All gone. He clenched his fists into his jeans pockets and stared out at the sun as it set on his hopes and dreams. But what could he do? He'd made the deal, that he'd abide by her decision and he would.

So as all the emotions crashed and burned inside him, he pulled himself together, knew that raging and storming would make it impossible for them to move forward as parents. 'I understand.' The words dark and weighed with a bleak truth because he did understand. 'We'll need to work out an agreement. Perhaps it would be best to leave this in our lawyers' hands from here on out. If you truly believe this is best for the baby and best for you then I accept that. This isn't the way I wanted it to pan out, but I hope you find what you're looking for, Stella, find something that is enough.'

She nodded. 'Thank you.' She opened her mouth as though she wanted to say more, settled for, 'For everything.' Her expression drawn and tired, her delicate features etched with sadness.

The walk back to the hotel spent as far apart as possible, such a far cry from just half an hour before when they'd strolled along hand in hand and he'd been so sure that the future held brightness.

A week later

Stella sat opposite her sister in her study in Salvington; relieved that her father had at least thawed sufficiently to allow his eldest daughter over the threshold.

'How is Dad?'

'I saw him earlier, told him you were coming and he asked to see you. He's sleeping now but Mum said she'd come and get you when he's up.'

'Is seeing me a good idea?'

'I think so. The heart attack—it's changed him. He seems more mellow, more resigned to letting things be, accepting the possibility that Salvington may be lost.'

'And are you OK with that? If you and Rob don't have an heir quickly.'

'Yes I am. Like you told me, we can't sacrifice our lives for Salvington. I love Rob, he loves me and we want to spend our lives together. And we deserve the chance to do that without the pressure of having an heir—if it happens great, if not that's OK. We won't let it embitter our lives.' She studied Stella's face. 'Now let's talk about you. Have you decided what you're going to do?'

'I told you.' Her sister had been the first person she'd

turned to and she'd told Adriana the whole sorry truth. 'I'm going to get on with my life, focus on being the best parent I can and I am sure Max will do the same.' She tried to inject enthusiasm into her voice. 'I've been in touch with him and we've got our first antenatal class coming up.' The prospect filled her with dread, the idea of being so close to him, of having to pretend, to hide the fact that she missed him with every fibre of her being. 'It will all be fine.'

'It doesn't sound fine. And you don't look fine—you look dreadful.'

'Gee, thanks.'

Adriana shook her head. 'Sorry, but you do, and I'm worried about you.'

'Please don't worry. I don't want to rain on your parade.' And she truly didn't. 'I am so happy for you and Rob.' And she was, even though every word of her sister's story, her happy ending seemed designed to further twist the knife into her own raw sadness. A tale of love and the fairy tale ending. But as she looked at her sister's face, illuminated and radiant with reciprocated love, Stella did feel happy, 'Happy that you finally have the love and recognition and happiness you deserve. And I'm sorry.'

'For what?' Her sister's face creased in genuine confusion.

'Sorry that it took so long, sorry I didn't stand up for you earlier, didn't stand up to Father and call him out for how he treated you. Sorry it's taken me this long to say sorry.'

'Whoa!' Adriana moved over to her sister and gave

her a massive hug, held her tight. 'You do not need to be sorry. You have always been the best sister I could wish for.'

Stella shook her head. 'I should have done something.'

'There was nothing you could do. We agreed on the plan—I'd be invisible, you'd keep Dad happy. And listen to me, I think you got the worse end of the deal in some ways. I got to wander around Salvington and do my own thing. You were in the limelight, having to do whatever he said. And, yes, it sucked what Dad did to me, what it did to my self-esteem and confidence but that's on him, not you.'

'You sound like Max.'

Her sister eyed her. 'So you've talked to Max about Dad and about how you feel about things?'

'Yes.' She'd confided things to Max that even her sister didn't know.

'So you trust him?'

'Yes, I do.'

Adriana took her sister's hands. 'Then maybe you should tell him the truth. I know you say you're worried that it will affect how you work together as parents, but from everything you've told me about Max being a dad is too important to him to jeopardise. I don't think he will let it affect how he parents. And neither will you, because you're going to be a great Mum. But if you don't tell him, you're living a lie and you don't deserve that and neither does Max.'

Stella stared at her sister, and knew that her sister was right—that Max did deserve the truth. He'd never got it from his mother, had no idea why she had done what she'd done and Stella herself had told him he deserved answers, deserved the truth. Just as Lawrence had. But Stella had been too scared to tell Lawrence the truth, that she had used him from the start. Too scared to tell her father the truth, that she disagreed with how he treated Adriana. Stella had always walked away. And now... Now she was still scared, and a memory hit of halving her fears and handing them to Max.

She looked up at the tap on the door and her mum entered. 'Your dad would like to see you now, if that's what you want too.'

Max looked down at the unopened letter in his hand; a letter handed over to him by a private detective, along with a report explaining his mother had been located, but didn't want to see him, though she had written him a letter.

Emotions struggled for ascendancy, hurt amongst them. But a hurt that paled beside the pain he'd felt since Stella's rejection, that wound still stung and ached, refused to subside. Constantly prodded by the continuous stream of memories that pretty much anything and everything provoked. A smell of vanilla, a low laugh, a blonde woman, the glint of a gold necklace...any food. Every meal he'd find himself analysing ingredients, thinking of texture, imagining her face as she tasted it.

He blinked, refocused on the letter, part of him wanted to open it, part of him dreaded the content.
Jeez, Man up, Durante.
Swiftly he ripped open the envelope.

Dear Max,
I am sorry. Sorry I abandoned you and sorry that I cannot see you now.

I was young. Your father tricked me, dazzled me, conned me into believing he was something he wasn't. I couldn't have an abortion, but neither could I keep you as an unwanted reminder of my mistakes.

Soon after your birth I relocated to India— my family brought me here to help me recover.

Many years later I married a good man and we have four children. But I never told him or them about you and I don't want to. He would feel betrayed and it would change everything, all my family relations, and they would see me differently.

So I ask you to please let me be and know I think of you every day and I am proud of your success and take comfort from the fact that your family took you in.
Rupali

Max stared down at the words and then folded the letter up and replaced it in the envelope. Rejected again, gently this time but there had been no doubt in that letter. Rupali wished him well, but she did not want him in her life. An unwanted reminder of her mistakes.

He could hear Stella's voice in his head. 'You're more than that.'

He shook his head. Only he wasn't to Stella—to Stella he wasn't enough.

But there were those words again. 'You're more than that.'

And dammit he was.

He would not let what his mother had done to him, as a baby and now, define him. Not let his uncle and aunt's judgement be the final one. He was more than an unwanted reminder, more than a chip off the old block. And maybe, just maybe he was enough for Stella, if he could find the courage, the strength to be honest. To be real.

And now he knew exactly what he had to do.

Two days later

Stella entered the restaurant where she had arranged to meet Adriana, glanced round in surprise to see how deserted it was, then went to sit at a corner table. Pulled her phone out and looked at the text she was painstakingly composing to Max. Rolled her eyes at her own hesitancy. She had to stop worrying that he would ignore her or refuse to see her. Stop wondering if she should sign it with a kiss.

Instead she pressed Delete, started again.

Hi, Max Could we meet up? Stella

Before she could press Send a waiter approached and she opened her mouth to explain she was waiting for someone. 'Good afternoon. The gentleman at the bar asked me to send this over with his compliments.'

She froze, her heart started to beat a little faster and, oh, so slowly she lifted her gaze to the man sitting at the bar. Dark, dark hair, tamed into a businesslike cut, eyes the colour of expensive chocolate, chiselled features and a jaw that spoke of determination. His body emanated a sense of power and a frisson of pure desire ran through her. She blinked—this wasn't Dubai, wasn't the first time she'd seen him and yet in some ways it felt like she was seeing him anew.

The waiter placed a drink in front of her, 'It's a passion fruit mocktini. And a note.'

She opened the envelope, read the contents. 'I'd like to talk.' That was it and now she looked up and his gaze met hers, unreadable. And then she lifted her glass in a toast and nodded and she saw relief flash across his features.

Then he approached, sat down opposite her and placed his glass on the table. 'Elderflower cocktail,' he said. 'And Adriana says she hopes you don't mind the subterfuge.'

'So you set me up.'

'Yes.'

'You could have just asked.'

He gave the smallest of smiles. 'I thought that lacked pizzazz.'

Her eyes widened and she gave a small breathless laugh. 'In which case I'm guilty of exactly that.' She put her phone on the table, showed him the text. 'I was about to send that.'

A quick scan and he looked at her. 'So who goes first?'

'There's only one way to decide that.' She reached for her purse and pulled out the coin, tossed it in the air as he called tails. 'Tail's it is.'

'Then I'll go first. There is something I want to ask you, something I want to tell you but first, if it's OK I'd like to, I need to tell you some things. About me.'

'Of course it's OK.' Her mind raced, whirred with curiosity, a dawning hope matched by equivalent trepidation.

He paused, frowned as if he was finding it hard to work out what to say or how to say it and she realised he hadn't rehearsed whatever it was. 'I told you that you could be real with me, that you didn't have to hide behind the persona you've created. Well this past week I've come to realise that I've been hiding behind a persona of my own. A success story I wove and spun— the Max Durante who overcame adversity, forgave his mother for leaving him in a cardboard box, was brought up by a loving family and built up a business empire.'

'You are a success story,' she said softly.

'Perhaps, but that's not how it happened. That's the spiel I put together.'

'I don't understand.' But she wanted to, leant forward, her gaze fixed on him, and she saw shadows in his eyes, but determination as well.

'After I was found in the cardboard box I was put into foster care, with a wonderful couple who I lived with for four years.' Stella held her breath, knew that this was something he had kept to himself, there had been no mention of this in any of his interviews. 'I can still remember them, remember a feeling of safety and warmth. They had just started proceedings to adopt me and then my uncle and aunt turned up. My uncle was my father's older brother. Carlos and his wife Annalise.'

'But surely by then you were bonded to your foster family.'

'I was but Carlos was my real family and blood trumped all. Also they were younger than my foster carers, they didn't have any kids of their own and they said they desperately wanted to adopt me. There was also my grandmother in the picture and she was very keen on the idea.'

'So they were allowed to adopt you?'

'Yes. Though it took time. I was removed from my foster carers and put with other carers whilst proceedings went ahead.' His dark eyes shadowed and she knew he was no longer seeing the restaurant in front of him, or the people on the busy London street outside. Instead he was reliving a tragic memory, and as he spoke she could see the small dark-haired boy he must have been, clinging to the people he'd known as parents, the people he loved. Being wrested away by unkind hands, dragged kicking and screaming away. To land in a strange, unfamiliar house with strange, unfamiliar people however kind and months later taken again to another place and told this was home.

'It didn't feel like home. I was five by then, and confused and sad and so very angry. With everyone. My old foster carers for "abandoning me", and my uncle and aunt for taking me.'

Stella blinked back tears, gently placed her hand on his arm, wished with all her heart she could go back in time and try to somehow explain things to the poor little boy. 'Were you allowed to see your foster carers?'

'No. I was told a clean break was better.'

'And your uncle and aunt? Carlos and Annalise?' she asked, could hear the desperate sound of hope in her voice. 'What were they like?'

'On the plus side they did provide me with food and clothing and a roof over my head. But adopting me was a mistake. They didn't really want to do it, they told me later my grandmother forced them to do it, threatened to disinherit them if they didn't. My father was the black sheep of the family and Carlos and Annalise hated him, but my grandmother had adored him, right up to the point he died in a prison brawl when I was four. That was when they found out about me. Carlos and Annalise couldn't have children of their own and I was a poor substitute, especially as my grandmother died very soon after the adoption went through. To them I was a chip off the old block, a carbon copy of my father. My father the career criminal. A liar, a womaniser, a gambler, a cheat…a drug user who ended up in prison on numerous occasions; he also had immense charm, charisma and good looks. Apparently I am the spitting image of him. And they believed that I was intrinsically bad and destined to follow in his footsteps.'

'Oh.' This was so warped, so horrible and Stella's hand clenched into fist. 'But that is so wrong.'

'In their defence my behaviour was appalling—I was so confused and angry that I lashed out, tried to run away, broke things...and it all fed into their beliefs. Plus they never wanted me anyway.'

'But how can you bring a child up to believe they are bad?' She couldn't wrap her head around it. 'You weren't your father, you were you and of course you were angry, you were tiny, a child, and... *I* am so...angry.'

'It wasn't all their fault.'

'How can you say that?'

'They hated my father. I mean really loathed him. And I think they had cause to. From what they told me there was no depth he didn't sink to and yet my grandmother always forgave him even though it was Carlos who did well, who studied hard, who did the right thing. But he couldn't provide her with a grandchild like my father did. They looked at me and they saw him. Just like my mum.' And again she sensed he was back in the past, looking back at a childhood strewn with cruelty. 'My aunt told me that my mum must have taken one look at me and she must have seen it in my eyes. That I was destined to be like my father.'

This got worse and worse. 'That isn't true.' But the young Max must have believed it was, maybe on some level he still did. 'If you look like him that is genetics, what is inside you...it's you. And you have made your own destiny and it is clearly nothing like your father's. Surely they must have seen that.'

'Nope.' He shook his head. 'I don't think anything could shake their convictions about me. When I was sixteen they asked me to leave, said their duty was done. Years later when I was beginning to be successful I contacted them, because I still hoped that maybe they would change their minds. But they wouldn't even see me. Said something along the lines of success doesn't make you a good person.'

'That must have hurt.'

'Yes, it did, though I didn't want to admit it even to myself—I told myself I didn't care, told myself I was bigger than all that, that I was successful, wealthy, ambitious. So it didn't matter what they thought. And so I built my persona, to hide the fact that inside I've always felt diminished. My mother had rejected me without even knowing me, and my aunt and uncle rejected me no matter what I did to try and win their love, or even their liking and that made me feel small, inadequate and I hid that behind the aura of success. And I decided that I wouldn't let anyone reject me again. Then I had a double whammy. You rejected my offer and then the detectives found my mother and she wrote me a letter. She doesn't want to be contacted, she's married with other kids, and she wants to keep her status quo as it is.'

'Max. I…'

'No. It's OK. Because it made me think. Rupali Patel is technically my mother, but she doesn't know me, she isn't rejecting me, or judging me because she doesn't know me. My aunt and uncle never bothered getting to know me—all they could see was the image they created, a mini version of my father. But you…that was different. You rejected me.

'And you were right. What I offered you *wasn't* enough, a marriage of convenience, a sham marriage, a persona of a marriage, built on a contract. I offered you the Max Durante persona because I was too scared that the real me wouldn't be enough, too scared to admit how I really feel.'

'How do you really feel?' Her heart pounded and hope burgeoned inside her.

'I love you.' The words tumbled out of him. 'I don't expect you to reciprocate, but I love you. I love you, the real Stella, the woman who cares for other people and wants to make a difference, the woman who tastes every item of food as though it is the most important thing in the world. I love your smile, your laugh, the way tears sparkle in your eyes. I love the way you give everything your all, the way you truly listen to people, the way you've made me re-evaluate and think about who I am. And I want to marry you, not for the baby's sake, but because I want to spend the rest of my life with *you*. I understand if that's not what you want, but I want you to know, know that's how I feel.'

Stella opened her mouth tried to find the right words amongst the tumult of happiness that jumbled inside her. 'But that's why I said I couldn't marry you.' Seeing his look of confusion she stopped, knew she'd better get the most important fact across. 'I love you. I am totally completely head over heels in love with you.'

'You are?'

But even as she saw happiness begin to light up his brown eyes she sensed a hesitancy. 'You promise this isn't because you feel sorry for me, don't want to reject me out of some misguided compassion.'

'I promise. I wouldn't insult your honesty with that

sort of "compassion". I love you. That's what I wanted to talk to you about, what I wanted to tell you. I refused your proposal because I love you and I couldn't go ahead with a marriage where I loved you but you didn't love me.

'I should have told you the truth in Mumbai but I was too scared, scared that it would mess up our co-parenting. And so for the past days I have tried to do the right thing. I started work and I've talked about paint and colour themes with a smile on my face, I've helped Adriana with wedding plans with a smile on my face. I saw my Dad.' She thought back to the conversation as she told it to Max. Her father looking so frail lying propped up on pillows. His voice soft as he spoke.

'I wanted to say I'm sorry for our last meeting. Nearly dying has changed some of my perspectives on life and I want to live whatever I have left differently. I'm just not sure how yet.' Even those sentences had tired him and Stella had stepped forward and kissed her father on her cheek.

'I know you'll work it out. But now focus on getting better.'

He'd covered her hand and squeezed it before falling back to sleep.

Now she looked at Max. 'And his words made me think, and I realised I wanted that for me too. To live the rest of my life differently. As the real me. And the real me loves the real you. And I realised that *you* are committed to our baby, that you would make being a Dad work no matter what, because you love our baby and you will be the best Dad in the world. So I could tell you the truth. That I love you... The real you, because I could see the real you just like you could see the real me. I love the man who cared enough about me to take half my terror and fear away on the aeroplane when he was in shock himself, the man who makes me laugh, the man who cares so much about his child. The man who showed me vulnerability, who confided in me to help me. And, yes, the man who has made so much of his life, who has drive and power and ambition, who is a success. The man who danced a Bollywood dance, the man who told me I could be a lawyer, could follow my dream. The man I want to spend the rest of my life with, wake up with every morning. I love you and if the coin had fallen differently I would have told you first, because you are enough, you've always been enough for me. I love you with all my heart.'

And now he plunged his hand into his pocket and in an instant he was in front of her, down on one knee.

'Stella Morrison, will you marry me? I promise to love you for the rest of our lives, to cherish you and talk to you and share the ups and downs. I want to raise our family together and I swear I will always be there for you, the real me with all my flaws and vulnerabilities and all my strength.'

'Yes. I will marry you and I will be there for you, stand by your side. Always. We will be a happy family full of love for each other, and I will always be there to share the good times and the harder times, the real me. I will never walk away from us.'

And then he slipped the ring onto her finger and she knew that this was the happiest moment of her life, knew that this choice was the best one she could ever make.

EPILOGUE

STELLA TOOK MAX'S hand as they entered Salvington Manor, ducking under the festoon of pink balloons that adorned the top of the front door.

'Look at that Bea,' Stella said. 'Balloons.'

The baby safely ensconced in the forward-facing baby carrier strapped securely around Max's chest gave a gurgle of laughter and Stella leaned over to drop a kiss on her daughter's downy-haired head. 'Balloons,' she said again, 'to celebrate your cousin Martha's christening.'

'Welcome.' Rob stepped forward, holding Martha in his arms, his face so full of pride and happiness that Stella's heart turned as she kissed her brother-in-law's cheek and watched as the two men exchanged a complicated handshake. 'Your parents and Adriana are in the living room along with some of the other guests.'

Before they could follow him, there was a knock at the door and Stella stepped forward to open it, gave a beaming smile as she saw the identity of the guests. 'Maxine, Chris. I'm so glad you're here.'

'Me too,' Max stepped forward and hugged the elderly couple, the foster carers who had looked after him for the first years of his life, released them as Rob reappeared and led them into the living room.

Stella held back for a moment and turned to Max. 'I'm so glad you contacted them.'

'So am I.' He smiled down at her. 'One of your excellent ideas.'

'But you did it.' And she knew it hadn't been easy, knew he'd feared rejection, believed that maybe Chris and Maxine hadn't really wanted to adopt him all those years ago. But it turned out they had wanted to, had fought as hard as they could until eventually they had backed down only because social services had convinced them his uncle and aunt were a better option for Max.

And over the years they'd assumed that decision to be correct, but *'It didn't stop us from missing you, loving you, thinking about you,'* Christine had said, tears spilling from her eyes at their first meeting. And since then they had become honorary grandparents.

'Which shows what a good team we are,' Max said now as he took her hand in his to enter the living room where more balloons bobbed from the ceiling, all pink. Every decoration a signal that a daughter was a welcome addition to the family.

Stella's gaze flickered to her father, who was listening to something his wife was saying; he nodded and smiled and then headed over to where Adriana had just taken Martha from Rob.

In truth Stella was unsure as to how her father truly felt about the fact that both his daughters had produced daughters, but all credit to him—Lord Salvington did seem to be trying hard to be a better person, a better father and a good grandfather.

Her father beckoned to her and she walked across, scooping Bea from Max as she did so, love swelling inside her along with confusion. How could Rupali have abandoned Max, how could her own father have taken a dislike to Adriana?

Lord Salvington nodded as Stella approached.

'I want to say something to you both, your husbands too.'

In an almost synchronised movement Rob took Adriana's hand as Max took Stella's and Stella was almost tempted to smile as she saw the protective aura that surrounded both men.

'I've made many mistakes in my life,' her father said. 'But I'd like to not make any more. I want both you girls to know that I will do my best to be a good grandfather to both my granddaughters. And your mother and I have decided we are going on a cruise as soon as the doctors give me the go-ahead, and if I can persuade her to give me another chance I will, but if I can't, I won't stand in her way.'

Stella saw he looked pale, but before she could move Adriana was there, an arm around him and Stella smiled at her sister, admired anew her kindness and capacity to forgive and care. But everyone deserved a second chance and when there was so much love in this room for these two beautiful, gorgeous, precious babies and so much happiness she hoped with all her heart that in their later years her parents could maybe rediscover love.

As for herself and Max and Adriana and Rob, Stella knew they were embarking on the rest of their lives, together with a guaranteed happy ever after. That was the deal and they would all make sure they kept it.

* * * * *

COMING SOON!

We really hope you enjoyed reading this book.
If you're looking for more romance, be sure to
head to the shops when new books are
available on

Thursday 2nd February

To see which titles are coming soon, please visit

millsandboon.co.uk/nextmonth

MILLS & BOON®

Coming next month

TEMPTED BY HER FAKE FIANCÉ
Kate Hardy

So what did you want to run by me?' Charlie asked.

'The wedding stuff.' She looked awkward. 'I know this is a big ask, so I didn't want to bring it up in front of Mum and Dad—but you said you'd be the face of the farm.'

'Ye-es.' He'd already agreed that. Why was she repeating herself?

She took a deep breath. 'Could you be our groom, too, until we get a real one?'

'A fake bridegroom?' That was a horrible idea.

His distaste must've shown in his face, because she said hastily, 'Fake's probably the wrong word. What I mean is, would you act as the groom in our narrative?'

His head was spinning. 'I...'

'Don't worry. I thought it was an ask too far,' she said. 'I was hoping we would save on the budget. If you'd do it, we wouldn't have to pay models or agency fees, but maybe I can call in a favour from someone.'

Her expression said it was pretty unlikely. And he'd rather the money for the marketing campaign was spent on something more urgent, like building the booking system and shopping cart. 'What would it involve?'

'We'd be cross-selling everything, showing that the farm's the background to every bit of a romance.

The story is that a couple stay on the farm in the accommodation, and watch the sunset together or the sunrise.' She spread her hands. 'Maybe both. A romantic dinner, a stroll in the woods or through the wildflower meadow, an afternoon cuddling newborn lambs. Then a proposal—I was thinking at the beach, to give people an idea of the wonderful bits of the countryside nearby. And we can have the barn all dressed up for a small intimate wedding.'

'And who would be the bride?'

'Me,' she said.

Elle, acting as his girlfriend and then his bride. His heart started to thud. Maybe this would put an extra barrier between them, making her safe to be around. And maybe it was what he needed: pretending to date, as the next step to actually dating. Finally moving on.

It wouldn't be putting his past in a box—he'd always love Jess—but maybe it might be the catalyst he needed. 'Who's going to take the photographs?' he asked.

'Of us? We are. Selfies,' she explained. 'I want to keep an intimate feel.'

Intimate. Now there was a word that made him feel completely flustered.

Continue reading
TEMPTED BY HER FAKE FIANCÉ
Kate Hardy

Available next month
www.millsandboon.co.uk

Discover more at millsandboon.co.uk.

Y059743

R   With
canyons and high alpine meadows full of wildlife

The item should be returned or renewed
by the last date stamped below.

Newport
CITY COUNCIL
CYNGOR DINAS
Casnewydd

Dylid dychwelyd neu adnewyddu'r eitem erbyn
y dyddiad olaf sydd wedi'i stampio isod

St. Julians